DANCING
IN THE RING

SUSAN E. SAGE

Black Rose Writing | Texas

ISBN: 978-1-68513-219-4
PUBLISHED BY BLACK ROSE WRITING
www.blackrosewriting.com

Printed in the United States of America
Suggested Retail Price (SRP) $23.95

Dancing in the Ring is printed in Book Antiqua

*As a planet-friendly publisher, Black Rose Writing does its best to eliminate unnecessary waste to
reduce paper usage and energy costs, while never compromising the reading experience. As a result,
the final word count vs. page count may not meet common expectations.

In memory of Bob & Kate
And my dear father, Robert Sage

ACKNOWLEDGEMENTS

Many thanks for the love and support of my husband, Tom Pugsley; dear friend, Jane Cameron; dear sister, Mary Lynne, and brother-in-law, Paul Wells. Also, much gratitude for their encouraging words after reading an early draft.

A heartfelt thanks to early readers, including my fellow author friends and beta readers: Patty Duffy, Faye Johnson, and Milana Marsenich. Their insights were invaluable!

And many thanks to Black Rose Writing—with special appreciation to Reagan Rothe and David King.

DANCING
IN THE RING

PREFACE

My great uncle, Robert Sage, was a boxer who later became a judge in Detroit, Michigan. He met my great aunt, Catherine McIntosh, when they were in law school together in the early 1920s. She was one of Detroit's first female attorneys. They married shortly after beginning their legal careers. To the best of my ability, I've reconstructed the story of their lives from the 1920s through 1940. Both families were of Irish descent. I had a lot more primary source information about 'Bob' then I did about 'Kate,' and therefore much of her family background is fictitious. My father, the younger Robert Sage, was an assistant prosecutor attorney for Detroit and Wayne County for many years. His colorful Uncle Bob may not have been the best of mentors, but he sure left a lasting impression on my father. Over the years, he regaled me with many stories about his locally famous uncle and aunt. I well recall him telling me that someday I should write about their passionate yet tragic tale. While I enjoyed hearing about this fascinating couple, I never had any intention of writing a novel about them. Once I began looking through old photos and letters, including my father's unpublished memoirs, there was no turning back. I've been as faithful as possible to the stories passed down to me—embellishing only when necessary.

~Susan E. Sage

"Being Irish, he had an abiding sense of tragedy, which sustained him through temporary periods of joy."
~William Butler Yeats

"Beauty and love pass, I know…Oh, there's sadness, too. I suppose all great happiness is a little sad. Beauty means the scent of roses and then the death of roses."
~ F. Scott Fitzgerald, *This Side of Paradise*

PART I
KATE & THE BATTLING BARRISTER

CHAPTER ONE

September, 1922

Catherine stared at an oak tree outside the classroom window without seeing the young man on the branch staring back in at her.

That humid early September afternoon, she was preoccupied with the fact that in less than a year, at age twenty-five, she'd be one of only four women in her graduating class. That is, if she passed all her remaining classes at the Detroit College of Law. She'd done well until this point, but anything could happen. Her single hope: to someday soon wear the cap and gown.

Then Catherine noticed the most handsome man she'd ever seen smiling at her from a tree branch. The oak tree was right outside the window, so she could see his brown wavy hair, the cleft in his chin, and even a dimple on his cheek. He wore a straw boater hat and tipped it her way when he caught her noticing him. She knew he was a fellow student as she'd noticed him before in the hallways, and at a few lectures.

He almost took her breath away, not because he was there on the branch, but because he was so darn handsome. "Only Valentino could compare," she'd later confide to Molly, her sister. She fanned her face when he persisted to stare at her. Throughout college, she'd prided herself on not having been much distracted by young men, but now she'd become a silly schoolgirl.

Somehow she knew he expected her to avoid his stare. Instead, she returned it. Five minutes left of class, so why not have a little fun? It was also the last day of classes for the term.

As Catherine predicted, he found it unnerving. He imitated an ape and began scratching his underarm. At this, she nudged a friend sitting next to her. "Joan, get a load of what's outside on the tree branch!" Enjoying even more attention, he began making loud ape-like noises. Then he almost lost his footing.

"Not that I hope he falls, but it would serve him right!" said Catherine.

"I think that's the fella who's been making a splash in the boxing ring. Bob Sage. Ever heard of him?" asked Joan, who seemed to know everyone.

"Can't say that I have," Catherine replied, unable to take her eyes off him.

When she left the classroom, sticky from the heat as well as the staring, he was waiting for her in the hallway with a red tulip. He extended the flower toward her.

"Thanks, but it belongs in a garden—no doubt the college courtyard."

"I always only take what needs to be plucked," he said, tipping his straw boater. She noticed he was wearing a vest with a gold watch chain. A bit too fancy for the trees, monkey boy…

With that, Catherine walked away in her usual brisk, no-nonsense stride.

His galling comment told her all she needed to know about him. What nerve! Who did this Bob Sage think he was? As she made her way through the crowd of exiting students across the campus toward the gate leading out to the noisy bustle of the car-laden avenue, she didn't know if she was uncomfortably warm from her anger or the heat of the late morning sun.

Refusing to acknowledge him, she looked down the road for the streetcar.

"Say, could we please start over, Miss Catherine McIntosh? While it may look like we've met by chance, I was actually looking for you. I sure as hell didn't mean to upset you."

"How do you know my name, Mr. Bob Sage?" she asked, shielding her large gray-blue eyes from the sun, and also his attention.

"How do you know mine? And by the way, it's Robert, but my friends call me Bob."

Hardly surprised by that she knew his name, he told her how he'd heard about her from his parish priest, Father Tim. Father Tim was also her parish priest, she told him. A good friend of the family.

"Father told me about how well you've been doing in law school, and how you'll probably wind up graduating with high honors. I'm hoping to graduate next June, too, but I almost flunked out this spring. Think you could give me some advice on how I can improve my study habits?"

"I shouldn't think tree branches would be the best places to improve study habits. Is that where you thought class was meeting?"

"I just got a couple classes changed. Since we'll be in the same ones, I was hoping you could help me out. Father Tim suggested that with your good guidance, I could do better."

"He did, did he? Hmm…"

Catherine could tell Bob was the type who refused to take no for an answer. If he went to the same church and rode the same streetcar home as she did, there was a strong likelihood that he, too, lived in Corktown—Detroit's oldest neighborhood.

Bob was telling her something about how he owned a car, but didn't drive it around downtown on the weekdays since so many cars clogged the roads. She nodded, unsure because of the street noise, if that's what he said or something else entirely. If he wasn't so good-looking, it would be easy to ignore him— remain cool and collected. That cleft in his chin was marked and his wavy brown hair, up close, was curlier than she thought. Not to mention his deep-set blue eyes.

They boarded the Jefferson Avenue streetcar and without asking for permission, Bob sat down alongside her. He kept smiling at her. She tried hard to keep her eyes straight ahead but found it nearly impossible.

Did others sense the electrical current between them? While she was no stranger to male attention, she'd fought hard to keep herself above the fray. This attention—okay, downright flirtation—would not turn her head. She would refuse to let it get the best of her. Besides, she still needed to study for exams.

The air on the crowded streetcar was close to stifling, even though they were close to the river. Catherine didn't know which was worse: the smell of body odor or factory smells wafting up from the river. The brash young man began telling her how he'd recently moved back from Wallace, Idaho with his older brother, Eugene or Gene, for short. The ding-ding-ding of the bells annoyed her because she couldn't hear all that he was saying – something about where they'd received their college degrees. And then how his family lived out West when he was little. Maybe he said they'd received their degrees there, but she wasn't certain. As she was about to ask, he added how he'd been born in a mining town, but she didn't catch its name.

He talked fast, too fast. Really, what did she care about where he was born or his brother's name?

Once he'd had four brothers, but one had died young from tuberculosis; another had fallen down a mine shaft, and the oldest had been a soldier shot down in the Great War. Gene was the only one who remained…

My God, was he about to kidnap her and force her to the altar? What was the point of all his blather? Having lived through the Spanish flu had toughened Catherine to tales of mortality, so feigning interest in relatives of this relative stranger now proved difficult.

Now he wanted to know about her family. Thank God he came up for air! She began telling him, but the din from the streetcar bells and voices kept getting louder. Her head pounded. She wanted to mention how she'd lost her younger brother and sister to the Spanish flu, but had three siblings still very much alive. Instead, she commented how she'd lost family members, too, but left it at that.

Before Bob could ask for specifics, the streetcar swayed as it crossed a rougher part of the track. Several passengers in the aisle slid sideways, including a wino that about wound up almost in their laps. Bob helped the bum stand upright and asked if he was okay with unexpected compassion. The poor fellow nodded without looking Bob in the eye. Bob smiled at him and then turned back to Catherine.

"Look, this probably isn't the best place to get to know each other. What say we grab a little lunch somewhere?" He pulled out the gold clock face from his vest pocket, and then stared at it, waiting for her response.

"Maybe *someday* we could get together at the library."

"Which day?"

"Don't press your luck, Mr. Sage!"

He didn't and she was grateful. Maybe he was a gentleman, after all. A dying breed, no doubt — especially in a big city like Detroit.

After reaching their stop, they walked to Corktown in relative silence, both trying to lessen the voltage between them. Once it had been a solidly Irish neighborhood, but in the past few years, Italian and Mexican immigrants had been moving in and the Irish moving out.

Like a shot from nowhere, Bob burst out: "Just know that one day I'm going to marry you!"

"I was starting to like you, but now I think you're plumb crazy. Beat it, would you? Scram! Don't even think about following me."

"I don't know where that came from. Honest, I don't." Bob's cheeks reddened, so possibly he was telling the truth.

Catherine clamped her hands over her ears, pretending not to hear him. When she turned left at a side street, he knew better than to follow. Still, something told them both that whatever this was, it wasn't over.

CHAPTER TWO

Why was Bob telling Catherine so much when he simply wanted to find out more about her? It was like words were flying out of his mouth before he knew he was saying them. Show some control, you blathering eejit! That's what his mother would say.

Meeting her in the library wasn't the same as lunch. Soon they'd be parting ways and he had to say something more — not only to get her attention, but to make him stand out from the male attention, she no doubt, regularly received. She'd be gone in a few minutes.

"Just know that one day I'm going to marry you!"

His shout caused all heads but hers to turn his way. He needed to run away. Fast. Why had he mentioned marrying her? He didn't even know her yet, though he felt like he did. Maybe all the boxing was affecting his brain.

. . .

Years later, Bob would recall how he couldn't help but stare at the auburn-haired beauty sitting at a desk close to the window gazing out of that classroom. How she hadn't seen him, at least not right away. He hadn't yet known about her propensity for a far-away look — as if she could see beyond this world.

He'd had no choice but to push a few people out of his way to catch up to her on the way to the streetcar. Catherine had to see that Bob wasn't some moron. Sure, pretty girls had no problem turning his head, but never had he behaved in such a silly manner. And he'd literally gone out on a limb for her, but only to see if she was in that classroom, as he'd been trying to track her down. Grabbing the seat next to her on the streetcar must have seemed somewhat forward, but he had to know more about her. Telling her he was going to marry her someday — now that, he never should have done.

CHAPTER THREE

Hot grease, like lava, bubbled up—then spat high above the stove. Some of it landed on the back of Catherine's pale hand as she reached for a coffee cup. She'd normally remember to run cool water on a burn, but not that Saturday morning. Her parents were arguing and no one was minding the eggs in the skillet, so she had to take over.

"I thought you said you'd already paid this month's rent," said Bridget, her green eyes narrowing. Her tense fingers raked through her gray curls. Once her hair had been auburn like her daughter's. While Catherine's eyes were steely blue, a similar fiery glint shone forth from both sets of eyes. This plus their determined jutting of the chin would remove any doubt they were mother and daughter.

"I said that it would get paid and it will. Enough of your yap, woman!"

"Michael Sean McIntosh, it's you who are full of blather and malarkey! When Ed stopped by, I figured he was merely paying us a social visit. Think, if that's possible for you, how it made me feel when he mentioned the payment being overdue." Ed O'Riley was their landlord, but also a friend.

Catherine served them their eggs and both parents stopped pecking each other momentarily to greet her with a quick nod. The two grabbed their plates and remained standing as they ate. They were standing a little too close to each other for Catherine to feel comfortable, but then the kitchen was small, like the rest of the house. Any chance of the three of them sitting together at the table for the meal was gone.

Her mother was taller than her father, but somewhat stoop-shouldered – as if she was self-conscious of her height. While they were the same age—fifty—her blue-eyed father appeared younger and quicker on his feet. It made sense: sorrow and hard work had had their way with her mother. Mickey never let much bother him.

Why did she have to continue listening to their blather? Catherine was the only one to sit at the table with her coffee.

The argument over rent was one Catherine had heard ever since she could remember. There never seemed to be enough money to make ends meet. One always blamed the other for raiding the cookie jar. She doubted her parents would ever move out of Corktown. Hearing them argue always made her tired and she longed to return to bed in the small dark bedroom that she once shared with Molly, her next oldest sister. When sleeping, she was unaware of the walls closing in. Hard to believe there'd once been six children living under this roof. Thank heavens for Uncle Gerry who'd paid her way through college and now law school. How limited her options would be had it not been for her father's older brother.

Just then Molly, popping in for a quick visit, appeared in the doorway holding the largest bouquet she'd ever seen. This didn't stop her parents from continuing their donnybrook.

"They're for you, Kate," Molly said in disbelief. "This must be a first."

"Are you sure they're for me?" Catherine asked.

"The card reads 'To Catherine,' so I'm assuming that's you. Then it says, 'From the ape in the tree.' Pretty romantic ape, I'd say! Do tell…"

"Only some fellow who ogled me from a tree outside a classroom window."

"Well, lucky you!"

It wasn't simply the largest bouquet Catherine had ever seen, but the loveliest and most fragrant. While her face grew warm from embarrassment, she no longer wanted to return to bed. Yet a few minutes later, she was seething at her parents. How many days had they ruined, beginning the morning like this? And neither of them had ever seemed to care if their children were caught in the crosshairs. At least her older sisters, Molly and Eileen, both had lives of their own. Now it was only Catherine and her nineteen-year-old brother, John, who lived with their parents. While Molly had recently married, she seemed oblivious to her parent's troubled marriage — dancing and laughing her way through life. In love with love...If only Catherine had some of her, what would it be called — romantic sensibility? Moon-faced Molly was pale like her, with curly dark hair.

"If I know our Kate, she's going to throw those pretty blooms away," her mother told the others.

"Dad, why don't you get mom some flowers? Maybe there'd be less arguing around here," said Catherine.

"Shite. Everyone leave me be, I'm tired of all you chatterboxes."

Mickey stormed out of the room, grabbing his worn brown derby from the standing hat rack and slamming the front door on his way out. It was early, but they all knew he was probably going to the downstairs of their family-owned diner, Mickey Mac's, for a pint. The basement was one of many smaller speakeasies in Corktown. During those days, the family speakeasy brought in more revenue than the diner.

Mickey was the only family member who tended the bar, though Bridget and their children had, occasionally, helped in the diner. Whenever he stood behind the bar, he looked taller than normal, his red hair wavier than usual. He had a way of making every customer feel no one was more important than they were. Sometimes Catherine barely recognized this handsome, affable man, for he didn't seem like the same person she knew at home.

After finding a glass jar for a vase, Catherine set the flowers on the worn living room coffee table. The day when she could have her own place couldn't happen soon enough. What did her future hold? Would she ever become a lawyer? Most of her family seemed to think so, as she'd been talking about doing so ever since her father's brother, Uncle Gerry, had shown her his courtroom. He was known there as the Honorable Gerald McIntosh. She had been impressed by his long black robe. When he let her sit on the bench and pound the gavel, she'd looked around the courtroom and decided she belonged in the legal world. After he described to her the job of a lawyer, her mind was made up.

Fairness had always mattered to her. When Catherine was five, her oldest sister Eileen had stolen their other sister's doll. Molly bit her lip but didn't tell their mother, as she knew it would only make matters worse. It had bothered Catherine for the longest time. Justice was finally served when Catherine found the doll hidden in a drawer and returned it to Molly. Tears beaded Molly's black lashes, veiling her dark blue eyes. The sisters hugged before Molly twirled her younger sister about the room.

• • •

Catherine had known other males besides her father, by this point in her life: several boys from the neighborhood and a couple of young men in college. Except for Danny, she'd given her heart to no one. Danny had lived next door when she was little. Her feelings for him had been more real than any she'd had since. His bedroom window was right across from hers. She'd stare through it when he wasn't home, craving his company. The loneliness went bone deep. Twice they'd kissed in the alley and once had pulled down their underpants behind a pine tree in a vacant lot. She thought for sure she'd committed a mortal sin and would burn in Hell after she died. It had been enough to stare without touching. Then Danny and his family moved away. The day they did, she cried so hard she worried she'd never recover.

No-nonsense Eileen told her: "See, that's all girls are good for: falling in love and having their hearts broken." Eileen had been in her teens, and Catherine was only ten.

Still, Catherine vowed to never fall in love again. Ever since she could remember, she'd planned on getting a college degree and doing something with her life. No way would she allow a relationship to muck up her plans.

She told Eileen that maybe God would forgive her earlier sins, and Eileen doubled over laughing. Eileen's laugh had been more of an evil cackle. It hurt all the more because Catherine looked up to her. Her oldest sister's eyes were the same bright green hue as their mother's.

Eileen wasn't able to discourage Catherine from either attending the University of Detroit as an undergraduate or law school. "You're not the one who should go. It should be John," Eileen had hissed. Catherine had grinned back and without a word, walked out of the room. Although John had been encouraged by family and teachers, he had little interest in book learning. Smart, but lazy.

At twenty-five, Eileen already had three little ones. She complained about how they needed her every second of the day, and sometimes at night. While Catherine, too, was no stranger to dark circles beneath her eyes, she'd never been the motherly sort. She recalled how lovely Eileen had once been with an hourglass figure and emerald eyes. Once Eileen had been called the most beautiful of the sisters, but now she was nearly as scrawny and nearly as stoop-shouldered as their mother.

Catherine now gazed down at polish-chipped nails. Fingers looked ready to detach from their hands, as they were always fluttering about. If she were to have a successful legal career, she'd have to develop more of a sophisticated style—though first, she'd have to discover her own style, whatever that entailed.

Would Bob Sage become part of her life? Speculating about it made her stomach queasy. Would he be any better a man than her father, whom she loved, despite his gruff and sometimes abusive nature? Maybe all men were little more than apes. Life would be better if women ran the world, of that she was certain.

CHAPTER FOUR

Catherine and Bob got together twice before what they would later refer to as their first 'real' date: first for coffee and dessert after exams were over, and then one Sunday afternoon they drove around the city's bumpy roads in his new Model T. Bob had enjoyed pointing out all the new construction projects downtown evidenced by all the cranes and scaffolding. What he wanted to ask was whether or not he'd made a good impression on her parents. He sure hoped so. Not only did he attend the same church but also, his ancestors, like hers, were from Cork, Ireland. Maybe he'd seemed too eager to say the right things.

It was during their second outing together, when they'd stopped for ice cream, that they told each other more about their family histories. Catherine thanked Bob for deciding to swap family stories in a quiet setting. He pretended like he didn't recall their exchange on the streetcar.

She rolled her eyes after he graciously allowed her to go first this time.

Some of the McIntosh family had been in the United States since the early 1850s. They were among that initial wave of Irish immigrants who'd been forced to leave Ireland because of the Potato Famine. Most were red-haired, brainy, and "tempestuous," Catherine said, raising her eyebrows up and down suggesting she was made of the same stuff, especially the latter.

She licked the melting ice cream as fast as she could from her cone before it trickled down onto her new blue summer dress.

After gallantly procuring a cup for her cone, Bob explained how the Sages had first been farmers in Saline, near Ann Arbor. After a few years, they moved west to Wallace, Idaho. It was before he was born, but his older brothers had often described the train journey.

"Did they see any Indians? Weren't they afraid for their lives?"

"This was around 1880 and much of the West was settled by then. Nothing sadder than seeing the poor Indians on reservations on my way back east a few years back," he told her.

"It should be their country," Catherine said. "Who did all the white folks think they were, barging in and forcing them from their land? After all, it's their land, or should be." Her already warm skin turned fever-hot, thinking about the injustice.

Bob, always a spokesperson for the disadvantaged, didn't disagree, but clearly didn't feel the same. "Look, Kiddo, our people came to this country only to escape starvation. It's not like we came here to kick out the Indians." The Sages, he continued, settled in Burke, a town near Wallace, Idaho. Bob's father had been sheriff of Burke.

. . .

Catherine decided against asking him further questions at this point and told him how her maternal grandparents came to the United States in the 1880s but died when her mother, Bridget, and her mother's sister were little. They'd been raised by their Aunt Colleen. According to her, their parents, Maureen and Sean O'Kelly, had died in an accident. When the girls began to ask more questions, their aunt would only say it was a blessing their parents had died together. Why a blessing? Their aunt, with a long sigh, would add how deeply they'd been in love.

Whenever Aunt Colleen would tell the tale, she rarely elaborated, but tears would trickle down her cheeks. Not wanting to make their aunt cry, the sisters never asked what sort of accident they'd been in. Aunt Colleen died a few years back and she was the only known family member. The sisters had always been close, though Vivian lived in New York. As for Catherine's father's side, well, that was a story for another day.

Despite Bob listening attentively, her skin was hot and prickly. Why had she prattled on so? She wasn't used to talking this much.

Licking the last of his ice cream cone, and forgetting exactly what he'd told her on the streetcar, Bob now repeated how his family had lived out West. Catherine didn't bother to stop him. This time, he added how most of the Sages had been brown-haired, fair-skinned, and muscular. They were tough, hard-working people. His mother's side—the Lyons—had been on the short side with delicate features. Most of them stronger of spirit than body, as many had perished when young from weak hearts. Still, they had an uncanny knack for seeing beyond the Earthly realm—or so his mother told him.

"That's all very interesting, but please don't call me 'Kiddo' ever again. I'd prefer Catherine, but if you must use a nickname, Kate will do."

While she was irritated by him being a little too familiar, at least he wasn't talking as fast as he had on the streetcar. At least he let her do some of the talking. For a moment Bob looked at her as if he'd been stung. Too bad, she wouldn't apologize because it felt condescending—as if she was a kid and not a grown woman.

"No problem, Kate…Will you be my date next weekend? I thought maybe we could go out dancing at the new Graystone Ballroom. My brother, Gene, and his wife, Violet, will be there. She's quite the dancer and a lot of fun. Everyone likes her. Gene's already an attorney, though he isn't a practicing one—at least not yet."

"Say, Bob, I didn't know that about your brother." Couldn't he have just asked Gene about study habits? Was his story about Father Tim recommending he get in touch with Catherine simply a ruse?

"Kiddo—I mean, Kate—he recently returned from living out West, so he wasn't around to ask. They've got a baby, a cute little tyke, named after me. So, whatcha say about going dancing? Be my gal?"

She winked at him, as she often did in those early days. The seductive little gesture sent him to the moon and back.

• • •

What Bob didn't tell Catherine that afternoon was that he was both 'a man's man,' as well as a 'lady's man,' making him something of a rarity. One of five brothers, he'd been the son most coddled by their mother. He was a 'born flirt'—his mother always liked to report. Not only did he catch a woman's eye with his dimples and taut muscles, but his long black lashes swept across his blue eyes as if to fan them. His lifelong interest in boxing could well have been because of defending himself from his brothers who teased him mercilessly about his gorgeous peepers.

At age seven, after openly crying over a coyote shot to death by his father, his brothers ganged up on him and called him a sissy.

That was the first and last time anyone dared to make that accusation.

No one, including Catherine, would truly know if his interest in women had more to do with trying to prove his masculinity. Unlike her, Bob lost his virginity early, at thirteen—out West in an abandoned cabin to Sally, a young woman, several years his senior.

. . .

While the two had fun dancing together at the Graystone Ballroom, it wouldn't be until late the following spring when they seriously began dating. For the first several months, they met weekly to study at the library, and only occasionally, would they go out for coffee or long walks. Catherine liked to insist to family and friends that they weren't a couple. She insisted a bit over-much, though she made sure never to wind up alone with him, as no man—not even Bob Sage—was going to take her eyes off the prize.

CHAPTER FIVE

June, 1923

A week after graduating from law school, Catherine and Bob boarded a steamship to Boblo Island with Gene and Violet. Almost a year had gone by since he'd ogled her from a tree branch. There were a few other amusement parks in the Detroit area, but according to Bob who'd been to them all, Boblo was the best. He'd been there several times, unlike Catherine who'd never been there or to any other parks with rides. Since her father worked seven days a week to make ends meet, there had never been money for 'trifles' — her mother's term for any unnecessary spending. Her girlish excitement had grown as the days had numbered down to their voyage, so that when the day arrived, she was exuberant and didn't care if the world knew it.

The two couples stood against the railing of the Columbia as it pulled away from the dock. Both men wore straw boaters and looked like twins. Catherine wore a sailor blouse and pleated skirt, while Violet had donned a red floral print dress for the occasion. While it was small in compared to the ships that sailed the Atlantic, it was the largest boat Catherine had ever seen.

Looking back at part of Detroit's skyline was breathtaking. "It's almost like New York's!" she said.

"Not quite," Bob had responded, "but some call it the Paris of the West."

She had no idea the city had so many skyscrapers. They watched the late afternoon sunlight dance on the wide river water.

Bob carefully poured a little vodka into their glasses of Coca-Cola. He told them how lucky they were because there would be a full moon that night. Violet's loud and high-pitched giggle caused a group next to them to turn in their direction. Bob had already pocketed his silver flask, not that it would matter much, as so many smuggled the prohibited alcohol aboard.

"And Vi, you know what happens to me when the moon is full, right? Your husband's told you, I suppose," said Bob.

Violet raised her thick dark brows and shrugged her thin shoulders. "No, Bob, Gene's never mentioned it. Something illegal? Maybe I should plug my ears."

Catherine couldn't help but notice Violet's large, long-lobed ears, despite her attractive, though overly made-up face. She shamed herself for being so critical. Certainly, Catherine had her own faults.

"I turn into a werewolf, so BEWARE!" Bob's bushy brows danced on his forehead.

Catherine rolled her eyes. Violet giggled again at an even higher pitch.

Bob, a bit irked, not to have provoked more fear in Catherine, continued: "Kate knows she'll be my victim tonight when we're out upon the silver sea…"

His audience of three had now grown to seven, counting the group next to them. Nothing he loved better.

Many of the passengers played cards at tables in a large cabin below deck. The stuffy air smelled of peanuts and popcorn. One of the more popular areas was a large dance hall. A small band played music—from Dixieland jazz to Ragtime—almost the entire way.

The captain, known as Captain Bob-lo, was a small man in stature—only three feet tall. While he looked cranky and out of sorts, he loved entertaining audiences with his Irish jig. Bob told Catherine that it was rumored he was related to the leprechauns. If he stared into your eyes, he could see your soul and possibly your future.

After spending some time on deck watching a boat parade go down the river, Violet complained about the wind messing up her black hair, even though it looked to be securely pinned and netted to her head. She then turned to Catherine:

"How's my crazy brother-in-law been treating you?"

When Catherine tried to respond, at first Violet feigned interest, but then quickly became distracted. She even interrupted Catherine to coax Gene into going below deck to play cards.

"Whatever you say, Doll," Gene had replied. Catherine knew Violet intended no ill will; she was merely excitable. Gene asked the other couple to join them, but they declined. This was Catherine's first time aboard the ship and Bob wanted to show her the giant steam engine below the passenger decks.

Once there, Bob explained what he knew about the mighty pistons. Because of several interested others, he was forced to stand behind Catherine. The loudness of the pistons made her cover her ears. He gently pressed against her and softly kissed the nape of her long smooth neck. She thought of inching away, but they were wedged in place from a growing crowd. She stiffened and then relaxed to his touch. Would they get a few private moments so they could kiss on the island? Everything went dark. She'd never fainted before. If she fell into his arms, she'd be another damsel in distress. She wasn't about to let that happen. After a few deep breaths, the feeling passed but left her shaky.

Shouldn't the trip to the island have taken longer than only a little over an hour? "It's because we're headed downriver," Bob said. "The return trip will take a lot longer, but there'll be more time to dance in the moonlight."

"There's never enough time to dance in the moonlight," Catherine whispered in his ear.

The two couples strolled around the amusement park side of the island. Bob, Catherine, and Gene rode The Whip and the roller coaster, though Violet had declined, saying she didn't much like rides. Violet remained seated on a park bench, fanning herself with a Japanese fan Gene bought her on the ship. She did look rather peaked. Catherine announced her love of thrills and the wild roller coaster fit the bill. Afterward, they rode the train around the island, and Catherine was enchanted. Bob reached for her smaller and smoother hand in his paw-like one and held it almost the entire way.

After the train trip, the twilight faded fast, but little lights illuminated the walkways.

"The fairies from Ireland settled here," Bob told the group, "At least that's what I've heard. I know Gene, why don't you and Vi choose your path, and Catherine and I—another? We'll meet back here and see who the lucky one is that finds the blarney stone."

"Bob, you're the one full of blarney," Gene said, but readily agreed, giving him a knowing wink. Gene was the 'straight man' to his younger brother's more expressive nature. Sensible, shy, and perfectly happy with being unseen, Gene liked a good joke, but couldn't tell one. While he admired his brother, Bob's antics and attention-seeking could become irritating. Now that there were only three left in the family that he'd been born into, Bob meant the world to him.

Bob knew the exact path that led to a private, cool grassy area surrounded by tall hedges and walls of white birch trees. It was almost perfectly enclosed. A large willow tree served as a back wall. Catherine leaned against it. The longer they kissed, the more he pressed into her. She swooned and got weak in the knees. Seizing the moment, he spread out his suit jacket on the grass. While it wasn't large enough to be a blanket, there was ample material to protect the back of her skirt. He'd been carrying the jacket around much of the time anyway, because of the warmth of the June day.

She surveyed the almost private enclosure and remarked what a swell place this was, maybe the most magical she'd ever seen. "Oh, Bob, I'm not so sure. What if we get company?" she giggled.

Bob, lying on his side on the grass, patted the jacket. She asked another question, but he then put his finger to his lips. Shush, my sweet one... And it was as if he'd cast a spell on her, as suddenly she was no longer hesitant.

They'd waited so long for this moment and could wait no longer.

"I'll show you even more magic, as I'm going to take you from here to Paradise in mere moments," he whispered, nuzzling her neck with his stubbly chin. Curling up to each other, they kissed some more. She rolled onto her back. Then he fondled one of her breasts. With slow but steady gentleness he lifted her skirt but picked up speed as he unclasped his belt, and unzipped his fly. Her pelvis tilted upward and her slightly trembling thighs rose to meet his muscular loins.

Catherine tried her best to straighten her skirt and smooth her rumpled blouse. She tried her best to keep from appearing dazed but kept pulling out little blades of grass that had become woven in her auburn hair. "You look fine, Sweets, quit worrying. No one saw us. I promise you." She wished they could remain on their private, sensuous island within an island.

In the public restroom, she did her best to dab the blood stain from her underwear. Most of it had probably gotten on the inside dark brown liner of Bob's jacket. She decided not to mention it; there was no need. Her cheeks burned, but not for long.

Later, she'd reason that she wasn't the first woman he'd taken there. The give-away was that he seemed to have known which of the many paths to take to find such a private area. She wouldn't ask, of course, but would always wonder. Was it good fortune that no one had disturbed their privacy? They both hoped so.

As they searched for the other couple, Bob saw an acquaintance. "See that fellow over there in line at the hot dog stand? He's bad news. We gotta steer way clear of him, Sweets." Still, in passion's fog, Catherine only nodded, as he told her about Bernie Schwartz from the infamous Purple Gang. She chewed one of her chipped nails.

There was still time to join Gene and Violet at a picnic table before boarding the boat back to the city. It was too bad, the four agreed, that there hadn't been enough time to dance at the large pavilion. They all ate elephant ears as the full moon rose higher in the sky. Violet giggled when Catherine mentioned the island was the most romantic place she'd ever been.

A young, blond-haired woman strode over to them.

"Why, hello there, Kate. I see you have a life outside law school. Good for you! How are you doing, Bob?"

Bob smiled and Catherine was quick to respond to her friend from the law school: "Hi, Joan. Let me introduce you to Bob's brother and his sister-in-law," she said, without acknowledging her classmate's remark. Maybe Joan hadn't meant to be sarcastic, so Catherine was willing to overlook it. Something about the way Joan looked at her made her feel guilty — like Joan somehow knew about what Catherine and Bob had been doing on the island. Catherine ran her fingers through her hair, realizing it was messy, and pulled a couple more pieces of grass from it. Joan, whose hair was always perfectly coiffed, noticed. Catherine felt like a fallen woman. Again, her cheeks burned.

Joan and Catherine had studied together countless times in the university's library over the past few years. While Joan's grades were higher than most, she believed a woman's first duty was to marry and have a family, though she hoped to become a law clerk someday, and then a trial attorney. Catherine liked her well enough but was irked. Why had she made the remark that she did? Did Joan think all she did was study?

After introducing her to Gene and Violet, Catherine could have sworn Joan batted her eyes at Bob. She wouldn't put it past her. While Joan was pretty and petite with a girlish giggle, Catherine doubted she was Bob's type. Maybe it was because Joan was forever clearing her throat and was sort of a know-it-all.

The blasting of the boat horn rudely announced it was time for the return trip.

"Remember, Joan, we're going to be like Lila!" Lila Neuenfelt, the first woman to graduate from the law school in 1921, now had her own practice.

"I don't know about that. There's only one Lila! See you two at the bar exam," Joan smiled.

Catherine came back to Earth with a thud, though Bob stood behind her on the deck as the steamboat made its way back to the hardworking city. With his muscular arms wrapped tight around her, they gazed at the full moon.

"I think Joan was flirting with you back on the island."

"So what if she was? I sure didn't flirt back. Dames like her don't interest me."

They danced to a band playing Louis Armstrong's 'Riverside Blues.'

"Kiddo, it'll never get any better than this." She scoffed at his nickname for her, but his remark delivered a powerful punch. She wanted to correct him, but how did he know? How did anyone know what the future held? Still, it was quite a time she'd had with Bob Sage on Boblo Island — her first time. And one she'd always remember.

· · ·

In the following few days, Bob began to feel bad about seducing Catherine outdoors. While he was pretty sure that her sexual desires were nearly as strong as his, he now told himself that they should have waited—if not for marriage than in the nearly guaranteed privacy of a hotel room. After their time on the island, he began having impure thoughts about ravishing her body. He could so easily picture himself cupping her breasts, sliding his fingers inside her underwear, and then stripping her of all garments. She didn't know what a gorgeous body she had. Had he not been so smitten with her, he wouldn't have been bothered by those thoughts. He'd had countless improper imaginings about women ever since he'd been wearing long pants.

He didn't confide his fantasies to her, of course, though he confessed his sins to Father Tim. Also, he decided not to tell her. She'd have to look after her own conscience; it wouldn't be right to force her into the Confession box.

. . .

Catherine no longer felt like a Jezebel. She blamed the moonlight and romantic atmosphere for their lust on the island. As far as her impure thoughts: it was no one's business but her own! Since they'd refrained since that time, she hadn't seen the need to tell Father Tim.

CHAPTER SIX

Bob didn't need approval from his mother. Still, it would be swell it would be if his two gals got along. So far they hadn't met, as he'd been waiting for the perfect time and place. Mary Ellen Sage was a small, yet mighty woman, known by many as Nana. Had you met her when she was seated at a table, you would've been shocked by her short stature. "I'm barely five feet in my stocking feet," she liked to tell new acquaintances.

Bob had wavy hair like his mother's, though it had been years since hers had been brown. He also got her deep-set eyes; though hers were more pensive, his were no less soulful. Despite her many losses, her small but startlingly blue eyes never lost their twinkle, nor did her words lose their kindness and good intentions.

One late summer night, Catherine and Bob strolled through part of Belle Isle – an island in the Detroit River. While they'd had several dates by then, they'd only had sex the one time on Boblo Island—not because of a lack of desire on either part, but because of their Catholic upbringing. Also, as neither lived on their own, convenient opportunities hadn't arisen. Nana, with her ever-watchful eyes, and Catherine living with her folks— didn't make it exactly easy for them to be alone. Bob wondered if his mother ever slept.

"Say, Sweets, you got plans for next Friday? How about coming to my fight next weekend? I've been reluctant about inviting you, but it would be a good time to meet my mother," Bob asked Catherine as they followed a paved walkway that led to the Belle Isle Aquarium.

Catherine had previously expressed more than a passing interest in seeing him in the ring, but until now he'd discouraged it by telling her it was "no place for a lady." He knew telling her this made her even more intent about going. Still, she made no bones about not being a sports fan—especially one of such a violent sport. Knowing how her mother had sometimes been roughed up by her father, Bob figured that could have something to do with it. Yet if Catherine had truly fallen for him, the way he had her—she needed to see him in the ring, by golly! More than making her proud, he needed to see this part of his world. If he didn't pass—God forbid—the bar exam, boxing would be his be-all and end-all. And, if for no other reason, he had to get her to see what a great sport it was. Of course, she didn't have to be as wild about it as his dear mother—Catherine just had to like it.

After pinning her against the trunk of a massive oak tree, she, at last, agreed to see him in the ring.

. . .

Catherine had heard Bob's description of Nana so often that she had little difficulty picking out the tiny bespectacled lady in the long navy blue coat. "Little but mighty," Bob had said and he was right.

"Hello, Mrs. Sage. I'm Catherine. Mind if I sit next to you?" Being in a crowd had already made her dizzy, and she could hardly wait for Nana to remove her large handbag from the hard seat.

Nana smiled, but then returned her gaze to the ring where two of the referees were talking between matches. She'd been saving the seat for "Bob's girl," who, in her estimation, had shown up a little late to the boxing event in Arena Gardens.

Catherine refrained from saying anything further, sensitive that the older woman had barely acknowledged her presence. She had no idea they'd be sitting ringside, but since Bob would be one of the main fighters that night, it made perfect sense.

While he'd only been boxing for a couple of years, Bob had quickly become well known as one of Detroit's top middle-weight champs, known for being quick on his feet, as well as for his jabs and double-jabs. But it was his powerful uppercut that had caused his name to be on the lips of local boxing fans. They knew that as soon as his opponent's head drooped, Bob would deliver a powerful blow with his left mitt.

Nana told her that Bob could be the next Billy Miske—the *St. Paul Thunderbolt*, or Harry Greb, known by fans as the *Pittsburgh Windmill*. He could even be the next Jack Dempsey, the little woman insisted, giving Catherine a sidelong glance.

"You've heard of Jack, right?" Nana burrowed her fierce little blue eyes deep into Catherine's eyes. Then the older woman let out a belly laugh. "Bob said you'd meet my stare, and gosh, you sure did, Lawyer gal! I like you fine and I can see you're more than simply a good looker."

"Why, thank you, Mrs. Sage."

"You can call me Nana, too. Most do. You read about the boxing matches in the newspaper, or are you too busy with your law books?"

Catherine had to admit that she didn't.

Nana feigned disappointment. "Honey, to be frank, I'm a bit surprised Bob wanted you to be here."

Aromas of salt, sweat, popcorn, and greasy hot dogs filled the smoke-filled, dimly lit arena. This alone made it worth the price of admission, Catherine decided, feeling a wave of hunger.

Then the lights of the ring switched on and two boxers entered the ring. From his corner, Bob threw kisses at Catherine and Nana. Nana whistled back at him. She was as loud as any man there.

Catherine chuckled in surprise and shielded her eyes with her hand as a visor. She'd never seen lights so bright. It made Bob and the other boxer look larger than life—like gods in the ring. Nana told her that her son's opponent, 'Ready Eddy,' was a light heavyweight—both taller and bulkier than Bob, the 'Battling Barrister.'

Almost everyone in Detroit's boxing world knew that Bob was going to law school and that he was paying for school with money from his boxing wins. The moniker would stick with him during his entire boxing career.

"It's not going to be a fair match, is it?" sweaty-palmed Catherine whispered to Nana.

"Guess we'll have to wait and see, my dear, but as you probably know: Bob has no problem throwing down a boxer double his size."

The referee introduced both boxers to the roaring crowd.

Then a voice shouted: "I LOVE YOU BOB!" Catherine's cheeks burned when after realizing it was she who'd just shouted the declaration at the top of her lungs.

"Did you hear that, Bob? Your gal loves you!" A man's voice shouted and the enthused audience cheered.

Bob stepped away from the center of the ring and waved at Catherine. She bolted out of her front-row seat and he squatted down to give her a quick smack on the lips.

"I love you, too, Kiddo! Now I have the luck of the Irish, plus you!"

The two boxers lowered their chins to their chests and began hopping like kangaroos. What an odd sort of dance they were doing! But Ready Eddy had the advantage and early on, knocked Bob out flat in the first few rounds.

Nana shouted in her ear: "He's only a slugger. Bob will outsmart him real soon!" She explained to Catherine that 'sluggers' deliver a hard punch, but they can't get far in the boxing world if that's the only move they're known for.

Catherine was certain she was going to faint. Her stomach tossed and turned as fast as the boxers' bodies moved.

By the fourth round, Bob made a comeback. Nana had been right.

Catherine chewed her nails. While she found it difficult to take her eyes off his glistening shoulders and his powerful legs, she doubted she'd be able to attend another match anytime soon. Still, she was proud to be the girlfriend of the Battling Barrister.

Ready Eddy proved he wasn't ready enough for the Battling Barrister. Between rounds, Eddy dared to call Bob a "Mick." Once Bob's Sage's ire was provoked — look out! Some say it only would have taken a single punch to knock him flat, but Bob kept punching long after his opponent was down. He knew he'd get a penalty for it, but he didn't care. Bob's manager and coach, Billy Watson, shouted at him.

The crowd roared.

The referee pulled Bob away from the not-so-ready Eddy's flattened pulp.

Bob had the killer instinct. Catherine was both proud and somewhat afraid of the beast that climbed out of him in the ring that night. She hoped that would be the only place where the beast could be roused and rewarded.

· · ·

During that busy summer, Catherine would attend two other fights. Bob won both because of his powerful jabs and uppercuts, as well as being quick on his feet. He said it was because she'd been there, but with his winning record, she doubted her presence had much to do with it. She'd been disappointed that Nana hadn't been at either of the other two fights. Bob claimed his mother had been feeling poorly and was concerned about a return of the 1918 flu. Luckily, it wasn't, but after several visits to the doctor, Nana was diagnosed with angina. She was under doctor's orders to rest, though it would remain unknown whether or not her condition would improve. Catherine often popped in to visit her, until she had to spend most of her time preparing for the upcoming bar exam.

Bob lived with his mother in an upper flat in Corktown, near where Catherine lived with her parents. Nana kept it as dark and cool as she could, though because it was an upper flat, keeping it comfortable in the summers proved a losing battle. The strong scent of cabbage and corned beef from a previous supper always filled the small rooms.

The stairs leading up to the flat creaked and Bob told Nana to use them as little as possible. He promised to run more errands for her now and do all the grocery shopping.

"Over my dead body!" she'd tell him, secretly pleased.

"No, Ma, I'm serious," he'd respond. She'd smile, pat his hand, and call him a good son.

Sometimes when he found her slowly making her way up the stairs, he'd scoop her in his muscular arms and carry her up the rest of the way. Her other son, Gene, wouldn't do such a thing, but he was, as she called him, "a good boy, too." While she made a bigger fuss over Bob, she lived and breathed for both sons, who were now her only living kin.

Nana had made a photo altar of the deceased Sage men on a round table in front of her living room window. Framed black-and-white photos were often picked up by tending hands—hands that dusted the glass frames almost every other day. During the first few times Catherine had visited, Nana had not only pointed out the photos on the table but also shared a small photo album and point out who-was-who.

The first picture was of her husband, Eugene. He died of silicosis, a disease common in miners, not long after they'd moved to Michigan. After reporting this to Catherine, she set the frame down and quickly moved on to the next photo. Catherine could tell she didn't want to say anything further about him. Not yet, anyway.

"Now this is my oldest son, James. We all loved him so much! How proud we were when he attended the University of Michigan for engineering. But then he died in the war. Some say he was the best of the boys—but they've all been my prizes. He took after my husband Eugene's side of the family because he was tall and slow to anger. And here's little Francis. He only lived to be a wee lad of three."

Catherine knew to smile and nod, but ask only a few questions, as she knew stories would trot from Nana's mouth unbidden. Soon, she was telling Catherine about Raymond—Bob's twin—in a mining accident out in Idaho.

"I dreamed about his death the night before he actually died. Poor lad was only fourteen. He'd chosen to go back west rather than remain in Michigan with the rest of us. Only fourteen...Do you believe in the spirit world, Catherine?"

"Mostly I do."

"Good. It's there all right. I know this from dreams and sensing the presence of those I've lost. Now, what say we chew that licorice you brought and we'll speak of other matters?"

Nana sat lengthwise on her plush rose-colored Victorian sofa with her short legs covered by a heavy throw, despite the heat. Catherine sat across from her in an armchair. She nodded and smiled, as she noted several crucifixes on the walls, as well as the Irish Blessing. Once the older woman nodded off, Catherine told her softly that she needed to leave so she could meet Bob.

"Before you go, dear, I want you to know something about Bob. Something he wouldn't tell you himself," said Nana, now wide awake. "The reason he's such a fine boxer can be attributed to his brothers. Bob was the scrawnier twin when he was little, and also the kinder one, but get his Irish up and look out! That gang—what do they call them—The Purple Gang? They once tried roughing him up after he found out about their bootlegging shenanigans. Most folks live in fear of them, but not so my Bobby. Well, one time, after Bob immediately bounced back after receiving a hard punch, the gang member who'd delivered the blow recommended he take up boxing. So he began taking lessons when he was about thirteen. Also, when Bob hears of any sort of injustice, it immediately flares up that temper of his. I've always made it my duty to keep him from getting too many bumps and bruises — both physical ones and bruises to his soul. Saints preserve him."

Then, taking both the younger woman's hands in hers, Nana whispered, "Think I can recruit your help? I need you to assist me in keeping his temper at bay. I worry that someday he's going to go off like a firecracker — or worse: a landmine. He thinks he's smart enough to rid the world of the bad folks, but I'm not so sure. It's that Purple Gang I worry about. He needs to steer clear of them."

Catherine hugged her close, assuring her she'd do what she could. It wasn't difficult to see where Bob got his feisty spirit from. Nana had entrusted her with the care and keeping of her son's heart — more than his body. Problem was that Catherine had little idea if she were truly up for the task, especially since she was far too ambitious to settle for becoming a wife and mother.

CHAPTER SEVEN

Toward the end of Catherine and Bob's first summer together, close to fifty guests showed up for the annual McIntosh summer picnic at Appleton Lake. Appleton was a small lake, a good two-hour drive west from the city. While the family never had money for trips, summer wouldn't be complete unless they hosted a picnic. Several family members and friends hadn't yet met Bob, though most had heard about him — especially those who followed boxing. This could explain the reason for the larger than usual gathering.

The day sizzled and the sun seemed to spat flames well before noon. Catherine's breezy blue polka dot dress revealed her knees. Her mother, dressed in a summery, long white gown, hadn't approved of her youngest daughter's short, sleeveless dress. "It's all the rage," Catherine told her, and Bridget eye-rolled her. Her daughters were always using that phrase, especially Catherine.

Every summer, the McIntoshes always got to the picnic area early to set up: red checkered tablecloths needed to be spread atop several picnic tables…balloons needed blowing up…tubs of ice had to be hauled from Mickey's truck. There was always enough bottled Vernor's Ginger Ale for an army, as well as bootlegged whiskey, gin, and beer. This year, like the last couple, Catherine and her mother spent much of the day before cooking chicken, making potato salad, and baking brownies — despite the heat. Now that both her older sisters, Eileen and Molly were married, it was Catherine alone who helped their mother in the kitchen.

Almost as soon as they'd arrived, John left them to go fishing without first helping his parents and Catherine set up.

"John could do a little more, Mother. He's positively spoiled. I've never seen him lift a finger at home or anywhere. Certainly never at our picnics!"

"Now, Catherine, if he catches those tasty little bluegills — that'll be his contribution," Bridget said, crossing her thin arms over small, but sagging breasts. Catherine was saddened by the havoc wreaked from childbearing on her mother's body. No way would she ever let this happen to her!

Why did her mother always have to defend John? He'd wink with those wide-set hazel eyes, and run his hands through his sandy curls. He was full of blarney, but girls always fluttered around him like moths to a flame. While Catherine loved him, there was no excusing his laziness. Why didn't the rest of the family find him as irksome as she did? Sure she loved him, but…

"You know he never catches anything," said Catherine, holding her ground.

"Now, girls, let's not quibble. May all the saints preserve us," said her father, mopping sweat from his brow. Both women smirked at him because he was always the peacemaker when the two of them argued.

Catherine had gotten little sleep the night before. She'd worried that Bob either wouldn't make it to the picnic — or that he would. She didn't know which would be worse. "You got a stack of Bibles? I'll swear on it that I'll make it," he'd told her repeatedly. Not that she didn't want him to show up — she did — but his injuries resulting from a match two nights ago had been worse than usual. Not only was his head sore, but he sounded like he was suffering from laryngitis. Still, he promised to not only bring Nana, but Gene, Violet, and their little Bobby Gene.

This was to be the 'last hurrah' of the summer — at least for Catherine and Bob — as they'd have to prepare for the much-anticipated bar exam. She looked forward to introducing Bob to Uncle Gerry — the Honorable Gerald McIntosh — and hoped that she, too, would have some time to speak with him. He'd always encouraged her to go to law school and had expressed utmost confidence in her intellect. Hopefully, he'd put her mind more at ease about the exam. Too much time seemed to have passed since her last course. What if her memory was like a leaky boat? More than a few professors had said that she had excellent recall, and her ability to both analyze and cite points of law was beyond compare. The portly and silver-bearded Professor Higgins once told her that her mind was "like a steel trap." She'd have to keep that in mind before the exam.

"What are you daydreaming about, my dear? That good-looking boyfriend of yours perhaps?" her mother teased.

"The bar exam, if you must know," said Catherine, hoping her steel trap of a mind sprang shut on her mother. Had there ever been a nosier person?

"Honey, it's too nice a day to worry about it. This should be a day of relaxation for everyone."

She wished her mother could rest after all the picnic preparations, though Catherine didn't hold much hope. If this year was anything like the preceding ones, Bridget would likely worry about whether or not everyone was having a good time. She wouldn't relax until she was home in bed. While Bridget hadn't gone beyond the eighth grade in school, she had an active mind and had always functioned on little sleep. Not only did she take care of home and family, but also the books for the diner.

"What do they call your new hair-do? Does Bob know about it?"

"It's called a bob, Mother, and no, Bob hasn't yet seen it." Catherine couldn't believe there were more questions from the interfering matriarch, as well as implied judgment.

"Don't be surprised if Bob won't like the bob! You know full well that a 'woman's hair is her crowning glory.'"

"I don't care if Bob likes it or not, Mother. It only matters that I do."

"I know you better than that, Catherine."

"Quit razzing our girl! Katy's beautiful, no matter whether her hair's short or long," said her father, coming to her aid.

"Thank you, Daddy." Catherine gave her mother a long, smug smile.

"I never said she wasn't," said her mother, sighing. "Just that men like a woman with hair. Not everyone's so fortunate to have such a lovely head of hair like you. All those natural curls."

While she knew Bob wouldn't be arriving soon, she hoped it wouldn't be long before her sisters and Uncle Gerry showed up. This superficial conversation with her parents was nearly as insufferable as the heat.

Uncle Gerry had never married and had always lived with his widowed mother, Grammy McIntosh. They lived together in a mansion, or so Catherine had always told her friends. When she was a child, she'd been the only one of her siblings to spend an occasional night at her uncle's large home in Grosse Pointe. The others had always been afraid of Grammy because her one eye, enlarged by her monocle, gave her a look that Eileen said "could wither grapes on the vine." Catherine disagreed and told them they should view her like she did—as an unusual antique.

Their father and uncle weren't the closest of brothers. Mickey had always had to scrape for a living, unlike Gerry. "He got all the brains but I got the personality," Mickey was fond of saying. Once he told Catherine how she was lucky because she wound up with both assets. He asked her not to mention this to her brothers and sisters. She never did.

Not wanting to join her mother in swatting at hungry flies swarming above the food, still covered on the tables, Catherine wandered off and sat with her back against a giant shade tree close to the water's edge. She daydreamed about Bob.

Her initial impression from a couple of years ago had sure changed. While he was a snappy dresser, she was relieved he wasn't the city slicker sort. The day they'd met, he'd worn the vest with the watch chain, along with the straw boater, simply to impress her. It had been no accident.

Already, they'd made so many memories. Good thing they hadn't met the first year in law school, as she would have either flunked out or refused to have gone out with him. Contemplating their future together made her dizzy. On the one hand, it sounded thrilling, but on the other — exhausting.

Their dreams were big ones: Someday, she would be a successful trial attorney and Bob — a judge, then perhaps even mayor of Detroit. They both longed to travel the world, buy a yacht, and live in a mansion (a small one, but large and fancy enough for lavish parties). They both wanted justice for the underdogs and equal rights for all — and this mattered to them both way more than material wealth. Still, people listened to those who were well-off. Once they became a high-society couple, it would put them in a position to fight for the poor and oppressed. Everyone should be equal, but they weren't. That they weren't upset her to no end. Why couldn't everyone realize their dreams in America? Shouldn't it now, in the twentieth century, be a place of opportunity for everyone? Did Bob feel as strongly as she did? She sure hoped so.

If someone had later asked Catherine how long she'd been sitting there in the tree's shade, she wouldn't have had a clue. As she tried to rein in her inner voice, she observed prehistoric-looking Sandhill cranes edging ever closer to the picnic tables, and a family of ducks swimming close to shore, and several sailboats out on the lake. The water lapped against the shore and a cooler breeze caused her to drift off.

When she returned to consciousness, she found it difficult to focus and make out the shadowy forms of family and friends. How long had she been asleep? Had Bob arrived yet? Why hadn't anyone come over to rouse her? It made her crabby to feel anything less than lucid at a social event.

There could be no mistaking her sisters, Eileen and Molly. Disconcerted from slumber, Catherine waved but doubted they'd yet seen her. Feeling wobbly, she balanced herself against the tree trunk. Then she noticed Eileen's brood of three: the two older girls were chasing the Sandhill cranes, and the baby, Matthew, crawling off a blanket spread out on the grass.

Eileen's husband, Tommy, was already searching for the hooch in one of the large tin tubs—and not watching Matthew. Eileen was yelling at him to do so. Then Tommy's eyes were on Molly, who thankfully had little idea of his attraction, though Eileen and Catherine were well-aware of it.

At last, there was Grammy McIntosh, which meant that Gerry must be there, too. Good, at least there'd now be someone interesting for Catherine to talk to. But now her mother was calling over to her.

"Come say 'hello' to my friends, Kate," coaxed Grammy McIntosh. Grammy's three friends, women Catherine had met on other occasions, all smiled at her now, but not exactly in a pleasant way.

"Catherine, I was just telling them how you've earned your law degree," her mother said.

"Hello, ladies. Actually, I do have one more test: the bar exam," Catherine told them.

"And then what?" asked pointy-nosed Nellie, the most critical of the three.

"My plan is to become a lawyer, of course."

"You think those bullying men are going to let you join them? It won't be easy, my dear, are you aware of that?" Leave it to Lenore to state the obvious.

"And did I just hear wedding bells ringing for you, too?" asked Sally, the friendliest of the group. If only she didn't giggle after everything she said.

"Now, Mrs. Merton, you shouldn't fall prey to my mother's gossip. Mother, may I please have a word?"

Bridget reddened as her daughter yanked her away from the twittering trio.

"Telling them about my law degree is one thing, Mother, but that I'm getting married? Bob hasn't even proposed. You've got to set them straight!"

"Now, dear, don't be so—so—petulant." Her mother looked proud of herself for using a several-syllable word.

"I don't think that's the word you're searching for. Please, promise me."

"Promise you, what, Catherine?"

"That you will tell them I'm not yet engaged." How could this woman seriously be so exasperating? Shite!

Uncle Gerry sat at a picnic table with Grammy. He waved in Catherine's direction and she took her leave of the three busybodies. Despite it being a hot day, Grammy's thin body swam in a dark blue coat. She pulled the collar up, which partly disguised her disgruntled expression.

"There's my favorite niece!" her red-haired uncle said. While he cared for his other two nieces, he'd made no pretense of trying to treat them the same. After they'd hugged, Catherine bent down to kiss the cheek of her stoop-shouldered grandmother. Grammy held the monocle affixed to a chain around her neck up to an eye to examine her granddaughter. She was such a formal woman—a force to be reckoned with—that Catherine found it strange that she was called Grammy.

"Kate—my Katy! How are you doing dear?" Grammy inquired in a friendlier tone than Catherine would have supposed. "I simply can't abide this heat. Did your father bring the hammock? I'd like nothing better than to collapse into it, though I don't know how I'll ever get out."

"He brought it, Grammy—just for you! Uncle Gerry, did you hear my friend, Bob, will be here?" began Catherine.

"Your *friend*, eh? Word has it that he's a bit more than that," said Gerry.

"Well, yes, I guess so. He recently finished law school, too."

"Word has it that he's a big shot, but believe me, Katy, he's in your shadow. I can't imagine how he could hold a candle to you, though I hear he's getting famous wearing those boxing gloves," said Gerry, turning up one side of his still-red handlebar mustache that always drooped a little more than the other.

"You flatter me, Uncle Gerry, but Bob's no slouch: he's quick in the ring, plus he can think on his feet."

"Well, I'm happy for you, my dear. While I'm genuinely hoping things work out, I hope you don't neglect your dream. You've got what it takes and having that Irish ire doesn't hurt you one iota. Between that and your smarts, you'll go far. That is unless society has its way with you."

"Don't let this son of mine say such a vulgarity to you, Catherine. Gerry, whatever did you mean? Society's having 'its way' with her? You're the bee's knees, my girl! Gerry, help me out of this winter coat. I didn't know it was going to be such a summery day."

Bee's knees? Catherine was surprised that her grandmother knew that expression.

"You know you don't have to be like that one friend of yours. The one who's never had a beau. Is it Margaret?" Gerry asked, helping his mother out of her coat.

"Maybe Catherine's friend doesn't like men. She could be a lesbian. Those women exist, though our savior, the Lord Jesus Christ, is the only one who could forgive such a mortal sin," said Grammy calmly.

Even unflappable Catherine was startled over her grandmother's opinion of a topic few discussed, at least in public. She wasn't sure how to respond and tried to change the subject. "You're right, Grammy, it's definitely too hot today, although it's a bit better in the shade. I can't wait for you to meet Bob, and also his mother. She likes to be called either Nana or Nana Sage. I'm not even sure what her first name is."

Grammy could be right about Margaret, but that was Margaret's business. Were all people as gossipy as Catherine's family? She couldn't wait to speak more with Uncle Gerry, but clearly, that wouldn't happen soon.

"I'll go see if my dad will put the hammock up between those two trees," Catherine said, pointing out two tall oak trees nearby.

By now most everyone was enjoying the smorgasbord of cold chicken, frankfurters, baked beans, cake, brownies, watermelon, pickles, as well as the cold lemonade. The spiked lemonade proved a smashing success. Catherine and her mother, for different reasons, still hadn't had a bite. Catherine took a few swigs of the spiked lemonade. Knowing she shouldn't drink on an empty stomach, she ate a pickle and some baked beans. Then she had a couple more swigs of the tastier than usual lemonade.

There was Bob's brother, Gene, Violet, and their one-year-old, Bobby Gene. They must have come without Bob since he was nowhere in sight. If Catherine got the chance, she'd ask about Bob's whereabouts, but not then, as everyone was milling about, all talking at once. She knew it would be awhile while before she could get a word in private with them.

Bobby Gene, known to disarm strangers with his dimpled grin, was doing so now with Catherine. He had a dimple in the same place as his uncle's. She returned his smile and he beamed all the more. Happy to see some of the Sages, Catherine then introduced them to her family.

But where were Bob and his mother? Shouldn't they be there by now? Had she imagined that he'd told her he'd be there around 1:00? Sure it was a long drive to the lake, but it was now well after 2:00. Violet was saying something about how she often broke out in a rash if she sat in the sun. Did Catherine know about a good skin cream since, like Violet, she was fair-skinned, too?

Although Bobby Gene couldn't actually chase the ducks, but waddled after them, in no time at all he'd made it down to the lake.

Neither of his parents appeared to notice, so Catherine tore after him, crying out his name. Luckily, he stopped just before reaching the water, and turned around, smiling — of course. He extended his chubby little hand for her to hold. Except for the dimple, he had the same black hair as his mother, though his eyes were hazel instead of his mother's dark brown.

Catherine took him over to look at the cranes, as being with Bobby Gene was more interesting than listening to more of Violet's prattle.

"Look at Katy," Eileen told their mother and Violet. "Think she'll be a mother someday? A Nervous Nelly, for sure, but she's certainly got the instinct."

The two other women nodded in agreement. (Catherine was glad she hadn't heard her remark; later, she got wind of it from Violet.)

Bobby Gene was now wandering off toward the parking area. Catherine again ran after him.

Then a howl resounded from the chatter of picnickers. Just as quickly as it was admitted, it ceased.

There on the ground, lying on her back was her grandmother's normally cheerful friend, Sally. No smile on her face now —

"I can't bear it anymore!" she shouted. "My one and only child—Bernadette—gone! My Frankie died from the 1918 flu and then she was all I had."

"Sally, what do you mean she's gone? She didn't die, too, did she?" asked Grammy McIntosh, clasping the woman's hand.

"No, but same as. Gone to her husband's side. No good gypsies they are!"

"Hear, dear, take a nip, you'll feel better," said Gerry. Little did anyone know, but she'd already had several nips—even gulps of the hard lemonade. She took another but then refused to budge from her prone position. Others, growing bored by her drama, returned to their previous conversations.

"I have no one and nothing now," Sally told Gerry and his mother, then rolled up her small body into a ball.

"Dear, you have friends. Think about that," Grammy McIntosh told the sad and tipsy woman.

"Friends—shmends!" was Sally's response. Her small audience fidgeted, so Catherine plunked down alongside her. After sympathizing with the elderly woman, Catherine told her how so many had suffered losses and how she'd lost a brother and sister to the pandemic. Sally then patted her arm and said how she recalled hearing about their deaths from her grandmother. After some cajoling, Catherine convinced Sally to follow her down to the water to dip her toes in. The older woman's mood visibly improved; she even chuckled at something Catherine said.

Next, Catherine put on her swimsuit in a rundown, but vacant shed everyone always used as a changing house. No point waiting any longer for Bob. Her black suit was a daring one and she could only imagine the disgruntled expressions on the older women. As she easily tucked her short hair into a bathing cap, she wondered what Bob would say, both about her suit and her short hair—that is, if he'd ever get the chance to see it.

Taking a dip in the cool water was truly the cat's meow! How nice to be away from the people, though Sally's words replayed in her mind. How dreadful to have no one in this difficult world! Catherine swam further and further out. She'd always been a good swimmer, and had few qualms about swimming into deeper water.

She stopped and began treading water. Who was that muscular-looking man in a one-piece black bathing suit? He began wading in her direction. Before even making a conscious decision to do so, the two swam toward each other as if their lives depended on it.

Bob pulled Catherine to him and she wrapped her legs around his middle. When he tried to French kiss her, she pulled away, more concerned than he was of the watchers from the shore.

"A gal's got to look after her reputation, right?" she asked.

"I know, I know," he said. "Say, what if we swam further out where we won't be seen?"

And so they did. Once they were in over their heads and had no choice but to tread water, Catherine expected Bob to feel her up and she was planning to comply. Instead, he told her to float with her head in the crook of his arm. Then he, too, floated on his back. Occasionally, he used his free arm as an oar and rowed them back into the shallower water. The weightlessness and coolness of the water was this side of divine.

"You told me once you were going to take me to Paradise. Well, this feels pretty darn close," she said, shutting her eyes. He smiled down at her trusting face.

Once he could feel the bottom with his feet, he began carrying her, as if he was rescuing her.

"Bob, what are you doing? I can swim with the best of them!"

He looked startled as if she'd awakened him from a trance.

"Sorry, I thought you were panicking out there."

She wanted to remark: "No, you were," but smiled and said, "I guess I am drowning in love."

"That makes two of us," he responded. She loved the feel of his wet skin.

Once they reached the beach, she removed her bathing cap, revealing her short bobbed haircut.

"For Pete's sake, who is this strange woman? Has anyone seen Catherine?" Bob yelped, causing several to look in their direction. He then whispered to her it made her look modern and even more beautiful than before.

Those who'd been there on that late summer day wished it would never end, with the possible exception of Bridget who would later claim that she was "beyond tired." The heat drove most into the water—even Nana, who'd discarded her black shawl and overskirt and went wading with her new friends. Bobby Gene had no other little ones his age, but Eileen's two older girls—Jeanne and Maggie—accepted him as part of their gang. By early evening, food was running low, as was the spiked and un-spiked lemonade.

An animated discussion ensued about whether alcohol consumption had gone up during Prohibition. Both Catherine and Bob argued it had, based on all the speakeasies now in the city. Neither of them saw the harm in it. Uncle Gerry cautioned them about condoning the Devil's brew, though he admittedly drank now and then.

"We need laws to curb the drunks—people too stupid to know when too much is too much," Uncle Gerry told them.

Bob knew better than to argue with him, as the judge had taken an immediate liking to him, and could readily see what a passionate, good-hearted soul he had.

"Now Bob, someday you'll have to choose between the law and boxing, or you won't do well at either. As fine a boxer as you are, there's no way you'll be able to keep up with the sport into your old age—unlike the law."

"Who knows if I'll even be around when I'm an old man?"

Uncle Gerry was at first alarmed by Bob's statement, but then slapped him on the back in jovial fraternity. Bob then told his fellow Irishman an Irish joke. Gerry's deep voice bellowed in laughter and the two strode off to the end of a dock to smoke cigars together.

. . .

Bob drove Catherine home after an enjoyable, but tiring day. On the way, she explained how the following two weeks would be long ones because she had to prepare her notes for the bar exam essay and wouldn't have a minute to spare.

"I thought we could work on our essays together in the library," he said.

"Now, Bob Sage, you know you'd wind up distracting me. And we already know how much I distract you! Remember, you barely passed a couple classes last semester."

"Didn't mean to get you worked up into a lather," he told her, looking dejected.

"You didn't. I guess we could try, but..."

"Never mind. Forget I said anything, okay?"

Catherine thought he'd understand, but Bob pouted like a little boy. He must have caught himself doing so because he was suddenly cool with her. He looked at his pocket watch once he pulled up in front of her house.

"Unlike you, Sweets, I minutes to spare, but not much more. I'd argue that even you won't need more than a week, but it'd be pointless since I can't win. How's about I call on you in two weeks?"

"Bob, why are you suddenly so aloof? I thought you'd say you'd miss me or something like that."

"Hell, Kiddo, I miss you already—even more than I do your shorn locks," he teased with tears in his eyes. Catherine would recall the tears over the next couple of weeks, and it would help get her through that time, as well as the single rose he left on her doorstep every day until they saw each other again.

CHAPTER EIGHT

Had it not been for the freshly clipped red roses she'd been receiving daily, Catherine would have had an easier time preparing for her exam. Not only did they distract her, but they also made her nose itch. Until she met Bob she had no difficulty focusing on her studies. No wonder there weren't as many famous women in the arts or sciences: once love had you head-locked, the game was over, the jig up. Somehow she doubted Bob was thinking of her this much. Could it be men were less affected, less waylaid by love? Damn them! It wasn't fair. The more she willed herself to get over being obsessed with him, the more front and center he became in her mind. And then there were her dreams of him, compounding the issue.

In one of them, Bob had perished in a house fire along with his mother. In another, a large cross was burning. Catherine woke up to what sounded like Nana crying for help. It turned out to be Jezebel, her parents' one-eyed cat, meowing at her bedside. The next night she'd dreamed she was watching one of Bob's fights. He was knocked out cold. When the referee finished the count Bob didn't open his eyes. The referee called the time of death like a hospital surgeon. In yet another, Bob was brain dead but alive, sitting at a table wearing a baby bib. Catherine kept trying to feed him from a teaspoon, but a whitish mush kept dripping down his chin. "Let me show you how it's done," insisted Nana, taking the spoon from Catherine's hand.

. . .

Eileen kept imploring Catherine to get in touch with Bob and thank him for the roses. "It would be ungrateful, Catherine, not to thank him. He needs to know you miss him."

"Well, Miss Nosy, if you must know, he agreed to be apart for two weeks." Catherine eye-rolled her sister.

"Why not write him a note and spray it with your perfume? That's what I'd do," said Eileen.

"Thanks, sis, but I think I can handle my own affairs."

"But can you? Maybe you're not as deeply in love as I thought."

"Not that you are or have ever been. Look, it's none of your beeswax," replied Catherine, finally shutting her sister down.

Catherine didn't let Eileen know about the telegram she wrote to Bob. It turned out tougher to write than her exam essay. She tore up ten drafts of it, as she couldn't communicate the depth of her feelings. Could it be that she was way more of a sentimentalist than she realized? Never would she mention to anyone (save Bob) the telegram she finally sent: *Dear Bob. Many thanks for the roses. Miss you! Love, Catherine.* After sending it, she regretted not having signed as 'Kate' — the nickname he'd recently begun calling her. That same day, received a telegram back from him: *Miss you, too, Kate. Your ever-loving, Bob.* Despite its brevity, she clutched his telegram to her heart and gazed out the window, lost in daydreams.

Now that she could settle down and focus on preparing for the essay, Catherine worked most of the day and into the early evenings at the dining room table, only taking breaks for coffee and her two-mile walks every morning. If the house was too inhabited, then she'd retreat to her bedroom and work at her desk, or even sit cross-legged on her bed. She usually studied in the dining room, and her parents soon learned to keep their distance, as did the usually pesky John.

•   •   •

While Bob missed Catherine more than she would ever know, he kept busy at the gym getting ready for an upcoming fight — and also preparing for the bar exam himself. He knew the exam wouldn't be easy, and that essay writing wasn't his strong suit, but when he put his mind to it, he knew he could do anything. If he won the fight, he'd be the next regional middle-weight champion.

Nights were hardest. More than once, he pulled all-nighters with a few friends in the speakeasies. Harry and Joe, he knew from the gym, and Bill was a law school buddy. Plus, he'd danced with a few pretty girls, though none could hold a candle to Catherine. He liked the way whiskey made him forget how much he missed her, the way it kept his self-doubts at bay. His fear of flunking the exam was the biggest of all, even though he knew he could retake it. Bob knew he wasn't putting in near enough time studying. And he also knew that Catherine was going to do well. She was the smartest person he'd ever met, though he never told her. Someday he would, though he worried by doing so, might make him look less of a man in her eyes.

•   •   •

"If Bob saw you like this, wouldn't you feel at all embarrassed?" Bridget asked. Her daughter shrugged. She'd been wearing the same pair of baggy trousers for over a week. Also, her tousled short auburn bob desperately needed washing. Who could do anything else when preparing an important case? In her essay, Catherine had to describe her defense of a hypothetical case. At first, she'd been thrilled because it made her feel like an actual lawyer, although she wouldn't be presenting to an actual jury.

"No, Mother. Why would I?" Catherine asked in an exasperated tone.

"You've been looking a bit like a ragamuffin these days. And when you doll yourself up, you're so pretty."

Why was her mother always so critical of her appearance? It wasn't like Catherine was going out in public like this, and even if she was—what business was it of hers? Deep down, she knew her mother wasn't being merely vain and superficial; she just didn't want Catherine to suffer the same financial difficulties that she had. How many times had she told Catherine that her father was a good and decent man and that it was only their financial woes that tried his patience? It was only being at the 'end of his rope' that caused him to take it out on his wife—and even then, it was mostly the drink talking, not him. If her daughters married men who were better off, it meant they'd likely have a better life. "Simple as that," Bridget often told her daughters over the years.

Catherine knew she was viewed as the last hope, since her sisters hadn't listened, and were now in circumstances similar to their mother's, especially Eileen.

Once she asked her mother if she wished she'd only had sons like Nana, but it wasn't a fair question as Nana had lost three of her five boys. Catherine knew she should go easier on her mother, as Bridget had lost two of her own—her youngest ones.

Catherine, too, missed Colleen (named after her mother's aunt) and Stephen. Those summer evenings in the neighborhood park when Molly and she would make up stories for them about fairies. They'd insist that fireflies were actually fairies, and how, if the little ones were bad, their souls would be snatched away by the meaner fairies. How large and wide their eyes became! And then five years ago, they were taken by the flu. Her sister and brother would have now been fifteen and seventeen.

Both Colleen and Stephen had been sickly children—matchstick thin with watery blue eyes. They'd struggled with asthma and had been prone to catching any virus in circulation. Catherine still felt guilty when she'd recall how much she'd once resented them for not letting her finish a book she was reading. Yet some memories provoked feelings of deep tenderness. They'd always seemed otherworldly, too, as if part of them had never fully lived on Earth.

Losing loved ones had caused her to adopt a harder view of life. They could be here one day but gone the next. Someday she could be the only one left and would have to fend for herself. She didn't want to rely on her parents, her uncle, or Bob. She had little choice but to rely on her own wit, grit, and gumption. Luckily, she had a lot of that in store. As much as she adored Robert Sage, she didn't want or need him—or any man—to be her meal ticket. Someday she wanted to be respected for that.

•　•　•

Catherine's essay, in defense of Jane Doe, had been based on the following scenario:

Jane Doe shot John Smith. Her defense hinged on the fact that Jane committed the crime because John assaulted her. According to Jane, her assailant asked for directions and then told her to follow him down an alley. He then grabbed her buttocks. She slapped him. He responded by pushing her repeatedly until she fell backward. She drew a pistol from her purse and shot him when he was about to attack her. The bullet entered one side of his face and exited the other—disfiguring him for life. Jane Doe insisted that he would have raped and possibly murdered her had she not taken such an extreme action of self-defense.

•　•　•

Thinking about the case made Catherine's blood boil. She couldn't help but personalize it. Not that one of her parents would murder the other, but there'd been at least a dozen times over the years she'd witnessed her father push her mother. Sometimes her mother had pushed back or slapped him, but she did so less as the years went on. Catherine tried to intervene when she was younger, but soon learned it only made things worse for her mother. Sometimes she'd hide with her siblings in the bathroom. They'd covered their ears and tried not to hear what was going on, but they always did. Catherine never understood why her mother didn't leave and take her children to Aunt Vivian's in New York.

One early evening, a couple of days before writing her essay in the law school library, Catherine's parents coaxed her into walking with them to an ice cream parlor. Had her mother and Bob secretly hatched the plan to get her out of the house? Catherine feigned being upset, but of course, would be secretly delighted to see Bob. He would sweep her into his arms...

It was a humid evening in late August. The line for ice cream snaked down one street and onto another. Her parents spoke about the hillside sign made of flowers out in California where they made motion pictures. Supposedly, it was made of flowers that spelled out "Hollywoodland." Wouldn't that be something remarkable to see? Maybe, said her mother, the family could take a trip out there to see it. Her father suggested maybe they could take a train west. But then the talk degenerated into how sticky the air had become. Could rain be headed their way?

Catherine began to no longer comprehend what they were saying and only heard the buzzing of their voices, as she recalled a few salient points she'd try to remember to make in her essay. It would be an easier case to prove if the shooting involved two men, rather than a man and a woman — or even two women. She would point out two similar cases and also focus on Jane Doe's sterling character and good family. Also, she'd address the fact that Jane had never been in trouble before.

Was that Bob sauntering down the road? The man had a similar gait, this side of cocky — a man about town.

"Mother, did you arrange this with Bob?"

Her mother raised her brows and turned around to see who Catherine was gesturing at. "Catherine, that's not Bob. You thought I was in cahoots with your beau, did you? Why, I'd never think of interfering!"

Oh, no, you never interfere, Mother — she wanted to say, but bit her lip. She was crestfallen but tried not to show it.

"Look, dear," Her mother nudged her father. "Kate is sad because I didn't ask Bob to join us."

"That true, Katy?" her father asked.

Catherine bit her tongue as they continued to tease her. She longed to remark how the last thing she wanted to do was to be there with them.

After they'd finally been served, the three sat on a bench outside and licked their cones in silence. Ed O'Riley, their stern-looking but kindly landlord, stopped to chat. He'd lost his wife a few years back and had always been especially friendly whenever Catherine was in his presence — a little too friendly, though he was older than her father.

Her mother wondered if she was enjoying the ice cream. Not wanting to disappoint her, Catherine tried her best to reassure her of its tastiness. The smirk on Bridget's face told her daughter all she needed to know.

It had been close to two weeks since Catherine and Bob had seen each other. Bob must have been well-aware that she was preparing for the exam. She worried he was spreading himself too thinly, preparing for both the exam and his next match. Still, he seemed to have more free time than she did. Had his head been swayed by another woman? Maybe a blonde at one of the speakeasies or out on Belle Isle? If he wasn't so friendly and had such a handsome mug, she wouldn't have been so worried. She fretted about their future together.

She asked if it would be rude of her to walk home by herself after the ice cream, as she didn't have time to dawdle. Her mother told her to go on ahead of them, and that it was just nice she'd for once agreed to join them on a family outing.

While the ice cream was almost worth the wait, Catherine ate her chocolate cone so fast it gave her a stomachache on the long walk home alone. She took herself to task, not for going out for ice cream so much as having such a suspicious mind. Keep your eyes on the prize and maybe someday you'll get lucky. Everyone was out sitting on their porches. Children shouted and ran around like they didn't have a bedtime. They'd been so noisy at the ice cream parlor. The lot of them: such loathsome little creatures.

As she soaked in the cool spray of the bathroom shower, she began framing her defense of Jane Doe so well that when she wrote her essay two days later in a classroom. The words seemed to have written themselves. Confident yet exhausted after writing twenty-five pages, she turned in her essay to a professor, who would then submit it along with others to the judging members of the Bar Association. Professor Higgins later confided that she was the second one to complete the essay. How much more satisfying it would be to defend a wrongfully accused person in a courtroom! One day, she would, despite the difficulties her gender faced in the legal profession.

CHAPTER NINE

"Catherine told me you're a pie fan, Bob. Tell you what: you can eat all the pie you want for free tonight. It's on me!" Mickey told him.

"Offer accepted, Mr. McIntosh. Thanks, sir." Bob jumped to his feet and extended his right hand to shake on the deal. Mickey first wiped off his hands on his slightly stained white apron. Bob then devoured slices of three different ones: blueberry, apple, and cherry—claiming they were all his favorites.

It was near closing time and most customers had left Mickey Mac's. Catherine's father would get a few hours off before tending the downstairs bar of his small, nameless speakeasy. Most nights Mickey would grab a bite to eat in the diner's kitchen and then head straight downstairs.

Bob kept laughing a little louder than Catherine remembered and talking between bites. She could barely get a word in. Still, she kept grinning at everything he was saying. Instead of spending his 'free' time studying, he'd gotten together with his friends, but mostly he'd walk the streets at night missing her. After swallowing his last bite of pie, Bob dimpled up and admitted that he'd also worked out at the gym. He added, sheepishly, how he'd won a couple boxing matches, but they were with a couple no-names.

They were trying to decide if they'd go out dancing afterward or to a speakeasy. If they ended up at a speakeasy, it wouldn't be this nameless one of her father's. They preferred the nicer ones, so rarely did they set foot in Mickey's — and besides, they didn't feel exactly comfortable drinking around Catherine's father.

Catherine sipped coffee and nibbled a piece of blueberry pie, leaving most of it on the small dessert plate. Her stomach rumbled. Clearly, they were both suffering nervous reactions since it had been two weeks since they'd last seen each other. She couldn't wait to tell him her news. The problem: when to tell him?

Mickey sidled over to them on the pretext of refreshing their coffee. In his eagerness to please, Bob encouraged him to sit with them.

"Only for a minute, I've got a mess to clean up in the kitchen."

Catherine bit her tongue as she feigned a smile. What Bob didn't know was that her father would not only take him up on the invitation, but after plunking down with them — he'd never leave. While it made her happy to see that Bob seemed eager to please him, she couldn't help but feel somewhat taken aback.

As the two men chatted, she noted a few similarities. Like Bob, her father was quick on his feet and was happiest around people; he didn't look directly into your eyes unless he knew and trusted you; and, he probably would've made a good boxer. She sure hoped Bob didn't have some of his other qualities.

Mickey said he knew the couple had lots to catch up on, so he bid them a good evening, and scurried off to clean the kitchen. Thank God, he hadn't spilled the beans.

Catherine could no longer contain herself.

"Guess what? I passed the Bar! Best news of my life!" she exclaimed, but then put her hand on his and softly asked, "Did you get your letter?"

"Not yet, but that's great you passed, Kate! Say, I thought I was the best news in your life," Bob said, batting his lashes.

"I meant 'best news' besides you, Bob-o! Here I'm being perfectly serious and you're teasing me. I'm sure you'll hear real soon."

Modesty was big in the Sage family. Compliments were doled out few and far between. Bob recognized this as one of those times; he hadn't meant to make light of Catherine's accomplishment.

"I'm truly proud. See, all that hard work really paid off, didn't it? Me, I'm just banking on the luck of the Irish," Bob said, after licking his lips following his second piece of pie. "Look, Kiddo, even if I don't pass this round — I'll take the exam again. At least I passed law school and can attend the big award ceremony and dance."

It only then occurred to her how worried he was about not passing it.

Bob then told her how he'd been 'raking in the dough' from his fights and that he wanted to buy her a new dress for the occasion. Tomorrow he'd take her shopping. Catherine pretended to refuse but soon relented.

"August has turned out to be quite the month, hasn't it? First, President Harding dies, we graduate from law school, and now you've passed the Bar! Life sure always changes," said Bob. Catherine told him he forgot to add how much softer the September sunshine was and how the nights had cooled down considerably.

"Any chance asking you for a favor?" he asked.

"You can ask…"

"Seeing as you did so well throughout law school, think you could help me prepare for the exam if I have to retake it? Maybe give me some help with my writing skills?" Bob asked, more hesitantly than usual.

"Sure, of course, I will, but don't give up all hope yet. You're welcome to all my notes, but when it comes to writing papers, you're on your own, buster."

"You're an answer to my prayers, Kate."

"You're plenty smart, Mr. Robert Sage, and if you didn't pass, I know you will next time around."

"Strange, isn't it, how I have plenty of confidence in the ring and other parts of my life, but not in the classroom?"

"*Other parts* of your life—you mean, like with the ladies, right?" Catherine teased, rolling her steely blue eyes. "And as far as your classes, since you've managed to get to your senior year, I doubt you need too much help, but sure I'll help you some."

"Thanks, Kate. It's different now. Got to keep my nose to the grindstone, you know? It'd be different if I didn't have boxing— and you." He gave her yet another dimpled grin, then switched gears and told her about the dream he'd had a few nights ago. In the dream, he hadn't been feeling well and had a fever.

"I was older, not old, but it was many years from now. A couple guys were visiting me and I felt this anger exploding inside me. Wound up shooting them. Don't know how badly I'd hurt them. I ran from the office and down a dark alley. Never have I had such a clear dream. When I woke up, I was still burning up. I ran out to the living room. Gene was there, waiting for our mother who was getting ready to go out for dinner. That part I recall, but a few days later he told me I acted like it had all really happened. I don't recall saying it, but I guess I told him we needed to get out of town. "

"Have you ever seen those men before?" Catherine was unnerved by his dream but tried not to show it.

"I don't think so. Their features weren't real clear. They looked alike: balding with beady eyes."

"Fever dreams are the worst! I don't think you should read too much into it. Still, maybe it's a warning for you to never buy a pistol."

"Honey, I have one. My father bequeathed me a fancy one with a handle made of pearls. In this crime-ridden city, a man needs to protect himself and his family. Let's forget about that silly dream. What say we go kick up our heels on the dance floor? Let's forget about crazy dreams and life's little uncertainties," Bob said, as his fingers danced on the tabletop and climbed Catherine's arms. She giggled. Something she didn't do often.

. . .

Anyone noticing the smartly dressed couple on the dance floor of the popular Graystone Ballroom would have said they looked perfectly matched, though the woman was a couple of inches taller. She wore an emerald green dress that followed her curves with a tight-fitting cloche hat. He was clad in a pinstriped suit and a bow tie. It was obvious they were in love, as they seemed oblivious to everyone but each other. She'd bend down a little to whisper something in his ear, and then he would murmur his response. No one would hear but her, and she would throw back her long neck and laugh. If you were dancing next to them, you might see their eyes in a half-closed swoon, and then how their eyelids lowered completely, as if to dispel some of the intense feelings between them—a passion that was close to overwhelming.

Catherine and Bob danced to song after song without taking a break. They couldn't get enough of the popular tunes from Al Jolson, George Gershwin, and Bessie Smith...Certain she was on fire, she asked him if he could put her in a tub of ice. He laughed, twirled her, then dipped her with such grace, that the other dancers stood back to admire their moves.

When Catherine's smoke-filled hair hit the pillow, she expected herself to fall asleep right away, but she couldn't stop thinking about Bob's dream. She wasn't able to convince herself that it was merely a dream. Were there more details that he hadn't mentioned? Had he had these kinds of dreams before? Nana had said something about spirits visiting her and dream visits from her late husband and the three sons who'd died. Maybe this sort of thing ran in the family.

CHAPTER TEN

It was early evening on a late summer night in 1923 when the Detroit College of Law celebrated its recent graduates with an award ceremony. Fifteen of the twenty-five graduates were being honored. The top three wore their graduation robes and carried lit tapers down the main aisle in the auditorium. Third in line was the lovely and lanky, auburn-haired, Catherine McIntosh. The actual graduation had been held back in June.

Tears wouldn't stop streaming down Catherine's cheeks as she attempted to keep her pace slow and even. While she didn't have a job offer yet, she'd smoothly landed—she'd finally arrived. A major goal had been accomplished. Why didn't she feel ecstatic then? Maybe she'd been tricked into thinking she'd landed smoothly, but was still airborne and about to go into a hurdling descent. *No. Don't be silly. You'll be okay, better than okay, as long as you keep your eye on the prize. Time to take your place beside the others... Shoulders back. Smile at the audience – those guests are kind enough to give up part of their evening.*

Catherine was one of only four women to graduate in her class. The dean, Honorable P.J.M. Hally announced that not only was she the third highest in her class, she also received the third highest honors of one-hundred and nineteen students statewide that took the bar exam that year. It was the first she'd heard that she scored higher than the rest of her class on her exam. She beamed, though her cheeks burned.

While Bob graduated in the same class, he did so without honors, and as he suspected, he hadn't passed the Bar.

How marvelous to sit down! The fifteen graduates being honored sat in the first row in front of the stage.

Catherine's parents were there, and also her sisters, brother, uncle, and grandmother. She turned and gave a small wave to them before the first speaker readied herself at the podium. While she appreciated family support, she couldn't help but wonder the whereabouts of Bob and Nana. Maybe he'd changed his mind. She couldn't blame him since he wasn't receiving any awards, but he said he'd be here — to support her. So why wasn't he? Almost all the other graduates were there. Maybe he felt unworthy, though he had every right to be proud. She hoped he was. Maybe something had come up to prevent him from...It was difficult to take a deep breath of the sticky and stagnant air. The pain caused by her pinching shoes was close to insufferable. At least that got her mind off feeling like she was about to spontaneously combust.

She turned again to give a head nod and smile to Gene and Violet, sitting a few rows behind her family. They must have known Bob wasn't receiving any awards, so this must have meant they were there for her. Such sweethearts they were! Maybe Nana was taking care of Bobby Gene.

Catherine counted herself fortunate to have alongside her, her good friends — Joan, Margaret, and Grace. The bond between them was a strong one. Did they feel as strongly as she did about staying in touch and becoming lifelong friends? Competing in a man's world wouldn't be easy, and having friends in the same profession would be, if not essential, certainly important for her own success. Focus, Catherine, focus...Lila Neuenfelt was about to speak, followed by Emily Schauber, both former graduates and now successful attorneys.

Their rousing speeches brought tears to the graduates' eyes, particularly those of the young women. Catherine clapped until her hands burned—and for a few minutes, she'd even forgotten about Bob. Then she kept turning around in her hard chair to search for him. If he couldn't be there, she wanted the entire event to come to a screeching halt. Without his presence, it no longer seemed meaningful. She couldn't tell this to anyone and especially not her friends. Her cheeks grew blazing hot. Bob had become her world, her mainstay, her purpose. Everything else— only icing, or the bow on the present...She couldn't keep her pale hands still in her lap; they looked like they wanted to fly away. Joan noticed and rubbed her arm.

The valedictorian, Ronald Blazer, gave a long speech about the need for justice and fairness in an unfair world. He mentioned that nine different nationalities were represented in the college and how proud he had been to be a student there. Catherine found it interesting that he didn't mention the breakthrough of women in the legal world. She couldn't stop shifting about in her seat. Clasping one sweaty palm into the other seemed to be the only thing she could do to appear calm. She couldn't seem to breathe evenly.

At the end of the ceremony, Dean Hally spoke about how Detroit, Michigan, and the nation, would benefit from these capable, intelligent legal minds who would fairly promote justice for the next half-century.

Before the dinner, there had been congratulatory hugs and kisses from family, friends, and acquaintances, and several bouquets. Referring to the latter, Catherine asked if someone had died—mind you, she'd had more than a few glasses of bootlegged bubbly. For this one night, she felt a little famous. If only Bob could be there to enjoy it, too.

The high-ceilinged ballroom was perfect for dinner and dancing. Family members could stay for the dinner, but not the dance. Catherine sat at a large round table with her family. Everyone seemed to talk at once. Was anyone listening? Knowing them, her guess was probably not. Since Bob loved to eat, he would've been here by now; therefore, he must have decided not to join the festivities. She needed to stop looking for him. She wanted to invite Gene and Violet to sit with them, but couldn't locate them in the crowd.

The heat and excitement kept Catherine from having an appetite, so she'd hurriedly gone by the buffet table, after taking small portions from a few of the serving platters. Her feet not only pinched but ached from her high heels. She hated how tall they made her appear and kicked them off under the table after setting the food plate down. No one would notice – or so she hoped.

Again, she scanned the crowd for Gene and Violet, as she continued looking for Bob. Her mother repeated the same question three times before it registered. Stifling a yawn, Catherine wanted nothing more than to go home and let slumber have its way with her. For the love of Mary, the entire event was taking far too long!

Finally, families of the graduates began left; including her own. As Catherine hugged and thanked her loved ones for being there, she came alive. While she'd been proud to wear the black robe, it now felt hot and bulky, and after eating what she could, she peeled it off as soon as possible. For the rest of the evening, she would sashay in the long and slinky peacock blue gown that Bob had bought her.

The crowd was now a different one – all law school students and professors. While it was nice her family had been there for her, maybe the fun could begin and she could finally relax.

The orchestra began playing and music performed its usual magic: it wound her up like a mechanical wind-up toy and then let her loose on the dance floor. Since Bob was there, at first she danced with her friends. She mingled with friends and laughed. How good it felt to laugh.

And then there he was.

Bob swept her off her feet, her bare feet, and onto the crowded dance floor. They danced both the Charleston and the Fox Trot. "They're all the rage," she told him.

"I'm so proud of you, Catherine," he whispered, hugging her tight. She couldn't believe he just used her actual name instead of one of her many nicknames. How nice it was to have his respect, as well as his love.

"In fact, I'm amazed, and you look dazzling in that dress." He twirled her, and then pulled her close again. "Sorry, I missed the ceremony, but I had to go see my mother. She's in the hospital."

"I'm so sorry! What's wrong? Is she going to be alright?"

"She'll be okay so long as her ticker holds out. The doc told us she may not have many years left. Gene and Vi were eager to see you receive your awards, but left to see her. They send their apologies for not staying long enough to see you afterward."

Catherine promised to visit her in the hospital the following day. Nana was only fifty-nine — not all that old.

"Wish there was a way I could make it up to you" Bob said, having a certain hotel in mind.

"Oh, I think there is...Plus, I know of at least two dinners coming up for us graduates."

"Absolutely, my love, but I also have reservations at the Book Cadillac for Saturday night," he whispered in her ear and then kissed her neck.

"Bob, we're not at a speakeasy right now. Easy there, fella!"

And then Catherine was whisked away for an interview and photoshoot with the *Detroit Free Press*. From the corner of her eye, she caught Bob laughing with a vivacious law school student. Catherine had noticed her in the halls, but they'd never been in any of the same classes. Next, he was handing the pretty brunette a glass of punch.

She didn't equate her anger with jealousy, at least not at first. It was all she could do to control her rage. Only once had she experienced this way before — back in sixth grade with Jimmy O'Neil had walked another girl home instead of her. Catherine never spoke to him again. She wasn't about to so readily let Bob off the hook. She'd dangle him first, and then smile at his descent.

As soon as her interview was over, Catherine strode over to him. Bob awkwardly introduced her to the sultry Megan, wearing a long burgundy gown. Catherine in a polite, but ever-so cool tone, told the young woman that she needed to speak with him alone.

Megan looked from Catherine to Bob, and then back to Catherine. She nodded and blushed a deep crimson — almost as dark as the dress.

She led him outside into the brisk autumn air.

"Now, Kate, I know what you're thinking."

"You do, Bob? Tell me, will you?"

"Megan's the sister of a friend of mine — Henry — from the parish. I couldn't ignore her."

"Well, aren't you the sensitive sort? Truly, why couldn't you ignore her? On second thought, don't answer that. Look, I think I need a break."

"Catherine, how could you say that? We just spent two weeks apart. You know I'm mad about you! No other girl means a damn to me. Won't you at least give me a chance to make it up to you?"

It wasn't that his voice lacked passion or intention, but he spoke so fast the words fired from his mouth like bullets. This made it easier for her to say what she did.

"Maybe. In a couple days. I need time to think. If you could, please take me home. I wouldn't ask if my parents were still here."

"Of course. I'd do anything for you, Kate!"

"Let's lay off the sweet talk for now — okay?"

The long silence on the drive home was painful for both of them. They'd never felt so uncomfortable with each other. Bob wanted to tell her what a knockout she was in her blue dress, but knew she'd probably punch him if he opened his mouth. He had little idea she had this side to herself; that she could get so jealous. She always seemed so self-assured. Catherine wanted to take back what she said about not seeing each other for a while — especially since they'd just begun seeing each other again — but it was too late.

She gave him a quick peck on the cheek before bolting from the car.

Catherine had known from an early age that no matter what she'd try her hand at — she'd excel. A teacher once told her she had the memory of an elephant. While she'd had to study — to really hit the books in law school — she never doubted herself capable of grasping the material, though she knew well that society didn't dole out the "Attagirls!" the same way it did the "Attaboys!" She knew Bob mistrusted his memory. Still, he also knew his bravado and charm could compensate. Would it bother him to sometimes be in her shadow? Would he wind up leaving her because it would bother him too much?

The ceremony should have made her feel like she was on top of the world, but she wound up at the bottom — devastated in her private hell of insecurities. She walked through the dark neighborhood, cursing the world and loudly ranting: "Thought you were too smart to goof up, did you? And now you've let a goddamn man bring you down. Just some stupid man!" It woke up one dog and then another. A chorus of barking only added to her fury — her Irish ire.

Lights came on in a dark house. It was late and she'd had too much of the spiked punch. She tripped, stumbled, and lost her balance. Her blue dress — her beautiful blue gown — had a long tear up one side. Hot tears streamed down her cheeks. The dress—her display of jealousy—casting Bob out of her life again...It all added up and she howled louder than the dogs.

"Lady, go home or I'll call the cops!" a man's gruff voice shouted at her from a porch. She could only see his heavy-set outline. She'd been pretty sure she didn't know who it was.

Instead of responding, Catherine removed her shoes so she could make it home faster.

CHAPTER ELEVEN

Bob tossed and turned on the squeaky-springed bed in his small bedroom. Strange to be in his mother's upper flat without her there, too…He wasn't used to being alone and didn't much care for it. Not for a second could he imagine being in the world without her.

This was the second time his mother's heart had acted up; today her angina had been so bad she had to be hospitalized. The first time was after she got the telegram informing her of James' death in the war. Her oldest son, at twenty-seven, had been killed by a grenade in France. She'd already lost Francis when he was only three.

Mary Ellen Sage had carried on and remained devoted to her husband, Eugene, and their three sons. But then she lost Raymond and her husband, not long afterward. With each loss, she looked tinier, like her spirit's physical home had caved in and was on the verge of collapse.

Bob couldn't imagine life without her. Lately, he'd taken comfort in that if something happened to her, at least he'd still have Catherine. But would he? Had he been unintentionally driving her away? As much as he'd fallen for her, he recognized she might be too intellectual and independent to make a good wife. He couldn't imagine his life without either woman. If Catherine and he married, they'd not only be lovers but best friends, who'd someday travel the world together. What could be better? And with their combined intelligence and passion for causes, they could help right the world's wrongs — help to create a more civilized society.

He needed to get some rest, but then he recalled how much fun he'd had eating ice cream with Catherine on one of their early dates. It had been a hot summer, humid in the way only Detroit summers can be. The stink of fish and oil from the factories had rolled up in waves from the river and had made them both feel queasy.

But then they got ice cream, so sweet and cold. It brought a pleasure to his tongue — almost as good as their long kisses would be as their relationship progressed. Licking the cone, he'd almost been able to forget the brutality of the steamy city, the guys selling weapons in dark alleys — all for smuggling booze across the river or sticking up for a friend who'd been wronged. Still, it was always related to booze. The ice cream soothed. It returned him to his childhood out West and a pharmacy in Wallace where his mother had taken him for ice cream after getting his first pair of leather boots. Sure people did evil things there, but they were more spread out, like the open plains. These brutal and busy city streets could wear a man down.

"Bob!" A voice shouted. Startled, he sat bolt upright. It had been a man's voice. One of his dead brothers? His father? Maybe they were shouting to him from the beyond. Then again, maybe it was Gene — here to tell him their mother had died. But no, it wasn't a relative, either living or dead.

Bob quietly took the pearl-handled pistol from his nightstand drawer. It could be someone was trying to break in.

He inched his way along the walls of the dark flat. There were all kinds of strange shadows on the living room walls from the street below. He looked for one in the shape of a human, but only saw his own. After going through all the rooms, he backtracked through each of them.

At last, convinced no one was there, he sat at the kitchen table and sipped a glass of water.

A fly buzzed around the light above the table. He stared at the pistol now resting on the red checked tablecloth. The startling voice dimmed in his memory, enabling him to make a sudden decision: Next time he saw Catherine, he'd ask for her hand in marriage.

CHAPTER TWELVE

The following evening, Catherine saw Bob at a weekday mass at Most Holy Trinity Church in Corktown. She was glad he didn't know she was there, as sitting in a back pew gave her a chance to observe him. The sanctuary was packed, so she doubted he'd turn around and see her. After initially stopping by the church to deliver her mother's brownies for a bake sale, she attended the mass.

While Bob had said nothing about it to her, she knew he was there to pray for Nana. Sitting forward against the kneeler with his head bowed, made him look contrite and vulnerable — hardly a tough boxer. A wave of tenderness passed through her.

The organ music stopped and Father Tim began saying the Latin mass.

She remained hidden behind the head of a curly-haired woman in the pew in front of her. She prayed Bob wouldn't turn around. Could he feel her eyes burning into the back of his skull?

The priest droned on in the comforting hum of Latin.

Confession would follow the mass, but Catherine wouldn't be among the confessors. Unlike most Catholics, she preferred to confess her sins directly to God, that is — when she needed to do so. She supposed she ought to ask God to forgive her for not confessing to a priest, but surely He would view it merely as a venial sin.

She continued to observe Bob, enjoying that he was still unaware of her presence. His bowed head made the back of his neck look vulnerable. While she'd never asked him how often he went to Confession, she had a feeling he did so regularly. Maybe she should confess her sin of jealousy from the previous night. No doubt it wasn't the jealousy that was the actual sin, but the ugly thoughts she'd had about the woman—Megan—with whom Bob had engaged in conversation at the graduation party. Certainly, it wasn't a crime for him to speak to another woman; even if Catherine and Bob were married, it wouldn't be. So next time a pretty woman caught his eye, she would at least *try* to turn the other cheek.

Others in her row were now going up to receive the Communion host. How could it possibly be this far along in the mass? She decided not to partake in the rite, as surely Bob would notice her. Now she was the only one sitting in her pew. The jig could be up.

Bob couldn't help but be friendly and outgoing. No doubt his good looks and charisma would always make him attractive to women unless he'd become disfigured from too many years of boxing. More reason than ever to help him with his studies. If boxing was an option, maybe he wouldn't have to enter the ring so often.

Part of her longed to join Bob in the pew, but she didn't dare disturb him. She couldn't imagine her father, hyper as he was, to ever come close to looking so lost in thought. Something else she now found to love about Robert Sage.

.   .   .

Not that evening, but the following one, Bob showed up right before dinner with a dozen red roses. Of course, Bridget invited him to stay for the meal. She'd made a pot roast and all the fixings—a meal usually reserved for Sundays. Mickey had closed the diner early, something he rarely did. John's good news would be announced at the dinner table, and so far no one knew besides Bridget. It was all she could do to contain herself.

Before dinner, the young couple sat on the porch swing and both apologized for their respective behavior at Honor's Night. Bob truly hadn't meant to appear to be flirting with Megan and no one could light a flame next to Catherine.

"You know that, right, Kate?"

She didn't answer right away. Part of her wanted to see him squirm, not-knowing whether his apology had been good enough. She didn't have it in her to keep him guessing for long.

"Sorry I got so ridiculously jealous. It's truly not like me."

"Sure, Kiddo, I know it's not."

She couldn't tell whether he believed her, but he gave her his winning smile. Women were attracted to Bob, and she couldn't blame them.

They held hands and swayed in the swing in a peaceful silence until they were called in for the meal. She leaned her head on a muscular shoulder.

At the table, John told them about his decision to join the seminary.

"But John, you're so young! Don't you want to date a little more first?" Catherine asked, egging her younger brother on. Girls had always found him attractive, and she'd always imagined that he found them to be equally appealing. Yet he'd never had a girlfriend longer than a month or so, so maybe he liked them best from afar. One had claimed that he had eyes that would sear your soul if you gazed back at him for too long. His dark blond bangs often fanned those treacherous orbs. Now, he'd have to swear off women entirely.

"I've thought about it a long time, Sis. Our Lord has called upon me to serve him in the priesthood."

True, John had always been the most devout among her siblings. He loved all the Catholic rituals with unusual zeal. It made perfect sense.

Bridget pulled out a bottle of brandy from the back of the cupboard and filled five brandy snifters.

"Let's raise our glasses to John!" she said.

Then Bob stood and said, "Let's also toast Catherine to her great success at passing the bar exam with flying colors!" Glasses clinked again but with hesitation. Catherine could tell they disapproved; she'd already been celebrated. They didn't approve of her stealing John's thunder. After all, he was the only son—the prince—the one to carry on the McIntosh name, or he would have, had he not been about to enter the priesthood.

After Bob left, Catherine helped with the dishes.

Her parents and John talked all at once with each voice vying to be heard rose about the volume of the others. The house felt like it was closing in; the small rooms became even smaller as the voices canceled out not only Catherine's voice but even her thoughts. It became hard to breathe and her heart felt like it was going to fly out of her chest. She had to get away from her family. Her mother wondered what was wrong, but only for a second before she began to monologue about flappers and their short dresses.

Catherine ran down to the cool and quiet basement. She paced and then sat on the bottom step, rocking back and forth. Grateful no one knew she was there except for the mice peering at her from a wall hole, no doubt wondering about the strange human in their midst.

CHAPTER THIRTEEN

One early September evening before the sun had set, the young couple drove to Belle Isle. Catherine snuggled up to Bob, who was behind the wheel. The air was less humid, though still warm. If you didn't know any better, you'd think it was spring—but a spring that brought with it an awareness of numinous death around the corner.

Bob said there was something he wanted to show her. She followed him through a wooded area to a clearing. There stood an ordinary door—except that it was painted ocean blue. Some of the paint was chipped, but the brilliant blue beckoned you. It stood by itself, attached to a frame, but with no walls.

Why it was there hadn't mattered to either of them.

The door was partly ajar, so they opened it further and glimpsed a wild, overgrown garden. He took her hand and led her through the doorway. Catherine declared it the most magical place she'd ever seen. A piece of paradise not far from the crime-ridden city…

Seated on a solitary bench facing the garden they gleaned an enchanted world, including a ribbon of the river beyond. She wore a gauzy, fairylike green gown, and he had on the same vest with a watch chain that he'd worn when they first met. He'd replaced the boater hat with a fedora.

He told her his mother would find this place, as the Irish would say: "all lure."

"What's 'all lure' mean, Bob? Alluring?"

"I think she says it when she's delighted by something. You're the alluring one, my Kate, and 'to be lured away' by each other is most alluring. If we look close enough, maybe we'll be able to detect the wee folk watching us from behind a tree or bush."

In the gloaming hour, Bob kneeled before her, removed his hat, and proposed. After his grandiose blathering about a term, his sweet popping of the question was all the sweeter. Later, he would say he'd heard the fairies applaud when she'd answered with a passionate kiss and a nod. He told her he'd ask her hand again once he bought a ring.

Afterward, they had their customary pie and coffee at Mickey Mac's. The diner's stark lighting hadn't allowed the glow from Belle Isle to follow them inside. Mickey, downstairs readying to open the speakeasy for business, had left his daughter in charge of the diner. Grateful to be the only customers, the couple spoke freely. It proved to be a perfect time to discuss their future. After covering a range of easier topics, Catherine told Bob she didn't think she ever wanted children.

For only a second did he feel gut-punched, and had recovered by the time he asked her quietly why.

"For a few reasons," she said, "but mainly because there's too much work to be done in their fight for justice in a world which favors only the wealthy."

Bob agreed, but then told her he'd assumed all women just wanted children.

"Not this one. If I get pregnant, well, that'll be one thing. Of course, I'd have your baby, but can you imagine me burping a baby while trying to write a legal brief? It'd be my luck the little one would upchuck on my legal pad!"

They agreed to use birth control, though the pope wouldn't be smiling about it.

"What say we just keep it our little secret?" Bob whispered.

"Mum's the word — not mom…" She said, making him wince at her pun. "Maybe at some point, we could get a cat," she added.

"Well, just don't expect me to get up for the midnight feedings."

Catherine threw her head back and guffawed, picturing him feeding a kitten a bottle.

Then they decided it was too soon to announce their engagement to family or friends. She was relieved and could truly feel excited about their engagement. Hopefully, Bob felt the same, but the goodnight kiss in his car was less amorous than either would have predicted, especially after his romantic proposal on Belle Isle.

CHAPTER FOURTEEN

"You and your friends out drinking again, Kate? Mom said this was the third night in a row you've been out with your law school pals. Is that true?" Eileen stood with her hands on her hips, looking for signs of drunkenness on her youngest sister.

"Don't worry, Eileen. I only sometimes drink to get drunk." Catherine was admittedly a tad tipsy, but there was nothing in her behavior that called for her sister's severe scrutiny. Plus, it wasn't any of Eileen's business.

"What do you take me for, just another dumb Dora?" Catherine asked her judgmental sister. "Anyway, what are you doing here so late anyway?"

Eileen responded by walking out of the room. She grabbed her purse and sweater from the cluttered dining room table.

"If you really must know, Mom said she needed to talk when Dad was out of the house. I guess they've had some issues lately. I'm sure you out carousing until all hours, doesn't help any."

"My life is tough enough without your high and mighty opinion!" Catherine shouted as her sister made her way down the front walk. She wondered why her mother had chosen Eileen to turn to rather than her.

"As if I care. I have enough trouble with my own brood. Good night to both of you," Eileen said.

Bridget, shaking her head, now stood behind Catherine in the front doorway.

"What am I going to do with you girls? Why can't you ever get along?"

Catherine wiled away more nights in the speakeasies than her fiancé in the early autumn of 1923. It gave her somewhere to go for some fun with other recently graduated cronies from law school. Most were women, as many of the men had already found jobs in public or private firms. The women weren't surprised by this, as they knew securing a position wasn't easy. It was about making connections in a man's world. Few women went to college—let alone law school—so it was important, not only to stick together but to support each other, especially at this time.

If Catherine didn't get out of the house at least four nights a week, she told Bob she'd more than likely go stir crazy. He sympathized, but then added that he was confident it wouldn't take her long to launch her career.

. . .

Bob, quick on his feet and almost as quick-minded, hadn't taken long to figure out how to juggle study time, boxing matches, and spending time with Catherine. Billy didn't think he practiced enough. Bob knew there was little point arguing with him, as his manager was simply doing his job. The intellectual rigor of law school had always energized him in the ring, and his occasional losses only further motivated him to buckle down with his studies. Billy knew this. Bob had discovered that too much drinking and dancing muddied his thinking, so he eased off, except for an occasional Friday night. Their 'big' date nights out comprised taking walks together, drives, or having pie at the family diner. Mostly, they got together at his mother's flat.

Nana had converted the dining room into Bob's office. They ate all their meals at the kitchen table. Occasionally, Catherine stopped by for dinner.

While both missed the fun they'd shared during their earlier times, they realized they'd now entered a new phase of both their lives and their relationship. Hopefully, better days would return. Catherine often remarked how their lives were like runaway trains: there was little either of them could do to get them back on track, and the brakes were broken. Bob didn't care for her analogy but understood her point. "We just have to roll with the punches," was something he often told her. Her first response was to agree: "Sure, Bob, sure." But then she'd always roll her eyes.

His reputation as the 'battling barrister' was growing and Detroiters loved his Horatio Alger-like story: a poor Irish kid from Corktown who began making money from boxing. That Bob had a decent intellect and had recently finished law school was especially impressive. His fans followed him because he was a wild card: sure, he had a fighting chance of passing the Bar, but he was also known to get 'punch drunk' and 'lose his marbles.' Catherine cautioned him to keep a low profile and "to wind his neck in," so as not to appear arrogant. He agreed and so would his Irish forebears—that is, the more rational ones.

Word was that because of his reputation, Bob would simply get a nod the next time he took the exam regardless of his performance. When she brought it up to him, he denied that there was any truth to the rumor and that he was against that sort of corruption.

"Who do you think I am, Catherine? What kind of man…the sort who takes bribes?"

"Certainly not!"

"If I don't pass the exam by my own wits, then I deserve to fail."

Bob paced, stopping only to glare at her—as if she was accusing him of being as dishonest as those poor Micks who had nothing going for them but an oily sort of charm. He had to remind himself that she wasn't the one spreading the outright lie.

· · ·

Catherine's frustrations surmounted that early fall. Sure, she'd graduated, passed the Bar, and become engaged, but her life felt far from perfect. It would prove to be Uncle Gerry, as well as her friends from law school that kept her self-esteem and spirits from floundering. Not Bob. Living with her parents had become nearly unbearable. While she loved them and would do anything for them, she could no longer withstand how they treated each other—especially the way her father treated her mother after he'd been drinking. Had she remained a day longer in their house, she reported to Bob and a few others, "It would have soured me on marriage."

She'd witnessed a scene that would remain with her for the rest of her days. One night, her father came home late from a speakeasy, drunk and loud, swearing at the world, but mostly at his wife. He'd been doing this twice a week for several years, but lately, it had been worse than usual. Bridget had been waiting up, chain-smoking in the living room in the dark.

"What are you waiting up for, fool woman?"

"Mickey—I was worried—"

"Shite. As if I'm a lad and need my ma's scolding. Feck off, will you?"

From a crack in her bedroom door, Catherine saw him slap her mother's face. When Bridget turned her back to him, he knocked her to the floor. Catherine had at first been too afraid to help her mother out.

"That's where you belong—on the floor with the dogs, you bitch!"

She ran to her mother's side and yelled at her father to leave her mother alone.

"Kate, I'm...I'm okay. This has nothing to do with you. Go back to bed... Mickey, would you like a cup of coffee?"

While she'd witnessed her father abuse her mother in the past, this time, Catherine couldn't believe her ears. Often, a month or more would go by in which the worst they'd do was to bicker, and only occasionally raise their voices. But then there were other times when push came to shove, followed by tears of exasperation and, finally—apologies. And the following day, no further word would be spoken about the matter. Had Catherine remained living there, it would have meant enduring another sleepless night, waiting for the fighting to begin again. One thing was clear: Bridget didn't want her daughter's help.

Catherine told Bob about the possibility of moving in with Uncle Gerry and Grammy McIntosh. It would be for only a short time, but since the wedding bells wouldn't be chiming any time soon, it seemed for the best. Uncle Gerry had made the offer back when Catherine was in law school. Bob now encouraged her move—especially since it implied they'd have more time to be alone together. All those beautiful rooms in Uncle Gerry's large home...

. . .

Grammy McIntosh lived with Gerry in his fashionable home on a tree-lined street in Grosse Pointe. It was the largest house that Catherine had ever been in—a near mansion with twelve bedrooms, two parlors, a living room, a library, an office, two dining rooms, two staircases, and several fireplaces (even in some of the bedrooms). The kitchen was as large as one of the parlors. She wasn't sure how many bathrooms it had, maybe three or four. Spacious lawns overlooked two ponds; one even had a flowing fountain in its center.

Bob drove Catherine up the long driveway that led to the house. It was his first time there and he had to admit feeling

DANCING IN THE RING

awed by the place. "It's a palace! Maybe one day we'll get a place like this. You game?"

"Too many rooms to lose you in, my love," she responded, kissing his neck before they got too close to the house.

She then suggested to him that while she spoke with her uncle, Bob could browse his law library.

While Catherine adored her uncle, she was always somewhat anxious in his presence. Maybe it was because he seemed to have a permanent scowl, even when he found something amusing. His thick, unruly red brows were constantly furrowed. He rarely laughed and was forever smoking a pipe and stewing about one issue or another. And he didn't just look at you from across his wide mahogany desk: his eyes burrowed into your soul. Truly, her uncle was one of the most fascinating people she'd ever met. Wise, yet humorous and kind.

"So, Katy, my girl, what brings you here today? Bob, it's nice to see you again." Gerry extended his arm to shake Bob's hand. His warm tone put his niece more at ease. He'd been nothing but kind to her. And the droopy side of his red handlebar mustache was more than a wee bit endearing.

She explained the situation at home and how impossible it had become for her. While he deserved the truth, on another level she felt like she was betraying her parents. Her cheeks burned.

"I'm sorry. I'd gotten wind of Mickey being that way with your mother, but that was a few years ago. You want me to have a talk with him? Knock the Irish out of that brother of mine? Admittedly, he's as full of blarney as his mother before him. For you, Katy—anything!"

Catherine could tell her uncle was sincere. Unlike so many, he was never anything but sincere. But he'd already helped her out by paying for college. She didn't want to feel more beholden than she already did.

"Uncle Gerry, I was actually hoping to rent a room from you. Temporarily, of course. I've been interviewing for a legal position, so I'll have no problem paying my way—"

He interrupted her. "My dear girl, as I offered before, you're more than welcome to stay, but your money's no good here."

"But you've already done so much for me. I don't know how I'll ever be able to repay you!" Suddenly, it was as if a huge burden had been lifted. He'd always come through for her; had believed in her abilities when others hadn't. Maybe it was because he didn't have children he'd put his faith in her. No matter. She would've been happy to pay for her keep, but that she would no longer have to endure life in her parents' small Corktown home made her feel that positive change was possible.

"Well, lass, how about by becoming the best damn woman attorney in the city?"

"That's the plan! There's something else, too. More news: Bob and I are engaged."

"Congratulations, my dear! That's what I'd first thought you were stopping by to tell me." His face reddened with emotion as he hugged his niece and shook Bob's hand. "I'm not surprised since I heard about it from your father just the other day. Let's have a toast, shall we? And let's find that wily grandmother of yours and all sit out on the patio."

The shady patio was surrounded by a garden still in bloom despite the lateness of the season. All four sat in white wicker chairs around a white wicker table. Catherine was amazed at how the patio brick was kept as clean as the floors of the grand home.

Silver-haired Grammy McIntosh, dressed in a long black gown that could easily have been made in the previous century, eyed the young couple with her monocle. Few could ever discern if she was smiling or scowling. The eye behind the monocle appeared ten times larger than normal. It was all too easy to see where Uncle Gerry got his serious expression from.

She loved to hold her guests in suspense. At last, she stopped peering out her monocle and smiled at the young couple. Not a dazzling smile like her son Gerry's, but it was the best one she could muster.

"Grammy, I know you already know our news—"

"I was going to act surprised, my dear, but as you realize, not much gets by me. Saints preserve us, I'm a wee bit taken aback by how soon you two became engaged. You've known each other for how long?"

"A year and some change," Bob interjected, but then hastened to add, "We probably won't get married for a year or two."

"Well, that's a relief. Catherine, it's good to know you're not in the family way. You're not, are you? I only ask because you've got a certain glow in your cheeks." Grammy waved a black lace fan in front of her face.

"Heaven's no, Grammy!"

"Then this calls for a celebration. Gerry, dear, fetch the champagne and glasses, will you?"

Gerry immediately disappeared into the house.

"You know what this means?" the elderly woman asked, placing the fan down, then picking it up again.

Eyebrows were raised in question.

"I should still be around until after the wedding, so I have at least another year or two of life in me yet. Don't shake your head, Catherine. You've now given me good reason not to hasten my departure from this mortal realm, ill as I am most days."

"Mother filling you two up with her prattle about her impending death?" Gerry asked, setting the silver bucket containing the champagne on the table.

"Now, Gerry, me lad, I was simply telling them how I have no plans to exit this world until after they're married."

"Good to hear. Brace yourself, Mother, there's more news." The droopy side of Gerry's mustache twitched.

Grammy McIntosh looked alarmed. She held out her black fan like a bird frozen in flight, but after her son informed her that Catherine was moving in with them, she smiled, fluttered her fan, and patted her granddaughter's hand. Katy, she said, was certainly welcome to stay as long as she'd like.

"But, it has nothing to do with that other son of mine does it?" she said, raising a bony index finger. "He's been hitting the moonshine too much, I'll wager."

Knowing how much Grammy still loved her younger son, Mickey, even though he wasn't her favorite, Catherine diplomatically explained how things had been strained between her and her parents. The matriarch thought for a minute, patted her granddaughter's leg, and said, "Well, what are you waiting for, lass? Go pack your bags!"

"But," the grand dame said, addressing Bob. She once again raised her birdlike claw of a hand. "Please be advised that Catherine will not be receiving gentlemen callers in her bedroom—not even if she's engaged to one of them. Do I make myself clear?"

Bob gave a vigorous nod. What was the woman, a mind reader? He'd been imagining opportunities for Catherine and him to be alone together. Catherine squeezed his hand under the table and he wasn't sure what she meant by it. Uncle Gerry removed the chilled bottle from the ice bucket and half-filled the glasses with a vintage Champagne.

"Let's raise our glasses, shall we?" Everyone did so. Then Catherine's uncle blessed their engagement:

"May your mornings bring joy and your evenings bring peace.
May your troubles grow few as your blessings increase.
May the saddest day of your future be no worse than the happiest
day of your past."
(Traditional Irish Blessing)

Afterward, the group clinked their glasses.

Catherine thanked her uncle for the blessing, though he apologized for not remembering it in its entirety.

. . .

Before leaving, Gerry escorted Bob to his law library and left him there, after which, he gave Catherine a tour of the ten available bedrooms. He stared at the hundreds of books in awe. Had her uncle read them all? How would he ever become as knowledgeable as Uncle Gerry? He pulled a book from the shelf, sat, and waited for Catherine to save him from all this erudition.

. . .

Catherine chose a large suite at the end of a hallway. Not only for its rose-covered wallpaper but because it held three full bookcases. Before law school, she'd always loved reading and now she hoped to have more time for it. A quick appraisal told her the cases held mostly Classics that she hadn't yet read. She found the aroma of all the old books intoxicating.

CHAPTER FIFTEEN

"Mother, you do realize I'll soon be turning twenty-six?" Catherine reminded her. Bridget had cried and carried on for hours. Her thin frame now sighed and sputtered like a mechanical wind-up toy before it abruptly stopped.

"I know, Katy…But time — where does it go? Such a bugger! Such a mean and nasty thief!" With that, Bridget broke down again. This time Catherine hugged her close. Even if she was forty, her mother would have the same reaction. No doubt it wouldn't have been as difficult had she not lost her two youngest ones to the Spanish flu in 1918.

She realized as odd that her parents — her mother especially — rarely spoke about Colleen and Stephen. What was left of them now? Only a couple of small photographs on walls and end tables, a beloved whistle of Stephen's, and a rag doll of Colleen's. Only a few memories, especially of them giggling and singing. Lives snuffed out way too soon. Her mother mentioned dreaming of them now and then, but she never described her dreams.

Catherine reminded her that her other two daughters had both been married by Catherine's age and Eileen had already had children. Her mother nodded, but then teared up again. Catherine then promised that when she became a bona fide attorney, she'd be more than happy to help financially. Bridget shuddered, but then smiled through her tears. While Bridget would have denied it, this seemed to quell some of her misgivings, and would hopefully prevent further tirades—or so Catherine hoped.

Still, Catherine's mother refused to be home the morning of the move. Instead, she'd chosen to spend those hours at a friend's house.

"Your mother wanted me to tell you, Kate, that your room will always be there for you," her father said as he helped carry boxes out to Bob's car. Since she hadn't known how long she'd be living at Uncle Gerry's, she'd taken only her clothes and a few personal items.

"I don't believe you for a second, but you're sweet to say so, Papa. I mean, it's sweet for Mama to let me know."

He grinned broadly at her. 'Papa' was a word Catherine only used on rare occasions. While he'd always taken his frustrations out on his wife, he never did more than raise an eyebrow with his children. When they were little, it was always Bridget who disciplined them. After any of them had misbehaved, she'd get out the 'spanking machine'—a wooden spoon and paddle them with it. Knowing how soft-hearted their mother was, the children had always pretended it hurt way more than it did.

Except for her mother's reaction, all went well with the move. She promised her father she'd stop by every Saturday for dinner—that is, unless Bob and she had other plans. Maybe you two won't argue so much, Catherine told him. He gave her a confused look. Come on, Father, she wanted to respond, but didn't.

Would he treat her mother better or worse after the move? What if something happened to her mother?

Once again, Catherine had to remind herself that it wasn't her job to be her mother's keeper.

Within days after of moving out, she received a job offer. She'd interviewed for two positions calling for a legal clerk and was offered the second one—as a law clerk for the Wayne

County Prosecutor. The building she'd be working in—the Wayne County Building—looked important enough to be in Washington, D.C.!

Catherine couldn't wait to get started but would have to wait another week. While she hoped to someday work for a law firm as a lawyer, her dream job was to someday have her own firm, though she knew well that few people—especially women—landed higher-level positions. At first, she worried the position would be secretarial. Her uncle assured her that not only did the position entail mostly research, but she might even present prosecutorial arguments in court—providing the prosecuting attorney didn't show up. She would welcome this stepping-stone opportunity. Bob was thrilled for her.

She arrived early on a sunny morning for her first day of work with a bad case of hiccups. Never had Catherine seen a more impressive building except in pictures of Roman architecture. She'd been here before to visit her uncle, but this time it was different. As she climbed the broad flight of steps, several smartly dressed people passed her on their way to their important jobs. She stopped mid-way and gazed up at the Corinthian columned portico. It must have taken her breath away for her hiccups had vanished! Was it her awe of the place or lack of sleep that caused the sudden dizziness? A kindly guard ushered her to a seat in the impressive lobby of marble and dark wood.

The last step up the stairs had been momentous: she had arrived. Pinching herself added some necessary reassurance. She took a deep breath and gathered her wits before reporting to her job.

Catherine returned to her uncle's home dog-tired. To celebrate, dinner would be held in the formal dining room of the McIntosh home. Not only was her head spinning from the newness of the job, but she still didn't feel at home at her uncle's. However, she knew better than to protest.

Rosa, the family cook, had prepared Lobster Thermidor for the occasion. It seemed a tad formal, but Catherine couldn't deny how regal it made her feel. The delectable cooking aromas wafting into the dining room from the kitchen made her salivate; she discreetly wiped the corners of her mouth with her cloth napkin. Grammy McIntosh loathed lobster, but it was Uncle Gerry's favorite.

Following the first course, a carrot and ginger bisque, Grammy excused herself, saying that her arthritis was acting up. Her silver hair, normally pinned back in a neat bun, looked as if a bird had been nesting in it. Before leaving the table, she beamed at her granddaughter and expressed how proud she felt.

"You'll be a regular Queen Maeve there in no time," Grammy said, patting Catherine's shoulder. As if there had been anything 'regular' at all about the powerful Irish queen of the fairies!

"Thanks, Grammy," she replied, briefly clasping the cold hand in her clammy one.

"Also, you'll be a shoo-in for a job as a courtroom attorney once you've had some experience under your belt," said Gerry, winking, before they enjoyed the tasty lobster meat in wine sauce. Catherine was much relieved they didn't have to crack the shells, as she'd never had lobster before.

"I know there aren't many women in the field yet, but besides my red hair and Irish temper, that's what's going to make them take notice of me." Catherine noticed her elbow was resting on the lace tablecloth and quickly removed it.

"You sure got that right, my brilliant niece! I promise you, the world will someday be your oyster shell."

"As long as it's not as tough to crack as a hard-shelled lobster!"

They laughed together before having a serious discussion about the recent rise in Detroit's crime rate.

Catherine had only seen Bob once that week. When she'd given him her news, he'd congratulated her, but afterward had acted distracted. She couldn't help but notice the contrast: Uncle Gerry had told her all the right things — the things she wanted to hear. Why hadn't Bob? True, he was busy studying law and had been boxing in more and more matches, but she wondered if he resented her getting a job. It wasn't like it put a crimp in their style, as they hadn't been going out much. It must have been because she'd entered the legal field before he did. And here she was a woman.

They wouldn't be able to get together until the following weekend. Maybe that was soon enough.

Lucky for Catherine, her uncle's courtroom was also in the Recorder's Court of the county building, so she could get a ride to work and back every day. She was happy not to have to ride the crowded Jefferson Avenue streetcar, plus she enjoyed chatting with Gerry about her job and hearing about his cases.

It wasn't long before Catherine had created a pleasant enough routine during the work week, though had she not enjoyed solitude, it would've been far more difficult. She spent most time at work doing research in criminal law, citing cases from law books. Assistant Prosecutors would then use the information she provided to help build their arguments to lock up Detroit criminals, be they, petty thieves or murderers.

The other clerks and attorneys were nice enough, but she kept mostly to herself. Needing occasional rest from scouring the fine print of thousand-page books, she daydreamed about seeing Bob. It hadn't taken her long to become adept at shifting her focus back to work.

Following a brief rest Catherine she got home, she'd join her grandmother and uncle for dinner. Afterward, the three would go their separate ways. Tiredness and eye strain prevented her from reading as much as she wanted to in the evenings, so she'd laze in the living room and listen to records on the Victrola.

She imagined spending time alone with Bob in the mansion. Grammy and Uncle Gerry — out for the evening, and Rosa —

gone for the night...She would meet Bob at the back door in a long silk negligee. After a brandy or two, they'd embrace, but before becoming intimate, she'd leave the room, and beckon him from the next room, divided by French doors. She'd lure him with whispers and one leg bared. Once he'd reached her, she would prance to the next room. Lights would be dim in some of the rooms, and off in others. The pursuit would end in her candle-lit bedroom, of course, where he'd slip off her nightgown straps, pull down her gown, and then kneel before her. Catherine would moan softly before arching her back and turning into a rare and exotic feline.

The ferocity of her sexual fantasies sometimes frightened her. They often came unbidden as she was drifting off to sleep. There was no one with whom she could confide. It had been ages since she'd seen friends, and even then, she'd feel too inhibited to mention this other side of herself.

Catherine visited her parents on Saturday afternoons, without Bob, as he was often at home recuperating from a fight from the previous evening. Sundays became the only day they could spend entirely together. They regularly attended a late morning mass, followed by lunch, and then a Sunday afternoon drive—often they drove out to the countryside. The times were enjoyable, but the silences between them seemed longer than ever before. Nothing was nicer than those lingering kisses on the roadsides. She could tell he wanted to do more than kiss, but she'd slap his hands and straighten her skirt. It was never the right time or place. She turned up the volume of her sighs.

After the drive, they'd sit together in his dining room to study and pore over her old notes and law books which entirely covered the table. He'd put his hand on her knee, and then almost always slide it up her skirt. She'd fish out the groping paw, giggle, but chide him in a stern voice: "Excuse me, but your mother's in the adjoining room."

. . .

Boxing changed Bob's appearance: his face was almost always a little swollen, making his deep-set blue eyes appear smaller. He knew he no longer had the most handsome of all mugs. It depressed him, but he'd always known it was bound to happen. His small nose had been smashed so much in the ring that it had been almost flattened. Bruises and broken blood vessels marred his complexion, though the most notable change was his voice. By far the worst injury he'd suffered so far was to his larynx. Blows to his neck became a regular occurrence until Bob learned the 'Dempsey Roll.' Still, in those days, his scratchy voice didn't prevent others from understanding what he was saying. Catherine often told him she found it "oddly sexy." It helped a bit.

. . .

One Sunday afternoon, sitting on a park bench on a sunny and unseasonably mild October afternoon, Catherine tried talking to Bob about the physical toll of the sport.

"For the love of Jesus, Kate, I never fancied myself a pretty boy! Did you?"

"I'm not talking about that handsome face of yours, Lover-boy, but what if there's something a doctor or time can't mend?" she asked, grabbing a paw that had removed itself from her own cool, tapered fingers. Not the first time she'd noticed that his hands—for a boxer—were almost delicate. His boxing mitts disguised this, so his opponents never knew.

"I know how to take care of myself, Toots. I always have, despite the concerns of you and my mother." Bob bit the toothpick between his lips, pulled it out, and, studied it for a few moments. Was it the late afternoon shadows casting on the side of his face or a bruise?

They watched a boy and girl trying to fly a kite in the field behind them. At first, there wasn't enough of a breeze, but at last, the kite was aloft.

"What if the day comes when you lose your voice for good? How are you going to persuade a jury in the courtroom?"

"Now, Sweets, I assure you that won't happen. Did I tell you how Jack Dempsey kept his crown in New York after it'd been temporarily stolen by that Argentinian, Firpo? It was a second-round knockout. But what Jack's becoming known for is the 'Dempsey Roll.' It's a move that's sure to do the trick and keep me safe."

"Too many 'down for the counts' and you promise me, you'll hang up your boxing gloves—are we clear, Bob Sage?"

"Crystal clear, Kate." He then gave her a kiss that not only took her breath away but almost caused her to be down for the count.

Afterward, Bob jogged over to the boy and girl whose kite had gotten tangled in the lower branches of a tree. Catherine watched as he gently removed it and then helped it become airborne once more. She couldn't hear the conversation, but it was clear he'd made a couple of young friends. He truly had a way with kids. How she longed for more time to be alone together.

Driving her back to her uncle's home, Bob exclaimed how he couldn't wait to sometime soon spend the night with her. Failing that, maybe they could find a private place for a few hours—like their time at Boblo. The sweet heat of that memory made her blush.

"You make me feel like I'm one of those wild flappers, even though I can't always act like one. Why does society force us to be so restrained and well-behaved?"

"You said it, Toots, you really did. Promise I won't quote you in the papers!"

CHAPTER SIXTEEN

"Robert, dear, your pacing is riling up our dead," his mother said, referring to their lost loved ones. She often made similar comments: "Your cursing is waking up our dead," or "Your bad mood is disturbing our dead." It was a way to manipulate his behavior, and it wasn't unusual for her to converse with them—especially when she thought he might be listening.

"Ma, for the love of Pete, will you please stop with the blarney? Catherine's over an hour late and I can't wait forever. If you recall, I've got a big match tomorrow."

"Of course, I remember, Bobby," she said, softening her tone. Ever since she'd been home from the hospital, she'd seemed more forgetful. "But I don't see why you can't open a law book without her at your side. How are you ever going to be a lawyer if you don't put in the work?"

"Don't you worry about that, Ma, I've always done okay in school, or did you forget that, too?"

She looked as if she'd been slapped.

"Now, Robert Edwardo, you know I think there's no one smarter than my sons, but time to wind your neck in," she said, rising with some difficulty from her overstuffed chair.

Catherine once asked him why Nana had chosen 'Edwardo' as his middle name and he shrugged, saying he had no idea, though his mother had always gotten a secretive little smile on her lips when asked. No doubt an actor's name, as Nana had always loved the stage.

For a few years now, she'd been working part-time as a theater nurse at the Bonstelle Theater. When the manager learned she could play the organ, Nana was talked into playing organ music before Saturday afternoon entertainment shows for children. The music helped settle them down before the show. While she'd never received formal nursing training, she'd been a hospital volunteer during the Spanish flu. But now, when not playing the organ, she could be found mopping up the vomit or helping to settle down a crying child.

Bob had places he had to be and wasn't about to bend over for this verbal caning from his wee but mighty mother.

"Look, the bar exam isn't until next week. I'll be ready for it. Say, if Catherine ever gets here, tell her to come find me at the gym."

His mother nodded and hugged him close. Could she feel the rapid beat of his poor, caged heart and spirit? He was pretty sure she did.

·   ·   ·

After throwing some jabs at the punching bag, Bob wound up sipping coffee alone at a downtown diner. It wasn't that he felt jilted, just more alone than usual. Shite. He pulled out a piece of Wrigley's Juicy Fruit gum and absently chewed as he gazed out the window at the inky night. No pie for him tonight. He took another slurp of coffee. Only an occasional car drove by.

He'd forgotten what it was like to be lonely. While he didn't deal with it as well as his mother or Catherine, he didn't mind it now and then—at least not when he could focus. It allowed him to think about how important it was to spend time on law classes, since being a prizefighter wouldn't be enough to live on for his entire life. He loved learning about the law, especially criminal law, and knew someday he'd make a fair judge, a 'sage' judge. He'd give second chances to the poor and unfortunate. Not all were born to wealth; not everyone could simply 'pull themselves up by their bootstraps.' And this era of 'get rich quick' would only bring the downfall of many.

Bob had been getting to know the kids at the gym where he trained. Some were good young boxers, but most went to bed hungry, and none had been given a fair shake in life. Once he became a lawyer, he was going to do his best to help them out. Maybe someday Catherine and he could open up a law firm together, and use some of their money to buy city land for parks or playgrounds. There weren't enough of them. After that, he'd help out with housing. Society needed to get rid of distinctions based on the color of skin or ethnicity or, by God, by gender, too. The Irish knew about struggle in America, but things began to look up — at least in Detroit. He could've easily been born a poor Colored woman. And had he been, what were the chances of dreams being realized? Pretty slim, he'd wager. He couldn't get over the one who graduated with Catherine — Grace Murphy — and could only wonder about the odds she must have faced working on her law degree.

Not even an occasional car drove by the diner. He headed home.

• • •

Catherine returned to her new rose-wallpapered bedroom earlier than she thought. While she was confused and somewhat let down not to have found Bob at home with Nana, she was more concerned over the prospect of having disappointed Nana. She felt bad for not staying for a longer visit. Nana had been so welcoming, too, but Catherine had only remained long enough to write Bob an apology. She'd had to work late and couldn't leave at her usual time.

Still, Nana must care for her, since she'd squeezed Catherine's hand before she left, telling her: "Bob's lucky to have a lass like you, Katy me-girl. Let's see if he can keep you!"

Nice as it was, this beautiful house wasn't her home. Sometimes she missed the feeling of lying in her old bed thinking about what she'd do with her life—all the possibilities that stretched out before her. Now there didn't seem to be as many of them. For the last couple of weeks, she'd avoided Saturday dinner with her parents, telling them it was because she'd brought some work home with her for the weekend. She had, but it was really that she wanted to spend more time with Bob. Despite how much stress they caused her, she truly loved her parents. Soon she'd make it up to them.

Her uncle knocked on her door. She opened it, but only partly.

"How about joining me in the library for a glass of sherry?" he asked.

"Thanks, Uncle Gerry. Be there in a few minutes."

Catherine joined him after switching from her robe to a pair of comfortable black palazzo pants. The comfortable yet elegant pants were her first purchase from her new job. She wished Bob could see her in them and wondered what he'd say. They were all the rage, that's what she'd tell him if he objected to women wearing pants. Too bad she couldn't wear them out. Perhaps one day.

"So how's your job been going, Katy, me girl? Since you've been staying late, I've missed our rides home together." She'd often take the streetcar home if it wasn't too late. If it was, she'd then get a ride from one of the other clerks.

The corner grandfather clock chimed the hour. The aroma from her uncle's pipe mingled with the hundreds of leather-bound books.

"It sure keeps me busy. I enjoy reading briefs and finding relevant legal cases for the assistant prosecutor to use in court, I just wish I could be that prosecutor. Sometimes it feels awfully 'behind the scenes.'"

"Your day's coming, just you wait! I wanted to let you know that I've been hearing about what a bang-up job you're doing. You've only been there about a month, correct?"

Catherine nodded and took another sip of sherry.

"You'll be running the place in no time, I'm sure," he further praised her, lighting his pipe.

"Oh, now, Uncle Gerry, maybe that'd be true if my gender wasn't an issue, but the men I'm around, usually think I'm part of the clerical staff."

"Want me to show up and set 'em straight? I'd be more than happy to."

Something about the way he said this made Catherine chuckle and then laugh. She couldn't recall the last time she'd laughed so hard she cried. It was such a release from her concerns. Life was always so serious, even during these madcap, flapper times. He gave her a sidelong glance, with one side of his red mustache looking especially droopy. She then confided how Bob hadn't been home when she'd stopped by Nana's flat. She knew he was as busy as she was—maybe more. Still...

"He'd be a fool not to be under your spell, my dear. Still, Bob's got a lot of promise. What would you say if I took him on as my clerk? Now, I'd only do so if you two are in it for the long haul?"

"That would be great, Uncle Gerry. And yes, it definitely looks like he's going to be my 'one and only.' Say, want to go with me to see him box tomorrow night? I guess it's going to be a big deal fight in the boxing world."

Gerry told her he'd see if his mother would like to go as well. Nana and Grammy McIntosh had now become pretty good friends, and no doubt Nana would be there. He added that Nana—whom he called Mary Ellen—was a "tough little bird," and a good influence on Catherine's grandmother, who had, as Gerry termed it, a 'sensitive constitution.'

Catherine took a copy of *Great Expectations* off the bookshelf, but only got a few pages in before the busy day and the sherry had their way with her. While she missed Bob, she sure felt less alone than she had in quite some time.

CHAPTER SEVENTEEN

Long metal tables had been placed end to end in the VFW banquet hall. Catherine and Bob arrived separately at the fish fry dinner held in honor of the vets from the Great War. While she was used to the plain furnishings of her family's diner, Catherine couldn't get over the stark atmosphere here. The tables had been covered by white butcher paper to conceal that the room was more a mess hall than a banquet room.

She'd been hoping for a more festive venue to wake her up after a long work day. At least she'd get to see Bob for the first time in a couple of weeks. Since he had a big boxing match tonight, it wouldn't be a long visit. Better than not seeing him at all, she kept reminding herself. Knowing she'd have to share him with so many others at the table made her feel out of sorts. She resented the way others robbed her of his attention.

Bob sat at one of the long rectangular tables with his mother on one side and Catherine on the other. He whispered he had a surprise for her after tonight's fight at Arena Gardens. Her mood perked up, but then he reminded her he could only stay for a quick bite before he'd have to get in some more practice before the match. Billy Watson had reminded him earlier not to arrive at the ring with a full stomach. One time Bob had and he'd lost the match. Now Billy would never let Bob forget that one incident.

"When did that happen, Bob?" asked Nana. "I never heard about it," she continued as if it had never happened.

Then Bob told Gene how he was dying for a nip of rum from his silver flask, but knew he couldn't have one—not here. Catherine wouldn't mind one or two nips herself. No sooner was she about to tell the others she was going outside with the men when Violet caught her eye.

"Kate, dear, we have more in common than just our good looks." Violet, sitting on Catherine's other side, pointed at runs they both had in their silk stockings. They had a good laugh over it. Violet always seemed to have a way of perking her up.

Catherine stayed put.

"Be sure you don't run off after the fights. Remember what I told you…" Bob, ready to leave, reminded her.

"I'll wait for you, Bobby. I promise," she replied, recalling a couple of matches in which she'd left before the end. It would be one thing if they could go out afterward, but lately, he'd been too tired and physically sore for their usual shenanigans at the speakeasies or dance halls. He wouldn't admit as much, but it sure seemed his opponents were getting harder to beat.

As soon as Bob left the hall, Catherine immediately noticed the loudness of the dinner din: all the voices and clattering of dishes. It reminded her of how she hated the noise of the hustle and bustle of downtown when she walked from the streetcar to her building: the jackhammers, cars, and sirens. Some days the discordant sounds were almost too much to bear.

While it was always nice to socialize with Bob's family, it was impossible to have a decent conversation at an event like this. Plus, the fish had been full of fish bones and the biscuits had been dry. She should have left with Bob and just milled about the arena until the others showed up.

Bobby Gene must have felt the same because he not only spat his food out but began crying at a high pitch. Normally, he was such a happy little boy, but tonight there was no pleasing him.

He was passed from lap to lap. It wasn't until he sat on Catherine's that he settled down, fascinated by a string of pearls around her neck. After she'd carefully pried open his little fist and bounced him on her lap, he'd looked up at her and flashed a devilish little grin. She imagined it was much like his Uncle Bob's had been at the same age.

"This tyke's such a little man, isn't he?" Catherine remarked. His parents readily agreed and thanked her for calming him down.

Violet then asked if Catherine and Bob would want to join them at a party after the fights. Gene elbowed Violet. When his wife persisted, he gently chided her for not realizing that Bob was rarely up for much after a match, adding that Catherine would probably be tired, too. Gene truly was a good fellow – more sensitive and caring than most. He confided that his passion was basketball and that he'd been reasonably good at it during his college days. After a game, he'd always felt energized, but he knew boxing was different.

Catherine suggested the two couples get together real soon. This appeared to satisfy them, especially Violet, who always looked forward to socializing and seemed to need the next good time to look forward to.

Gerry drove Catherine, his mother, and Nana to the Arena Gardens. Gene and Violet, the first to arrive, had saved them several ringside seats.

The arena was hot, smoke-filled, and even more crowded than usual. Uncle Gerry at first sat between Nana and his mother, but early on, had to switch seats so they could chat together. Nana was quieter than she'd been at Bob's last match. She sat quietly chewing red licorice, occasionally offering others a piece from a paper bag.

Catherine noticed Grammy didn't have her monocle with her and seemed more interested in talking to Nana than watching the fight.

Her uncle told Catherine that Benny Tandler, a middleweight champion from Indiana, was better known for delivering hand punches.

"He's what's known as a slugger," Gerry explained to Catherine, sitting next to him. "Your boy's called a boxer-puncher: he has the power of a slugger, but is also quick on his feet and quick with the jabs. Bob should beat Tandler without much of a fight."

By the fifteenth round, Bob had him down for the count, but Benny was fancier with his footwork than Catherine's uncle had realized.

Nana, Grammy, and Catherine hid their faces behind their hands.

The crowd, all Detroiters, gasped as one punch caused Bob to go down hard—his forehead smashed to the ring's hard floor. He was down for the count. Catherine winced and looked away to find Bobby Gene staring at his uncle in what appeared to be open-mouthed awe. How could such a young boy possibly follow even part of a boxing match? It was something to behold.

Family members stood around the lobby, for what seemed an interminable amount of time, waiting to hear how Bob was doing. The somber mood made Catherine feel like someone had died. At last, Billy stopped by. Bob was going to be okay, he said, but the arena doctor had to sew a few stitches on his forehead.

"Will it leave a scar?" she gasped.

"Honey, that's the nature of this business, but I'll wager it'll be a small one."

She was relieved when most of the group finally went their separate ways. Gerry drove the two older women home, and dropped off Bobby Gene at Nana's, as he was spending the night there. Gene and Violet waited with Catherine a while longer before she convinced them to leave for their party.

Catherine had never been so dead on her feet, though Bob looked even worse than she felt. He held an ice pack to his head.

"Thanks for waiting, Sweets. Got a few stitches and the good doc says I've got a wee concussion," said Bob.

"So that's why you look so pale, my darling. You ready to hang up those mitts of yours?"

He laughed, but less heartily than usual.

"You said something earlier about a surprise?" she asked.

"Not here, but I'll surprise you on our drive home."

At that moment, Billy was walking by and overheard Bob. "You're seriously not going to drive in your condition, are you, Bob?"

Catherine immediately agreed and said she'd drive him home.

"But there's not enough room for you to sleep at my ma's place unless, of course, you cuddle up with me. Something tells me she won't go for that."

"You could stay at my uncle's since there are plenty of beds."

Then Bob looked like he was having some difficulty processing what she was saying. She finally got him to agree. His manager looked perplexed, which made her even more concerned.

He was quiet on the drive and said nothing about the surprise. Once they pulled up at the Grosse Pointe home, Catherine again asked him about it. After a minute or two of silence, he fished for the right words and finally said that tomorrow night he was going to take her to a fancy hotel. She pressed him for specifics, but his lips were sealed. As they climbed the porch steps, he tripped and fell backward – hitting the back of his head against the cement.

"Bob! Are you okay?" she yelled, running over to him.

He scrambled to his feet in no time, claiming it was nothing — maybe the worst was just a muscle pull in his neck. But it was the second knock to the head in one evening. That couldn't be good. Gerry offered to take him to the hospital, but Bob refused. When Gerry then insisted he spend the night in one of the guest bedrooms, Bob didn't put up much of a fight. He even let Catherine tend to his wounds. While she'd smoked a bit before then, it was that night that smoking became a habit. Uncle Gerry gave her a pack of Lucky Strikes.

CHAPTER EIGHTEEN

"Hey, sweetheart, bring me a coffee, will you? Cream, no sugar," said Jim Dolan, an assistant prosecutor, to Catherine on a mid-morning Monday. Her shoes were already pinching, and the wool of her new black checked dress was too heavy for the early November day.

She'd been working in the Prosecutor's Office for over a month, but still couldn't get used to the fast pace or the demands of certain male attorneys. While she'd had office jobs in college, and had worked several summers at Mickey Mac's, she'd always had some time for herself during her work hours. It seemed wrong that prosecuting attorneys — and their law clerks — didn't have more time to prepare their cases. Still, that didn't give the attorneys the right to treat clerks, as she called it — "like shit on a shingle." Catherine wanted nothing more than to tell Jim Dolan to feck off. Instead, she hatched a plan so he wouldn't dare ask her again.

On the way to the small coffee room, she was stopped by Emily Schauber, one of the top assistant prosecutors. Emily was the boss of over forty male assistant prosecutors.

"Got a second, Catherine?" Emily asked.

"Sure do, at least for you, I do, Miss Schauber." Catherine's cheeks burned. Could it be that she felt flustered merely by being addressed?

"Please call me Emily. How do you feel about trying a case in court?"

"I'd love to, but I didn't think law clerks could."

"Well, the ones who've passed the bar exam sure can! If—or shall I say—when—one of the assistant prosecutors doesn't show up to court on the day cases are distributed, the case can be given to one of the qualified clerks, provided another prosecutor doesn't get to it first. With Detroit's ever-growing crime underworld, they're all too busy to jump at the chance. Anyway, I've heard you're pretty fast at thinking on your feet, so I promise to soon 'throw you a bone.'"

"Oh, Miss—I mean, Emily, I'd truly welcome the opportunity. Thanks so much!"

Catherine awkwardly hugged her. Emily looked somewhat taken aback but then smiled up at the tall new clerk. She was Catherine's senior, but only by a few years. You could tell she became fully engaged with whoever had her attention by the way her large, deep-set brown eyes penetrated theirs. Catherine's mood significantly improved. Before returning to the four open law books on the table in the office library, she carried out her plan regarding Jim Dolan.

"Here you are, Mr. Dolan," Catherine said handing him a cup of coffee, interrupting his conversation with another attorney. Her auburn hair looked distinctly redder in the light pouring through the large office window.

"Thanks, Miss...I'm sorry, your name is?"

"Catherine McIntosh."

"Oh, that's right. Now, if you'll excuse us..."

She stood in the doorway, watching as he took a sip of the cold coffee without cream.

"Say, wait a minute. This isn't exactly what I asked for, Miss McIntosh."

"I'm sorry, but I'm a little busy to oblige, Mr. Dolan, as I'm not a secretary."

Catherine turned on her heels, telling him to 'feck off' under her breath. He chased after her down the hallway.

"Forgive me, Miss McIntosh. You're one of our law clerks, aren't you? The smart one everyone's talking about."

There were dozens of assistant prosecutors, but only half a dozen clerks. If Catherine ever became a prosecutor, she'd immediately learn the names of the indispensable clerks.

"Can I make it up to you? What say, I take you out to lunch sometime soon?" Jim Dolan implored. They were the only ones standing still in the long hallway.

"Kindly back off, Mr. Dolan. I'm betrothed to Bob Sage. Maybe you've heard of him?"

"*The* Bob Sage? The boxer? Well, I'll be. That prizefighter sure has won the prize now, hasn't he? But, my dear, I simply want to make up for my rudeness."

"Good day to you, Mr. Dolan."

Catherine walked away, trying hard not to wince from the pain. It had been over a week since she'd last seen Bob after he'd fallen off the porch. Worrying about him had kept her from getting enough rest at night; it was all she could do to get up in the mornings and go to work. But when it had seemed like sheer drudgery, opportunity had come knocking: she could now look forward to getting the chance to shine in the courtroom.

• • •

Bob returned home that evening to receive some bad news. He opened the envelope waiting for him on the dining room table. After reading it, he tossed the brief letter on the floor.

"What is it, son?"

"I didn't pass. Again." The dark circles beneath his eyes looked darker than normal.

"But you'll keep trying, right? I'll pray to the saints, but remember, we're the fighting Irish!"

CHAPTER NINETEEN

Bob showed up at the Prosecutor's Office with a bouquet of yellow mums. Catherine wasn't surprised to see him standing at her desk, though she'd been delighted by the flowers. That very morning she'd received a progress report about him from Grammy McIntosh who'd been downtown shopping with Nana the day before.

Catherine hugged him and they lingered in the embrace before she remembered where she was. There were a couple of others in the back of the office—a secretary and one of the assistant prosecutors. Had they witnessed them hugging? Too bad if they did! Still, she tore herself away and brushed invisible crumbs on her skirt. Bob, knowing exactly why she was doing so, threw his head back hoarsely guffawing. There was no hiding the glow to her skin, her ear-to-ear grin.

Bob whispered—though a little loudly—that he wanted to make good on the promise of spending a night at the Tuller Hotel. Catherine put her index finger in front of her lips, nodded, and gave him a smile more provocative than demure.

It had taken him longer to recover, he said, not only because of his previous fight but from his spill off the porch. Bob's head injuries had caused him to have a hard time studying law or concentrating on much of anything. Stuck at home and bored, he'd mostly paced and daydreamed about Catherine. He didn't tell her this, but maybe he would at the Tuller.

"I'm feeling like my old self. Well, almost."

"That's great news, Bob! It seems an eternity since we've been together."

They ducked out of the office for a cup of coffee at a nearby diner. At first, he'd been unable to look at her as he told her the bad news about not passing the bar exam for the second time. She kept stirring and stirring the cream in her coffee cup. He watched the flow of customers coming in and leaving the diner. Finally, he quietly stated that if he didn't pass on his third try, he'd apply the three-strikes rule and think about a career as a boxing referee.

. . .

Catherine put her hand on top of Bob's, then rubbed his forearm, but didn't encourage him to be persistent in his legal career. Why not? He found that curious, knowing she must have felt bad for him. After all, he wanted to pass it, as much as she had — maybe even more. At least he had a fallback plan. She asked how his mother had been doing. He could tell she was disappointed in him. Why didn't she just sock him in the kisser? It would have hurt less.

. . .

She decided against telling him her good news about someday soon getting an actual case to prepare and — hopefully — try in court.

Bob walked Catherine back to the lobby in the Wayne County Building. After making quick plans to rendezvous after the work day, they hugged, though this time kept it brief.

After she'd returned to her desk, two attorneys asked her how serious her romance was with Bob. Catherine knew they weren't asking out of sincerity, but because if they knew marriage was in the cards, there could well be an opening for one of their law school cronies. She couldn't blame them for thinking that way, as so many women were expected to give up their careers the minute they got married. Not her. Why would any woman or man give up what they'd spent years preparing for? It made no sense, except that women were expected to have children. One of her crusades was going to be to educate the public on the importance of birth control. Neither she nor Bob believed sex was simply about procreation, unlike many of their fellow Catholics.

"Bob's my fiancé. We don't have a wedding date yet. End of story!" Catherine told the three men pretending to admire the flowers on her desk. She was hoping this weekend, Bob and she would come up with a date, though they'd tell no one but immediate relatives.

· · ·

One Saturday afternoon Grammy caught Catherine readying to leave the house by taxi with a small suitcase. Catherine's voice quavered as she informed her she'd be spending the night with a girlfriend. Grammy gave her a dubious smirk, adding that she hoped she'd have a "fine time." The blush on her granddaughter's face told her all she needed to know.

Was she now short of breath because of the sight of the impressive hotel or in anticipation of her night there with Bob?

He'd informed her the day before that he'd made reservations at the Tuller under the assumed name of Robert Bennett, so she should simply tell the clerk she was Mrs. Bennett. She'd raised her eyebrows. Bob had quickly explained how he'd be couldn't get there until later because of a meeting with his boxing manager. Catherine could get there first and slip on her finest gown. "We'll meet in the Arabian Room for a late dinner," he'd whispered, then nuzzled her neck. How did that Bob Sage always know exactly what to say?

The hotel sounded like it was out of a fairy tale and now here she was.

It was the first time she'd ever set foot in a swanky hotel and got dizzy taking in the enormous tapestries on the lobby walls, as well as the large and intricate chandeliers. There were more people than she'd expected to see milling about the lobby, so she purposefully didn't linger. Should she have shown up in disguise?

The Tuller was known as the "grande dame of Grand Circus Park," as it was situated directly across from the park. Catherine told the young man at the registration desk that she was Mrs. Robert Bennett and was given the key after signing the form with a shaky hand. A friendly bellhop, who reminded her of her brother, assisted with her suitcase. As they rode an elevator to the tenth floor, he told her how the luxury hotel had eight hundred rooms and each had a private bath. He unlocked the door to her hotel room and remained standing there.

"Is there anything else I can do for you?"

Mister, you'd better back off — her look suggested — but then she remembered she was supposed to give him a tip. Her blush burned her cheeks. Maybe he thought she wanted him to do more for her. She immediately opened the clasp of her black purse. Luckily, she had two quarters.

The room had long burgundy velvet drapes, mahogany furnishings, and real rose petals covering the bedspread. The rose scent almost concealed a mustiness there before the roses. It occurred to her that Bob must have contacted the hotel and had someone scatter the petals. Such a sweetheart to splurge on her! It reminded her of the roses he'd sent when she was studying for the bar exam. How nice to now thank him in person instead of by telegram!

She wished she had more time to enjoy the ambiance before meeting Bob in the dining room. After a steamy bath, she changed into a black satin evening gown. She slowly combed her bobbed auburn hair before generously applying her deep red lipstick.

They hadn't seen each other dressed up since their law school graduation, but that was different.

Tonight they had each other's sole attention. In her black evening gown, Catherine was the most glamorous woman Bob had ever seen. She'd never seen a more ruggedly handsome man than Bob Sage in his pin-striped suit, with his thick hair combed back—glistening from the pomade. The slight cleft in his chin and his dimples were noticed well before his two or three small facial scars, which were almost invisible in the dimly lit dining room. No one would have guessed him to be a boxer.

Dinner was delectable. Over small talk, they first enjoyed an appetizer of Oysters Rockefeller, followed by the main course comprising of a chicken breast stuffed with Camembert and pesto. Catherine tried to forego dessert, but Bob ordered two slices of Black Forest cheesecake. Sinful yet divine.

Afterward, wiping the corners of her mouth with a cloth napkin, she asked: Can you believe some people eat this way regularly? If so, there ought to be a law against it! Following Turkish coffee in the tiniest cups she'd ever seen, the band started up.

Without question, they made the best-looking couple on the dance floor, though they proved not to be the best dancers. While Bob was light on his feet, Catherine tripped a few times—luckily, no one got injured. She was self-conscious because she was taller, and her two-inch heels made her feel like a giant. When they danced in the speakeasies or dance halls, she always wore flats shoes. Could it be true that a woman should be shorter than her male escort? She visibly stiffened when he twirled her.

"Just relax, my darling girl," he whispered, not once, but a few times. Once she did, the other dancers cast envious glances at the handsome pair.

But after a while, Catherine complained of her shoes pinching her feet, so they sat down.

"I have an idea," Bob said. "What say we excuse ourselves and retire for the night?" He batted his long dark eyelashes.

"I like your plan. Let's make a break for it."

Once they'd entered their cozy haven for the night, they kept the lights off except for a small table lamp. They slow-danced cheek to cheek, pressing into each other. Then she kicked her shoes off.

"My dear you're an absolute knockout in that black satin dress."

"You made me feel like a million bucks since I was dancing with the most handsome man in the room."

Catherine purred and Bob growl-purred.

They rolled in the blanket of rose petals. He slowly undressed her, unzipping the back of her dress, kissing a shoulder, and then unclasping her bandeau brassiere (flappers were known for flattening their breasts). After cupping her cool breasts in his hot hands, he picked up a petal and slowly drew it up and down her arm. Then, ever so tenderly, he kissed her neck causing her to catch her breath and shiver. He gave her breasts a slight squeeze before his lips attached to one, while his hand kept hold of the other.

Bob's touch made her feel like a goddess.

She mimicked his slow languorous movements, stroking his hair and nipping an earlobe.

Unzipping his fly, she brought his swollen member deep into her mouth. And then he cried out to the gods.

Side by side, they lay next to each other, taking drags from the same cigarette. Bob figured it was time to tell Catherine about Cuba.

"Say listen, Sweets, I've got an upcoming match down in Cuba. I've been meaning to tell you."

"You're going there just to box?"

"A lot of money's riding on it. If I win, it'll help with our savings for our wedding trip to Europe. The bad news is I'll be gone for a few weeks. I'd ask you along, but now with your new job, you probably can't take the time. By the way, I'll be clerking for your uncle as soon as I return."

"A few weeks? Something's always coming up, Bob...I never get your undivided attention for long, do I?"

"Katy, I promise it won't always be this way."

A long silence ensued. She pouted and avoided eye contact. He began drumming his fingers on the desktop. At last, she spoke.

"Glad to hear you took my uncle up on the job offer. Still, you could've asked me if I wanted to go, though you're right about me not being able to get away. Sure takes the wind right out of a gal's sails."

"Oh, I thought I'd put enough in your sails to keep the boat afloat."

"Well, since you sprang this on me, how about we figure out a wedding date?"

"Now, Kate, that's not fair...Not that it's below the belt, but..." Bob looked like he hadn't seen the punch coming. He sat sideways on the bed and for the first time, couldn't look at her.

"You think I'm with you tonight like some two-bit hooker?"

That got his Irish up and he slapped her.

In a fury, Catherine flew off the bed, but then crumpled up in an armchair by the window. She cried and then sobbed. Bob hadn't figured her to be the sort to do so.

Almost overcome by guilt, he walked over to her and put his hand on her shoulder, but she threw it off.

Once before Bob had slapped a woman and vowed at the time he'd never do it again. It wasn't the way he was raised. His mother said if his father ever laid a hand on her in an unfriendly way, she'd cane him. All the Sage males, her husband included, had been careful to never provoke her ire. Once she'd witnessed her mother get beaten by her father. It was worse than stories you hear about people beating their dogs senseless. She vowed it would never happen to her. Bob admired his mother's self-respect. She wouldn't be pleased with what he'd just done to Catherine.

Now would be the time to apologize, but he couldn't. He was backed into a corner. Sure, he wanted to marry her, yet to commit to a date made it all so real—too real. He loved her, of course, and she had to know he wasn't just fooling around. Maybe she didn't. Still, she'd called his bluff, so he had to concede.

"C'mon, Kate, let's not ruin our otherwise perfect time. Sorry about the slap. It was just..."

"Just what, Bob? I had it coming to me. Is that what you were going to say?" It sure sounded like a page right out of her parents' playbook. But Bob had never slapped her before; she had to trust that he never would again.

They picked out a Saturday next June on his pocket calendar. He circled the date.

After a nightcap, they slept in each other's arms like there would be no tomorrow. Catherine dreamed a fire had burned down her family home. It would be the first of many dreams she'd have about fires.

CHAPTER TWENTY

Arms crossed behind his head, Bob stared up from his hotel bed at the slow swirling ceiling fan. He marveled at how a week had gone by since he'd been lying in a hotel bed with Catherine and now here he was at The Saratoga in Havana.

He sure could get used to this slower pace, the salty smell of the sea, the tropical beauty of the palm trees, not to mention the Cuban women, the tropical flowers, the parrots—their amusing chatter and squawk. He enjoyed wearing a straw hat with a black ribbon brim, so common among Cuban men. Nothing better than walking the narrow streets to one bar and then another. Little, outside of sex, did he find finer than puffing on Cuban cigars in the bars or at the horse track. And the rum drinks! Catherine would love them. Yes, Havana was sure a haven from his busy life back in Detroit. A great place for a honeymoon, he planned on telling her, though they'd already made tentative plans for Chicago. He'd send her a postcard or two—maybe it would help convince her. She liked birds, if not tropical heat. Maybe he'd send one with a pink flamingo on it.

Bob loved the freedom to fantasize about the two women he met on the train from Detroit to Florida: Polly, the blonde, and her dark-haired friend, Mary. Both had been lovely ladies and delightful to flirt with—not that the situation would've gotten out of control. To be flattered by their attention had been enough (well, almost) and they'd seemed to like his stories about having grown up out West and being a boxer. Turned out they were traveling to Cuba, too. He'd planned on meeting them for a drink, but they'd stood him up. Guess they'd been a couple of dizzy dames after all.

Then there was that other woman he met on the ship. One he'd have to tell Catherine about. A Romanian woman who'd settled in Chicago. While her English wasn't the best, she could communicate that she knew the notorious gangster, John Dillinger. He'd cautioned her she should keep better company, though he ended up telling her about Detroit's Purple Gang. He was even more surprised when he asked her for her name and she said — Anna — Anna Sage.

"Now, that's a coincidence!" Bob's voice boomed almost as loud as the ship's horn.

She told him she didn't know what that "hard to say" word meant, so he explained.

"Why would be that?" Anna asked. Then he told her how they had the same last name. She explained how her actual name in Romanian meant something else, but she'd shortened it once she got to America. She asked his family's country of origin and after telling her it was Ireland, she said it made "the sense perfect."

He now pictured Anna lying naked next to him in bed. She'd been okay looking, but not beautiful by a long shot. But there'd been something about her. The ceiling fan swirled slowly as he stroked himself. How little that fan did to cool the humid air.

Bob took himself to task for even thinking of cheating on Catherine. He'd go to Confession here at one of the Catholic churches; then he could return home with a clean conscience. After he got married, would he feel free enough to at least fantasize about other women? Would marriage feel like a prison? If so, maybe he wasn't the marrying sort. Better to throw the white towel in the ring now rather than later. But then yesterday he'd begun missing Catherine — to deeply miss her. So there was his answer. He hoped she felt the same about him, and those assistant prosecutors weren't giving her the third degree over drinks in a speakeasy. And he sure as hell hoped she wasn't dancing the Charleston with any of them.

Good thing he'd brought some of Catherine's law school notes. A little studying would keep him from obsessing about her. Later, he'd take a stroll down the avenue, and then tonight he'd get to see the boxing match. Luis Firpo of Argentina would fight Heavyweight champion, Jack Dempsey. Bob wouldn't be surprised if the entire population of Havana showed up to watch history being made. Tomorrow night, Bob would fight another Middleweight, someone he'd never heard of, but then again, Bob's name wasn't on the lips of anyone here except for a few of the other boxers and referees. He'd gained a few pounds (all muscle) and it wouldn't be long now before he made light heavyweight status.

It sure got hot here, especially when the breeze died down. He didn't need any grease in his hair, as it almost felt like it did in the ring. Something told him Catherine wouldn't be able to withstand the steaminess of the tropics for long. He rather enjoyed it. Still, he sure wished he could share this incredible place with her. After studying her notes on Constitutional law, he drifted off and dreamed that Anna Sage had talked him into joining John Dillinger's gang in Chicago.

CHAPTER TWENTY-ONE

"Mother, will you please let me help?"

"Just pull up a chair, Katy. You're a guest here now."

Catherine knew there was no point in defying her. Sitting with her father at the kitchen table cluttered with ingredients for a spaghetti dinner, she watched her mother scurry about— talking as she chopped an onion. Mickey shielded himself from his wife by holding the newspaper in front of his face. The women knew he was pretending to read. He'd lower it now and then for Catherine's benefit, and dance his eyebrows—then roll his eyes, before returning to the page. She knew this habit of his and was secretly amused.

Her mother continued to chatter as she browned the onion in a skillet, and then as she wiped the sink. Such a familiar scene, Catherine felt as if she'd never moved out. She chuckled, reminiscing how seldom her mother had ever let her help in the kitchen. True, Catherine had never expressed much interest in anything domestic. It occurred to her she'd have to cook for Bob once they were married. Weren't mothers supposed to show their daughters the way around the kitchen? Maybe Bridget had instructed her sisters, but she sure hadn't passed along any of her culinary secrets to Catherine, who was okay at making scrambled eggs and toast, but anything more complex: forget it.

Over a week had passed since she'd stayed at the Tuller with Bob. Had they become engaged or had she only dreamed it?

"I have news."

Her mother stopped wiping the sink and her father put down the paper.

"Bob and I are engaged!" She beamed, feeling somewhat breathless. She hoped that by telling her parents the reality would sink in.

Her father hugged her, and her mother was about to, but stopped and asked: "Where's the ring then?" Catherine had an urge to throttle her.

"Mother, he asked for my hand in marriage. I said yes. Do I need to spell it out for you? We're hoping the ceremony will be next year. Maybe in June. Please don't ask me to be more specific. Bob is planning on a more formal proposal when he gets a ring."

Her mother could be so exasperating. Why was she so hard to deal with? Catherine was regretting having told them the news.

"You'll have your wedding at either Most Holy Trinity Church or St. Mary's, right? You simply must have Father Tim marry you, so it'll have to be at Trinity. But what about the reception?" Bridget paced back and forth, and finally remembered to mix the onion in with the spaghetti sauce. Had she always been so frantic?

Father Tim often dropped by the house for coffee. Catherine had never seen such watery eyes. If you didn't know him, you'd think he was crying, though he was usually the first to laugh at a joke. When she'd first heard it, she thought for sure the song "When Irish Eyes Are Laughing" had been written for him. Something told her that her mother wouldn't wait for Father Tim to drop by; she'd arrange a visit as soon as possible.

"Quit the wedding gears from turning so fast, Mama! We only just decided."

"For the love of Jesus, Mary, and Joseph! Will you leave the girl alone, Bridget? Here, she just stopped by to pay us a visit and you're doing what you always do."

Catherine thanked him. Her mother smirked but kept pacing.

"It's all right, Papa. I expected as much. What's new with you, two, anyway? Mama, will you please sit down for a second? You're making me nervous!"

Bridget finally sat down with her back to her husband. Boiling the water for the spaghetti noodles could wait, as it was too early for dinner anyway. She brought Catherine up to date about Eileen's difficulties. It seemed her husband had "gone cold on her," and Eileen's two older ones had had daily temper tantrums. Then her mother added how she'd enjoyed the quiet since both Catherine and John had moved out. He'd recently moved into a dorm at the seminary. Ouch, Mother—Catherine wanted to say.

"Still, we get lonesome. Luckily, John comes home twice a week for dinner," Bridget hastened to add. Why did she always have to rub it in? The good and devoted son forever contrasted with the neglectful daughter. Catherine sighed and told herself it was always going to be this way.

Her father kept wiping invisible food from the corner of his mouth with a napkin. He only half listened to the two women, as he looked out the backyard window at one blue jay attacking another.

As her mother finished cooking dinner, Catherine set the table. She told them how Bob was in Havana for a boxing match and wouldn't return for another week.

"Oh, Kate—just think of all the traveling you'll get to do once you're married!" said her mother.

"We've talked about taking a couple of trips, but if he goes somewhere explicitly for boxing, he won't have much time for me. I do have my own career, you know?"

"Now, Katy, your mother meant no disrespect." What? He was coming to his wife's defense for once? Catherine only smiled in response.

"Mickey, lend me a hand, please." It was unusual to hear a purr in Bridget's tone.

He immediately jumped up to help serve the spaghetti and meatballs. He'd been sitting at the table, shifting about, with one of his knees twitching. Funny, how he hated to sit still and he'd had that twitchy knee as long as Catherine could remember. Still, in the past, Mickey never would have helped serve a meal. Nice to see a positive change in their relationship! She probably should have moved out years ago.

Her mother had overcooked the noodles. Still, the dinner was better by far than anything Catherine could cook up by herself. The three chewed in silence. When her father offered her more, she politely declined. He gave her a knowing look and smiled.

"You're all skin and bones, Kate. With your short hair, you're beginning to resemble a bird with few feathers."

Catherine put her hands on her hips and gave him a scolding look before she propelled her arms as if preparing for flight. All three laughed.

"It's nice seeing you both...and nice to see you're getting along!" Her parents beamed before her mother stood to gather the plates.

Before leaving, after assisting with the kitchen clean-up, Catherine promised to stop by more often. Was it her imagination or did her mother hug her longer than usual?

She appreciated her father driving her back to her uncle's, as getting to either her parents' home or her uncle's, involved a long walk after getting off the streetcar. Besides, she didn't feel safe riding alone at night. It wasn't often she was alone with her father. While he was always kind and interested in how she was doing, they rarely had much to say to each other. Ever since she'd been an adult he'd seemed nervous around her. When he wasn't drinking, he had a much calmer presence than her mother.

Catherine remarked how it must have taken forever for people to get around before automobiles and public transport, but then cities weren't so large as they'd now become. Mickey told her how he well-remembered the days of horse and buggy.

After thanking him for the ride, she admitted how she was both excited, as well as afraid, of what life had in store.

"Ah, my girl, it gets tough, but then it eases up some before getting doubly tough. Some days, I haven't a baldy notion of what life's all about," he said. He suddenly looked older and more life-weary.

"Thanks for your honesty, Papa." She hugged him before getting out of his black Model-T.

"I love you, my Wild Irish Rose! Keep up the good fight!" he shouted, his brave Irish eyes watering a bit. She meant to declare her love for him but was overcome by his words.

She hurried up the walk to her uncle's front door. Wiping away tears, she bit her lip, hoping no one inside would notice.

· · ·

Catherine's legal research for the prosecutors often felt like studying once had in college, except now there were always interruptions, though thankfully, no exams to take. Still, it was like she was constantly preparing for one, as she searched through books and files for relevant laws and statutes to cement the prosecution's arguments on any given case. Once she found what she'd been searching for, it became a matter of interpreting the legal jargon. It often seemed like she was translating a foreign language. She pictured old British men in powdered wigs from an earlier century. They always struck her as pompous and vain, though who knew how her generation of attorneys would appear to the ones in the future; at least a few women had now joined the ranks, but only a few.

She knew well that she was constantly being tested by the men at work. When there were discussions in the break room, they'd address each other and pretend she wasn't present. That was, until she was about to leave.

"So, Catherine, what do you think about the decision in the case of Moran vs. Lake?" Jim Dolan asked, thinking he'd caught her off guard. He winked at a male colleague sitting across from him at a large table.

"I'm so glad you asked. Isn't it pretty much identical to the Stoper vs. Philips case back in 1921?" she asked.

"Oh? Bill, do you think she could be right?" Jim asked, amazed.

Bill nodded, looking impressed.

Later, she mused how she'd been lucky to have known about the Stoper versus Philips case, but after going through a similar scenario in which she was again correct, the men backed off a bit.

"Guess we caught a whale in Catherine, and not just some little fish." She overheard one of them say to the other, though she pretended she hadn't.

Without seeing Bob on the weekends he was away, her life settled into predictable tedium, though she knew it wouldn't remain this way once he returned. She enjoyed the occasional sherry and cigarette with her uncle. But then came a morning when Emily Schauber raced up to Catherine in the law library. Catherine was sitting at a large wooden table with a few small mountains of books.

"Catherine, could you fill in for Michael Sullivan in court? He didn't show up in court today to receive the file of an upcoming case. I think the man hits the hard stuff a bit too often. Anyway, if you're able to, I'll fill you in on the case."

"I've been dying for the chance. I so appreciate it!"

Emily, still breathless, sat down next to her.

"Don't thank me yet, but I appreciate your readiness. It's an Assault and Battery charge. Let's go to my office and I'll explain the case before handing you the file."

Catherine was surprised to find this lead attorney's office to be so modest and small. The only decorations were Emily's framed diplomas on one wall. Her desk was predictably cluttered with case files and legal pads. Two uncomfortable looking chairs, way too large for the cramped room, were positioned in front of the desk. She motioned for Catherine to take a seat before telling her about the case. Catherine, who'd brought a pencil and legal pad, prepared to take notes.

"Just listen to my summary of my longer report. You can make your notes later," Emily told her and then launched in:

"Two men had been fishing from a small boat in the Detroit River. They were the only ones on board. Evidently, Joe and Henry were both interested in the same woman and started to argue. Joe threatened Henry, telling him he was going to knock him overboard if Henry didn't "shut his trap." And the very next second, according to Henry's testimony, Joe did exactly that. An acquaintance of Henry's had been motoring by in his boat and had witnessed the two men arguing. He then saw Henry go overboard.

Henry further claimed that Joe tried to drown him by beating him over the head with an oar, though the witness couldn't verify this. There were no other witnesses."

Catherine raised her eyebrows, but then waited for Emily to continue.

"Joe, of course, denied doing anything of the kind. Henry wanted Joe to be charged with Attempted Murder, but an Assault and Battery charge would be the only one that had a chance of standing up in court."

Catherine took a few minutes to digest what she'd heard and then told Emily that it all sounded fairly straightforward.

"It is, Catherine, but look out for Leon Freemont's snake-in-the-grass tactics," Emily said and explained that he was the defense attorney.

It hadn't taken Catherine long to go from feeling flattered to sinking her teeth into the case. After asking a few procedural questions, she then took the file folder back to her office. She had to appear in court for a motion and then the following week, she would try the case. In that time, she'd try to interview Joe and Henry, and also Henry's acquaintance. Leon Freemont had had a few months to craft his argument.

Her good day at work culminated in an even better evening: when Catherine returned home, Grammy handed her a postcard from Bob. She stared in amusement at the pink flamingo, but then even longer at his tender love note.

"Oh, to be young and in love again!" Grammy said, making the sign of the cross. "If only the saints could preserve us."

Catherine giggled and Grammy tried not to grin.

She got little sleep those nights before the trial. While she appreciated the encouragement from a few of the assistant prosecutors, she sure wished Bob had been around to shore up her confidence.

Questions about Bob's fever dream about shooting people and having to leave town occurred to her the following night. There were similarities between Bob's dream and her case. Had Joe wanted to kill Henry? Had Bob intended to kill those men in his dream? Normally, she thought dreams mere silly leftovers from the day's events or difficulties. This one sure had bothered Bob. Where had the shooting occurred? Could he remember their faces? Was Catherine in the dream? She recalled that he'd mentioned telling Gene about it. Maybe she should speak to him and see if he recalled details that Bob hadn't told her.

It must be because of the upcoming trial that she was now recalling the dream.

If Henry's story could be proven, it would be Attempted Murder, a far more serious charge than Assault and Battery. Yet, if there was no evidence of intent, except one person's word against another's, there was little hope of making the murder charge stick. In Bob's dream, Bob had possibly committed murder. Despite how busy she was working on the case, she had to take some time and discuss Bob's dream with Gene.

She closed her eyes tight as if doing so would induce sleep. What if she recalled the dream because something was wrong with Bob down in Cuba? What if he'd gotten into a bar fight and his life had been threatened? He'd never spoken of shooting anyone, but he had that red-hot temper. Her heat felt like it was going to race right out of her body.

No point thrashing about in bed. She went downstairs and had a nip of her uncle's brandy. Tomorrow, she'd laugh at her crazy thoughts — or so, she hoped.

CHAPTER TWENTY-TWO

Violet greeted Catherine at the door with Bobby Gene at her side. He almost knocked his mother over so he could be the first to hug his soon-to-be aunt. What a friendly little guy! After they hugged — and to Bobby Gene's great delight — Catherine picked him up and twirled him around. He planted a kiss on her cheek, clearly smitten.

"What a little Valentino!" Catherine adored Bob's namesake.

"He's never like that with his own mother," Violet said. "Come on in, Kate."

"Thanks, Violet. Say, is Gene home? There's a matter I need to discuss."

Violet yelled out to Gene, who must have been in a back room. It was only the second time Catherine had been to their house, a small bungalow. Neat as a shiny pin, it smelled of furniture polish. After greetings were exchanged, Violet informed her she was just about to take Bobby Gene to a friend's house. They'd only be gone about a half hour and would Catherine still be here when they returned? Catherine rather doubted it and apologized for stopping by unannounced.

"When every family has a telephone, won't it just be the bee's knees?" said Catherine.

"It sure will! If I don't see you when we get back, let's get together soon, okay? Gene, be sure to offer our guest a piece of pie," Violet said loudly to Gene who was standing only two feet away. Catherine wondered if he was a little deaf.

Bobby Gene began to cry when his mother yanked his arm. "Quit your dawdling, Bobby Gene!" Violet scolded. He morosely followed her out the door.

Catherine perched on the sofa edge and took out a cigarette from her purse. Gene immediately jumped up to go in search of an ashtray. She'd forgotten that neither Gene nor Violet had the nicotine habit. The smoky air might bother Violet. If so, at least Catherine wouldn't be there to hear her complain. She glanced around at the tidy living room, and at the several little glass figurines on end tables. The room was stuffy and warm. It barely looked lived in: nothing was out of place or had a speck of dust on it. How could people live in a place like this? How did Violet keep it that way with a toddler running around?

Catherine couldn't help but comment.

Gene laughed and said Violet had so much nervous energy that she cleaned day and night — hardly ever took any time to sit down. She wanted to ask how he ever felt comfortable, but didn't.

"Sure makes me glad to have an office job," he said. Like her, Gene worked downtown. While he'd earned his law degree, he worked as a probation officer rather than an attorney.

"Funny, we both have law degrees, but don't really need them for the work we're doing — except I'm now working on my first case." Catherine described it in some detail and couldn't get over what a good listener Gene was. Also, he had a calm presence and was almost nurturing — much like his mother. Had she fallen for the wrong brother? After a short discussion of Bob's trip to Cuba, she lit another cigarette and explained the reason for her visit.

Gene rose from the chair he'd been sitting on and moved closer to her on the couch. Had he sensed her attraction?

"It's about Bob's fever dream from a couple months ago," she said.

"I almost forgot the apple pie. Would you care for a piece?" Gene seemed in a hurry. Was he nervous being around her or was it just that he didn't want to discuss it? If it was the latter, why not?

Catherine smiled and nodded, trying to put him at ease.

"Oh, right. Bob told you about it, did he?" Gene asked, leaving to the kitchen. When he returned with the pie, he suggested having it in the backyard. No doubt afraid that Violet would complain about any crumbs on her carpet.

She followed him outside to a small, well-manicured backyard and sat next to him at a patio table. It was more like a day in early October rather than mid-November. They remarked on how they didn't even need to wear coats. She exclaimed over how tasty the pie was, saying she didn't know that Violet liked to bake. Gene chuckled, saying it was a recipe his mother always made. Then scratching his chin, he added he didn't think his wife had baked anything her entire life. "Girl after my own heart," she confided. He nodded in understanding.

The brothers had the same noticeable cleft in their chins, as well as dimples. Gene took out a toothpick and gnawed on it just like his brother often did after a meal. After a few minutes, he removed it before speaking.

"Bob had been ill with a high fever a couple days after a fight in which he received a blow to his head. He's suffered a few of them, hasn't he? Anyway, I'd been over visiting our mother, and she'd just gone to bed, when he came rushing from his room. He begged me to leave town with him—right away—because he'd shot two men. A couple of no-good swindlers..."

Catherine again lit a cigarette and listened intently. After exhaling a plume of smoke, she tried to compare Gene's version with what Bob had told her.

"That's pretty much what he told me. Any other details?"

"If I recall correctly, he said he'd shot them with a pistol in a room—an office. Bob paced and seemed pretty upset. He kept telling me to open a window because the room was on fire. I got him a glass of water and told him over and over how what he'd had was a nightmare due to his fever. Finally, it seemed to register on him, but he still couldn't get over how real it seemed."

"Well, it was one of the strangest things Bob's ever told me," Catherine said, trying to rub the goosebumps from her arms.

"Don't forget, we saw a lot of rough stuff out in Idaho. Lots of people got killed or died tragic deaths down in the silver mines. Has he told you about Raymond?"

"His twin who died, right?"

Gene nodded. "They'd just celebrated their fourteenth birthday a few days before Raymond fell to his death. I don't think Bob's ever been the same since. He once said it was like half of him died that day. Bob and I are close, but not like Raymond and he had been."

"He's rarely mentioned him, but Nana has told me a few stories."

"I guess you could say Bob's on the secretive side."

"Maybe I'm with the wrong brother." The words were out of her mouth before she realized she'd said them.

"Maybe I shouldn't have told you so much, Catherine. I'm sorry if I've upset you."

Then Gene leaned over and kissed her softly—not on her cheek, but mouth. More a peck than a kiss. He pulled away and looked at his watch, clearly flustered. Then she leaned forward and stroked the back of his wavy brown hair. It was a lot like Bob's but styled with less pomade. He relaxed for a moment, but then looked startled—as if he'd heard something. They looked enough alike that they could have been twins. While Bob was the better-looking one, Gene was more of a gentleman, more patient and kind. He had little desire to be on center stage.

Her face felt flushed. Why had she let him kiss her? Violet could be home any second. She jumped up from her chair and told him she had to get going.

"Catherine—the kiss—I'm sorry. I don't know what came over me. Please stay. I won't let it happen again."

"No, it sure won't! But know that it wasn't just you—I kissed you back. Our secret, okay?"

"My lips are sealed. I promise."

If she knew anything about this man, it was that she could believe his promises.

She was relieved to leave before Violet and Bobby Gene returned, for Violet would have seen Catherine's rosy cheeks.

Catherine wasn't able to return to the rose-covered walls of her bedroom and ponder over her time at Gene's, as she had to refresh her memory with some of the details of the case. Tomorrow was her big day in court. Little did she know then, but she would recall Bob's fever dream for the rest of her life.

CHAPTER TWENTY-THREE

Bob returned tanned and rested after his trip. While boxing had been taking a toll on his looks, his spirit remained strong. One of his ears now appeared more misshapen than the other, and a new gash near his bottom lip was deep enough to cause a permanent scar. Also, Bob's small nose looked decidedly more flattened. He brought back boxes of cigars, candy made from sugar cane, and some smuggled bottles of rum. But the best of the bounty: a diamond ring he bought at a discounted price in Havana.

One late November night, beneath a full moon, Bob drove Catherine to their favorite bench overlooking the Detroit River on Belle Isle. He removed his fedora, got down on one knee, and proposed for the second time. After she fawned over the large diamond, they shared a long, lingering kiss. Less than a minute later, she told him about the court case—her first case—and how she'd won: the accused was found guilty of Attempted Murder.

Bob nodded, disconcerted, not so much by her quick dismissal of the romantic moment, but in her ability to switch gears. Why did she do this? It wasn't a sucker punch, but it threw him off balance.

He gave her a quick peck on the lips, and then launched into an account of a horse race he saw in Havana.

Catherine tugged down the brim of her cloche hat, lowering it as far as possible on her forehead.

Bob was retaliating for her bringing up the court case. Still, she couldn't help but feel slapped by his dismissiveness. She'd only mentioned the case because of how excited she was to get it. Gene never would have reacted this way. She nodded at what he was saying and politely asked a few questions. Was the great passion they once had for each other already diminished? Was it gone?

Again, she pulled down the brim of her hat.

The following day was one Catherine would regret. Try as she would, she'd never be able to forgive herself for something more egregious than her insensitive reaction after the proposal. It would be one of many blunders that would cause her to tell others: "We're all our own best friend and worst enemy."

Every couple of weeks she'd made it a point to visit Nana, often showing up with a pack of fresh red licorice. It mattered less if Bob would meet her there for a study night. The very day after receiving her engagement ring, Catherine stopped by, even before showing it to her own family or friends. Doing so made her realize how much she valued the older woman's approval.

Nana turned on the end-table lamp to see how the diamond glistened. She clasped Catherine's long, pale hand and exclaimed over the ring's beauty.

"And all he brings me are flowers, for Lord's sake!" Nana pouted as she pointed at the pink roses Bob gave her for her sixtieth birthday, a few days earlier. When Catherine commiserated, Nana burst out laughing, telling the younger woman that, of course, she was delighted by her son's attentiveness. Then they giggled together like school girls.

Then Catherine, out of nowhere, brought up Bob's fever dream, certain that Nana must have known about it. "Why do you think he'd dream about shooting a couple men? Did he ever describe the men or anything about it to you?"

"What are you talking about, Catherine?"

"It was a dream, one that he'd had when he was sick. I thought you knew about it," she said rapidly, suddenly sick to her stomach.

"This is the first I've heard of it. Pray with me, child," said Nana, looking pale.

Catherine folded her hands as if to pray. She was burning up. The room spun.

"No, he's said nothing about it," said Nana, holding off on the prayer. She continued in a whisper, "My dear, I've had dreams like that and so did my own Irish mother. They're portals into the future. Visions. Now that he's spoken of it—it's too late. We can only try to keep a gun out of his hands, but we're dealing with Fate here. Oh, how I wish you hadn't told me, but I'll seek advice from the dearly departed. Maybe they'll tell me how to proceed."

Catherine fanned herself with the most recent edition of *The Ladies' Home Journal*.

Nana walked over to the table of family pictures and began muttering aloud to them. Afterward, she sat down, and rocked back and forth, praying and crying. Catherine mustered all her courage to remain seated next to her. Why hadn't Bob told his mother? Nana closed her eyes, as if in a trance. Then she took Catherine's hand, still with her eyes shut. At last, Nana spoke.

"Child, I forgive you for revealing what you did, but you must take care and seek help from the saints. It was revealed to me that many difficulties lie ahead. To avoid an early death—take heed."

Catherine's entire being went numb. A sudden chill filled the room. While Nana didn't specify a date or time of Catherine's demise, she might as well have. Did she say this to be retaliatory, or did she actually have a vision?

Next, Nana poured a shot of Irish whiskey for Catherine and herself. And then another. Catherine couldn't keep her hand still enough to hold a cigarette.

"Now, Kate, I'm just a silly old woman. What do I know? I didn't mean to frighten you so. I'm not a fortune teller— sometimes I just get a feeling, a hunch. It's not like I saw anything in a crystal ball, so what I told you could be sheer nonsense. The ramblings of an old woman…"

Later that night, Catherine tossed and turned in bed, not knowing what to believe. Whispering the 'Our Father' over and over, at last, helped her drift into slumber.

• • •

Bob stormed over to her uncle's house the following evening. In a booming voice, he told Catherine they needed to talk. She could tell he was seething. Uncle Gerry and Grammy McIntosh stood motionless and mute in the hallway. Catherine's cheeks burned.

He refused to speak in the car and drove them to a small nearby park. For several minutes they sat in uncomfortable silence and he wouldn't look at her.

"Say something, would you?" Catherine asked.

At last, he said, "Let's walk."

Bob led the way to a picnic table, and sat down first, gesturing for Catherine to sit across from him. Still, he couldn't find the words to express his fury. After pounding the wooden table, he stood up and began pacing. The silence was painful. She had a hard time swallowing. Thankfully, no one else was around when he let her have it.

"How dare you!"

"What do you mean?" She gotten little sleep and her foggy brain couldn't fathom why he was this angry.

"Don't play Miss Innocent with me, Catherine McIntosh."

She racked her brain. It had to be more than simply mentioning the dream to Nana. Had someone told him she'd had lunch with Art Johnson, one of the assistant prosecutors, when Bob was in Cuba? Maybe Bob had gotten wind of her visit with Gene and he didn't approve of her seeing Gene and Violet without him. Had Gene mentioned the kiss?

"You're aware of how close I am to my mother. How could you?"

She gulped. Nana must have told him about their conversation.

"Shite, Bob, it was just a dream. You said so yourself!" Catherine said, rising from the hard bench. This was ridiculous. She needed to leave.

"Where do you think you're going? Sit back down. You know my mother. She talks to dead people and believes they talk to her. Not only does she believe in Christianity, but Irish lore. You basically told her that someday I'll leave town because I shot a couple people. For the love of Pete, don't you get it? Nana thinks it means that I could wind up dead — that would make four dead sons and a dead husband. I did the best I could to make her see it was only a dream from when I had a fever, but she was pretty upset. You've betrayed an important trust."

Bob looked down at his hands, avoiding Catherine's questioning stare.

Had his mother mentioned that the spirits had revealed that they might both die before their time? She must not have. Catherine certainly wouldn't tell him about it now, though maybe he wouldn't care or give much credence to his mother's premonition. Curiously, Nana seemed shield her son from bad news from the Other Side, though she had no problem telling Catherine. She must have known that Catherine would say nothing of this to Bob, too, though she hadn't sworn her to secrecy.

Bob finally spoke: "Now, I'm the one who needs to think things over. Maybe we should call off the wedding."

"What? Over me spilling the beans about a dream?"

"Like, I said, there's more at play. It's the principle, don't you see?"

When Catherine didn't answer, Bob went back to his car without even looking back at her. He delivered a blow that would knock her flat and he wasn't about to help her stand back up in the ring. She had it coming, he told himself. There was no point chasing after him or even waving at him as he drove away.

She walked back to her uncle's house, sobbing in the dark. Just when everything had been going smoothly—this had to happen. Here, she'd won her first court case, had been making friends, and doing her best to stay in touch with her family. It occurred to her that maybe life would be better, simpler, without Bob Sage mucking the otherwise gentle waters. Maybe she should be the one to break the engagement. Why give him the upper hand?

But a few days later, a dozen red roses were delivered to her office with a little note: "Forgive me? I love you now and forever. -R. Sage"

And of course, Catherine forgave him.

CHAPTER TWENTY-FOUR

January, 1925

Catherine marched down the endless aisle of Old St. Mary's church. At long last, the big day arrived. Well over a year had passed since Bob had first proposed. Her traditional long white gown was simple—without lace or beads—except for its exceptionally long train. And her short bobbed haircut had grown out and now auburn curls reached her shoulders. Thankfully, the netting on the long veil concealed her fatigue and nervous smile.

Had it not been for Father Tim waiting at the altar, Catherine might not have made it. His sweet face and watery blue eyes—his dear familiarity—helped calm her down. He'd recently been transferred to this downtown church from his Corktown parish.

While she knew she wasn't the first to suffer from insomnia before their wedding, Catherine's nerves were especially frayed because last night, Bob had a fight in the ring. She'd begged him to bow out. He said doing so was impossible, as it wasn't a small fight: it was for the first world title fight in twenty-one years. He'd be up against one of the champs: Harry Greb. Harry had been favored to win and Bob knew the stakes, but claimed it good luck to have a match the night before the wedding. Catherine wasn't so sure. The what-ifs had kept her tossing and turning: What if Bob lost and his mood sunk low? What if Harry further disfigured Bob's face? And even worse: what if Bob's injuries wound him up in the hospital? While unlikely, she knew the possibility remained. No way was she going to postpone the wedding after all the planning.

Still, her excitement over becoming Catherine Sage far outweighed her worries. Only a few hours ago, Bob sent her a telegram. It read: "Lost fight but won you! See you soon."

She'd almost made it to the altar, though Father Tim still looked miles away, along with waiting bridesmaids and the hundreds of guests. Again, the what-ifs. What if Bob was late? How bad she'd feel for the priest and all the guests. What if, during the long wait, she changed her mind? She'd heard of that sort of thing happening: a last-minute change of heart. Maybe Bob had changed his mind.

The lump in her throat turned into a bigger lump. She could barely swallow. Her stomach felt queasy and try as she might, it was impossible to take a deep breath. Where was he? Should she turn and run? If he didn't show, it would solve the potential problem and she wouldn't have to make a run for it.

After what felt like an eternity, but turned out to be a delay of only a few minutes: Bob arrived. Following his groom's men, he made his way down the aisle in a black tuxedo, top hat, and gloves. Still, as handsome as ever, despite whatever injuries he'd incurred. Knowing Bob, he'd have a few. Yet his suffering would, as always, be concealed by his wide smile. One thing she loved most about him was his bravery, though she was still miffed at him for being in the ring last night.

Eileen, Molly, and Violet made lovely bridesmaids in lilac-colored satin gowns. Eileen looked less dour than usual and Violet — if you stood too near her — seemed almost as jittery as a bride herself. And the three groom's men made dashing counterparts for the women: Gene, John, and Billy Watson. Like the groom, they wore tall black top hats, as did the bride's father.

Both the McIntoshes and the Sages looked pleased by the ceremony, particularly Catherine's mother, though she sobbed audibly throughout. Nana could be heard giggling by some, though she'd later deny doing so. Mickey stood more erect than usual, proud to be giving his daughter away. He even spoke for over five minutes to his brother, Gerry, at the reception— something he hadn't done in years.

A lavish reception was held at the Belle Isle Yacht Club. The drive from church to the reception was an easy one. As luck had it, the winter had been a mild one. When Catherine carefully stepped out of the car, Violet and Molly assisted her by holding up the long white train.

Several reporters had gathered with open pads, pencils, and cameras poised and ready.

"Mrs. Sage," said one of the top reporters from the Society Page, "Mind if we call you the Belle Isle Belle?"

"I'd love it!" Catherine flashed a camera-ready smile.

"Is it true that Battling Bob had a match on the eve of the wedding?" "Did he lose the fight?" "Where are you two lovebirds going on your honeymoon?"

Catherine wasn't prepared for the barrage and was grateful that Bob had now finished saying something to Gene and was headed her way. After taking a few questions and agreeing to pose for photos, the newlyweds waved at the now-growing crowd of well-wishers and headed into the yacht club. Gerry had again assisted his dearest niece: it turned out that the yacht club's manager owed him a favor. Catherine's parents at first wouldn't hear of it, but after purchasing her dress and the many flowers, they gratefully, though reluctantly, agreed.

Neither the bride nor the groom would remember much about the day. They could blame it on their nerves and the whirlwind of the wedding, but the simple truth: they'd both gotten smashed. Bob had cut a deal with the Detroit cops so they wouldn't be arrested or fined for having alcohol at the reception. Several of them were friends of Bob's and had attended the wedding.

There had been several hundred guests at the wedding, and even more came to the reception. Besides family and friends, guests included: Judge Frank Murphy, Father Tim, several attorneys, professors from the law school, various community leaders, a few members from Bob's old Irish gang from Cork Town, a few guys from the Purple Gang, and local boxers. Several newspaper reporters tried their best to get quotes from the gang members, but as soon as they'd been seen at the crowded reception, the couple had vanished. Billy Watson was mistaken for being part of the gang and took a swing at one of the reporters.

Still, a memorable time was had by all, and for some — maybe too much of one. One reporter described Catherine as a radiant bride and Bob, as a dashing groom. And another one remarked that the head-turning couple could one day be as fascinating as Zelda and F. Scott Fitzgerald. The guest to whom the remark was made begged to differ, as Catherine and Bob, though attractive, weren't movie star material.

. . .

When the newlyweds boarded the early morning train for their Chicago honeymoon, neither had slept since two nights before the wedding. Bob snored on the train, but Catherine remained awake until she collapsed on the bed in their suite at the Congress Hotel. She slept for twelve hours without stirring.

And then the following morning Bob accused Catherine of having snored most of the night. She threw a pillow at him. He then tried to reassure her she wasn't all that loud — that the sounds she made were "little lady-like snores." She hurled another pillow, but this time he caught it and flung it back, almost knocking her off her feet.

After enjoying a room service breakfast, which Catherine declared "divine," Bob suggested they get out for a walk, only because Catherine had claimed she couldn't wait to stroll through the shopping district. While they knew Chicago was called the 'windy city,' they hadn't known how bitterly cold it could be walking down streets near Lake Michigan. They weren't outside long before heading back to the welcoming hotel.

"Let's just stay in, why don't we?" she asked.

"Sweets, I've gotta show you the sights. Be a sport, won't you?"

"Sure, Bob." But she wasn't so sure.

Instead of walking, however, they took cabs to restaurants and speakeasies. Catherine couldn't hide her joy upon discovering that the speakeasies here were larger and more populated than the ones in Detroit. She claimed the live jazz and blues were "truly the cat's meow." They slow-danced to "It Had to Be You" and later agreed that it was "their" song. Bob hinted that maybe someday they'd move there and she readily agreed.

Still, she later complained that they hadn't stayed in their luxurious hotel suite long enough, but admitted to having had, overall, a grand time. The best part, Catherine told her friends, had been being enfolded in Bob's muscular arms in bed. The hard part was returning to Detroit and moving into a cramped studio apartment with a Murphy bed. Its two windows overlooked a dark alley. Bob assured her it would be temporary and they'd move someplace nicer as soon as they could afford it.

· · ·

It would prove to be a dizzying time.

After receiving the good news in a telegram, he spun Catherine around the small apartment.

A few days after returning home from Chicago, Bob retook the bar exam and finally passed after his two earlier attempts. He almost stopped mid-twirl to drive over to give his good news to his mother. But it was almost as if in spinning Catherine, he sent their lives together into an ever faster spin. He'd been clerking for her uncle ever since returning from his trip to Cuba. While he didn't mind the work, he was ready to practice law and knew he now had enough contacts to set up his practice since he'd passed the Bar.

Two large parties were held in his honor. Both started out tame but soon turned wild. A couple Purple Gang members crashed the second one. Catherine and Bob had just finished taking a whirl on the dance floor of a rented hall when Bob recognized one of the more notorious members.

"There's bad news, Kate, and then really bad news. See the guy in the three-piece suit? That's Joel Breen. It's said he doesn't know the meaning of playing nice."

He'd no sooner said this to her in a whisper, than Joel was standing there, tapping him on his shoulder with his cane. He politely told Bob that if he had a second, he'd like a word, and then began walking toward the back door.

Bob jumped up and immediately followed Joel out to the alley. She tried to follow them, but Joel's buddy—a big and tough-looking sort—made sure she stayed put at the table.

"Your lover boy will be right back," he told her, pulling out the chair for her to sit down. He took Bob's chair and introduced himself without asking her name. He probably knew it.

"Call me Frank," he said in a high-pitched voice. She gave him a brief nod and looked away. Worried that Bob was being roughed up in the alley, she couldn't think of anything to say.

"C'mon, Sweetheart, I hear you're a lady lawyer and good with words. Lighten up."

Catherine wanted nothing more than to punch him in his kisser.

"So about that couple hundred you owe me," Joel said to Bob in the dark alley. The smell of garbage and cat urine filled his nostrils.

"You got the wrong man."

"Think real hard, Bob. That bathtub gin you ordered. I'm told it was for a party you threw a few years back."

Bob recalled being told the hooch was a gift, and now that he recalled it, Joel hadn't been the giver. It was from one of Bob's pals from the Corktown neighborhood—Jack Nadell. He was Herman's brother. Neither were bad sorts. So the brothers were members of the Purple Gang? No such thing as a rum-runner in Detroit unless you were connected to the gang. Bob should've known better. He slicked back his hair from his forehead and couldn't look the well-dressed man in the eye.

"Jack sent me on this mission. Knowing you were a poor kid in college, he cut you some slack. Bobby boy, you got a week to pay up, or else." Joel pretended his index finger was a knife in front of his throat by making a straight slice motion.

Bob wouldn't discuss the matter with Catherine. She gave him the third degree, but he didn't want to involve her in the shady deal. He paid Joel three days later, by coming up with half of it himself. Gene loaned him the rest. Had he known Jack or his brother were Purple Gang members, he never would've accepted the gift. One of life's many lessons, he told himself.

.   .   .

Despite their proclivity toward hedonism, by summer's end, they began their law practice together. Sage & Sage leased office space in the impressive skyscraper—the Lawyer's Building. Popular boxer that he was, The Battling Barrister had no difficulty procuring clients. Catherine, with her red hair, wonderful wit, and newfound confidence, had become almost as magnetic. (In summer, her hair was always more red than auburn.) Sage & Sage was up and running. Soon they found themselves swamped with clients.

In the fall, they moved into a luxury apartment at the Whittier, near the Detroit River. Catherine let out a joyful yip as she looked out a window from their spacious apartment to the river below; then danced Bob around the spacious living room. Not only did their windows have great views of the river, but there was also a mezzanine with little shops, a doorman who held the lobby door open for you, as well as a parking attendant. The only problem was that she always felt like a guest in her own home— like she was staying at a grand hotel in a famous city. While this feeling lessened after a while, it would always remain.

While they were constantly on the go, they found time for climbing into bed with each other. They explored their passion for one another through sex, be it tender, rough, romantic, or silly. Not only did they become more skillful over time, they also enjoyed teasing as much as pleasing the other when naked between the sheets. Feeling uninhibited together became an essential way for both to relax from their stressful daily lives.

Catherine sometimes worried their birth control methods— vinegar douches coupled with withdrawal—might not be foolproof. It made her enjoy everything leading up to intercourse more than the act itself. Bob confessed to enjoying it all. Both loved relaxing with a cigarette afterward and had long conversations ranging from social justice to travel dreams.

While ocean liners were the best way to get from one part of the world to another, she told him that someday they'd be able to take luxury airplanes anywhere they wanted.

"Just think about it, Bob. We'll wake up in Detroit, and a few short hours later land about anywhere in the whole wide world!" she said, lying on her back blowing smoke rings.

"Still, a long way to China, my dear—we might get there a bit quicker if we just began digging!" he said, kissing her long neck and then one of her bare arms.

Bob continued to box and crowed about his new light heavyweight status. While he no longer won most of his matches, he continued to love the sport. While she promised to attend them — especially the bigger prize fights — Catherine often made up excuses for not showing up. Her eyes would often glaze over when he'd come home and describe his latest one.

She sometimes complained about not getting together with her pals from law school, and there being little time left for family. Often a month or two would go by before they'd get together with anyone. It bothered Catherine more than Bob, though he still saw his mother.

Most of their time was spent on building their careers. He tried to assure her it wasn't always going to be like this. Once they were well-established, things would ease up. She had her doubts.

Besides covering the costs of the reception, her uncle had also given them a handsome check for their wedding and two large, glass-covered bookcases filled with classical literature. Catherine lovingly scanned the titles, but there was little spare time for books. She hungered to spend time reading and complained to Bob. He'd tell her to take a day off and her comeback was always, "I will if you will." At that time in their lives, they never did. Time sped up at an alarming pace, but any attempt to stop it — unthinkable.

CHAPTER TWENTY-FIVE

"Wouldn't you agree that Lon Chaney makes a spectacular opera ghost?" Catherine asked her friends after leaving the Fox Theater. They readily agreed that the movie had been enchanting.

It was a different sort of Saturday for Catherine because she spent most of it with her friends. She met Joan, Margaret, and Grace under the marquee one autumn afternoon. All four had shown up wearing dark wool coats and cloche hats. They complimented each other on having such good taste and chatted while standing in line for tickets to see *The Phantom of the Opera*.

Bob had sulked when Catherine told him she was going to see it with friends, but she'd ignored his protestations. Once her mind was made up, he knew there was little he could do to convince her otherwise. "Why can't you see another movie with them? I really wanted to watch it with you," he whined more than a few times. It put an end to his grumpiness when she agreed to meet him later at Mickey Mac's and then stop by a speakeasy or two.

Afterward, they had an early dinner at The Embers, a new restaurant, located downtown near the Fox.

The swanky downtown restaurant wasn't crowded, but they were seated in the back near the kitchen. They were well aware of the main reasons: In society's eyes, Grace was 'a Colored,' and the women didn't have male escorts. Mostly, it was because of

Grace's skin color. Catherine, incensed, wanted to complain to the manager, but the other three women convinced her not to say anything. Doing so wouldn't get them a better table.

"So tell us about how Sage & Sage is going, Catherine," Grace prodded her, hoping this would get her mind off the social inequity.

"We're just getting established," Catherine said with a sigh, "But you know, Bob—he knows half of all Detroiters by name, so of course, clients are spilling out the door!"

The clatter of dishes and voices coming from the kitchen made the women raise their voices to be heard.

"Got any juicy cases?" asked Margaret, who was now working for a successful firm. Her voice, the loudest, caused a waiter to scowl at them.

"If only! So far, Bob's just given me a few petty theft cases, one's a larceny, but nothing exciting. What about you?" Catherine asked.

"Honey, do you have any idea what it's like to be the only woman working with a bunch of men? I'm downright lucky if they throw out enough seeds for me to peck." Margaret replied. The three others laughed, nodding in understanding.

"Say, what do you three think about that Ossian Sweet case?" asked Joan. The Sweet case was the talk of the town, especially among the lawyers and the residents from the Black Bottom. There was palpable relief among Sweet's supporters that Judge Murphy had ruled that the Sweet brothers had a right to defend themselves against the KKK-inspired mob. The judge had been persuaded by Clarence Darrow. Catherine and her friends couldn't have been more inspired and pleased by Darrow's incredible defense.

"Too many mobs and gangs seem to think they rule this city. Let's see if this doesn't settle them down some," Catherine said. The others heartily agreed. She was surprised and somewhat saddened that Grace didn't add her thoughts about the case, but

Catherine understood why. Despite fulfilling her own personal ambitions when few women did (no matter their skin color), Grace often kept her opinions to herself. Catherine knew that had it been just the two of them conversing, Grace would have been more forthright.

The restaurant now bustled with customers and a larger wait staff, though the four friends, enjoying their conversations and fruit cocktails, barely seemed to notice. Catherine wished they could enjoy real cocktails and her stomach rumbled with hunger—and thirst. The others seemed more patient with the slow service. She made a concerted effort to do so herself.

Joan, pregnant with her second child, requested another bread basket while they waited for their main course. Her peach complexion glowed. Maybe it was because she knew Catherine better than the other two, as she didn't hesitate before asking when Catherine planned on starting a family. After Catherine shrugged and tried to change the subject, Joan interrupted her and continued:

"Actually, your sister Eileen told me you don't want children. Is this true, Catherine? Why ever not? You could still practice law once they're in school."

For the first time, Catherine noticed Joan looked frazzled, and her blond hair a little more unkempt than usual. Motherhood had changed her appearance.

"I could, but Bob supports my decision and doesn't want any either. Maybe I'll change my mind one day, though I—"

"Sweetie, you're not getting any younger," said Joan, sounding like Catherine's mother and Eileen. Catherine's cheeks reddened, as she lit a cigarette and deeply inhaled. She was the only one in the group who smoked. Was it the smoke in the air or was Joan's blond hair prematurely turning gray? She bit her tongue.

"When's this new baby of yours due, Joan?" Margaret asked, removing Catherine from the hot seat—for the time being.

"In about five months," Joan replied before launching into a monologue about "what a sweetheart" her husband was and how she could always count on his help with their toddler. She kept clearing her throat as if something was trapped in it, all the while insisting that he'd be a great father with their new little one, too. Catherine sensed a tone in Joan's voice, this side of a quaver, that made her think that Joan could have doubts. She knew better than to pry, but couldn't help but wonder if Margaret and Grace had noticed.

"Sounds like you've got it made," stated Catherine. "Not all women are so lucky."

"Oh, I'll bet Bob would come around if you wanted kids," said Joan, continuing, "It's not like I didn't try to have a legal career first. I applied at countless firms in my first year after graduating from law school. Like my Frankie always says, it doesn't mean the door's closed for good." Her annoying habit of hacking was noticed by a couple at the next table.

Whatever unexpressed insecurities Joan had about her situation, Joan truly believed Frankie to be a good man.

Margaret changed the subject to the number of new speakeasies that had sprung up in the city. Catherine seemed to be the expert on the best ones. She exclaimed about the ones in Chicago. The others looked at her somewhat askance. Again, her cheeks burned. Maybe it would've been better to have spent the day with Bob—not that she didn't enjoy being out with friends. If Joan weren't so critical, she'd be having a better time. Plus, The Embers' service was slow and now they were all ravenous.

At long last, the waiter brought them their dinners. They'd all ordered chicken entrees, except Joan who'd ordered ham. The chicken on Grace's plate was burned to a crisp. Catherine swapped plates with her and asked for the manager. He immediately removed the plate and was most apologetic.

The waiter, a bald man with a bulbous nose, approached Grace and whispered to her: "Thought that's how all you niggers like it done over there in the Black Bottom." Grace pretended not to hear him. She wiped the corner of her lip with the cloth napkin. Catherine's fury made her skin sizzle; she felt like she could self-combust. It was all she could do to contain her Irish ire. Again, she motioned for the manager.

"Please, Catherine, say nothing more. It'll only make matters worse," whispered Grace.

The other two women agreed with Grace, but Catherine continued to inwardly seethe.

"I swear, Detroit's little different from the South," Catherine said.

"At least there are factory jobs here. Life down there is way worse," began Grace, but then she changed the topic back to the movie. The four exhaled and told each other their favorite parts.

• • •

After spending the afternoon and early evening with her friends, Catherine met Bob at her father's diner. He'd been waiting for quite a while, though they hadn't said a specific time to meet.

"I thought you'd stood me up," he said, just as Mickey stopped by to give his daughter a hug.

"We almost sent your brother out searching for you," Mickey said, winking at his son-in-law. John had recently dropped out of the seminary to become a police officer. He'd missed the attention of the fairer sex, he said, and confided that the celibate life wasn't for him. While the family had been at first shocked by his career change, John seemed suited to be one of the men-in-blue. Less burly than most coppers, he soon became known by most of the force as Gentleman John. How long he'd last in the crime-ridden city was anyone's guess.

"And they say females are the sillier gender!" Catherine scolded them both.

Before leaving them to wait on another customer, Mickey reminded his daughter: "Don't forget to come around and visit your mother sometime soon, okay? She's been sorely missing you, Katy."

"You know I'll visit," she responded, amazed at how much easier it was to get along with her parents now that she was married. Eileen had been right. Even when Catherine had lived at Uncle Gerry's her parents had been less appreciative of her than they were now.

"Hate to bud in, but I'm starving. How about you, Kate?" asked Bob.

"Remember, I ate dinner with friends, my darling, but you go ahead."

"Sorry, sweetheart, but I need more fuel for my tank before we dance the night away!"

Catherine eye-rolled her energetic husband, then continued to sip coffee, as Bob wolfed down meatballs and mashed potatoes. The sight of the food made her queasy. She longed to be home in her peignoir having a nightcap with him, looking out at the lights of the barges floating down the river. Those nights didn't happen often, as Bob always had to be on the go. While she enjoyed their nights out, he was the more restless one. On those rare weekend nights when they were home, he listened to the fights on the radio with the volume turned up so loud it made her wonder if his ears had been boxed one too many times.

She sighed.

Bob seldom spoke while eating, and preferred Catherine not to, as well. It was so unlike the spirited times at her parents' kitchen table. At first, this had annoyed her, but then she grew accustomed to the silence. Little wonder her mind drifted. After lighting another cigarette, she inhaled deeply.

"Why the sighs, sweetheart? Say, you know you could always read me a newspaper story while I eat." Bob daubed his mouth with the napkin.

"Knock off treating me like your personal secretary, why don't you?" she said in all seriousness.

"So where'd you want to go first, Kiddo?" he said, ignoring her remark.

Almost every weekend, they'd frequent the better speakeasies. They both enjoyed the larger ones with dance floors, though they were the ones more vulnerable to raids.

"I was in a raid once, back before we met," Bob said, adding that he'd had to hop a fence to get away from a cop. He didn't know why his buddies were all laughing at him when he finally caught up with them. Turned out he'd split the seat of his pants wide open. They'd laughed all the harder because he hadn't noticed it.

Catherine forced a laugh but found his anecdote less amusing than usual.

"I've been wearing these high-heeled pumps all day and my feet are aching. What say we skip the nightlife tonight and just go home and relax?"

She couldn't talk him into it, though at last, he agreed to stop by their apartment for her to change her shoes.

The five minutes alone in the bedroom with the door shut proved vital for getting a second wind. Catherine slipped into her favorite knee-length dress. She called the slinky, silver garment her 'flapper' dress. They loved to dance the Charleston together and her energy almost always recharged once they got on the dance floor.

She gazed at him with fire behind her silver-blue eyes.

As Catherine donned a coat to wear over her silver dress, they went to Jacoby's, their favorite place. Not an easy choice, as they were also big fans of Tommy's Detroit Bar and the Painted Lady Lounge. While there were many others to choose from, they preferred the ambiance of the ones with dark, cozy seating, ritzy furnishings, and dance floors. First, they'd have a couple rounds of drinks at a table for two.

Bob immediately saw friends even before they were seated. Being as gregarious as he was, he always ran into people he knew. That night she found it especially annoying.

Once the band started up, they excused themselves to the dance floor. As usual, they were the first couple on the floor, though it wasn't long before others joined them. They usually danced the Charleston, the Fox Trot, and a host of others before the night was over.

Bob must have noticed that Catherine was looking more tired than normal, and after a few songs, he led her back to their table.

"Aww, Bob, you're no fun! Can't we just dance to one more song?" She protested, but he refused to listen.

If a speakeasy didn't have a dance floor, they enjoyed their drinks and would then make their way to a legitimate dance hall. Typically, they'd dance and drink the entire evening. Sometimes they'd circle each other like two boxers before collapsing in each other's arms. Lately, Bob 'held his liquor' better than Catherine. She didn't seem to realize it. After two drinks her personality transformed; not only did she become opinionated, but she also lost all reserve. And after three or four, she lost all seriousness and usually developed hiccups and a high-pitched giggle. Sometimes Bob liked her drunk, but more often — not.

The drinks that Saturday night affected her almost immediately, no doubt because of her long day. Catherine told Bob about the way Grace had been treated in the restaurant. He immediately agreed that it was wrong and that everyone should be treated with respect.

"The worst of it, Bob, is that Negroes are being made to stay in Black Bottom. It's like society's keeping them in a pen."

He agreed, but she continued to argue the case.

"Here, Grace is an educated woman but she's treated like dog shit! Hard enough being a woman, but try being a Negro woman and you're asking for double the trouble. Sure, we have the right to vote, but do we? I've heard that Negro women down South aren't able to cast their votes. You say you care, but how do I know you really do?" Catherine's voice was getting loud. Everyone was staring at them.

"For the love of Pete, can you quiet your voice a bit? I love discussing issues with you, but..."

"But what, Bob? When you're hot about something, you talk loud, too, plus you get in the ring and throw punches. I don't have a ring, and have to put my dukes up with words...So, c'mon, let's have a go around!"

"But we're on the same side of the issue, my Katydid."

A three-piece jazz combo was warming up. The music somewhat mollified Catherine, but then she lit up another cigarette and continued.

"Since you're a man, you can't possibly know or understand."

Bob tried hard to switch gears by telling Catherine a joke, but instead of it doing the trick of making her laugh, she emitted a howl that even made the men in the band look her way.

"Wind your neck in, Kate, and let's get out on the floor."

She hated when he used that Irish expression, no doubt a favorite of Nana's, but she finally agreed to dance. "Maybe just...for this one...song, my darling," she said, hiccupping.

The music swept them away and took them to a better place.

The apartment was stuffy when they returned, so Bob opened the bedroom window, though the outside air was almost as humid as a summer night. Catherine decided not to argue about it. Instead, she stretched out on her back across the double bed, staring at the wooden blades of the ceiling fan. The effects of staring at the ceiling, the alcohol, and being tired made her feel almost paralyzed, though she was sure if someone yelled "Fire!" she'd still be able to run from the room and escape. Bob was saying something to her from across the room, but her throat and mouth were frozen, too. Maybe it was for the better, as she'd grown tired of her own voice after such a long day.

. . .

Bob lay next to her on the bed and tried to mimic Catherine's inert state, but she exuded a scent, both sweet and musky, that made him crazy with lust. He kissed her neck and gently pried her legs further apart. He knew she wanted him to do this — wanted his fingers to discover how moist she was, how ready.

Instead, she abruptly pushed his hand away. What a tease! Catherine had never been this cold, though it wasn't the first time she'd let Bob down. Sometimes she'd say she had a headache, or even more often — it was because of the time of the month. He knew it was a lie because there was no evidence in the bathroom wastebasket, plus no odor of menstrual blood. Despite the number of times boxing had flattened his nose, his sense of smell had always been strong. Lately, he'd been trying hard to be more gentle and patient with her, but she didn't even acknowledge it. Still, he could tell she no longer liked sex as much as she once had. Maybe because they were married or because she didn't want a baby...Hell, her reasons didn't matter — just the end result: rejection. Like a lot of women, Catherine could be a dizzy dame when drunk. Truth be told — he wasn't feeling all that hot about her either.

He sprang out of bed, telling her he was going out. She didn't respond, except to blink, and kept staring up at the ceiling fan.

"Kate, did you hear what I just said?

"What?"

"I said I'm going out for a breath of fresh air. Don't wait up."

"Fine, sure. Whatever..."

. . .

The following morning, Catherine woke up still wearing her short silver dress. Bob hadn't returned. Had he left her? Left her for good? Shite. She rose slowly from her prone position. Her limbs were stiff and her head throbbed. She lit a cigarette and sipped hot coffee. Since she had a profession now, she knew she had to conduct herself more responsibly—especially when in regards to drinking. Changes must be made. Had they argued last night? Maybe they had at Jacoby's, but not the apartment, though she couldn't recall their exact exchange. He'd tried to get amorous and she hadn't been in the mood. Why hadn't he understood how tired she'd been or how many drinks she'd had? All she could do now was to wait for him and come up with a plan for drinking less. Perhaps she should sign up with Carrie Nation's crew. She burned her finger lighting a match, as she reached for her next Lucky Strike.

CHAPTER TWENTY-SIX

The following morning, Bob returned with a dazzling bouquet of red roses. He told Catherine that he'd spent the night at his mother's and had done a lot of thinking. Maybe they should scale back their wild times—difficult to do during this jazzy, flapper era.

"If we took better care of each other, think we'll stop going downhill so fast?" he asked, a used toothpick dangling from his lips.

Catherine reluctantly agreed. After all, they'd be thirty in a few short years. It was obvious he'd been talking to Nana and she'd given him some 'sage' advice. And so they agreed to drink only on the weekends—and even then they would scale back to one or two drinks. Also, they planned to frequent their watering holes twice a month instead of weekly.

The autumn of 1925 and winter of 1926 turned out to be happy and productive seasons. Not wanting to disappoint the other, they both kept to their plan of moderation. No doubt it helped that they joined a group of like-minded others interested in social justice. It was composed mainly of professors, students, and Catholic activists. Grace, having heard about their support for Dr. Sweet during the trial, joined the group and promised to encourage others from the Black community.

The couple also began playing cards with Gene and Violet once a month.

While Catherine cared little for children, she couldn't see enough of the adorable Bobby Gene. He pulled his latest stunt, one cold winter day when he was out for a walk with his Nana. At first, Nana had chuckled at how cute her four-year-old grandson looked in a policeman's cap, which had been left at their house by one of his father's friends. He also carried a policeman's whistle given to him by his father. Such self-importance Nana had never seen in such a young lad, not even those rascals she'd raised. Not having to share the limelight could well have been a contributing factor.

But then Bobby Gene made a break for it by running ahead of her. Nana shouted his name, but he either couldn't hear her or chose not to. One of her hips had been bothering her, forcing her to walk with a cane. More worried that her grandson could get hit by a car, she threw cane and caution to the March wind, screaming his name, as she raced to the scene.

By the time she reached the wide road, a small crowd had gathered.

There he was, directing traffic like a policeman.

Once Bobby Gene had made his way to the always busy Livernois Avenue, he strutted into the middle of the avenue. He blew his whistle and raised his little palm at oncoming vehicles.

A newspaper photographer witnessed the scene and pulled over in his car. Bobby Gene would get his first picture in the paper. Nana told a reporter that after getting over being shocked and terrified, she'd been most proud. Her grandson had reminded her of one of her own brave sons.

Officer McIntosh thought it was the cutest story ever. Someday soon, John promised to give him a ride in a police car. When Bobby Gene got a little older, he'd even give him a tour of the jail.

Not only did Catherine and Bob pick up several copies of the newspaper story, but for a long time, they'd tell the story to everyone they knew. Bob loved telling people that the little boy was his namesake.

• • •

Outside of winter colds, family members remained well. There were more family dinners at the Sages and the McIntoshes than ever before or after that time. The law firm of Sage & Sage took off. They credited Bobby Gene's stint as a traffic cop as being instrumental to the rise in their clientele. Catherine successfully tried a few cases. She turned out the better trial attorney — more eloquent and logical than her husband. Still, Bob's ability not to get bogged down by details allowed him to have a crystal clear sense of justice. Catherine suggested he run for judge in a few years. Days later, he told her he had a great idea: he'd run for judge, not right away, of course.

"That's what I told you to consider doing. Just last week, in fact," Catherine responded.

He wouldn't acknowledge that it had been her idea, though he wanted to know if she thought Uncle Gerry would want to discuss it with him over brandy.

Catherine and Bob looked forward to someday taking two trips — both would be extensive and needed much planning. One was to go out West. He longed to take her back to Wallace, Idaho, near where he'd been born. The other excursion would be to Europe, especially Ireland, their ancestral homeland. They decided that their first trip would be a journey west by train. If all went well, maybe they'd be able to go the following summer. A little more forethought and cash would be needed for their European adventure, but they could narrow down which countries they'd like to visit.

There was talk of Bob boxing overseas, most likely in England, but the planning got put off because of their increased legal business. As a light heavyweight, he had fewer fights in the ring but brought in larger cash prizes when he won. Still, his deep-set blue eyes had further receded in his face and looked smaller, as if weary of looking into the faces of opponents in the ring or adversaries in the courtroom.

Fewer nights on the town meant more nights at home. Catherine's culinary skills improved somewhat and Bob was most appreciative. For a time she marveled at his tenderness and joked with friends about the truth to the cliché "The way to a man's heart is through his stomach." He bought her a fur coat and she was especially cuddly in appreciation. After making love on Saturday nights, they whispered into the wee hours of the morning. "Katydid — these are our salad days!" She had only a foggy notion of what he meant. Still, she nodded as she fell into dreamland.

CHAPTER TWENTY-SEVEN

One snowy, late winter night, Catherine was forced to sleep in her childhood bedroom. It was now a guest room. Besides Jezebel, the cat, wandering in and out, the only reminder the room had ever been hers was Hannah, a porcelain doll dressed in a dusty frayed dress. Hannah now eyed Catherine from a corner shelf. A pastel floral bedspread covered a double bed that had replaced her old single bed. There was also a crucifix hanging on a wall, along with the Irish Blessing. She suspected that when her parents argued, her mother wound up sleeping here — a whiff of her mother's perfume confirmed it.

After leaving work, snow had fallen, but not enough to change her plans to stop by and see her parents and her sisters. It would be the first time they'd all been together — minus John who was working nights — since Christmas. Lately, Catherine had realized how much she'd been missing her family. Also, she was curious to see how the Christmas present Bob and she had given her parents 'worked.' It was an electric washer and her mother had seemed thrilled by it.

There was yet another reason for the visit: Catherine's big announcement.

At first, she was horrified and didn't even let Bob know. After finally telling him, she was relieved and more than a little surprised by his obvious delight. She'd assumed he felt the same way about not having a child as she did. He was Catholic, but then so was she. He began treating her with a new tenderness she hadn't experienced since the early days of their courtship, which both pleased but dumbfounded her.

She'd known she was pregnant for almost a couple of months. For the past week, she'd been having trouble keeping food down and her breasts were swollen and sore.

Their previous birth control methods worked well — until they didn't.

Bob had wanted to be there when Catherine gave her family the news, but he had a boxing match at Arena Gardens. No way could she keep it from them until the following weekend. He'd teased her about it but understood — pleased that she was proud of her condition. With the way the snow was falling, she hoped he'd stay there and sleep on a cot in the Garden's medical clinic. Certainly, he wouldn't try to make it home.

When she told her family at dinner that snowy night, her feelings about being pregnant had changed: not only was she pleased to announce it — she couldn't wait! Her parents and sisters hugged her, and her father teared up. The mood was almost as celebratory as a Christmas morning. Molly had been the only one who'd looked deeply into Catherine's eyes, trying to figure out how Catherine felt about having a baby.

"Surely, you'll stay at home and forget about that lawyer side of you, right?" her mother had asked once the news had been digested.

"I don't see why I can't take the baby with me to the office," Catherine said. How dare she try to tell her what to do! Didn't other professional women take their children to work if they had no choice?

"Before doing that, I'm sure you'll first try to get a nanny, right? I've heard that's what the rich do," said Bridget with venom in her voice.

"We're hardly rich!" said Catherine.

"Oh, but you two are well on your way to becoming well-off, if you aren't already. Too bad you'll miss out on the fun parts of having a child. Not that there are many fun parts," said Bridget.

"Are you even being serious, Mother? I can't even imagine how you raised so many!" said Catherine. This probably wasn't the time to ask her if she wouldn't mind sometimes watching the baby.

"It's a woman's lot in life, and you'll need to simply accept it," Eileen remarked, forever the joyless eldest. Her green eyes had turned a dull gray.

"I predict that one day it'll no longer be 'our lot' as you say, but our choice. Birth control methods will get better than they are now." Catherine was now ready to put up her dukes with her oldest sister, as well as their mother.

"I agree with Catherine," said Molly.

"Oh, you always do," began their mother. "Why are we quibbling? Now, who would like a piece of Sunshine Cake?"

Eileen did the honors of slicing their father's favorite yellow cake with lemon icing. For once she sliced generous pieces of 'sunshine' for all. Not wanting to feel queasy, Catherine only allowed herself to swallow a few tiny bites.

· · ·

And now it seemed like Hannah was staring at her in the moonlit room; it was as if the doll wanted to tell her something. Catherine lay on her back with her hands gently cradling her belly, trying to listen to whatever it was Hannah had to say.

She was over three months along. Maybe it was too soon, but shouldn't she be feeling some movement by now? Her mother or sisters should be able to let her know when she could expect to feel the baby moving about inside her.

Still, she worried about what would happen to her career — if she'd still even have one. She also worried about how pregnancy would change her slim figure. Would she suddenly look dowdy? How many Hail Marys would she have to say because of her vanity? Way too many, if the priest knew her real reason for confessing.

Catherine and Bob both liked to be seen and admired. Despite her being the more bookish one, there was another side of her that wanted applause for her efforts — whether on a dance floor or in a courtroom. She didn't think that would extend to her efforts at either becoming or being a mother.

After a few restless hours, and hearing no words of wisdom from the doll, Catherine finally fell into a dreamless slumber.

. . .

The next night, back in the bedroom of her apartment, Catherine dreamed she was in a fire. Tendrils of flames wound up her legs and torso. She screamed but couldn't move. How frightening to be both burning up and frozen at the same time! She could see Bob's face through the haze of smoke; he seemed far away and she didn't know how to reach him.

"Sweetheart, I know you're weak, but let me help you to the chair while I change the sheets." His scratchy voice reached her and his face came into focus. Catherine discovered there was blood on the sheets, and also on her hands. She was no longer pregnant. And now she wanted nothing more than to drift back to sleep. Maybe when she woke up again, she'd find out that she'd had a nightmare. Bob's voice kept nattering at her, not allowing her to return to sweet slumber. Why couldn't he leave her alone? Her cramps had worsened.

She dragged herself to the bathroom.

Bob asked if she could walk okay.

Silly man, of course, she could. When she stood up from the toilet, more blood filled the bowl. She sat on the floor and cried uncontrollably.

He insisted on taking her to the hospital. Despite feeling weak, she refused to stay any longer than she had to and returned home the same day.

Later Catherine would complain that a nurse had looked at her as if she'd done something wrong—like the miscarriage was her fault. After hours of cramping and heavy bleeding, she was exhausted. All she wanted to do was sleep.

The following day her mother and Eileen came by to help her out. Why did they say so little and look at her in disgust? Eileen stayed only a couple of hours, but her mother stayed the day since Bob had to go to the office. She kept barging into the bedroom to ask Catherine if she could get her something to eat. Catherine would moan and turn on her side to face the wall. After she finally gave up, Bridget sat in a corner bedroom chair praying aloud for the miscarried baby's soul and then for her daughter.

"Please tell her to go home," Catherine whispered to Bob after he returned home. These were the last words she would speak for over a week.

She kept the bedroom blinds shut and wore an eye mask— day and night. When not asleep, time slowed down. She tossed and turned. So this was what it meant to hate your life.

Now and then, Bob coaxed her to have some broth or to sip some water, as she never finished what he brought on a tray. He wound up working from home at their dining room table and canceling all his appointments during that time.

She knew he was waiting patiently for her 'return,' but she simply wasn't ready.

Then Nana stopped by to visit. Bob tried telling his mother that while it was nice of her to check up on Catherine, his wife needed to rest. She adamantly refused to leave and pushed her son aside, as she made her way to the kitchen to make what she called a 'tea elixir.' It smelled like licorice and other spices which Catherine couldn't quite discern. Nana told her it would give her more energy, more pep — especially if she inhaled the steam before sipping the hot beverage.

The older woman plumped up her pillows and then moved her chair closer to the bedside. Catherine, trying her best to be attentive, sat up a little straighter.

"So you know about Houdini?" Nana asked.

"Sure, doesn't everyone? He died here in Detroit, right?"

"Last fall, on the thirty-first of October, to be exact. He was really something. I've told you about my dream visits with the dead, right? Well, don't say anything to Bob, but I was visited by Houdini's spirit."

"Why would he visit you?" Catherine was more perplexed than surprised.

"I guess he'd been trying to contact his wife. He'd promised to contact her from the Beyond. Instead, I heard from him! I don't know why. Then I found Mrs. Houdini's address and sent her a letter. I'm sure she thinks I'm just some crackpot."

"So what did the dead magician have to say?" asked Catherine, looking intrigued, but wary.

"It was most strange. He told me I'll have a great-granddaughter who will be born on the twenty-sixth of May in 1956. This great-granddaughter — he didn't know at what age — will also suffer from an appendicitis attack in Detroit, but she won't die from it. It'll also occur, like his, on a Halloween night. He kept 'seeing' the number three, though he didn't know why. After telling me this, he instructed me to let his wife know I'd heard from him. The odd part is that I won't be around to tell the girl, so YOU will have to be the one."

"Well, it's not like forewarning your great granddaughter will do any good — if what he said was true," said Catherine.

"No, but don't you see? It will prove to you that there's an afterlife. I think you need that sort of evidence — lawyer that you are," said Nana.

"Well, it's certainly strange, I'll grant you that. Just in case there's something to this, I'll write myself a reminder note to let my grand-niece know about her connection with Houdini. Let's see, I'll have to be around in the 1960s or 70s. That's a long way off, isn't it? Guess it cancels out what you told me about an early death, right?"

"I'm sure it does, my dear."

"Marvelous tea, but the way. I definitely have more zip!"

Nana giggled. "I knew it would do the trick!"

Catherine was back at work a few days later going through case files. It occurred to her that Nana's great-granddaughter would more than likely be Bobby Gene's daughter. She probably wouldn't try for another. Violet had recently confided that Bobby Gene was all she could handle, so that left one of his descendants to be the likely one to fulfill Houdini's prophecy. That is, if there was anything to it.

CHAPTER TWENTY-EIGHT

"What's life without some fun?" Bob asked Catherine one Saturday morning. She readily agreed. The question would become one of his favorite refrains.

Saturday mornings at downtown's Eastern Market proved to be among their better times that year and during much of the later 1920s. Lively weekend nights proved not to be their only way of enjoying themselves. The large farmer's market was one of the best around, and shoppers who arrived early could buy the freshest of everything available. Whether it was meat, seafood, cheese, produce, spices, or fragrant flowers—this outdoor market had it all.

Because of their wild Friday nights, they rarely wandered around it as early as they would have liked on Saturday mornings. Still, it became their habit to arrive well before noon.

Despite her occasional hangovers, Catherine loved how her senses came alive from the bouquet of aromas, as well as from the visual feast of crowd-watching. It astonished her to see so many appear as if they'd only recently arrived from the Old World. The curiosity and wonder in their eyes belied their weathered faces. She didn't quite share her husband's love of people watching for its own sake, and never would she have ventured here on her own.

It was too chilly and windy to stay outside for long, but they did their best to saunter through the large outdoor area.

Afterward, they did some shopping at the new Hudson's Department store.

"Don't look now, Kate, but over there by the flower stall is none other than Joe Zerilli doing business with Abe Bernstein."

In Detroit's crime family, Joe was considered Detroit's 'boss of bosses,' and Abe was the leader of the Purple Gang.

"You know why they call them The Purple Gang?" Bob asked.

Catherine had no idea.

"Because purple's the color of bad meat," he said, steering her away from the two criminals. This was common knowledge, but he loved to give her what he hoped was new information. "But some of them aren't so bad," he added.

"Name one," she said, looking dubious.

He could, but he didn't. Instead, he explained how one of the fringe members had snitched to Bob about a rum-runner who'd been making a lot of money in his trade. Supposedly, there was a drowning incident—only one of the two bodies had surfaced. Everyone seemed to think Harry—the rum runner—had left town, but Bob thought he saw him last week at the Market.

Catherine asked him who gave Bob the information, but again he refused. And no, he didn't know Harry's last name.

"Careful, Bob. You don't was to play with the big boys. I don't want to see you go looking for trouble."

"I know what I'm doing. See, this is why I wasn't going to say anything. Don't make me sorry, I did."

She made a fist and pretended like she was going to use it.

On mornings in late spring and summer, they'd have coffee and donuts at a café table near the market. Bob became so busy watching the crowd milling by that Catherine didn't bother trying to have any extended conversations. She enjoyed watching how animated he became as he watched the wild bobbing of the human sea.

They now spoke of returning here sometime soon and having more of a leisurely time. For now, they had other errands to run.

Although it was April on the calendar, a leftover winter wind whipped up from the river. It slapped their faces as they crossed Woodward Avenue, trying their best to hurry into Hudson's. Bob chased after Catherine's blue beret as it flew down the street. Thanking him, as he handed it back to her, she then tucked it into her coat pocket.

She couldn't get over that a single store could be twenty-five stories tall. They'd been there a few times in the past and were enchanted by its glamor.

Bob joined Catherine in her section of the large revolving door, showing her he could be as playful as he'd been during their early days together. She giggled, as he tried to remain poker-faced.

He followed her through the formal dress department chewing his toothpick. The saleswoman assisting Catherine was what he'd call "a looker" — stunning with high cheekbones and brown hair in a French twist. He whispered in his wife's ear that she was European, probably French.

In an accent that indeed sounded French, the saleswoman asked how she could 'ah-seeest' Catherine. Bob gave his wife a knowing look. Once the woman—Simone—knew the sort of dress Catherine was looking for, she disappeared for a while, and then returned with several fancy gowns. Garments were kept in a back room and brought out to customers.

Good thing Catherine was busy trying on dresses and didn't see her husband ogling pretty women. Had she, it would've been no big surprise. He tried to be discreet, as she'd emerge from the fitting room to 'model' the dresses. He'd motion with his stubby index finger for her to twirl around so he could see how the dress looked from behind. If he liked a particular one, he'd give her a whistle. Catherine would flash him a smile, but Simone smirk as Bob's whistles annoyed her, as she continued assisting Catherine with zippers and buttons in unreachable places.

Now that money was rolling in from their law practice, and also from Bob's boxing matches, they'd both turned into big spenders, particularly Catherine. Bob would often spoil his mother and nephew, along with buying himself an occasional new suit or fine cigar. But his spending habits were nowhere near as frivolous as Catherine's—according to him. She was always buying flowers for their dining room table, shoes, nightgowns, and hats. "How many do you need for Christ's sake, Kate?" When they'd been courting, he'd often spoil her with little presents, but his gifts meant little—or so it seemed. Occasionally, he'd splurge on something for her, but now it was mostly on birthday or Christmas presents.

She finally decided on a long slinky black-sequined gown for their next formal event—a charity ball. Over lunch in the department store's formal restaurant, he suggested she donate her dress to charity after the ball was over.

"It would be fitting, wouldn't you agree, Sweets? After all, it is a fundraiser."

"You're mean and spiteful, Bob Sage. I will do NO such thing, as I like this dress well enough to wear dancing at a fancy hotel in New York City, or at least to the Arabian Room at the Tuller." Catherine pouted, lighting a cigarette from one she'd just stubbed out, while they were waiting for the food check.

She loved reminding him of their next 'sometime soon' trip. It wasn't the first time it occurred to him that his wife had changed—and not for the better. Shortly after her miscarriage, Catherine acted disappointed with him and the rest of the world. Was she turning into one of those people who complain from early in the morning until late at night? Once she'd been so easy to please. She'd turned into quite the petulant child. If he accused her of being one, he knew he'd never hear the end of it.

Maybe it was because she'd lost the baby. If so, maybe that meant she'd someday return to her former self.

"What do you say we begin a fundraiser among our attorney friends? Maybe throw a ball to raise money to buy land in the city. Then how about we put in a playground for poor kids?" Bob asked.

"Sure, my darling. Sounds like a good idea," Catherine replied, nodding. "But why are you bringing this up now?"

"Only because we've got to watch our spending. Not only do we have to contribute to our cause, but we may also end up being its major contributors—especially when springing for playground equipment."

"Your timing could be better. Here, I just spent money on a fancy dress, we just finished this pricey lunch, and my next stop was going to be the perfume counter, but now you're making me feel guilty. Thanks, Bob. Thanks, a hell of a lot."

"Kate, don't you have enough perfume? And say, that's your conscience causing you to feel guilty, so don't pin that on me."

"I wouldn't buy perfume for me, but for your mother. Her birthday's coming up. Remember?"

"Nice of you to think of her, Kiddo, but it's not until the end of the summer. Trying to pull a fast one on me, eh?" Bob's voice had become loud—even louder than intended. His face reddened. How tired he was of her malarkey! "Okay, you win. We'll buy my mother some French perfume. And if I know you, you'll get a bottle for yourself—but why not? We only live once."

"Now, my dearest, why ever would I do a thing like that?" Catherine replied, batting her long lashes, then widening her steely-blue eyes. She laughed, a little too loudly, as they browsed at the perfume counter. It sounded like a cross between a vixen and a hyena. He cared little for either, but laughed, trying to be good-humored.

Catherine sniffed her wrists after applying sample after sample. Bob stood behind her, tapping his foot and rolling his eyes, feigning impatience.

The young blonde who waited on them was sweet and innocent, or seemed so. He couldn't help but bat his deep blue eyes at her and slip her one of his business cards. Why did women lose their innocence in the first place? It messed up their sex appeal.

Catherine noticed the way Bob's hand brushed against the girl's hand when she gave him two bottles of Chanel No.5. The one for Nana was gift-wrapped. She couldn't wait to get back to their apartment, put her feet up and sip a cocktail. Maybe gin and sweet vermouth...

CHAPTER TWENTY-NINE

After they were married, Catherine and Bob began spending more time with the Sages than the McIntoshes. They speculated about why this was the case. Bob thought maybe Nana being a widow had something to do with it. Catherine added that it could simply be because of his side being smaller in number. But it was even more likely because they enjoyed being around dear little Bobby Gene. Whatever the reason, they usually felt more relaxed with the Sages. Catherine sometimes resented Bob's closeness with his mother, though never for long: Nana was so big-hearted, who wouldn't be charmed by her?

While Bob and Gene were both a lot like their mother, Bob's Irish temper could get out of control — much like Catherine's father. No one could accuse Bob of not being passionate, but affection was reserved for his mother and children, and only rarely displayed with his wife.

Gene doted on his wife like Nana did her sons. And, over time, Violet became that way with Gene, or 'Genie,' as she called him. But the demands of their son were too much for her high-strung personality. No one doubted her love for little Bobby Gene, though there was consensus that she was mostly interested in the next party she'd be attending. Catherine initially thought Violet enjoyed socializing because of the hard work of being a mother, but over time she came to believe that Violet was born a *good-time gal*.

•   •   •

Bob was pretty certain Catherine didn't love him the way his mother did. Not that he wanted his wife to be his mother, but Catherine hadn't turned out to be as sympathetic as he'd hoped — anyway, not with him. She became crabby whenever he wasn't feeling his best. Like it was his fault! If he didn't feel like going out on the weekends, she'd always wonder what was wrong with him. They both worked long hours. Why wasn't Catherine as tired as he was after a long week? True, Bob was physically more spent because of boxing. Why couldn't she see it and give him a break? And when they were out on the town, if he wasn't as talkative as she was, she'd natter at him to tell him more about what was on his mind. Nothing, dear, nothing but sleep...He longed to tell her, but couldn't.

•   •   •

It became part of their routine to have Sunday dinner with Violet and Gene. Violet, while not much of a cook, was always a generous hostess, and as Bob would say: "She could put out quite a spread." If she wasn't in the mood to cook, the five of them would go to a restaurant for a midday meal after Sunday mass. One particular Sunday in the early fall, Violet and Gene didn't show up at church. Afterward, Catherine and Bob rushed to their house. They were saddened to find Bobby Gene sick with a high fever and a bad cough.

Nana sat by his bedside holding a cool, damp cloth to his burning forehead. Bobby Gene gave a brief wave to his aunt and uncle, but that was all he could muster. His tousled black hair contrasted with the pallor of his skin. She calmly informed them that his throat was almost swollen shut.

"Okay, Nana, we're going out for a meal. Bobby Gene didn't want breakfast, but try to make him sip some Vernor's ginger ale," Violet said to her mother-in-law in a loud, agitated voice.

Nana nodded and shooed the three from the small bedroom. Gene was waiting patiently for the others in the living room. He looked concerned, but not overly so.

"Vi, maybe we shouldn't go out. The little guy's looking pretty rough," said Bob. He'd developed quite a soft spot for his namesake.

"No, I need to get out for a while. He'll be just fine in Nana's hands." Violet's dark brown eyes darted about. She was more worried about the others backing out than she was about her son.

When they returned almost two hours later, Bobby Gene's fever had spiked. Nana, a semi-qualified nurse, had seen little children die with similar symptoms. She didn't mention this to the boy's parents, though she later told Bob.

"Time to give him an ice bath, Gene," Nana said, preferring to address Gene rather than his wife.

"He's going to be okay, right?" Violet shouted as Gene removed a large chunk of ice from the ice box while the older woman began running cold water in the bathtub. Nana ignored the question.

"Ohhh, my poor baby!" Violet wailed, even louder this time.

"Vi, let's sit out on the porch until we can be of some help," Catherine insisted.

Once outside, Catherine watched through the window as Nana carried the pale and limp little boy to the bath. Violet mopped her forehead and played with her rosary beads. She didn't want to see her son like that. Without saying as much, Violet looked at Catherine for answers.

"Hopefully, he'll be fine," said Catherine. It was all she could think of saying to reassure the frantic mother. Bob joined them on the front porch. He patted Violet's shoulder with one of his paw-like hands, his brain fumbling for the right words.

"I need more of a promise. Bob, do you think he'll be okay?"

"Sure, I do. Give him a day or two, he'll be swell," Bob finally said, almost biting his toothpick in two. Violet tried to smile back, as she daubed the perspiration dripping from her brow. She leaped from the porch step and began pacing up and down the driveway.

How had he been able to make that kind of promise? Catherine lit one cigarette after another, almost as nervous as if she was Bobby Gene's mother. Had she been, she would have been right there for him, unlike the nerve-frazzled woman next to her.

Bobby Gene woke from his fevered state screaming because of the ice-cold water.

"We need another towel, Vi. Hurry!" shouted Nana. But it wasn't Violet or Catherine who rushed inside to get them; it was Bob.

After Catherine and Bob went home to their apartment, they sat in the living room with only the dimmest light on, not knowing if their little nephew would make it through the night. They smoked and drank and said little. In a slurred speech, she told him she was about to pass out. After helping her to bed, he remained awake all night on the couch.

They received a telegram the next morning: "Bobby's fever broke. Weak but doing okay."

Catherine let out a cry of relief and then began sobbing. Bob put his arms around her. They realized how much the boy meant to them, to the entire family.

"Sure am glad we don't have to worry about a kid getting sick," Bob said.

"I suppose you're right, though we've been as worried about him as his parents."

Catherine gazed out the window, almost as if she was in a trance. Bob wondered what she was thinking, but knew better than to ask. He wanted to embrace her, but worried that she'd push him away.

Bobby Gene's recovery was a slow one.

• • •

No one else in either family came down with the flu that autumn, but everyday life began taking its toll on the couple, as they'd been working longer and longer hours. Bob found fault with Catherine, particularly with what she was wearing. Her clothes, he claimed, were too clingy or loose. "Kate, it truly looks like your skirt's going to fall right off." Also, her far-away gaze, which at first had seemed so mysterious, bothered him now: it made her seem absent and he missed the attention she'd once paid him.

Catherine had grown tired of what a *showboat* he could be — how he always had to be the funny one and *one-up* everyone in the room. And why couldn't he ever enjoy being home in the evenings? It was like he feared the world would end if he sat still. While she didn't complain about going out every weekend, their wild times had become *old-hat*.

They'd entered a new phase of their marriage: one of uncertainty. It caused them both to drink and smoke more than ever before. Bob began talking about her behind her back, telling people she'd become a lush — even a drunk. She got silly and slurred her words. One night he became so disgusted that he pushed her. When Catherine didn't respond, he slapped her.

"Get a grip, Kate. You're turning into a booze hound!"

"Pot calling the kettle black, eh Bob? Just leave me the hell alone."

He was turning into a mean drunk. Their sparring had taken a serious turn.

. . .

Catherine confided in Grace over coffee at Hudson's restaurant one afternoon.

"One day I'm going to snap. I just know it."

"What'll you do then?" Grace asked, looking at Catherine with fear in her eyes.

"I can see myself up and leaving him, so he act nicer. Here I am, an educated woman."

Grace nodded, as she listened without commenting.

"I've got to do something about it before I lose my dignity. I've loathed no one more than I presently do Bob Sage. I regret ever having married him."

"And here I thought you two were a match made in Heaven!" Grace said, shaking her head.

"Hardly," said Catherine, feeling jittery from drinking too much coffee. She'd chewed her fingernails down to nubs.

CHAPTER THIRTY

Catherine knew Bob was at fault for—as she called it—"getting a little rough" with her. But since it usually happened after she'd been drinking—and Lord knew what a sloppy drunk she could be—she was partly to blame. If she wanted to save her marriage, she'd need to quit drinking altogether if she couldn't keep it to one or two drinks. Even if she could do so, her new plan was to hold off until the weekends. She couldn't hold her liquor. She knew this now, but for reasons unknown, it came as a shock to her.

At first, she told no one about how Bob would try to—literally—slap some sense into her. After a couple of months, her secret became too much to endure.

. . .

Catherine visited her mother and sisters one Saturday in November at the McIntosh home. She'd been looking forward to seeing them since it had been a while since they'd gotten together. Never a tidy home on the best of days, it now looked like a cyclone had hit. A living room curtain had fallen off a rod to its death on the floor; end tables were cluttered with newspapers and yesterday's half-filled coffee cups; unfolded laundry spilled from a wicker basket.

Catherine stood in the small entranceway observing this, while both sisters continued to pick up the mess. Something wasn't right. "Well, don't just stand there gawking!" Eileen snapped in her usual fashion.

Bridget's normal pallor was chalkier than usual, so Catherine could see that she was in pain. She sat on the couch with an ankle propped up on a cushion. In a quiet voice, her mother told her how she'd twisted her ankle on the back landing steps. The accident had occurred the previous day. Those steps have always been slippery, she complained. Anyone would have fallen. The other two had already heard the story, but all three daughters now nodded in sympathy.

It bothered Catherine that Eileen and Molly knew about the accident before she did; they must have learned of it shortly before she'd arrived.

The three sisters insisted on the original plan of enjoying a pot roast supper together — that was if their mother was up for it. "You girls shouldn't trouble yourselves..." Bridget said, smiling despite herself. She looked pleased to have her daughters wait upon her. Eileen had brought over a homemade pie. For once she'd left her children home in her husband's care.

Knowing the girls were going to be there, Mickey made a quick exit. As Bridget would have ample help, he'd keep the diner open and get a necessary break from his wife's moans and groans. Although a fine cook at his diner, Mickey was curiously useless when cooking at home, claiming he didn't know his way around his 'wife's kitchen.' He said he'd try to make it home for dinner, as he'd love to see his three girls.

Ordinarily, Catherine wouldn't let Eileen boss her around, but today she dutifully followed her oldest sister's directions, as Eileen knew her way around the kitchen more than her sisters — especially Catherine. Catherine mainly stirred the gravy and boiled potatoes, trying her best not to look bored.

They waited as long as possible for their father to return home, but then finally ate without him. Bridget remained on the couch with a food tray on her lap. Since the kitchen and living room were so close together, it was easy to carry on discussions between the two rooms. Everyone spoke at once, as always, but when Bridget said anything, they listened more respectfully. Light banter replaced the normal bickering.

Eileen brought the others up to date about the trouble her two older ones had gotten into. Yesterday, she caught Maggie and Jeanne rifling through her clothes drawers. "Oh, boy, did they get a walloping from their father when he came home!" she added.

Molly, who now worked at a furrier, regaled them with stories about wealthy old dames who seemed to be more *on the hunt* for a mink stole or fur coat, rather than merely shopping. There was no pleasing them.

And Catherine described how Bobby Gene was still somewhat peaked after his bout of influenza. It gave them all pause, silently recalling the younger sister and brother they'd lost. While the family had lost several friends and acquaintances, losing siblings had been truly devastating. As usual, they chose not to discuss their losses. Eyes blinked back tears and upper lips stiffened.

It was then that Catherine changed the topic, and told them about Bob's bad temper, saying that these days he was having a hard time leaving boxing in the ring. Occasionally, after arguing, he'd even slapped her.

Her hands shook as she tried to light a match. After a couple attempts, she lit her cigarette and deeply inhaled.

"What did you say to upset him so? Maybe you still need to learn when to keep your mouth shut," Eileen said.

"You're saying I deserve to be treated this way? Oh, come out of the Stone Ages, why don't you?"

"Now, girls, please don't argue," their mother interjected, as she often did when attempting to keep things from getting out of control. "We know you like a drink now and then, Catherine. Has this sort of thing usually occurred—after being out drinking and dancing?"

"Mother, what's that matter?" asked Molly, the only one who Catherine could count on. "Or is it because that's when Dad knocks you around?"

"We all know I hold my booze better than Catherine holds hers. And that I drink far less. Your father's been much better these last few years," said Bridget.

"Didn't he give you a black eye just a couple months ago?" asked Catherine.

"Yes, we'd been fighting, but I was the one who started it," their mother admitted.

"That doesn't make it right for him to do such a thing!" said Catherine blowing smoke rings. Her sisters nodded in agreement.

"Surely not, but we were talking about your marriage—not mine. Please answer my question, Kate. Does this usually happen after you've been drinking?" Now both sisters raised an eyebrow, awaiting her response.

"I suppose so," Catherine said, bowing her head. "Look, I've cut back. And the last couple of weeks, I haven't had a single drop, except a little on the weekends. Bob hasn't laid a hand on me, lately, but we haven't been exactly getting along all that great either. Sometimes I think I should just pack my bags." It made her blush to recall many of the intense moments they'd had in the bedroom after a fight. Of course, she wouldn't mention this to her family, or even friends.

"Good for you!" Molly exclaimed. "At least you're an independent woman and don't have to put up with it if he ever lays a hand on you again."

Eileen and Bridget looked at Molly askance.

"While us women shouldn't have to live with a brute, it's important to remember our wedding vows. We must accept our husbands 'in sickness and in health,'" said Bridget, looking sadder than usual. She brought the evening to a close. "My dears, thanks so much for the meal, but all this visiting has tired me out, so if you'll please excuse me...Oh, and please no more smoking in the house. Look at how smoky it got in here!"

Her brood of three nodded obediently, though Catherine had been the only one smoking. They scurried about as she hobbled to her bedroom, wincing in pain. Each daughter tenderly pecked her cheek. Catherine was the last to say her goodbyes, and Bridget remarked in a weary voice, "I'm sorry for your situation, dear, please don't think I'm not."

"I know, Mother. Stay off your ankle as much as you can, okay?" Catherine couldn't help but notice the three crucifixes on the bedroom wall. It reminded her of Grammy's bedroom room at Uncle Gerry's. Like mother, like daughter, she couldn't help but think.

The three, now tired, women washed up the dishes in silence. Since they weren't vying for their mother's attention, they were no longer combative with each other. Before leaving though, Eileen remarked, "Kate, did you have to bring up your marital woes with Mother? From now on, let's just mention such things between us. It's not as if she doesn't have enough to worry about with Grammy being sick, plus being laid up with a twisted ankle."

Grammy McIntosh was sick? Why hadn't anyone told Catherine? Shite. Left out again – and here of all the grandchildren, she was closest to Grammy. The anger rising inside her got tamped down by worry. How sick was she? Neither knew.

"Knowing Mother, she'll pay Grammy a visit soon despite her swollen ankle. What if she says something to Grammy about my marriage?" Catherine fretted.

"I really wouldn't worry," Molly said.

"Then Nana will get wind of it and I'll fall out of favor with her. Mother won't intend for it to happen, but it will," Catherine said, almost dropping a plate.

Eileen smirked but said nothing.

Catherine chastised herself for being more concerned about herself than with her grandmother's poor health. In the future, she would confide in friends rather than family. She wouldn't make the same mistake again.

CHAPTER THIRTY-ONE

1928

Catherine and Bob rang in the new year without imbibing as they had in prior celebrations — or at least not as much. They did, however, toast to the future success of their law practice, as well as to the health and well-being of their families and themselves. Bobby Gene was finally feeling as energetic as other children his age. How could he possibly be going on six in a few months? Grammy McIntosh rallied and Nana immersed herself in her two sons' lives, and also the spirit world. She told Bob that she foresaw that Kate and he would soon take a wonderful trip by rail.

"But, Ma, I told you we'd be going!"

"And it would be all the better if you took me along." Nana giggled like a young girl.

"Well, now maybe we can. Tell you what: we'll buy you a ticket."

Nana was giddy with delight, though Catherine, while she loved her mother-in-law, was a little annoyed, though she never let on.

The three raised their champagne glasses to new adventures.

.   .   .

No easy task knowing who'd been most looking forward to their trip west that spring: Catherine had never been on what she called a 'big trip' before; Bob couldn't wait to show his wife his hometown, and; Nana felt like she was going home.

All three enjoyed watching the ever-changing landscape and the way the rumble of the tracks rocked them into wonderful slumbers in their sleeping berths. Nana's arthritis bothered her some, but she rarely complained. "Nothing a little red licorice can't get my mind off," she often said. She'd brought along quite a supply, fearing it wouldn't be available in Idaho.

Then they all exclaimed over the way the plains gave way to the breathtaking mountains. Yet it wasn't long before the train's gentle rumble lulled them into a stupor. The novel that Catherine had brought with her remained closed on her lap. She did, however, read several poems from a collection by William Butler Yeats. Once in a while, she'd read one aloud. Nana exclaimed over her lovely reading voice. But every time Catherine would read to them, Bob would close his eyes—as if to better enjoy the lyrics and ponder the deeper meanings. She knew better: it gave him an excuse to nod off.

Nana kept tearing up, saying that Michigan had never felt like home the way the West did. "The West has my heart!" she cried out more than once on the trip. Bob readily agreed.

As the train chugged along, Bob and Nana recalled explicit memories from their lives in Idaho and regaled Catherine with many a story. They avoided talking about Raymond's tragic death and instead conversed about all the mischief the twins had gotten into when they were little. Nana described what it was like raising all boys and being married to a sheriff. Had it not been for their father, they would've all been "little hellions," she added, laughing, "They could get wilder than the so-called savages! One night their sheriff-father swore them in as deputies. They simmered down for a spell after that—that is, until they found out they didn't have the power to arrest anyone."

"You remember being a deputy, son?" Nana asked her son.

At first, he shook his head, but then said he recalled wearing a badge. He never knew what became of it.

"That's right. You boys loved those badges!"

Catherine wondered how they'd treated—and been treated by—the Indians. Nana told her that her husband, Eugene was—mostly—a peacemaker and had been respected by area Indians because he was fair in trade deals. Also, he didn't hesitate to put whites in jail for mistreatment or unlawful behavior. (He'd hung two white men for raping a woman from the local Shoshone tribe.) The Sages learned several Shoshone words and terms, and Bob and his mother told Catherine a few they could still recall. Catherine could tell that his kindness and sense of justice came from both parents.

"My husband, Eugene, could be a bit rough on the boys, especially if they were discourteous with me. Once he even put Bob in jail for a night."

"Ma, must you tell Catherine about that?" Bob asked, blushing and preferring to look at distant mountains.

Nana nodded, pulling a new strand of licorice from a paper bag, and continued, "If I recall correctly, Bob had a swearing and peeing contest with a boy from school. Jack was his name. Well, Jack was too fast and got away, but Eugene hauled Bob off by the earlobe and locked him up, leaving Bob to stew in his juices. It was only for the night. You see, the two had had their little contest right in our front yard and they were old enough to know better. What were you about fourteen, Bob?"

"Twelve, Ma. I was only twelve. And by the way, the boy's name was Dave."

"Catherine, if you ever wondered how he got such big earlobes, now you know." Nana laughed and nibbled the licorice. Catherine snickered at first, and then the women laughed in unison, both delighted to have a new partner in crime

Bob blushed and eye-rolled his mother.

Catherine was "over the moon," by the picturesque scenery of the area around Wallace, Idaho. Earlier spring rains had given way to glorious sunshine and flowers in bloom. She hadn't expected Wallace to be surrounded by mountains. Nana and Bob were excited to be back in their old stomping grounds.

Catherine squealed in delight when they entered the hotel. It couldn't be called luxurious, like a big city hotel, but it had even more charm than she'd supposed — with four-poster beds, velvet curtains, and rockers in all the rooms. After they freshened up, Bob rented a car and drove them to where the family homestead once stood in the little town of Burke, not far from Wallace. A friend from the area had written to Nana a few years earlier with the news that their little house had been torn down.

While it made mother and son sad to stand on the ground where it had once stood, seeing once again those spectacular views of the mountains made them both joyful.

As they inched down Memory Lane, Catherine's mind wandered, but then returned as Bob explained how Wallace had been a booming gold rush town in the 1880s, though the Great Fire of 1910 had destroyed a third of it.

"No one knows exactly what caused it," he said. "Some say that embers thrown from trains were the culprits."

The next day, when Nana was visiting old friends, Catherine and Bob stopped at a two-storied Victorian house a couple of blocks from downtown. A young woman came to the door and Bob asked her if Isabelle Prevost still lived there. Catherine had no idea why he'd wanted to take her there.

A few minutes later, Isabelle, a well-preserved older woman in a dated long gown of purple and black lace, came to the door. It took her a second or two to recognize Bob. Then she clutched him to her bosom like a long-lost son or lover — Catherine couldn't decide which. Bob seemed terribly fond of her. After introductions were made, Isabelle grabbed her shawl and scurried them down the street to a restaurant.

It was there, through casual conversation, that Catherine was informed that the house was a brothel and that Isabelle was the madam, and had been for many years. Catherine stopped sipping her Coca-Cola and her eyes grew noticeably larger, which amused Bob. Swallowing her hamburger became near impossible. Everyone seemed to know Isabelle and fawned over her at the restaurant. Bob and she spoke of many people that Catherine had never heard of before. It got annoying. While Catherine found her fascinating, she wondered why he hadn't visited Isabelle on his own.

They discussed Isabelle back in their room at the hotel. "The way people treated her, you'd think Isabelle was a dignitary or royalty," Catherine said.

"In a way, she is," Bob replied. He then told her how most of the Wallace madams (and there were quite a few) were well-respected, as their money was used for many a good cause.

Catherine loved the shops in Wallace, as well its slow pace. Such a contrast to Detroit! She could hear herself think here. As much as she loved the cool mountain air and the quaintness of the town, there was no way she'd ever want to live here.

"Bob, you know me — I'd be bored silly."

"No one's asking you to move here, my dear," he said.

There were moments when the romance rekindled between them, though with Nana in the room next door, the flame didn't last long. Sometimes they'd hear her talking through the thin walls. Catherine told Bob that Nana was no doubt chatting away with spirits. Bob reluctantly agreed.

One evening during their week-long stay, the couple returned to their hotel room in a jovial mood after a stroll past the shops and a tasty dinner out. Catherine declared it the best river trout she'd ever had. She remarked how the friendly townsfolk had made her feel at home. I told you they would, Bob replied. Then he batted his eyes at her and she winked back.

Once again, she'd sent him—as he then said to her—"to the moon and back."

She collapsed on the four-poster bed and pretended to fall into a deep sleep, replete with fake snores. Bob lay next to her and kissed her smooth and slender neck, doing his best Dracula impersonation. She squealed and he put his hand over her mouth, pointing with his other hand at the wall between their room and Nana's. Soon, the two drifted off, facing away from each other.

Besides visiting splendid views from the mountains, which included several waterfalls, they visited the abandoned silver mine where Bob had lost his twin.

"We'd just had our birthday. Raymond had to work in the mines the following day. We couldn't wait for his next day off to use the new fishing poles and tackle that we'd been given as presents. But he never came home from the mine. Turns out he'd fallen down a shaft. Only good thing: he died upon impact. I don't know when it was I took a fishing trip, but it must've been that same year. I went alone and the loneliness of being there without Raymond was more than I could bear. Never went fishing after that."

Bob tried to mask his sadness behind facts of another mining tale. Catherine learned Wallace had once been an important union town. The mining company, not about to relinquish its power, kept the wages of the workers low and refused to recognize the union. Not only did one-thousand workers go on strike, but they also blew up their company's mill. Lives were lost, but luckily none of the Sages. Bob's grandfather had been one of the proud but angry men. Any soft edges to life on the new continent became lost to the new immigrants. The lush scenery of the wilderness now seemed foreboding and more the stuff of nightmares than potential romantic backgrounds for picnics.

. . .

While there were no hills to climb back on Belle Isle, the long walk from the parked car to their favorite picnic spot tired them both out. A few months had passed since their train trip west, and it was now mid-summer. There were several shade trees with river and lake views, but finding the right one — according to Catherine — took a while. Bob teased her for being, once again, so sensitive and picky. She didn't deny it.

They were both surprised by their shortness of breath and concluded it was due more to the humid air than how much they'd been smoking. A typical Detroit summer, he reminded her. Lately, Bob had only been smoking the occasional cigar or cigarette. He needed all the air he could get to his boxer's lungs. Catherine was rarely without a cigarette in hand. She usually smoked Lucky Strikes, but wouldn't say no to Chesterfields.

They collapsed to their knees on the red-checked tablecloth he'd spread out on the lawn. Bob was delighted she'd remembered to pack the wicker picnic basket that he'd bought her for her birthday a couple of years earlier. They usually forget it. It had been an especially lovely summer, despite the sticky air, and they'd gone on several picnics in shady parks.

Sitting on her knees in her gauzy yellow sundress, Catherine unpacked the cold fried chicken, grapes, and cheese, along with a flask of brandy. Bob rolled up his shirt sleeves, undid the top few buttons on his shirt, took off his shoes and socks, and then stretched out on his side. He felt like a lion and she looked quite the lioness, he told her, adding a contented roar in his gravelly voice.

She giggled.

"Do it again, Kate!"

"What?"

"Giggle! Remember how you once did? Hearing your laugh makes me desire you all over again."

"Well, take me on picnics more often, my darling, and maybe you'll get your old girlfriend back," she said, laughing again in that lilting way she once had. Then she sighed—if only life's difficulties didn't so often interfere.

Bob wanted to tell her how much he missed the passion he felt leading up to make-up sex with her, as well as the sex itself, but hadn't known how to explain it without sounding like a sex maniac. Only sometimes did they *do the deed*, but it was usually in the middle of the night, and only barely recalled in the morning. It frustrated him not to talk about it more directly.

One of the shocks of his life was learning women enjoyed 'making whoopee' almost as much as men. They could be such little vixens, so why wouldn't he be seduced by their very presence? Also, Bob was surprised—if not shocked—that being married had only slightly reduced his attraction to other women. It wouldn't have surprised him if Catherine felt the same about men, not that she'd admit it for one hundred years. He doubted she would act on her desire—and if so—he didn't want to know. Something told him they were sinners of the same degree. Someday soon he'd broach the subject of them going to Confession more regularly.

Bob closed his eyes while Catherine fed him first one grape, and then another. Gulls flew by overhead and the sound of a large boat horn sounded in the distance. A flock of puffy white clouds, like sheep, followed each other slowly across the sky.

They reminisced about the train journey they'd taken the previous spring. What a time it had been!

A question had been eating at her, burning up inside her, ever since the trip. How often had he, in the past, visited Isabelle or her girls?

Bob refused to tell her.

"Over ten times?"

He smiled at her, lying on his back in the late afternoon sunshine, his eyes closed.

"Over twenty?"

"Countless!" he said, plucking a handful of grass and throwing it at her.

"Shame on you, Bob Sage!"

"I feel no shame. See what Catholicism has done to you, my dear?" he said, only half in jest. Maybe if Catherine had been raised in or around Wallace, she'd be more natural about sex— they'd have had a better sex life. Yet, he wasn't shamed, though it was a shame. He knew he was losing his edge in the boxing world and turning into a damn *palooka*. Nothing helped better than the long, sultry looks from women, their lingering stares, letting him know he still had what it took—that intense virility of youth.

. . .

On that long train ride back home Nana and Bob had discussed how they were now ready to put their past behind them, or at least in perspective. Catherine returned with a clearer understanding of their lives out West. Despite their difficulties, she remained fascinated by this family she'd married into. The Sages, like many, at first arrogantly believed they were going to conquer the West. But their losses had broken them. And it was only by breaking that they learned to see the difficulties faced by those marginalized indigenous souls. The surviving family members had become more compassionate than they would have otherwise. And this was the real reason their spirits burned brightly. Catherine knew she shouldn't get too near the flame, but knowing better wouldn't have been enough to prevent the future domino effect.

She wanted to discuss this, too, with Bob now, but sure that he'd think she was poking a hole in his masculinity, giggled as best she could, at a ridiculous joke he was telling her about an Irishman named Finnegan.

CHAPTER THIRTY-TWO

Little did they know, but slipping beneath the sheets together after their Belle Isle picnic would also mean slipping away from each other: it would be the last time they would be physically intimate with each other for a long time. Tenderness, too, seemed to have fallen to the wayside. Still, they refocused their passionate natures.

During the fall of 1928, they both—though especially Catherine—became ardent in social justice causes. They championed the underdog and became a voice for those who were mistreated and lost in the justice system. Catherine worried about the tenuous strides women had made toward independence. Molly and she had once celebrated in a jubilant parade on August 18th in 1920 after women finally got the right to vote. Yet Catherine soon realized that Black women— especially in the South—couldn't exercise that right. She launched a letter-writing campaign to legislators.

Lately, she'd been wondering why women weren't more supportive of each other and would frequently bring it up for discussion informally and at meetings. Catherine and her friends once again wrote letters, but this time, they were addressed to women encouraging them to be supportive of other women. Too many women, in her estimation, who remained home to raise children, were against other women entering the professional world—even those with college degrees. They often scoffed at women who had. Yet if they stayed at home, how would they ever be treated as equals?

Men didn't seem to understand the issue. They often complained that women would never be happy, even if it became acceptable for them to wear pants — or breeches, as they were called — in public. One evening Catherine had several friends join her for a letter-writing campaign in her living room. After stuffing, sealing, and addressing envelopes, she told her friends maybe they could influence every woman who didn't wear breeches, to start doing so — both literally and figuratively.

"Like Amelia Earhart! Sure, she was a passenger on her flight to Europe, but they're saying she could be the first woman to fly there solo. If she does, she'll inspire the next generation, and those little girls will grow up and realize they have options and don't have to settle for being a wife and mother if they don't want to," Catherine said.

"And it's not like Amelia's the only female pilot," Grace added, and then told the others about Bessie Coleman, one of America's earliest pilots. She was both female and Black. "Few people know about Bessie. She died in a plane crash a couple years back."

•   •   •

Catherine often expressed her feminist views to Bob. He'd argue and tell her she was crazy. He'd get her 'Irish up' by egging her on with a devilish grin. "You women won't ever give up, will you? Not only can you vote — you can get an education and good jobs. What more do you possibly want?"

"What more do we want? I'll tell you what more —" Catherine would argue back in a calm but icy tone.

Bob knew he'd never hear the end of it. "Kate, have you ever heard of the devil's advocate? Certainly, I believe you women should be equal to men. I thought you knew me better."

Then he'd pretend to act hurt. But other times when she got on her soap box he'd nod, but then listen with only half an ear.

He was dreaming and scheming about the gym that he'd one day own. Recently, he'd become a boxing instructor at a downtown gym. Not only did he teach older kids how to box, but he'd also begun spending time with a few of them after their lessons. All were from poor neighborhoods. Bleeding heart that he was, he'd often dole out dollar bills, no strings attached.

The law firm of Sage & Sage was now located in the newly constructed Penobscot Building. It was one of the most impressive skyscrapers in Detroit—the eighth tallest building in the world at the time it opened in 1928. Despite working in the same office suite, and even though they had separate offices, Catherine and Bob spent little time there together. When he wasn't at work, he could be found at the gym, boxing arena, or at one of the less known speakeasies. He'd hide in the corners with one young woman or another. They were mostly bubbly, giggly, and impressionable—easy to compliment, kiss, and then escort to a flea-bag motel.

Catherine heard the rumors and decided not to say anything. They were mostly getting along okay, even if passion had dwindled from their marriage at an even more alarming rate than their bank savings. She began frequenting events put on by the Prosecutor's Office and looked as lovely as the days she'd worked there as a clerk. Jim Dolan had been most pleased to see her again. At a party, he confided how he still had a crush on her and hinted that Catherine should leave Bob for him.

After they began going to lunch together, Catherine confided how Bob had become sometimes "worse than just gruff" with her. While Jim sympathized, he began encouraging her—even begged her—to leave Bob. She had no issue telling Jim she needed to take things slow. If he continued to be pushy, she'd have to back off altogether. It bothered her that he was forever rubbing his eyes, sniffling, and clearing his throat. Even more irritating: he never looked at her directly. How could she trust someone who couldn't look her in the eye?

Jim was single and was eager to have a wife and begin a family. When Catherine told him she didn't want children, he'd looked at her aghast and they discontinued their lunches.

A month later, she met Richard O'Brien at a party. He, too, was a lawyer but unaffiliated with the Prosecutor's Office. Could she have simply fallen for him because he was a tall Irishman with green eyes and black hair? No, it couldn't have been Richard's looks alone, though his eyes were almost as soulful as Bob's — deep wells she could easily drown in. When he spoke, he often gesticulated with long, tapered fingers. She kept meaning to ask if he played a musical instrument, like a cello. (He didn't.) He'd once lived in France and had traveled around the world. Recently, he'd bought an airplane. Maybe someday he'd take her for a ride. Catherine couldn't wait!

Still, she hated how tongue-tied she became around Richard, and when she could find her voice — she often stuttered. Eating with him became an almost impossible task. She fell harder for Richard than she had Jim. Way harder.

Should she tell Bob? It would hurt his feelings and certainly his pride, but she owed it to him. How could she keep it from him? Maybe he wouldn't care because of his own dalliances. Besides, their marriage had been on the rocks for a while now. How unfair it was that men could play by a different set of rules! Then there was Bob's temper to consider. So much in life boiled down to the timing; if she timed it right — no one would get hurt or killed. But if she didn't...

She soon began encouraging Richard to leave his wife. He told her that he hadn't had sex with her in five years.

Catherine and Richard met once a week at a church parking lot. He'd drive them from there to a small hotel outside the city. While Bob was a passionate man, Richard was a skilled lover and could do things to her body that could send her to the moon and even over it. Was it love or sex? She never knew, but their affair went on for over a year. Even at work, she couldn't stop thinking about him. Her cases were stacking up and she wasn't paying attention to details the way she should. She realized, ever so slowly, that Richard would never leave his wife. The happy little world they shared in the hotel room would never expand.

Their last time together, Catherine knew she couldn't take it any longer—not another minute! She flew into a rage and threw a lamp at a wall, as well as the Bible. She called Richard names and in her fury, used words she didn't realize she knew.

At first, he'd laughed and when he no longer found it funny, quickly dressed and before leaving said: "You come near me again, Bitch, and I'll get a warrant out for your arrest."

Catherine collapsed in a heap on the wrinkled white sheets. Her body heaved and shuddered with her sobbing. Then she lay still enough to make a decision: she'd go to Confession. It would be the first time in a few years. No matter how many Our Fathers and Hail Marys she'd be given, she wasn't optimistic about it releasing her from the weighty guilt. During the affair, she'd been able to justify her actions, but now since Richard had rejected her, she could barely look at herself in the mirror. She couldn't even muster any anger. Still, the Church was now her only hope of salvation. She knew she was a strong woman despite being a sinful one. No other options: she would salvage her marriage and refocus on her career.

She splashed water on her face, ran a comb through her hair, straightened up the squalid room as best she could, and then took a taxi back home. What had she done? She'd never blamed other women for having affairs, but she hated herself for now being a fallen woman. How could anyone else respect her if she couldn't respect herself? Was her life ruined?

She had the driver let her out half a block from the apartment building. She planned to tell Bob—if he were home—that she'd gone out to dinner with friends, but hadn't felt well, so they'd driven her home. It was still early evening.

Bob, thankfully, wasn't there when she arrived. Towel-drying her hair after a long shower, she listened for his footsteps. She called out to him but got no response. As she sat in the dark, watching the lights flickering on the river, she had one nightcap, and then another. It was almost midnight. Tired of waiting, she finally went to bed. Never again would she betray her wedding vows. Was he somewhere now with another woman? Not that she could blame him.

Catherine got up, turned on all the lights in the apartment, smoked in the living room, and waited. He walked in the door at 12:55.

"Where've you been?" she asked in a sultry voice. She took a deep drag on her cigarette and then exhaled smoke rings.

"I told you this morning, Kate. I went over to Gene's to play some cards. There were several of us. Bobby Gene stayed up late, watching us play. We had a helluva good time. How was your day—and night?"

"Long. Glad it's over. You don't know how glad."

"Let's call it a day," Bob said, turning the lights off in all the rooms and checking the lock on their apartment door, a habit he'd acquired early in their marriage. At one time it had amused Catherine, but now she was grateful for the routine.

·   ·   ·

Bob refused to believe his wife had been seen with other men. The rumors couldn't be true. Of course, Catherine had denied it, looking him straight in the eye. When he once saw her getting into a man's car in the church parking lot, he thought she must have been getting a ride home after visiting the nuns. Maybe the driver was a visiting priest—or so he hoped. Still, part of him knew their marriage was 'on the ropes,' and eventually it would be time to 'throw in the towel.'

Despite having shared a pleasant time with Bobby Gene when they took him to see 'Steamboat Willie,' and afterward giving him a yo-yo, darkness had long ago settled in the gulf between Catherine and Bob.

CHAPTER THIRTY-THREE

January, 1929

As the clock struck midnight, they welcomed in the New Year with a lingering kiss on the dance floor of the popular Grande ballroom. It was like they were floating as they danced the night away, though this could have mostly been because of the floor having been built on springs. For a moment neither heard the hoopla from the hundreds of others packing the ballroom. Anyone there would have thought them madly in love. Only family and friends knew their problems were significant enough to destroy the marriage. Still, had they witnessed the couple's embrace, they would have seen the spark and heard it crackling.

Father Tim had reassured Catherine there was hope for her salvation—yet only if she paid penance, not only by going to Confession regularly but by continuing to do God's work in the city. His watery blue eyes gazed deeply into hers. She'd suffered for her many sins, so there was a squeak of a chance that the Lord Jesus Christ and the almighty Father in Heaven might absolve her wanton ways.

It turned out to be a vulnerable time for Bob. He had a big match coming up with renowned champion, Harry Henderson. Never had he needed support from others, as much as he did now. The match would occur in March and it would make or break his career. The stakes were high. Bob knew he wasn't in the best shape of his career and that he only had a year until he turned thirty—the peak of his athleticism would be behind him. He would do what he could to defy the odds. Also, his lifestyle of smoking cigars, frequent drinking, getting little sleep, along with his philandering, were all strikes against him. In the past, Catherine had provided reassurance like no one else—not even his new coach, Nick Riordan. (His former coach, Billy Watson, had moved out of state.)

Here it was only the second day of the New Year and Nick was already after Bob about getting in better shape. Nick, tall and trim—the very picture of Mr. Perfect, needed Bob's wife's help. He urged Catherine to coax her husband to get more sleep and eat lots of protein. Then he recommended that Bob should have sex—but not too much. She wasn't sure if Nick was joking or not, but was too embarrassed to ask him. Catherine, who'd always been emotionally loyal to Bob, followed through with most of Nick's advice.

The couple began spending more time together and also resumed seeing family on the weekends. Both were careful to avoid any topic that would lead to heated discussions, especially if it involved prior affairs or flirtations. One Sunday afternoon while Catherine was helping Violet get supper on the table, Gene cornered his brother.

"Say, Bob, think Kate and you could help the wife and me out by doing stuff with Bobby Gene sometimes? Vi's nerves have been getting worse lately. She's been getting these rashes and thinks it may have to do with always being around the boy."

"I'd love to spend more time with my namesake, Gene. Just been waiting to be asked."

Gene explained that he thought Violet needed a night out on the town on occasion, adding: "I'm sure you know how marriage can be a tricky business."

"Sure do, brother."

Catherine and Bob welcomed the opportunity. Every other weekend, they'd take Bobby Gene out to eat or to see a show.

Occasionally, on Saturday afternoons, they'd take him to the Bonstelle Theater to see magicians perform. Nana would be there, playing the organ in her nurse's uniform before the curtain would rise and at intermission. "My Nana's famous!" the little boy would declare.

In the late winter, they drove him across the new Ambassador Bridge to Canada. Bobby Gene admitted to having been a little nervous when the customs official had stopped them. When the official asked if they had anything to declare, Bobby Gene, sitting in the back seat, said in a squeaky tone: "I declare my love for Nana." Later, they stood at the bank of the river in Windsor. After having a good laugh about Bobby Gene's declaration, they marveled at the Detroit skyline and then watched a freighter go by. There were still blocks of ice floating down the river.

"Look, we got icebergs!" shouted Bobby Gene. The couple laughed and then sighed, both wondering if they should again try to become parents. They gave each other a knowing look, realizing that the other wouldn't dare bring up the topic. At least not soon.

Then Bob showed the boy where the tunnel was being built and promised to drive him through it once it was completed. Bobby Gene wasn't so sure about that. "What if it caves in while we're inside it?" he asked.

"You've got a point there, Bobby. You know I lost one of my brothers — your uncle — down in the mines out West."

"Don't make the boy afraid of the tunnel! Bobby, it'll be just as safe, maybe safer, to go to Canada through the tunnel. The builders nowadays know how to make things so they last."

Despite Aunt Catherine's reassuring words Bobby Gene had his doubts.

"Say, Bobby, what do you like better: that yo-yo we gave you on your last birthday, or going to Windsor?" Bobby had to think about it, but then admitted that he liked Windsor better because someday he was going to become a traveler. The couple chuckled and nodded in agreement. Uncle Bob made a promise to Bobby (now at age seven, he'd recently insisted on being called Bobby), that in a few years he would take him on a trip out West.

After returning to Detroit from Windsor, they again took him to the movies. The two Bobs enjoyed 'Popeye' more than Catherine did. Since Bobby was a sickly boy, heroes became increasingly important. He loved telling people that if he ate all his spinach, one day he'd be as strong as Popeye.

Bobby wanted to know why they didn't have children, and Catherine's response was, "Why then we wouldn't have time to go places and do things with you." Bobby never brought it up again.

• • •

Catherine and Bob attended mass one Sunday with Nana, and Uncle Gerry. The previous Sunday, Gerry had reported that Grammy McIntosh had taken a turn for the worse from a bout of the flu. He didn't think she'd recover.

Nana and Gerry accompanied them back to Catherine's parents' home for a pot roast dinner. The mood was somber and conversations were more stilted than usual. Catherine told the story of Bobby Gene seeing icebergs in the river and it fell on deaf ears. She was the only one who laughed. Bridget gave her a scolding look for saying something inappropriate. Before leaving, Gerry thanked his sister-in-law for the leftover Irish stew, saying that he'd gobble it down the following day. He then told Mickey how hard it was to see their mother "wasting away." The brothers gave each other an awkward hug.

Sage & Sage had fewer cases than they'd had in a long time. The *Detroit Free Press* did its best to cover the Battling Barrister's fights. Previously, the sport's page editorial had always helped their law practice, but now the free advertising no longer worked its former magic. No doubt because of Bob no longer being in college and not winning as many fights. He became short with Catherine over the smallest of issues, telling her she needed to wear more make-up. Cover up that pale face with more lipstick and rouge, you look like a ghost! Why didn't she ever think to change her stockings when she got a run in them?

"I married the wrong brother!" Catherine once screamed at him after he'd been hounding her. "Gene never would've spoken to me the way you do. Why are you always so critical?"

Bob apologized, but a few days later, once again began harping at her. Catherine dreamed about fires again. On her better nights, she dreamed of dancing with handsome strangers. And once more, she turned to the bottle to help knock her out from the cruelties of her husband and the world.

CHAPTER THIRTY-FOUR

One late winter afternoon, Catherine gingerly made her way up an icy sidewalk. She was carrying an apple pie still warm from her mother's oven to Nana. She would've made it herself except she didn't enjoy all the fuss involved in rolling out the dough. Climbing the porch steps, she was grateful for what was left of the opalescent light in the sky. But something wasn't right. Her uneasiness made it hard to get a deep breath. The sense of foreboding that she'd had earlier in the day had become increasingly intense.

Over the years she came to view Nana as something of a fortune teller since many of her predictions seemed to turn out to be true. Part of her wanted to hide from the older woman, but she also couldn't help but be intrigued, as well as comforted by her warmth.

She knocked hesitantly at the door with her free hand. Nana warmly hugged her daughter-in-law, asking Catherine to remind her later to give her a pack of red licorice, as she had extra. But after that Nana looked deep into her eyes and fell silent. It made Catherine blink and gaze down at her chipped nails.

Catherine's sense of something being not right intensified.

Over tea and slices of the apple pie, Nana took both Catherine's frozen hands and squeezed. Then the older woman closed her eyes, inhaled deeply, and slowly released her breath.

"My dear, we're going through a dark time which, I'm sorry to report, is only going to become darker."

"You mean 'we' as in the family or as in everyone?" Catherine asked, forgetting how to breathe.

"Our families — all families, sadly."

Catherine sputtered for air.

Nana rose and motioned for the taller, younger woman to join her at the window. Together they stared out at the pitchfork branches of winter trees and a cloud-filled sky. A chill went down Catherine's spine. Nana wrapped her arm around her daughter-in-law's slender waist.

"We must face it the best we can. Not only in my dreams have I heard the warning but in the cloud formations. See how the pearly ones are getting edged out by the two larger dark ones?"

Catherine nodded, though more convinced by Nana's dreams than by her interpretations of ever-changing clouds. This time of year was usually pretty cloudy, the skeptic in her wanted to say, but it was probably best not to mention this.

She longed to ask Nana whether or not she'd had any further premonitions about Catherine's death. No time like the present.

"That's intriguing for sure, Nana, but can you tell me about what I can do to avoid an early demise? Last time you spoke of it, you brushed it off due to the news from Houdini that I'm to pass along to my great niece in the 1960s or 70s. See why I'm somewhat confused?"

"Do you keep a diary, my dear? If not, begin one, and write about your dreams. What I saw about you — some time ago, if I recollect — might not have been your actual death, but the death of a certain time in your life. I meant to tell you that at the time. It was more about taking precautions, my girl, like keeping healthy. But maybe don't listen to me, Katy me-girl, for I'm hardly an expert," Nana said and then emitted a rather loud and long belly laugh. Afterward, she wiped tears from the corners of her eyes. "But the main thing for us is to be as brave as possible, as I deeply sense the road ahead will be very bumpy."

Catherine nodded, stole a breath of air, and sighed. She wondered about Nana's ominous words. Could this be why she felt like she did before the visit?

They then discussed the logistics of attending Bob's next day's boxing match.

· · ·

Catherine sat in the middle of the ringside seats reserved for the families of the boxers. Nothing lonelier than being in a crowd. The giant wave of noise and smoke almost overwhelmed her. Was she about to faint? Hit her head upon the hard floor and lose consciousness? As she struggled for breath, she had difficulty making sense of what even those seated on either side of her were saying. Nana sat on one side, and her father on the other. Also seated in the same row were Gene, Violet, Bobby, her mother, and uncle. They all seemed to be talking at once. As uncomfortable as Catherine was, she still welcomed the distraction of family being near. Looking at them helped to regulate her breathing. Maybe she'd get through this after all.

Bob had reminded her over coffee that morning that his opponent would be Harry Henderson. Strategist that he was, Bob planned on felling Harry with the 'Haymaker' punch. If done properly, Bob's arm would swing sideways like a scythe cutting hay. He'd never tried this before.

"So long as I don't wind up feeling like a total palooka—or worse—afterward."

"Or you could use your powerful uppercut when he drops his head."

"For the love of Saint Michael, when did you suddenly become my coach—huh?"

They hadn't spoken to each other the remainder of the day.

After seeing Nana the night before, she tossed and turned in bed like a horizontal windmill. Nana's words about this being a dark time about to get even darker kept repeating in her mind. As much as she adored her, who was Nana to make such dire pronouncements? Catherine looked over at her now, proudly waiting for her son to enter the ring, and seemingly not at all bothered by her prediction from yesterday.

The match was over before it began. Bob started off quick on his feet, as usual — especially for a light-heavyweight. Harry and Bob danced and hopped like two kangaroos. Following a double-jab and a lead hook — just as Bob was about to go for an uppercut — Harry knocked the wind out of him. Bob fell but staggered to his feet. Then he got slower and slower with each successive round and did the dance of a dying kangaroo. Sheer stamina and willpower kept him upright. The crowd couldn't wait for him to go down; it had completely gone insane.

Catherine couldn't bring herself to watch the final round. She could imagine the headlines: 'The Battling Barrister Debarred from Ring'…'The Battling Barrister Defeated.'

Afterward, the family waited anxiously in the lobby to hear from Nick about how Bob was doing, hoping none of his injuries were serious.

"His pride sure took a beating, that I can tell you, but physically I think he's going to be okay," Nick, at last, informed them. The crowd had long since left the building. "You knew he wouldn't win this one, right?" he asked them, adding that Bob had enjoyed a better career than many boxers. Was he implying that it was over? Did Nick tell Bob it was? She fought the urge to punch Nick.

. . .

Catherine waited up for her husband, knowing he'd be off somewhere drowning his sorrows. And though she couldn't blame Bob if he were, she sure hoped he wasn't in the arms of another woman, some bimbo. Not that she could blame him...She'd been sensing for a while that he was nearing the end of his fighting career and knew he must have been feeling likewise. And if so, it couldn't have been a complete shock for him. Maybe they could plan another trip or beef up his business. He could become a professional coach or manager himself. They could move to a house with a yard and get a puppy. If he wouldn't go for a dog, then maybe he'd agree to a cat. They had options about the way forward.

But where was Bob?

Catherine smoked and played game after game of solitaire at the dining room table, wearing the floor-length blue silk robe that he'd given her as a wedding present. Time had stained it, and ripped the sleeves and a shoulder. It reminded her of an old boxer.

Hard to believe they'd only known each other for six years, for some days it seemed like a lifetime.

At 4:00 a.m., Bob finally staggered in. Catherine had never seen him looking so rough—his face was swollen and the dark circles beneath his eyes had their own dark circles. He looked like a dying owl. His clothes were disheveled and his hair— normally slicked back—looked like wild, but dead, seagrass. She would have almost believed him had he said he'd been in a hurricane. What she definitely knew was not to ask him where he'd been.

"My boxing days are over, Kate," he said in a weary, yet frightened voice. She noticed how heavy his face had become, how it had lost the chiseled look of younger years. He then wandered to the bedroom, fell across the bed, and slept for fourteen hours. She never slept until the following night—and even then, she drifted off only briefly, afraid to dream.

CHAPTER THIRTY-FIVE

For the next few weeks, Bob rarely left the apartment and rarely uttered a word. He visited Gene two or three times but didn't take her with him. When he returned home in a slightly better mood, she attributed it to having seen their nephew. After that time, he returned to work, but only a couple of days a week, while Catherine continued going in daily. She didn't mind at first, but it began to annoy her. Their total number of clients had dwindled, so it wouldn't be a problem to take over his. Still, it was the not-knowing that kept her awake at night. Boxing had meant so much to him and was such a part of his identity. She wished she had a tender and soothing temperament like his mother.

Bob promised her that soon he'd 'buckle down.' When Catherine asked him where he went when he wasn't at the office, he insisted he'd been at meetings. Oh, and what was discussed? Lately, whenever she questioned him, he'd tell her he was "taking the Fifth," and would leave the room. She decided not to pester him. At least Bob wasn't sitting around the apartment in his pajamas all day. While they slept in the same bed, he'd become a stranger. Catherine longed to touch him but knew that he'd recoil, so she didn't bother.

Could he be having a nervous breakdown? She didn't want to let on how worried she was.

Then one evening, Bob could no longer withstand the silence between them and confessed that he'd been playing poker with 'the boys' downtown once or twice a week. Catherine didn't bother asking who he'd been playing with, knowing it was unlikely that she'd get a straight answer. At first, he'd made a tidy profit, but then his luck changed—putting him in the red. His gambling days were over now, just like his boxing days, he admitted, hanging his head. She tried to be sympathetic, but it was all she could do to keep a lid on her fury.

Bob stayed away from the boxing world, as his ego was shattered like never before. Then he recalled the neighborhood kids—the ones with no dads around—who were counting on him. It didn't seem fair to let them down.

One particular afternoon, his young fans jumped up and down when he walked into the gym. He'd had such a good time horsing around with them and showing them boxing moves, that his good mood followed him home.

After telling Catherine about his time with the kids, Bob asked her to think about where she'd like to travel next. Life hadn't just been tough on him, but on her, too.

"I'm sorry to have been such a rat these days, Kate."

"With business not exactly booming, are you sure it's the right time for a trip?" She smiled and squeezed his hand.

"Why not? Let's live each day to the fullest. That's my motto and it should be yours, too. I'm thinking Cuba. It's both exotic and pretty cheap."

"But we'd need a good two weeks. Can we afford to be gone that long?"

"Must you always be the voice of reason? Bo-ring! Kiddo, you've turned into my conscience. How am I ever going to take you to bed again if you're that shaming voice in my beat-up boxer brain?"

Catherine laughed and shook her head in denial. Hers was hardly the voice of reason. Still, how wonderful it was to see signs of the old Bob! Maybe it wasn't too late and they were still attracted to each other after all. Maybe the dying embers could be fanned until the passion between them revived— at least a little.

Then Bob suggested Chicago, knowing she loved it there as much as he did. He had a renewed interest because of the St. Valentine's Day massacre. Wouldn't it be fascinating to see the spot where seven of Bugs Moran's gang had been shot down, no doubt by the infamous Al Capone?

She raised an eyebrow. Maybe there wasn't that big a difference between those who break the law and study the law.

"Let's take the train tomorrow! Go pack your bag, Sweets, and I'll get the tickets."

"I can't wait, Bobbo! Don't you just love the Windy City?"

Maybe their lives would get back on track and better times were just around the bend. She told this to Bob who said she wasn't all that 'punny.'

. . .

Catherine rested her head on Bob's shoulder on the early morning train. She dozed and thought of other trips they'd taken, their honeymoon to Chicago, and then the long trip out West. What a shame they couldn't travel more often! They always got along so much better than they did in their daily lives. Bob hadn't been rough with her in a long time, even on his bad days. Whenever they went somewhere together, he was tender and funny, not to mention passionate.

As if reading her mind, he slipped his hand inside her blouse, and then inside her bra—he knew this aroused her, as much as it did him. She pulled his face to hers, and they kissed slow and deep. The vibrating rumble from the train made it difficult to sit still. Just as he was putting his hand up her skirt, the ticket-taker was standing in the aisle next to their seat.

"Your ticket, miss," requested a stern-looking, double-chinned man in a uniform.

"Sure. Give me just a second." Catherine rifled through her purse, still lost in the fog of desire.

Their room at The Congress Hotel overlooked Lake Michigan. The room itself, while small, had large windows with cushioned seats from which to watch the boats go by. They also had a perfect view of the beautiful Buckingham Fountain across the street. It felt like a second honeymoon.

A good part of the first day had been spent in bed dozing, laughing, ordering room service after having a 'roll in the hay' — as Bob called it, and afterward sharing a smoke. Later, both got restless, so they ventured out on the town, crossing the new Michigan Avenue Bridge to the shopping district, dining out, and then dancing in jazzy speakeasies that easily outdid the ones in Detroit. The city was as windy as they'd remembered. The gangster atmosphere made them feel reckless and wild. "What say we throw caution to the wind?" Bob would often ask her.

In one of the clubs, they met a couple who claimed to have been friends of Al Capone's, though when asked, their lips were sealed about the horrific massacre back in February. Then Bob pointed out a woman with red hair.

"I met that dame on the train south to Miami. Her last name is Sage. Isn't that something? Her first name, I've forgotten. Maybe Amy or Amelia, possibly Anna..."

Bob recalled fantasizing about her in the hotel bed in Havana. This, of course, he'd never tell his wife.

Catherine gave him a nod to signify that it was okay for him to speak to her.

"Hello, again, Miss Sage."

"Do I know you? Oh, yes...I met you on train. Your name, it is Bob. Bob Sage?" Anna said, smiling at her memory of meeting him. She turned to Catherine, standing awkwardly behind Bob. "I'm Anna and you would be?"

"I'm Catherine, Bob's wife. Nice to meet you," she said in a monotone, not feeling at all happy to meet an attractive woman of Bob's acquaintance. How much time had they spent together? Had they gotten beneath the sheets? That Anna had the same last name made it all the worse by establishing an intimacy between them. And then it would be all too easy for Bob to make a move.

Anna Sage said, in broken but understandable English that while it had been nice to see Bob and meet his wife, she couldn't talk long, as she was already late for a meeting. After Anna left, Catherine tried to hide her jealousy, which would've been easy had the woman had a different last name and been on the homely side. Her red hair had been striking, more so than her own. Bob saw right through it.

"If you're wondering, my dear, she doesn't even hold a candle to you. She's just a moll."

"I wasn't wondering."

"Sure you weren't, sweetheart...Whatever you say, but just know, I never even stole a kiss from her."

Still, the encounter dampened the mood until they took a cab to a steakhouse with burgundy velvet booths. Bob whispered sweet nothings into Catherine's ear that were really 'somethings'; the spell it put her under transfixed her for the rest of the trip. "What a swell city!" she'd later remark, "And to think it made such a comeback after the Great Fire."

CHAPTER THIRTY-SIX

And then the Study Hall fire in Detroit killed twenty-two and injured fifty. The Study Hall wasn't a place to study, but a place to dance. It ranked as one of Catherine and Bob's favorite Detroit haunts, until one night in late September. They knew several who were there at the time. Two of Bob's friends had perished in the flames. While Bob had many friends, to lose even one caused him — as he termed it, "deep soul-crushing anguish." The fire was speculated to have started from a discarded cigarette in a stairwell.

Bob had known Joseph and Johnny ever since he'd first moved to Detroit. The twins had always reminded Bob of his own twin. He enjoyed being around them, not only because they were fun-loving guys, but because they often finished each other's sentences. It reminded him how Raymond and he had once done the same. These two had kept Bob's unspoken memories alive.

Although Catherine had barely known them, she was all broken up over their deaths. She sobbed at the funeral, and again on the drive home. There had to be some other reason for her tears. Bob grew increasingly annoyed with the way she was carrying on.

He jabbed his finger into her side. He couldn't help himself.

"Look, be my guest and shed a few tears, but they were my friends, so don't you think I should be the one crying?" he asked, though he didn't expect an answer. She continued to blubber, so steering with one hand he poked her again with his other one, this time on her arm and with more force. She slapped his hand and then he slapped her face. Hard. Why didn't she understand his grief?

When they got home she ran into the bedroom, slamming the door behind her. No one slammed the door on Bob Sage. No one.

He downed one shot of whiskey after another. Their apartment was a pigsty. Catherine hadn't cleaned in weeks. In the small kitchen, dirty dishes were piled up in the sink and on the small counter. Filthy ashtrays and old newspapers added to the clutter. Thick layers of dust and ash had settled on the carpet and table tops.

She had plenty of time to clean on the weekends, so there was no excuse for her laziness.

His mother's voice was in his head scolding him for what he did to Catherine. "That's not how you treat a lady," she kept repeating. She was right. His temper sometimes got the best of him. Catherine was a lady, a damn fine one, and he was lucky she married him. She could leave him and he certainly didn't want that. True, there were other dames, but no one could replace her. The next day he'd talk with Father Tim before it was too late. The priest knew her well, probably better than he knew Bob. While Bob wouldn't tell him everything, he'd give the priest a clear enough picture. He knew he could count on this man of God to help him through this time, certainly better than his mother.

Catherine crying over his friends' deaths was no big deal, nor was the messy apartment. Still…

. . .

Her tears finally stopped flowing, but Catherine wasn't ready to deal with Bob, so she dozed for a while. The wells of her gray-blue eyes were finally dry. She slipped out of the dress she'd worn to the funeral and into silk pajamas. While she could understand how upset Bob must feel over losing his friends to the fire, in no way did it justify him for slapping her simply because she'd been emotional. It's not like she'd been drinking.

Living in the Whittier still made her feel like a wealthy woman. Tomorrow she was having her hair done at Pierre's Salon, one of the wonderful little shops on the mezzanine. This perked her up some, as did what she found in a box in Bob's sock drawer: a pearl necklace. Christmas was still a few months away, and it was unlike him to buy a present this far in advance. Maybe he intended it to be a surprise, a "just because" gift. Bob could be a real charmer when he tried. Then she recalled his unkind words and not only how he slapped her, but had jabbed her with his finger. She wouldn't let him off the hook—not right away. His finger could easily have been a knife.

Catherine replaced the lid and slid the box to the back of the drawer. Then she touched something cold behind it. Opening the drawer a little more, she saw the steely nose of a pistol. She knew he had one, but the one she'd seen before was smaller. She shut the drawer fast—as if the gun was alive and could go off by itself. If she mentioned it, he'd accuse her of snooping through his things. Come to think of it, he always fussed about putting away his clothes after they'd been washed. Now she knew why.

When she peered into the bathroom mirror she saw a red mark where he'd slapped her. The badge of the battered. Tomorrow the bruise would be purple, and no matter much powder she'd apply, she wouldn't be able to cover it. She'd have to make up a story for Pierre at the salon.

That night, Catherine woke up screaming—sure their bed was going up in flames. Her silk pajamas were drenched in sweat.

And then that fall, the Stock Market crashed and the roar went out of the 1920s.

On the day after what would come to be known as Black Tuesday, Catherine and Bob were shocked to hear about the crash. They heard about it on the new radio he'd recently brought home as a surprise. Sitting as close to it as possible, they listened to a broadcaster report how crazy it had become on the Wall Street trading floor. Not only had fistfights broken out, but some of the traders had collapsed; the chaos was causing the nation to lose its collective mind. While the market hadn't been doing well all autumn, few realized what the fallout would entail.

"Looks like the country's gone belly-up, Kate. If everyone pulls their money out of the banks, they're speculating that the banks won't have enough to dole out. Good thing we don't have much in our savings account."

"About how much?"

"Fifty dollars and some change."

Big spenders that they were, they usually loaned or gave away what they didn't spend on themselves. Bob kept a small safe with cash in their apartment.

"Good thing we don't know many wealthy people, except Uncle Gerry."

"Maybe we better check up on the poor guy."

They stopped by to see Gerry the weekend after Black Tuesday. Gerry's life savings were completely wiped out. He looked like he'd aged ten years. All he had left was his house. He had no idea if he'd be able to keep it, or its value if forced to sell. In a hushed tone, he told them to please not mention this to Grammy. They gave him their solemn promise.

Then Uncle Gerry died suddenly of a heart attack right after Thanksgiving. No one wanted to break the news to Grammy. When Mickey finally did, she took it so well they wondered if it had even registered. Yet she wasn't well enough to attend the funeral of hundreds of mourners. For a couple of weeks, a family member stayed with her at night. Most often it was Catherine.

Like Grammy, she kept speaking of her uncle in the present tense; though unlike her, Grammy never shed a single tear. Mickey speculated it was because she couldn't accept Gerry's death.

Gerry, a man of good habits, had seemed healthier than most. Catherine always wondered if he was lonely. If so, he'd never complained. Her father once said Gerry had been jilted by a woman at a young age and it had broken his heart, though she rather doubted he'd had much interest in women. As close as she was to him, she never would've dared to bring up his romantic life, or lack thereof.

Catherine would never forget how kind her uncle had always been. Grammy, too, though she wouldn't have extended the offer for Catherine to live with him, had it not been for him. Catherine's life at the time had flourished — getting her first real job, being in love with Bob. Naively, she'd expected it to only get better from then on. Not only did she mourn her kind uncle, but losing her younger self. She could do good things in the world, but its rocky surface was a lot craggier than she'd supposed.

For Christmas, Bob gave Catherine an orange kitten she called Mr. Mercedes. He gave her the cat, but not the pearl necklace. While she adored the kitten, she had to bite her lip to keep from asking what he'd done with the necklace. He must have either returned it or given it to another woman since it was no longer in the drawer. She guessed it was the latter.

She longed to strangle whatever lovely neck was now wearing it.

Having fewer clients than ever before, they wondered how they'd be able to continue to live at the Whittier. Those who owed them money weren't able to pay them back, though promises were made. While the couple never looked shabby, their clothing looked a little worn. Gone were the days of splurging or buying new things. Catherine spoke about possibly returning to her clerk's job at the Prosecutor's Office in the winter, and Bob toyed with the idea to work for a larger firm. He took up playing poker again with friends, but only on the weekends. None of the players could now put much in the pot. Still, when you won, you were a winner, no matter how small the winnings, he'd often say.

Catherine finally had time to read a few of the novels Uncle Gerry had given her, including *Hard Times* and *Great Expectations*. It took her mind off her grief. She often stayed up late reading and waiting for Bob's return. Sometimes she thought about the pearl necklace and the wearer.

"It's just you and me, Mr. Mercedes." The blue-eyed orange kitten looked up at her in gratitude (as much as any feline can). It hadn't occurred to Catherine until then that Bob had given her the kitten so she'd have a companion. She often drank and smoked until she eventually passed out with Mr. Mercedes purring on her stomach.

One Saturday night when Bob was out playing poker, she received a telegram from her father stating that Grammy McIntosh had died.

PART II
TURA LURA LURAL

CHAPTER THIRTY-SEVEN

1930

Sitting at a table next to the restaurant's kitchen, Catherine and Grace had to raise their voices to hear each other over the clatter and din. They were used to being seated in the backs of restaurants when they were together. Grace told her she wouldn't dare go into one without a white friend unless she was in Black Bottom. They joked about how at least they weren't given the boot, which no doubt they'd get if they dared to sit together down South.

"And can you imagine what would happen if I tried to exercise my right to vote?" Grace asked, rolling her eyes.

Catherine shuddered to think of the horrible possibilities that could—and did—occur to anyone with dark skin.

They hadn't seen each other in over a year, and had much catching up to do. A button on Grace's lovely pale pink blouse was missing and there was a stain on a sleeve. Catherine's dress had a small tear at the shoulder and its hue of forest green had now faded like a parched lawn in late summer.

Catherine couldn't help but notice that while her friend still had her former elegance and grace (her name was so fitting), she looked older—maybe because she was thinner and had a more noticeable crease between her brows. Catherine's own worry lines on her forehead were now etched deeper than the laugh lines near her eyes.

It took the two friends mere moments before seeing beyond those surface changes.

Despite the kitchen racket, the restaurant of Hudson's Department Store wasn't busy, as few were during that time. Menu selections were pared down, making it easy for them to decide on what to order. Canadian cheese soup, a small Maurice Salad, and fresh bread sounded just fine.

An elderly couple seated at the next table eyed the two women. The man wore a monocle that reminded Catherine of the indispensable one once worn by Grammy McIntosh.

Catherine smiled back and continued doing so until they turned away. Her cheeks reddened.

"Just ignore them, Kate. So, I guess the last we saw each other was at your uncle's funeral," Grace began.

"It meant so much that you came. Could you believe that large turnout? I'm sorry we didn't get a chance to talk, but I sure didn't feel all that social."

"Of course, you didn't. I know how much you thought of him, and he of you."

"Uncle Gerry was far too young for his heart to give out. Fine one day and dead the next...We were all shocked. While it was sad to lose Grandma McIntosh, she was no doubt ready to go, but not him. Hard to believe they've been gone for so many months."

Catherine confided she wished she'd spent more time with Grammy and that she'd been as close with her as she was with Nana. But Grammy hadn't been close with anyone except Gerry.

Grace gave her an encouraging nod, so Catherine continued: "She'd been at her most hospitable when she allowed me to move in with them, but after I got married, she pretty much shut the world out. She'd get together with Nana and go shopping now and then, but you couldn't call it a friendship."

Death's sting was still fresh and Catherine was disappointed that Grammy and Gerry hadn't even been showing up in her dreams.

"And they died within a month of each other? I'm sorry I didn't make it to your grandmother's funeral."

"As I recall, you sent lovely flowers. Can you believe it was just a month to the day between their deaths? Of course, Nana had seen it in the clouds or tea leaves or wherever she foresees such things. At least, that's what she told us after the fact."

Grace laughed, as Catherine had hoped she would.

"Have you ever lost anyone close?" Catherine asked, having little knowledge about Grace's family.

"Hasn't everybody? Let's see...My mother, when I was young. All my grandparents are gone, and also several aunts and uncles. I never knew my father, so I have little idea if he's alive or dead."

"I'm so sorry, Grace."

"After a while, I guess we just get used to loss. While he's still alive, it sure feels like my husband passed away, too."

"Sam left you? Why?" Sam always seemed to have worshipped the ground Grace walked on. Her appetite was suddenly gone.

"Pride, I think. I hear from him now and then. He said being married to a 'lady attorney' was too fancy for him. Not that it matters much lately, as my paychecks are puny. Plus, some of my work's always been pro-bono." Catherine remembered how Grace had been giving free legal advice to women who couldn't afford to pay for it.

"Sam still working at the Ford assembly plant?"

Grace nodded and rubbed her hands together, as if a sudden chill in the air. "He sends me cash sometimes. That is, when it suits him."

Catherine had only met him once and Grace had rarely mentioned him. Her bitterness was palpable and who could blame her?

"Will you get a divorce?"

"I sure hope so, but I doubt he'll grant me one," said Grace. Rubbing her forehead, she continued, "I don't have the energy to cheat on him, and, sadly, that might be my best recourse. Then he could divorce me for adultery, though that would end my career." It was then that Catherine noticed how her friend's nails, while clean, looked chewed and unpolished — much like her own.

"Things aren't quite that bad with Bob, though he's had affairs," said Catherine. Grace's eyes widened. Catherine continued, "The good news is they never seem to last long. Say, why don't we run off to New York? We could work for one of those big law firms."

"Sure wish we could! But no one can keep us from dreaming about it, right?" asked Grace, one tear rolling down her dark cheek, followed by another. She wiped them away with the corner of the cloth napkin and forced a smile. Catherine wondered if she should tell her friend about her two affairs, but decided against it. Maybe someday she'd confess, but for now, she wanted Grace to think the best of her.

"From what you've told me about Bob, I wouldn't blame you for leaving him."

Catherine was ready to tell all, but just then, two young men approached the table. Were they going to say something mean? Maybe what the elderly couple had been thinking?

The taller one asked if Catherine was the wife of the famous boxer, Bob Sage, the Battling Barrister. Catherine unfurled her fist.

"Could you please let Mr. Sage how in awe of him we are?"

Catherine blushed and nodded. After they left, the women laughed about the timing of Bob's fans stopping by when they did.

She told Grace how she was back clerking for the Prosecutor's Office and Bob was working for a large firm.

"Good for Bob, but that's got to be tough on you."

"It's work. I truly don't mind the job, though I'd prefer being an actual attorney."

"Still, after all the experience you've now had practicing law…" Grace shook her head and sighed.

"And we both have jobs, Grace, though you're not being paid what you should. They're paying me a pittance, too. I've heard women around the nation are back to being housewives. I know, let's make a toast with our water glasses."

The two women raised their glasses.

"One day we'll both be working in the Big Apple and the world will be ours!" said Catherine.

"One day." Grace smiled, but it was a wan and weary smile.

The soup turned out to be more broth than the advertised Canadian cheese soup. They did their best to enjoy it, as they caught up. Catherine filled Grace in on Margaret and Joan. Margaret had been doing well at a large firm. That was, until a certain Mr. Benedict Draper—the head of the firm—got word that Margaret was a lesbian. After being fired she battled severe depression, and now lived with her elderly parents.

Catherine mentioned how occasionally she'd been having lunch with Joan, but their conversations weren't what they'd once been and it was sometimes hard to talk.

"You never would've known she'd once gone to law school, as she only talks about her children," Catherine reported.

"Well, it sounds like she has a pleasant, if not boring, life. What I wouldn't do for that! We were always afraid that would happen to Joan," Grace said.

It had been quite some time since the four friends had gotten together. Catherine and Grace then checked their appointment planners and came up with possible dates for lunch the following month. Hopefully, the other two women would join. Since finances were tricky for almost everyone, why not have it at Catherine's apartment? Grace readily agreed, noticing how Catherine returned her planner to a dingy and worn purse.

"I know, let's take ourselves shopping and see what we can find," Catherine said, trying to change the serious mood. Her friend readily agreed, but then added that she had little money for purchases.

As they were counting out coins to pay their lunch bills, the elderly couple who'd been staring at them earlier now stood at their table. They stared down at the two women.

"There ought to be a law keeping Coloreds out of such a fine establishment. Milly and I are putting in a complaint to the manager. We thought you two should know in case you decide to dine here again."

"There's no such law, nor will there ever be, at least not in Detroit. And how do we know? We're both attorneys and we protect folks from people like you." Catherine's voice was low, but quiet and steady. Had the couple not turned on their heels and left, her Irish ire would have known no bounds. She apologized to her friend.

"Catherine, let's not dwell on stupid people. What say we do some shopping?"

The store wasn't crowded, despite Hudson's ad campaign about their new layaway policy. While uncertain if they liked the idea of the store 'holding' items until they could purchase them, both women easily chose a few skirts and blouses to test out this new concept. In a month they'd—hopefully—be able to return to pay what they owed. Besides, it gave them another reason to get together for lunch—not that they needed any.

CHAPTER THIRTY-EIGHT

1932

Unlike many during the Great Depression, Bob and Gene had greater job security than many and remained lucky to be employed. Although Gene wasn't a practicing attorney, both brothers got hired within a month of each other by a large and well-respected law firm. Bob preferred private practice and missed working with his wife, but certainly, during these tough times, he'd be more secure working with a group of attorneys. Gene continued to work as a probation officer with an eye toward one day handling legal cases. Sometime soon, we'll open up our own practice—with or without Catherine—Bob would say. Gene would smile, but clearly had misgivings.

The large firm, a duplicitous one like many during that era, defended professional criminals, while determined to bring down the city's criminal underworld. Sadly, the waters got muddied: mug shots were taken of both those who were hungry and just trying to feed themselves and their families, along with the professional criminals. Bob knew which cases to take and which ones to pass along. His name recognition and 'fighting' personality helped bring in more cases. While his pro bono work for juvenile offenders was frowned upon, the three men running the firm turned a blind eye so he could continue helping the disadvantaged. Also, they more than appreciated his scoops about the dealings of the Irish gang.

Catherine, besides working for the prosecutors, gave free legal advice to poor women — especially regarding divorce and abusive husbands. Grace and Catherine often worked together in Grace's office late into the night. Tired and anxious women sat in the waiting room, willing to wait hours hoping to speak to either of them. When no chairs were left, a line would form. Many of the stories were heart-wrenching. Having suffered abuse from their own husbands, Catherine and Grace were all the more empathetic. Catherine's guilt over her privileged lifestyle could never be expunged. It was something she wished she could talk about with Grace, but she never did.

Catherine often came home exhausted to the waiting Mr. Mercedes who jumped into her lap as soon as she sat down.

The couple had scaled back from their little indulgences, specifically their wild nights on the town and new clothes. In no longer wearing perfume daily, Catherine learned how to make it last. Bob rarely showed up in the back-room poker parlors, and now had little time for cavorting with women. Still, there was always plenty to eat. They could continue living in the Whittier, though they'd decided against buying a house, especially since they wouldn't have children. They laughed at how neither of them was any good at home maintenance, and marveled at Gene and Violet's immaculate yard and neat-as-a-pin home on the city's west side. Bob continued to spoil his nephew at Christmas and birthdays. Young Bob's favorite present had been a springer spaniel who — much to Violet's protestations — became her son's constant (and often only) companion. The two Bobs often took Tippy out for long walks together.

Bob had several friends, but few close ones, despite his involvement in the male-dominated boxing world. He remained a 'lady's man' and preferred their company to the all-too competitive and tough guy types he knew. Some thought it was because he didn't want it known how soft-hearted he was, though those who knew him best believed he couldn't care less about how others perceived him; he simply found women's company preferable. He enjoyed how alive he felt in their presence. But lately, on weekends, he could be found at a boxing gym downtown, coaching young boys.

Despite Catherine's loss of Grammy and Uncle Gerry, she no longer drank excessively, though Bob didn't like how secretive she'd be on those nights she came home late. He knew about her volunteer work, though she rarely discussed it with him. While he admired her ability to keep friends, it wasn't long after she began working again at the Prosecutor's Office when she began having frequent lunches or shopping trips with Grace. Kind of odd, as she never brought home any packages. Wasn't there a guy who'd been sweet on Catherine the first time she'd worked there? When Bob had asked her about it, she outright denied it.

He knew plenty of private investigators. It might be the right time to contact one—just to keep tabs on her.

One Saturday night after returning from an outing with Bobby, he confided in his brother.

"You recall that fellow—the PI—Jay Riley? We knew him from the neighborhood," Bob said, referring to their stomping grounds in Corktown.

"Sure, do. A good guy with a nose like a beagle's. What makes you bring him up?" Gene asked.

Bob explained.

"You'd really have your wife tailed? What'll you do if you find out she is seeing someone? How do you plan to keep that Irish temper under wraps?" Gene wasn't surprised that men found Catherine irresistible. He sure had, though he'd known better than to pursue his brother's wife.

"I don't know. Curse of us Irish—all except you, Gene. Wish I could be a mild-mannered gentleman like you, but we're born who we are, right? Haven't you ever had to wonder about Violet? I mean she's a looker and goes off to play cards with friends twice a week. Doesn't that sometimes make you wonder?"

"No, can't say it worries me much, seeing as I drive her to her parties. But if she did even act—suspicious—and cause me any doubt, I'd let her go to them, knowing she'll always come home to me."

"Gene Sage, you're certainly the better man! Mind you, you haven't talked me out of contacting Jay, but you've given me pause. I love Kate to pieces and maybe that's part of the problem. She's mine, but I don't own her. These modern dames, brother, they're hard to fathom. Kate's complicated and has this wild side like no other. I should've married a gal more like Ma or Vi."

"Don't be so hard on Kate. You're lucky she gave a Mick like you a second look."

Bob knew his brother was right and laughed his soundless laughter, because of his damaged voice box. Gene did likewise— not to poke fun at his brother, but just because he'd adopted the habit. They both chewed on toothpicks.

Bobby witnessed this as he was coming back into the room from his bedroom with a model plane to show his uncle. He laughed aloud at the silent, near hysterics of the two men. Then he snickered some more when he noticed their toothpicks.

Bob cuffed the younger Bob on the head before taking leave.

"You're all right, kid," he said, handing Bobby a dollar from his wallet. Bobby's eyes became sage-green saucers in his pallid face, before running off to put it in his piggy bank. When the boy was out of earshot, the brothers made plans to take him to the newly opened Detroit Zoo.

CHAPTER THIRTY-NINE

Catherine left work early to spend time with her sister, Molly. Taking time off work was something she rarely did, especially with people — particularly women — getting sacked from jobs in ever-growing numbers in the early 1930s.

The streetcar was full of grim faces. Catherine had never seen the sky so gray. The gulls circling overhead looked more like buzzards in an industrial graveyard. Even the ding of the streetcar sounded weary. What had happened to Detroit's charm? So much for Paris of the West...

A week earlier, Molly had doubled over in labor pains at seven months along. She knew it was way too soon. Following several hours of intermittent cramping that continued to worsen, Molly convinced her husband to take her to the hospital.

Edward loathed anything to be out of order in his life. He was annoyed that Molly had interrupted his nightly routine. His mood worsened by her moans whenever she took a step, as they readied to leave for the hospital. Seeing his grimace, she readily apologized. Catherine knew her sister adored Edward — or Eddy — as she called him, and always tried to please him. She couldn't fathom how Molly could love such a man.

Several days later Catherine visited Molly in her darkened bedroom. Catherine sat at her bedside holding her hands, clueless about what to say. Then Molly had asked if the baby would have lived had she gone sooner to the hospital. Catherine repeatedly reassured her that the infant wouldn't have survived since the umbilical cord had become detached. This seemed to relieve Molly, though she remained listless on her bed.

Catherine partially opened the drapes, and Molly cringed, as she veiled her face with her hand.

"Kate, you don't have to stay with me. I'll be okay. If you're worried, I'm going to hurt myself — you needn't be." Molly's lips were chapped and her skin had a worrisome pallor.

This was precisely why Catherine planned on regularly visiting her sister, as she'd made several veiled suicide threats to loved ones in the first few days following her miscarriage.

"How about if I read aloud to you, as I refuse to budge, big sister?"

"Go ahead. I'm just going to shut my eyes while I listen."

Catherine, sitting in a bedside chair, began reading a story from *The Saturday Evening Post* about a search for a missing dog. Molly loved stories even, more than Catherine, and had been penning her own ever since she was a girl. She'd shared several — especially the ones for children. Catherine's favorite was a recent one about a woman — an artist — who murdered her older sister who'd always criticized her artwork. It was more than obvious that Molly had described their sister, Eileen (though both believed Eileen incapable of murder). Molly never shared her stories with Eileen, and certainly wouldn't this one. Catherine encouraged Molly to publish them, but she lacked the confidence.

Molly's eyes popped open once her sister finished reading. Unlike Catherine's gray-blue eyes, hers were a startling sapphire blue.

"Did I tell you I'd been planning on resuming my search for her?" Molly asked, barely audible.

At first, Catherine hadn't known who she was speaking about, then realized her sister was referring to the baby from Molly's first pregnancy. Molly, at fourteen, had given the baby up for adoption. Their parents had forbidden her to show her face in public during the entire pregnancy. The day following the birth, they'd whisked the newborn away from her. All Molly had been told was that suitable parents had been found, as well as a wet nurse. Molly claimed her mother was still ashamed of her, though Catherine claimed otherwise. No one had ever spoken of the baby again, except Catherine.

"Had it not been for your kindness, Kate, I know I would've killed myself," she whispered.

Catherine, speechless, leaned across the bed and clasped her sister's hands again.

She was the only one Molly would turn to during a crisis, though Eileen was forever trying to recruit Molly into taking sides against her.

In Eileen's eyes, Catherine was a well-educated woman, but 'loose' and a 'floozy,' which was way worse than Molly, who'd only once made a mistake. While Eileen would never directly accuse Catherine of having less than a sterling character, there was always an undercurrent of judgment. Once Eileen had called her a 'sodden whore' under her breath, but loud enough for Catherine to hear. She, naturally, denied saying it. Eileen knew better than to poison their parents' view of Catherine—to them, Catherine could almost walk on water. Still, Eileen always helped in a family crisis; no one could deny that she was a good and caring mother. She was mostly bitter that no one had encouraged her to attend college. Eileen viewed herself as smarter than her two sisters put together. Maybe she was.

How could Catherine not have been there for Molly? She'd held her hand on Catherine's first day of school. Two years older, Molly had always been like a little mother. Before bedtime and when Catherine was sick, she'd read aloud to her, and complimented her whenever she did something well. Catherine hadn't been in school long before she'd zipped past her older sister in all subjects—except music and art, in which she'd never had much aptitude. But until Molly became pregnant, Catherine had always followed in her footsteps. And now it was Molly who followed in hers.

Molly sat bolt upright in bed. "That's it. No more children for me. I'm done," she said in an emphatic and determined tone. Catherine knew better than to disagree. Another pregnancy could ruin Molly's health, as another one could ruin her own, as well.

"Have you told Edward?"

"Not yet. Eddy will try to argue since he loves kids. Once he understands my feelings, he may try to coax me into adopting, but I don't have the energy. I'm not like you, Kate, with your good health, despite your evil ways!" Molly said, laughing for the first time, though it was more of a nasally snicker.

Catherine joined in. "I do have evil ways, don't I? But seriously, don't let him bully you into doing something you don't want. Lord, I hate how pushy men can be!"

At that very moment, their mother and eldest sister walked in, wearing worried expressions and carrying bags of groceries. Catherine knew Molly wouldn't share her thoughts on the subject with them. After a few minutes of family updates, Molly pulled the blankets up to her chin and shut her eyes. Her mother and sisters quieted their voices and darkened the room again by pulling the drapes shut tight.

"Kate, dear, you needn't leave work early to see your sister. It's easy for Eileen and me to stop by," Bridget said, as they were leaving.

"Speak for yourself, mother," said Eileen. "Don't forget, I've got a job at home, though I don't get paid for it."

"Eileen, you know what I meant. Seriously though, Kate, why don't you just stop by after work?"

"I guess it's because Edward's home by then. Look, we all do what we're able to. I'm sure Molly won't need us to come over so much as the days go on," Catherine replied.

. . .

The chilly March day of the burials wasn't nearly as brutal as on the day of the Hunger March. Although Catherine and Bob couldn't attend the march, they now stood at the cemetery in solemn solidarity with thousands of like-minded others. They wore their dark and drab winter coats like many others. Bob's cashmere coat and her furs were tucked in the back of their clothes closet. The sobbing of the mourning families at the fresh graves burst into the frigid air, subsided, and then bellowed again. The rawness of their grief was both distressing and incomprehensible.

The Ford factory laid off two-thirds of its workers by March of 1932. At one time, it had been the largest employer in the area. The layoff wasn't the single-most factor but a major one, leading to hunger and frustration. Detroit got hit especially hard by the Depression. Henry Ford refused to meet the protesters' demands. According to many, the wealthy man had blood on his hands after the 'Ford Massacre' at the Detroit Hunger March. Four men from the Young Communist League had marched peacefully only to have been gunned down by Dearborn police and Ford's hired hands. Many others were injured.

Catherine and Bob were shocked and then outraged. They had no choice but to attend the burials. Also, the day before, Bob had been hired by the family of one of the young men who had been killed.

Bob had become even better friends with Frank Murphy, who was now the mayor of Detroit. Mayor Murphy had allowed the march, though he'd never explicitly given a permit for the event. Bob claimed the sympathetic mayor felt terrible about the outcome of the march, though afterward Frank Murphy, too, would receive some of the blame.

Despite their lack of closeness during this time, the couple bonded over the event. They both helped spread the word by passing out leaflets about the cemetery gathering. Many would later claim that up to sixty thousand gathered at Woodmere Cemetery, to both pay respects and show unity for the cause. While the wealthy Henry Ford couldn't be blamed for the Depression many now viewed him as evil. Catherine wondered how Ford would be recorded by history. Would people remember how he'd treated his workers?

After the day of solidarity, she was ready to join the Communist Party. Bob talked her out of it, telling her it would prevent them from ever being able to hold public office. "C'mon, Kate…You don't want to be known as Red Kate, do you?" He also added that her timing was bad because of the pending case. She claimed not to give a 'rat's ass,' yet decided against becoming a card-carrying member. And it was Catherine who helped him frame the argument for the family, which ultimately held up in court.

Afterward, the long line of Ford cars inched their way down the streets next to the cemetery. Catherine and Bob had been amazed at how long it took to drive home. They were encouraged by the number of people who, like them, refused to sit idly by while the world turned upside down.

CHAPTER FORTY

Standing alongside Nana as she ladled out soup gave Catherine a new resolve to remain there until the last in line had received their share. If this older and somewhat frail woman could do it, well then, so could she. It was a damp, gray day in late October and Catherine's third time that fall volunteering to help feed a hungry city.

No one in the Sage or McIntosh families had—so far—lost their jobs, though incomes had dwindled. Both families, especially the Sages, felt the need to support Boystown - a Catholic orphanage for boys. But as far as Catherine was concerned, donating money after Sunday mass didn't go far enough, nor did the free legal counsel she gave out whenever a client couldn't pay. Yet standing here, helping those most in need, at least gave her some satisfaction.

It was the first time she'd gotten out of bed in three days since the funeral.

She still couldn't imagine being in the world without her friend. Never would they take that trip to New York together.

Almost a week ago, Grace's body had been found hanging from a noose in her living room. After not having seen Grace for several days, a neighbor from the next-door apartment pounded on her door. When there was no response, the neighbor, Louise, a sweet elderly woman, had twisted the knob and found it unlocked. How typical of Grace to have been thoughtful, that way.

Grace had been a brilliant attorney who'd lost her job simply because of the color of her skin. Had times not been so tough, maybe she would still have her career—would still be here, but Catherine knew there was more to it. Her friend hadn't had enough support—either emotional or financial—to keep living her difficult life. Sam, her estranged husband had been as jealous as he'd been mean. Grace would've been willing to overlook those qualities had he moved back in with her, but no way was she going to quit her job just so he could 'save face.' Her few remaining family members lived in the South. Besides Catherine and their small group of friends, she'd had no one else to turn to.

Louise said Grace only had a rotten potato and a crust of dry bread left on her pantry shelves.

Louise called Catherine because Grace had Catherine's phone number written on a pad next to the phone.

Catherine was certain she'd been a lousy friend. A better one wouldn't have let this happen. Why hadn't Grace let her know about how bad things had become? When they'd last seen each other the previous month, Grace had only hinted about her situation. Looking back, she had seemed quieter than usual, less animated. They'd mostly talked about Molly's miscarriage. Catherine should've done more to make her friend open up; she had failed her.

Bob, initially sympathetic after hearing of Grace's suicide, hadn't understood why Catherine had taken it so hard: refusing to eat, pacing, and smoking like a chimney.

"The losses add up, Bob. While I haven't had a best friend—besides you—Grace was next in line."

"I had nothing against you being friends, but a close friend? She was a Colored!"

Catherine was floored by his remark. It was like he'd punched her and knocked the wind out of her. At last, she recovered: "What's that got to do with anything? Did that really come out of your mouth?" It wouldn't have surprised her had steam poured from her nose and mouth.

"Calm down, Kate. I meant nothing by —"

"You sure did! You sound like some southern Cracker!" Catherine's skin crawled just before heating to a boil.

"I know plenty of folks here in the North, Kate, who wouldn't be nearly so understanding if their spouse was friends with one of them."

"Good to know where you stand. Guess I'm a little surprised — all those boys you coach..."

"I don't see how that's at all the same."

"Leave me be, please, Bob. I was completely exhausted before this conversation even began." How fast her anger turned into despair.

Bob backed out of the bedroom, slamming the bedroom door behind him.

Then there'd been Grace's funeral. It was held at Grace's Baptist church. The funeral had been well-attended because she stood out — not only as a female in a male profession but as a Black woman. Several pews were filled by law school alumni. Curious, as most hadn't remained in contact with Grace. If even a few had, maybe there would've been no need for a funeral. But she was gone and there was no changing that. It was Catherine's greatest hope her friend would be included in the history books, though something told her that was a tall order.

Bob attended the funeral with Catherine and held her hand throughout. It meant more than she let on, though she was still angry with him over his earlier remarks. Joan and Margaret sat next to them in the pew, clutching damp handkerchiefs. Professor Higgins and Dean Hally sat in the row behind them. Catherine openly wept.

. . .

Catherine had spent part of the previous evening with Nana who'd encouraged her to help in the soup line. She'd held Catherine's hand in her candlelit room. They'd closed their eyes for only a few moments when Catherine experienced a momentary rush of warm air. Her eyes sprang open.

"Nana, did you feel that?" she whispered.

"It was Grace's spirit," began Nana. "She had a message: 'My dear Catherine, will you?'"

"Will I — what?"

Nana's messages from the Beyond could be so infuriating!

"When you opened your eyes you must have interrupted the whole message. Let's try again," whispered Nana.

For several minutes they waited for Grace to return and finish her question, but it soon became apparent to Nana that Catherine's friend was long gone. Catherine would wonder about her friend's request for the rest of her life. Still, Grace had called her 'Dear,' so at least Catherine knew her friend had cared for her.

Before Catherine left to meet Bob for a drink, Nana gave her a bear hug. Catherine felt a burst of energy, a wakefulness she thought she'd never experience again. Maybe that's what Grace had wanted.

"Anytime you'd like me to help you get in touch with Grace, I'm more than happy to assist. Still, we never know about spirits, they can be a bit flighty," Nana said, smoothing the collar of Catherine's jacket.

"Nana, I certainly appreciate your — abilities. It truly helps reinforce my faith in an afterlife, but now that she's communicated — even though we didn't receive her full message — I think I'll just look for Grace in my dreams."

"Well, if you change your mind, my dear, just let me know. How early are you able to meet me at the soup line in Grand Circus Park? They'll have the food ready around noon."

"Then noon it is! I hope my heart doesn't further break when I see all those hungry faces."

"Catherine, you're one of the fighting Irish! Do remember that our ancestors made it through a potato famine. Not much worse than that. We've all got tough hides."

"You're right, Nana. I'm certain you are."

Catherine relayed Bob's mother's 'sage' words to him over a drink at the bar of Tommy's Detroit Bar, a legendary basement speakeasy. Bob threw his head back and roared with near silent laughter. He couldn't have looked more like a lion, even if he'd had a mane.

"She thinks she's so tough, Kate, but she's got the softest heart I know."

While Catherine agreed, she couldn't help but feel a twinge of jealousy. It was obvious Bob's feelings for her had diminished in their close to ten years together. Too many other issues clamored for her attention, so she refused to cater to the green-eyed monster within.

"By the way, Kate, I wanted to apologize for questioning your closeness with Grace."

"Apology accepted. I guess most wouldn't understand. The prejudice against Negroes sure has been getting worse since the Depression began...Think you'll find some time to help us out tomorrow? We could always use an extra pair of hands and some of your friendly bluster," Catherine said, lighting one cigarette from the butt of another.

Bob said he'd see what he could do to fit it into his busy schedule. He had a court appearance, plus a meeting with a couple of clients—hard to say how long the meeting would take. Catherine's hours clerking at the Prosecutor's Office had been reduced and she was only working a few days per week.

Tomorrow was one of her days off. Ordinarily, she was helping in the free legal aid clinic, but helping the needy was way more important.

Bob suggested a nightcap, but Catherine declined for once because she needed her energy for the next day.

He told her he was proud of what he hoped was her new resolve. Maybe he'd cut back, too. All too easy to become a booze-hound in the fast-paced world they lived in. Neither of them had the energy they had in their youth.

. . .

The many small bare trees of downtown's Grand Circus Park weren't protected much by the surrounding tall buildings. There stood the Tuller Hotel where they'd stayed so long ago. Staring at it now, as she poured soup, she recalled their — mostly — romantic evening. Where was Bob? It was going on two and he said he'd be here by now. She wasn't surprised. It had nothing to do with him not wanting to help, but because his meetings had probably lasted longer than he thought — or so she hoped. He was also trying to be the main breadwinner since her income, while reliable, didn't amount to much. Bob was at his happiest when busy, but not her. She craved solitude and a good book.

Nana introduced her to a few friends of hers — nurses like herself. And Catherine was pleasantly surprised to see some acquaintances from law school. They were women who either hadn't become (or yet become), successful as attorneys, despite their qualifications. Two had given up their careers for motherhood. Catherine counted herself lucky to have a part-time job in the legal world, even if she rarely got the chance to try cases.

She couldn't get over the many pale and ashen faces, most with sunken eyes and despair beyond sadness. One after another, they slowly shuffled their way up to the soup table.

Only the younger ones showed trace amounts of hope. Not all looked skeletal, but all were hungry and jobless. She'd never seen people in such rough shape. While her family had never had much money, they'd never gone hungry.

Following her shift, Catherine couldn't wait to return home to soak in a hot bath. Maybe she'd more remembering of that bygone time at the Tuller. She would help ladle soup again, but just not right away. Later, she'd realize how it had kept her mind from dwelling on the loss of her dear friend and her sister's miscarriage.

CHAPTER FORTY-ONE

1933

While Bob couldn't help at the soup line that day downtown, not only did he join Catherine on several other occasions, but together they also sponsored clothing and food drives. They championed those who needed financial help by persuading landlords to allow renters to live rent-free until assistance began. The new President, Franklin Delano Roosevelt, gave hope and stamina to a weary nation. Together, with like-minded others, they helped make his message a reality. This helped to strengthen their bond — for a time.

Bob decided not to hire a P.I. to follow her. Still, Catherine laughed less often and he'd become less affable than his former self – gruffer than ever before – not only with her but everyone except his mother.

One night, Bob returned from a poker game with a cut lip and a blood-smeared, torn shirt. He had a wild look in his eyes. At first, Catherine couldn't get him to stop pacing so she could tend his eye.

"Please just sit down so I can see if you need stitches."

At last, he complied. As she cleaned the dried blood from his cheek, he told her about what had led up to the fight.

"This guy — Jimmy Calhoun…you remember him?"

"That attorney who owns a few apartment buildings?"

"Yeah, that's the one. I can't believe he calls himself a landlord. Told me he's going to soon start tossing his tenants out on the streets. Seems none of them have paid up. Who would want to move into the dingy, squalid places? I asked Jimmy, but he didn't have an answer. Since so many come up from the South, they'd be pleased with any old roof over their heads, he said. I repeated myself, and told him he wouldn't find anyone else to live in them, so why not let them stay? He considered it for a second, but then said his mind was made up. I slugged him right in the chops. For the love of Christ, it felt like the old days, but now I had a good reason to make a guy lose a tooth or two!"

Catherine told him next time maybe he could just work a little harder at his power of persuasion.

With that, Bob got up from his chair and chased her through the apartment. Thankfully, his wounds were superficial ones. A giggling Catherine shrieked once they'd reached the bedroom, and began pelting pillows at him. He threw them back at her and then threw her onto the bed. Wild abandon ensued. A couple months later, both would recall their passionate night and knew that must have been when Catherine got pregnant.

Before knowing she was pregnant, she lost her job at the Prosecutor's Office. While crime in the city was up in January of 1933, Catherine was among several — mostly women — who were laid off. While she knew better, at first it seemed like she'd been fired for poor job performance. She gulped her gin drinks and chain-smoked. Bob reminded her over and over not to take it personally. He wondered if she was going to look for another job. Of course, she would, Catherine told him, though it could take a while to find one in the legal field. She joked that if she couldn't, she'd consider prostitution.

Bob slapped her and she fell backward. She turned away from him and sobbed into a pillow.

This time he felt justified and didn't console her. She'd become an opponent, and an unworthy one at that.

DANCING IN THE RING

Then Catherine slept deeply for several hours and afterward was queasy and had a problem staying awake. She sipped coffee at the dining room table, while he ate bacon and eggs. The coffee and food aromas nauseated her. Could she once again be pregnant?

"No way!" Bob said.

"Oh, there could well be a 'way.' Recall that night after your poker game?"

He did. After they got over the shock, they waited a month before telling anyone. Strangely, that month proved one of the happiest—though groggiest—of Catherine's life. While she didn't stop drinking entirely, she cut way back. Lucky Strikes smelled strange, so she only smoked a few per day. She slept in and daydreamed about how happy the news would make her family—especially her mother and sisters. It amused her to think how they'd once been opposed to raising a child.

Bob became less gruff—tender almost, kissing his wife before leaving for work and a hug every evening when he came home. Sure, she recalled how he could get when he lost his temper, but maybe fatherhood would change him. She found herself humming. They began searching for a house with two bedrooms, hoping to find one in the nice little neighborhood on the west side of the city near where his brother lived. She would make curtains for the windows, and tend a vegetable and flower garden. Bobby would have a cousin. Maybe she'd even learn how to knit booties. By the time their child would be in school, the economy would have picked up, and their law practice would again be prosperous.

Most of Catherine's family was thrilled by her announcement, as were the Sages, and Joan and Margaret. The world truly seemed to have righted itself. Was it too much to hope that Eileen and she would now feel closer? A few weeks earlier, Catherine learned Molly was pregnant again, too. Catherine hadn't told her about her own pregnancy.

"Mum's the word," she said to the rest of the family. She wanted to be the one to tell Molly when the time was right. They agreed. She hadn't wanted to overshadow Molly's good news.

Then she invited Molly over for lunch one day.

After hearing Catherine's news, Molly almost spilled a spoonful of soup onto her lap, but then quickly regained her calm, after hugging her younger sister.

"Let's hope the cousins will be friends someday!" Catherine told her. "Maybe the toppled-over world has righted itself again!"

Molly gave her a nod and a half-smile. Only a few months along herself, Molly's recent miscarriage must have still been on her mind.

"Katy, I haven't seen you this jolly since I don't know when," said Molly. The sisters silently ate the small meal of tomato soup and grilled cheese sandwiches. It was too bad her Molly wasn't happier for her, but Catherine understood why. It had been important to inform her in person with no one else around.

"I beg your pardon, sis, I thought I was just being optimistic. I'm a little nervous, of course, but why worry? I must admit that I'm somewhat surprised you tried again," said Catherine, wiping the corner of her mouth with a cloth napkin.

"Who said I was even trying? Like yours, my pregnancy wasn't planned. I'm glad you're excited, Kate, I really am, but maybe cut back on all that running around you do and keep your feet up as often as possible."

"I promise, big sister, but isn't it kind of fun being pregnant at the same time?"

Molly smiled, but then changed the topic. Catherine looked outside at a gull riding on a block of ice floating down the river. The wintry sun poked its face in and out of bulky clouds.

.   .   .

But then on an early spring morning, Catherine woke up to a huge bloodstain on her white sheets. She was burning up. In a dream, she'd been sitting next to Amelia Earhart in the cockpit of a plane. They'd both gaped in awe at the Earth below. Was there blood because they'd crashed? Was she dying? She screamed like she never had before.

Bob drove her to the hospital and the doctor confirmed it: she'd lost the baby. Why did they have to call it a 'baby'? It was Catherine's second miscarriage. She'd been three months along in the pregnancy. The room spun. It felt like the bottom of the world had fallen off. She loathed the man in the white coat wearing a stethoscope. Who did he think he was? Bob kept petting her damp, snarled hair, so she knocked his hand away. She longed to be alone in a dark cave. Why couldn't they all just leave her alone? Then again, being alone with her thoughts would be the worst. How could life be so cruel?

At least Molly hadn't miscarried. A jealous wave passed through her entire being, almost drowning her.

Catherine sobbed in Bob's arms. He cried silently, much like the way he laughed, heaving slightly as he did. He'd make sure to never let her know the depths of his despair.

As the days went by, Catherine returned to her former habits, except this time she'd lost all interest in conversing. She preferred quiet nights spent smoking in the dark. The only person she wanted to talk to was her dead friend, Grace. Her other friends, Joan and Margaret, were simply friends to have lunch with and reminisce about law school. They didn't know each other on a deeper level, the way Grace and she had.

Bob told Catherine she was suffering from a nervous breakdown. While she'd been telling herself it was grief, she nodded in agreement. He suggested she think about going to a sanatorium. There, she could take her time recovering and slowly regain her strength. She adamantly refused. Don't you think, Bob, if people went to one every time they suffered a loss—there'd be almost as many sanatoriums as houses? She didn't, however, have the energy to say this.

Molly and Nana stopped by for a visit, but not her mother. Nana admitted that while she hadn't foreseen Catherine having a miscarriage, she'd sensed that the family was in for a period of dark times. She tried to reassure the younger woman by telling her that the light would soon shine again. Molly did her best to soothe her troubled sister. She brought up the time they'd put a mouse in their parents' bed, and another when they'd witnessed their parents outside dancing in the rain. Catherine smiled wanly and then gazed out the window. Her older sister left before an hour had elapsed.

Catherine was convinced that her mother was ashamed of her—beyond embarrassed. She felt as if she'd betrayed her family, even though it was her body that hadn't complied with her dreams and desires. She was jealous of Molly. The thought of physical intimacy with Bob made her queasy. She only longed for booze, cigarettes, and Mr. Mercedes. She played the popular Louis Armstrong song "All of Me" repeatedly on the Victrola. "Why not take all of me?" she hummed along.

CHAPTER FORTY-TWO

One night in Corktown, Bob sat in a back pew of Most Holy Trinity Catholic Church. He'd become almost a regular attendee at Printer's Mass and was amazed at the number of fellow Catholics there so late at night. Printer's Mass was a special mass for printers and other workers unable to attend the regular Sunday mass. Not wanting to be seen, he'd chosen to sit in a pew at the back of the sanctuary. He leaned forward, resting on the kneeler, and then rested his head in his arms on the empty seat in front of him.

Bob wept and prayed for the little soul who'd spent so brief a time in his wife's body. He wept and prayed for Catherine. He'd been amazed at how excited he'd been about having a child and how he'd so looked forward to their lives being forever changed. While he had his doubts about her ability to be as domestic as his mother, he didn't once doubt her maternal instincts. He knew she'd make a loving mother, despite a few shortcomings. It was then—weeping like a child—he concluded that sex was for procreation. Bob had been taught this, of course, but before, he'd always overlooked that piece of information because of how enjoyable sex could be. Catherine told him the previous night how she definitely wouldn't want to try again and suggested they adopt. He'd readily agreed, though now he'd mostly lost interest in having sex with her. Surely, it wasn't a good idea to raise a child in a sexless marriage. He'd be surprised if she didn't feel the same.

Bob shuddered. Again he dropped his heavy head, realizing how much he envied his brother. Gene could be slow as a turtle, but it would be Gene who would win the race. His life was stable: he had a good wife, a son, a decent career as a probation officer, plus he was a homeowner. His temper never got the best of him. In short, he'd proven to be the better son. Bob Sage was a flash in the pan—a one-trick pony whose glory days were gone. Gene would live to a wise old age, but he doubted that he, himself, would be so lucky. No doubt his mother knew this, too, and pitied him. He shuddered again and wiped the tears from his cheeks.

He was the last to take Communion, and the last parishioner to leave the church. A couple of guys—acquaintances—lingered on the church steps and yelled out to him. Bob waved but kept walking. Sometimes it was important to keep a low profile. He walked against the wind that cold, late winter night. Hard to believe it could be spring. What he knew now and doubted before was that he loved his wife, he truly did.

CHAPTER FORTY-THREE

1934

"C'mon, Bob—it's Friday night. Let's go kick up our heels! I've got some new dance moves I'm dying to show you!"

"Sure, Doll-face, but give this working man time to snooze first, okay?" Bob yawned like a tired lion. Catherine snarled but let him rest.

Over a year had passed since Catherine's miscarriage and nervous breakdown. She'd recovered most of her former energy. The support of family and friends had helped get her through the darkest days. It was a nervous, frenzied liveliness, but her desire to kick up her heels on the dance floor surprised herself, as well as Bob. She wasn't down for the count, after all. Now that Prohibition was over, new dance halls that served liquor sprang up around the city. Still, she'd eased off the heavy drinking.

Could a changed outlook so renew the world? It sure had proved to truly be a lusty month of May. Flowers burst from their buds; blooms were twice the size as the previous year.

Catherine pouted but reluctantly played solitaire, while her husband snoozed with Mr. Mercedes fast asleep on his stomach. All that afternoon she'd pictured themselves as Zelda and F. Scott Fitzgerald. She wondered if they had a cat. Not only because Bob and she could get a little crazy like the famous literary pair, but because Catherine had been writing poetry lately. And while Bob didn't pen his tales, he'd always been a storyteller; she was most certain F. Scott would enjoy his wild and bawdy stories if they'd been sitting together at a bar.

What she truly longed for was to get the past behind her. While she wanted to get back to volunteer work, she also wanted to feel that former zest for life — that joy — which gave her the energy to help others. Maybe they could begin planning their next trip — even a European adventure.

Catherine could hear him snoring away from the bedroom. After an hour of solitaire, she loudly began to whistle 'All of Me.' Bob stirred and rolled over, but continued to snore. Unable to wait any longer, she tickled his feet.

With nearly the speed of a bullet, he flew from the bed. "What is it you want, Kate?"

"You promised we'd go out."

"Yeah, guess I did…But never tickle my feet again or I swear to God, I'm gonna slug you in your kisser!"

Instead of flinching, she smirked, and then made a fist. Don't even think about it, buddy. She quietly pouted until he got up and readied himself for a night on the dance floor.

It was on this sultry, late spring night they danced with others, though they promised to come home with each other. Attention from the opposite sex and even a little flirtation was harmless, Bob proposed. Catherine agreed. Not a mortal sin. It would make them feel young again, both silently thought.

Catherine, in a gauzy silver gown — less flashy than the ones she wore in the 1920s — danced with four other men besides her husband. She didn't catch their names. Bob interrupted one of her partners, but he was too busy twirling on the floor with one particular woman to give much notice to his wife.

On the way home, Bob told her the woman's name. Sophie. She was a ballet dancer and didn't drink. Also, she was a young widow with a little boy who looked somewhat like Bobby — at least from a photo. What he didn't say was that he found Sophie to be the most graceful woman there.

He pulled up to a fountain in front of the Tuller Hotel. They spoke wistfully about their night together there. Before getting teary-eyed about their early days, Bob suggested they run through the fountain to cool off. As they laughed and splashed about, they almost forgot their changed relationship. Catherine told him how this was exactly something F. Scott Fitzgerald and his wife, Zelda, would do.

"Couldn't you compare me to someone more of a man's man like Hemingway, not Fitzgerald."

Laughing, she admitted that he might have something there.

Bob then spoke further about Sophie, as if Catherine was a buddy and not his wife. She felt like he'd slapped her. Why was he rattling on and on? He must have had more to drink than usual, but his words hadn't sounded slurred and he'd had little problem driving the car home. It was different this time—must have been the liquor talking. This must have been like what F. Scott would say to Zelda when he'd tell her about his interest in another woman.

Catherine no longer wanted to be Zelda. "Why are you going on and on about Sophie? All I asked was her name."

"But my dear, I'm merely being honest, like we agreed. Isn't it refreshing not to hide things?"

"How much did you drink, Bob?

"One—no, I guess, two. You think my telling you about Sophie is because I've had too much? Do I sound drunk?"

"No, I suppose not, but are you trying to make me jealous? Just shut up about her, will you?"

"If you'd found some man interesting, I'd want to know. Putting my cards on the table is all I'm doing, my darling."

Not so long ago, Catherine had lost a good friend, her job, and a miscarriage. Bob had the audacity to go on and on about another woman—a woman he desired more than her? The world had gone to hell, make a quick exit now?

From the passenger seat, she grabbed the wheel and began veering toward a large tree.

Bob, quick with his hands, grabbed the wheel back in the nick of time. "What the hell were you thinking? Were you trying to get us both killed?"

Catherine didn't answer. She looked down at her hands and folded then in her lap. Shouldn't they be trembling? That they weren't would bother her for the next several days. She'd wanted — in that moment — to kill both Bob and Sophie. Later, she would think — why bother — as Bob and Kate as a couple had already died, and their two bodies were only going through the motions of being alive.

Shaken to the core, he could barely look at her. Earlier, Catherine seemed almost like her old self and he'd felt relieved that she could still enjoy life. While he wasn't anywhere nearly as attracted to her as before, he cared for her — yes, even loved her, even though his passion had all but vanished. Where could they go from here?

CHAPTER FORTY-FOUR

Catherine woke up certain her nightgown was on fire. She kept swatting at invisible flames, before recalling the nightmare of landing a plane in a dust storm. She'd had it before. The plane became engulfed in flames and she couldn't get out of the cockpit. She felt ill. This time it wasn't due to a miscarriage. Did she have the flu? Had the pandemic of 1918 returned? Maybe she was dying. Her life was over and she was still young. She lay stone-still for the longest time. When she didn't expire, she called out to Bob in a kitten-weak voice.

She had no other symptoms besides a fever, except for a headache. Bob, at least so far, hadn't caught it.

After the mystery virus dragged on for several days, he begged her to go see a doctor. Catherine refused. She could barely eat and drank only the smallest sips of water.

During this time, Bob went out less, though she wished he would have, as he nearly drove her insane the way he constantly checked on her. She was too weak to protest.

When her mother telephoned, Catherine had been sleeping and Bob hadn't wanted to disturb her. He forgot to mention the call. Another time, Molly phoned, but Catherine was in the bathroom. Again, it slipped his mind to mention the missed call. He discouraged them both from visiting. It wouldn't have mattered so, had she not felt neglected. When Catherine told him that no one in the world seemed to care for her but him, he confessed that he'd forgotten to tell her about the calls and implored her to forgive him.

Too sluggish to blame him, Catherine agreed that if she was catchy, she sure wouldn't have wanted to get anyone sick. Still, she'd never been so lonely, but that was when she was awake. All she wanted to do was sleep. During unsuccessful attempts to lose consciousness, she visualized Bob together with Sophie — going to all the places Catherine and Bob had been together. She even began making up pet names that Bob would call Sophie...Sexy Sophie...My darling dancer...Try as she might, she couldn't keep herself from being obsessed.

When her fever finally broke one morning, she was listless, yet lucid enough to make a decision.

Catherine wistfully recalled her tentative plans about going to New York with Grace that last time they'd gotten together. They'd spoken of a large New York law firm that was always searching for smart attorneys — particularly women. She'd recently heard they were still hiring, and that female applicants even had an edge on males, despite the grim economy. Maybe she stood little chance, but wouldn't Grace have loved that Catherine realized their dream? She would do this for Grace.

If everything worked out the way she hoped, she was in for some big changes.

A few weeks later, Catherine surprised Bob with the news of her interview at the New York firm of Ruderman and Stevens. She hadn't mentioned that she'd even applied. He winced, but never one to be rendered speechless, claimed it a fine idea. If she got the job, maybe she could put in a good word for him. Was he trying to bamboozle her? He was probably only feigning interest in both working for the firm, as well as a possible move to the Big Apple. He'd never be able to sever his ties to Detroit. Either he didn't know himself very well, or he didn't think she did.

But Bob's bigger, and certainly more hurtful deception, was that he was no doubt having an affair with Sophie. While he'd stopped rattling on so much about the young dancer, he'd been coming home later and later from the office. She knew that could mean only one thing. Bob claimed that he'd been spending time at the new horse racing track. She rather doubted it.

When Catherine informed her parents of her decision to accept an interview in New York, her mother had broken down and cried. Then she shouted and accused Catherine of being heartless.

"We'll only get to see you about once a year — if that. Do you enjoy putting your parents in an early grave?"

Why didn't they realize that if she didn't follow through, she'd put herself into an even earlier one? If only she could tell them about his affair.

"First, I don't even know if I'll get the job. Plus, there's no reason we couldn't get together a few times times a year. I'll pay for your train tickets. You must admit, we haven't seen all that much of each other, anyway."

"That's only because you don't stop by very often. It's not like your father and I can just pop by your apartment since you two are always so busy. Well, go on with you then, Catherine Elizabeth! You've had a stubborn streak ever since you were born, and there's no stopping you once your mind's made up. You'll be staying with Vivian, I hope." Vivian was Bridget's older sister.

"Yep, I told her I'd be in New York, and then she invited me. Come to think of it, she sounded happy to hear I wouldn't be bringing Bob with me." Bob and Aunt Vivian had had a falling out the last time she was in Detroit, and still hadn't made amends.

CHAPTER FORTY-FIVE

A porter helped Catherine onto the train, relieving her of a large suitcase, though she still lugged a hefty satchel down the narrow aisle of the train compartment. In her excitement, she'd taken no notice of the bag's heaviness. It was the first time she'd ever traveled alone. The sky had never appeared such a sapphire blue as it had that early September morning before boarding the train. She was ready for the adventure.

According to stories told to Catherine, her grandmothers had originally come to America from Ireland with their children, but not their husbands. Their husbands came over in advance and did everything they could to get settled. The ocean journeys made them all tougher for the resettling in America. She wished she knew more about them and their families.

Catherine's senses were electrified—she'd never been so awake. It must have been similar to the way her grandmothers felt as they headed toward places unseen, though certainly their lives had been completely upended. She scolded herself for equating herself with her truly brave, hard-struggling ancestors. She'd only seen Aunt Vivian a few times before. Her mother's widowed sister worked as a librarian in a private all-boys school. Eileen was said to resemble Vivian: beautiful, yet sullen, with a penchant for scolding. Providing she allowed Vivian to boss her around, Catherine would do just fine, her mother advised. Also, she should, by all means, never disagree with her aunt. *Promise me, you won't. I promise you, Mother.*

She continued thinking about Aunt Vivian as the train left the station. Only now did she notice the soreness in her arms from lugging the heavy bag of books, along with a suitcase, through the station. Bob had driven her there, but she'd declined his offer of helping with the luggage. She'd taken little notice of his somber expression behind the steering wheel.

Catherine was relieved that no one, at least at the Detroit station, sat next to her on the train. She could use the seat for her book satchel, for the time being. The large tapestry bag contained not only books but several sandwiches. She'd made a few peanut butter ones, plus a few with cheese.

An older man wearing a monocle and handlebar mustache sat across from her, but thankfully not directly across. Recalling Grammy's monocle and Uncle Gerry's red mustache, she sighed. So much time had passed since she'd lived with them. She deeply missed them, especially her uncle.

The stranger on the train held a newspaper in front of his face. Once in a while, he'd lower it to peer at Catherine. She couldn't stop fidgeting and squirming about. "Sorry, I'm not used to sitting for so long," she apologized. He gave her a brief nod and resumed reading the paper.

During the long, eastbound journey, she would read and reread the first couple paragraphs of the novels. There were several books by Fitzgerald, Hemmingway, Woolf, Poe, and Austin. She wasn't sure why she hadn't settled on taking only a couple of them. Catherine finally decided on Fitzgerald's *This Side of Paradise*. Once, long ago, Bob told her on Belle Isle that he'd take her "from here to Paradise." If only there'd been more of those moments. She glanced out the window at a farmhouse and barn— blips on the landscape and then were gone. The only return to Paradise for her would be emerging herself in what looked to be a titillating book.

Catherine spent most of the time gazing outside, preparing for the interview. Her experience should speak for itself, but she knew, too, that she'd have to sell them on her personality. How much easier it would be if she were younger—before she realized her character flaws. There were so many. Maybe she could pretend to be someone else. She'd always loved the theater, so maybe she could pull off acting the part of a strong and confident, though non-aggressive, woman.

She struck up a conversation with the man across from her when she could no longer tolerate the silence. Harry Holden turned out much friendlier than he'd first appeared. Like her, Harry was traveling to New York.

Their brief conversation relaxed her enough to doze for a time, but when she woke up, she couldn't get Bob off her mind. No doubt he'd be spending most of his time with Sophie. Regardless of how the interview turned out, Catherine would have to ask for a separation. No way would she give him the chance to ask for one first. What if he asked her for a divorce? It would simply be too much to endure! Who would be the one to move from the apartment? If she did, where would she go? Certainly not to her parents' house—especially at age thirty-three. Maybe Molly would let Catherine stay temporarily in her guest room. If Molly said no, maybe she could turn to Joan or Margaret.

Bob had asked her to call him from her aunt's telephone as soon as she got settled in. What if he didn't answer? He promised he would. Still…

She needed to wake up from this bad dream. While she wouldn't classify her life as a nightmare, it sure wasn't turning out the way she'd hoped or planned.

Catherine ate two of the five sandwiches and gave one made with cheese to Harry. The bread was dry, but unlike the peanut butter ones, those with cheese and mustard were fairly tasty. Harry heartily agreed. She confided she wasn't much of a cook, but sandwiches were her specialty. Harry shrugged as he couldn't care less. Tears welled up in her eyes.

Two men flirted with her on their way to the club car. The younger-looking one asked her if she would care to join him — if her father didn't mind. Catherine declined, feigning that she was coming down with something. Why not let them think Harry was her father? Harry played along by raising a brow at the brash lad. After he left — and hopefully for good — Catherine and Harry laughed themselves silly. She threw a bag of peanuts at Harry, and he pretended to be upset by raising an eyebrow over his monocle-covered eye. She hadn't known train travel would be so enjoyable.

New York had more skyscrapers than Chicago or Detroit. On the taxi ride to her aunt's from the train station, Catherine mused how sidewalk crowds there were far larger than she'd imagined. A combination of the driver's body odor plus the peanuts he was snacking on filled her nostrils. Too bad the peanut aroma couldn't cancel the human stench. She tried her best to breathe into her gloved hand and only hoped he wouldn't notice.

At first, nervous in the back seat, she kept nodding to everything the driver said as they moved slowly through the bustling city. She told him how she'd never been to New York before, how she'd never taken a taxi. He nodded and turned into a tour guide, pointing out the many amazing sites, including Times Square, the Empire State Building, and Central Park. She was sorry to see even longer soup lines and more downcast faces here than in Detroit. Maybe it was because New York was larger.

Pulling up to an apartment building, the driver told her: "So here we are in the upper west side of Manhattan." A few smartly uniformed doormen stood ready to assist. Catherine was impressed at its great height — it was nearly as high as the several skyscrapers they'd passed along the way.

Aunt Vivian greeted Catherine with a hug, but a stiff and brief one. Her face was more lined and she was shorter than

Catherine had remembered. While her aunt had never had children, she looked many years older than her slightly younger sister. True, it had been a few years since Catherine had last seen her.

Catherine wished she was back in the cab driving around the city with the friendly cabbie.

She sat stiffly on the edge of a living room chair and answered a few questions about the train trip. Then her aunt asked for details about how everyone was doing back in Michigan. How could she be so cruel? Catherine hated to be prodded. Then, showing some mercy, Aunt Vivian remarked how tired she must be and escorted her to the guest room, telling her to take her time freshening up. There was something formal and queenly about the way her aunt moved. Her erect posture made her now look younger than her slump-shouldered sister.

She wondered if she'd ever be able to relax around the older woman.

After unpacking and using the spotless small bathroom next to the guest room, she joined her aunt once again in her simply decorated, yet elegant high-ceilinged living room. No sofas, but a few wing-backed chairs, a lovely round coffee table, and a mantel clock on a faux fireplace. Three windows overlooked a cathedral and a large park. Could it be Central Park? Catherine would have to ask.

Catherine mentioned how the Depression was taking its toll on people.

Aunt Vivian and her two Siamese cats, gazed at Catherine with Mona Lisa grins. No doubt chiding her for being naïve—

"Well, my dear, many of the homeless vagabonds could work, they simply choose not to."

Catherine, ready for battle, was about to launch her first verbal assault when she remembered her mother's words about never disagreeing with the woman.

"Let's hope that prosperity's around the corner. Aunt Vivian, tell me about your school year at Hutchinson's Boys' Academy. I've always loved hearing your stories about some of those boys."

"Let's have a deal. How about you call me Aunt Viv and I'll call you Kate? Vivian sounds too formal — wouldn't you agree?"

Catherine told her she'd try her best. Aunt Viv smiled for the first time. She then told one school-related anecdote followed by another. One involved a chauffeur forgetting to pick up his wealthy employer's seven-year-old son at the school and how the boy spent the night there. There was another one about twins who'd rarely attended, as their parents wanted them to see the world. Since the tales were so polished, Catherine concluded her aunt had told the stories many times and relished each re-telling.

Aunt Viv proved to be kinder than Catherine had expected. She completely understood why Catherine would need to call Bob. "Don't worry about calling long distance. I'm happy to pay for your peace of mind, Kate."

Catherine placed the call with the operator who informed her that no one was answering. The two women visited a while longer before she called again. It made her sick to her stomach knowing that Bob was no doubt with Sophie. No point in mentioning her troubled marriage, as it would get back to her mother. When she tried a third time, Bob finally answered. His voice sounded far away and the static kept her from hearing much of what he was saying. Something about being glad she called and good luck at the interview.

Waiting for Catherine on the bed of the guest room had been a long peach-colored nightgown and robe. The room had a sweet, but not overpowering flowery scent. She discovered some sachet in an empty drawer of a bureau that her aunt had said she could use for her clothes. Her aunt had turned down the corner of the bedspread. Now sleep sounded even more divine. The ambiance helped Catherine drift off, but didn't prevent her from waking several times during the night, worrying about the interview, as well as her marriage.

The following morning, when Catherine first arrived at the law firm of Ruderman & Stevens, she'd been surprised at how alert she felt after her fitful night's sleep. Aunt Viv's strong coffee had worked its magic. Here she was on the 40th floor of the Chrysler Building — the second tallest skyscraper in the city, falling just short now of the Empire State Building. What were they in, a race to the sky? The lobby walls were made of African marble... Her head was whirling. Soon she'd be interviewing for a possible dream job. She had to pinch herself to make sure she wasn't dreaming.

Betsy, a young receptionist with pale blonde hair, told Catherine to have a seat and that Mr. Ruderman would be with her shortly. Betsy smacked her chewing gum most annoyingly. A custodian took the longest time vacuuming the carpeted floor.

A half hour early, Catherine had expected to wait. This would give her time to go over points she wanted to make about her work history and legal expertise. She then noticed that one of her nails had chipped. Luckily, she'd brought a nail file in her purse, so she had time to smooth the jagged edge. She worried her nail polish was too close to 'fire engine red' and not the deeper, more subtle shade of 'raspberry,' although the small bottle had claimed it to be the latter. Her tweed suit made her skin itch and the white blouse beneath the jacket refused to stay tucked in. Hopefully, the jacket covered it.

The coffee now made her stomach grumble.

At least she had time to use the restroom. But there was more time to kill after she'd returned to the hard-cushioned chair in the waiting room. Time to re-do her raspberry lipstick, not once, but three times. Time to twiddle her thumbs and have doubts about what the hell she was doing here. Shite.

She checked with Betsy after an hour of waiting, and then once again after an hour-and-a-half.

Two hours after arriving, Catherine was shown into Gary Ruderman's large office. Writing on a legal pad, he didn't bother to look up for another fifteen minutes. She folded and unfolded her sweaty palms. His name was fitting, for he sure was rude. He raised an index finger when he thought she was shifting in her seat a little much—no doubt a strike against her. And keeping her waiting was all part of his evaluation.

"So, Miss or is it Mrs.? Umm...Ah, yes, Mrs. Catherine Sage, tell me a little about yourself and why you've applied to our most prestigious firm," Gary said in a most uninviting tone, after puffing a cigar. He glowered at her once, glasses at the end of his hawkish beak, as he waited for her to speak. After she told him about herself, he again looked down. Now he was writing on her resume, occasionally saying, "I see..." and "Uhmhmm..."

Betsy interrupted to say he had a phone call, which he took, of course.

Catherine could feel her temper rising. She reminded herself that she'd come a long way for this interview and as rude as Gary Ruderman was, she had to keep doing her best, no matter how ill-at-ease she felt. Powerful men were often this way, so truly his behavior came as no surprise. But it wasn't until after his long phone chat with the room hazy from his cigar smoke; and even after he commented how he loathed women trying to climb the professional ladder—when she could no longer contain herself.

"You know what?" she asked, allowing plenty of wait time. Her profuse perspiration did the trick of cooling her a bit.

Finally, he responded, "No, what?"

"You, Mr. Ruderman, can take your job and shove it up your arse and after that, you can go feck yourself!"

Catherine saw his face turn beet red. Fire engine red. Before could respond, she fled from the office, from the building, and two days later—from New York.

CHAPTER FORTY-SIX

Bob stirred in two sugars, and then a third, into his refilled cup of coffee at Darla's Downtown Donuts while waiting for Catherine. He was glad it wasn't named *Detroit* Darla's Downtown Donuts, as that would've mucked up the catchiness. He'd already scarfed down one donut and would probably have another inhaled once she got there. It worried him he couldn't smell the coffee or fresh donuts. Had too many fights taken away his sense of smell? It sure hadn't messed with his sense of taste. Since he no longer boxed professionally, putting on extra weight had been all too easy. It wouldn't be long before he'd have to buy the next suit size up—and he'd already gone up one in the last six months. Soon he'd get back to the gym and cut back on the sweets.

Sophie had been all the 'sweets' he'd needed and now she was gone from his life.

During the past few weeks, Bob had lost a lot of money at the racetrack. While his conscience was less troubled, his despair was intense.

Where was Catherine? Fifteen minutes late, according to his watch, but this was nothing new— she was probably still sore over the whole Sophie situation. He couldn't blame her. If things had turned out the way he'd planned, he wouldn't be in the booth waiting for her right now. Maybe he'd have even moved out.

Almost a month had gone by since Catherine had been back from New York. When she'd first returned, he'd planned on telling her that he wanted a divorce. He knew the Church and his mother would've clobbered him, but what other choice did he have? Surely, divorce was better than cheating on his wife. But then, Catherine had beaten him to the punch by asking him for a separation. It sure had surprised the bejeebers out of him. They'd spoken like two sane adults about it, too. Both calmly agreed they'd had a good marriage—until they didn't. They'd experienced more in their ten years together than many couples do in a lifetime. They reassured each other that they'd always love each other—as friends. They were both passionate people who simply couldn't exist without passion.

Then Sophie cut him out of her life in such a cold, heartless way. Two weeks had now passed. Someday—provided Catherine and he were still together—maybe Bob would tell her all about it. She knew it was over with Sophie. At least he hoped she did. To save face, he'd made it sound like he'd been the one to call it off when it had actually been Sophie. She'd jilted him for Ted Tilson—an up-and-coming young boxer. A kid really; he couldn't be older than twenty. Sure, Bob Sage had become somewhat of a local legend, but boxing was now in his past.

Sophie turned out to be a flighty dame. A regular flibbertigibbet. Sure, he was the one committing adultery, but still. She'd turned out to be Catherine's opposite: malleable as putty, sweet without ambition, and a woman who wouldn't diminish his manhood (or so he'd first thought). Someone he could've even pictured himself raising a child with, even though she already had one. Had they married, he would've had a ready-made family and that would—would've been—swell. The thought of one day having their own children had often occurred to him. But Sophie had tricked him. For her, it was only a roll in the hay until she landed a worthy successor.

Catherine, still living in the apartment, hadn't spoken of the separation for several days. Had she not been there during this difficult time, maybe he'd have taken the pistol from his desk drawer and called it a day. While he didn't remain in bed the way she often did when depressed, his spirits began sagging more than the worst fleabag mattress. She'd been pretty blue, at first, following her disastrous interview in New York. She still needed him, too, despite two-timing him in the past. While married love sure wasn't all it was cracked up to be, he was still her husband. He needed to step up to the task, as he didn't want a separation or divorce.

Bob knew a thousand 'Hail Marys' and 'Our Fathers' wouldn't be enough penance to absolve him from the mortal sin he'd committed. But he had an idea which he'd tell Catherine about as soon as she got here. They'd linger over coffee a few minutes, and then he'd suggest they plan their excursion to Europe. But what if another woman were to come along someday and turn his head? How would he be able to resist? Now, that was a question for another day, as Catherine, just walking through the door, was smiling his way. What a looker she still was!

CHAPTER FORTY-SEVEN

That Christmas at the McIntoshes would prove one of the best in Catherine's adult life. While they'd shared many enjoyable ones, often the memories ran together, like the ones of holidays often do. For the first few years of married life, she avoided lengthy family visits, but not so for the 1934 celebration. Had there not been a good-sized basement, there was little way all seventeen could have comfortably fit in the small house.

The succulent aroma of the roasting turkey filled the rooms of the small home. Everyone brought a dish to pass, which relieved Bridget from the burden of being the sole cook. Laughter filled the home like it hadn't in a long time.

The atmosphere was more festive than it had been in a long time, as several family members had good news to share, as well as plans for a rosier future.

Rose, Molly's little girl, recently had her first birthday. She'd been named after their maternal grandmother—the grandmother Catherine and her siblings had never met. It was said that little Rose was Catherine all over again: the same red hair, steely blue eyes, and hot temper. Bob was smitten and this amused Catherine. She'd splurged on her niece, as well as her other nieces and nephews, as she'd recently been rehired once again by the Prosecutor's Office. Supposedly, once the Depression was over, she'd be made an Assistant Prosecutor.

Bob informed them that in a couple of years he was going to run for judge of the Common Pleas Court. And before or after becoming a judge, he was going to turn vacant lots into playgrounds for poor kids.

John, rarely at family dinners, told Bob that he'd help with the fundraising and do anything else in his power to help. Maybe he could get several other Detroit cops to pitch in. After all, they had a vested interest in seeing kids off the streets – maybe it would keep them from turning into delinquents. Bob was pleased by John's excitement. Maybe there was more to the kid, after all. He'd always seen him as Catherine's kid brother, but clearly, there was more to him. John had a big heart.

Bobby, now twelve, found everything fascinating: Uncle John, the new baby, his colorful Aunt Kate, and Uncle Bob. He was also nearly intoxicated by the food aromas. Despite his pants being too short, his large ears, and a permanent look of embarrassment for taking up space, he was turning into a handsome boy. He had a good personality and laughed easily.

After hugging Aunt Kate, he planted a smacker of a kiss on her cheek because he was overwhelmed by all this wonderfulness. Normally, he was bored during the holidays spent at home with his parents. Why couldn't Sages have these sorts of feasts and lively conversations?

"So, kid, you getting ready for the trip?" asked Uncle Bob.

"Trip?" Bobby had forgotten about his uncle's offer, as it was made a few years earlier, and was never brought up again. Then Bobby remembered and grinned from ear to ear. "When are we going, Uncle Bob?"

Bob senior laughed in his gruff way. He nudged his wife. Catherine had forgotten about his promise to the boy, as well, but now recalled Bob saying something about it when they'd taken him to Canada over the Ambassador Bridge.

"I'm thinking maybe in three years. How old will you be then?"

"Fifteen." Bobby wanted to ask if they couldn't go on the trip a little sooner, but then remembered his manners.

"Well, kid, you better save up, as we're gonna be gone for several weeks." With that, he gave Bobby a Christmas card with a twenty-dollar bill inside. The boy had never received that much money. He held it up to the light.

"Just checking to make sure it's not counterfeit," Bobby said, raising one of his thick black eyebrows.

"Would I kid a kidder? No, Bobby, it's the real McCoy."

"Did I hear a 'thank-you,' Robert Eugene?" Violet rarely sounded so stern.

"I already thanked him, Ma, you simply didn't hear."

"Well, I want to hear you thank him again. Money doesn't grow on trees, you know? Give it to your father for safekeeping until we get home." Violet, shrill as always, but given today's verbal cacophony—few even noticed it. Bobby blushed and thanked his uncle.

Mickey strongly suggested that a few of the younger guests take their food plates down to the decorated basement, telling them that "it was plenty warm down there, and decorated, too." It was almost impossible to move about—it didn't help that the Christmas tree took up well over a corner of the small living room.

Bobby and Elaine's three children, wondered about the present opening. After being told this would only happen if they remained downstairs, they smirked and grumbled loudly as they headed down to the lower level. The festive basement was replete with ribbons, wreaths, and red and green paper covering a couple of card tables.

Elaine's children were all older now. The youngest, Matthew, was only a little younger than Bobby, and his sisters were now in their early teens. All three were sullen and long-faced, though Bobby—the life of the party, like his uncle—could bring them out of their shells. The sisters kept rolling their eyes at his jokes, which only egged him on into telling yet another, with his voice getting louder with each one. He laughed uproariously after getting to the punch lines and at last got the girls to giggle.

Jezebel, now an old one-eyed cat, kept looking for somewhere to hide. At last, she found a closet door half open.

At last, Catherine had the chance to have more serious conversations with a few adults. She mentioned to Molly and John how she'd been having nightmares about fires again.

"Did you hear about the Kerns Hotel fire in Lansing earlier this month?" she asked.

"I read in the paper that it killed thirty-four people," said John.

"Including several state legislators," Catherine added.

"Almost as bad as the Little Sisters of the Poor fire in Pittsburgh a few years ago," John reported. According to him, the Little Sisters of the Poor had been a religious institute designed for women to care for the elderly. Neither Bob nor John knew whether the institute had yet been rebuilt.

Hearing about this didn't ease Catherine's fire fears, but the monotone of her brother's voice droning on had a calming effect, as did the spiked eggnog—her father's secret recipe. While John had become a police officer, his religion mattered to him almost as much. He attended church regularly and loved to recruit those he picked up in his paddy wagon.

"Kate, did you try one of my chocolate chip cookies? They're all the rage!" exclaimed Nana with a plate of cookies. Catherine declined but promised to take a few home—if Bobby didn't eat them all first. Nana shrugged and sidled up to Molly.

Lately, Catherine's rapport with her mother-in-law had been strained. After her trip to New York, she'd visited the older woman and while she hadn't told Nana outright about Sophie, she'd hinted about Bob's unfaithfulness. Nana had crossed her arms in front of her well-endowed bosom and let Catherine know that her loyalties to her sons came before anything else.

Catherine knew better than to say anything further. After losing so many brothers, he was a mama's boy for a reason.

"What's this about a trip to Europe?" Nana asked.

"We don't know exactly when, Nana, but we're thinking maybe next summer or the following one. I'm hoping it'll be before he takes Bobby Gene out West. Has Bob already asked if you'd like to join us?"

"What's that, Katy me-girl?" Nana asked, playing dumb.

"Has he asked if you'd like to come along?"

"I know I'd likely be a burden. But let me sleep on it..." A smile, both smug and devilish, crossed the older woman's face. Catherine felt a deep and tender love for the frail but mighty Nana. If Catherine had truly believed they'd take the voyage, she doubted she would have extended the offer.

CHAPTER FORTY-EIGHT

1935

The tougher life got, the more Catherine dug her heels in — that is, on the days when she wasn't hungover. She never viewed herself as a *sloppy drunk*, though some would have disagreed. But then she began taking a small silver flask inside her briefcase to work in the mornings, allowing herself only occasional sips to steady her hands. Co-workers never suspected her of drinking during the workday, though she admitted to Molly that once or twice she got "a little tipsy" on the job. Before this time, she'd confined her drinking to home, and only on weekends — that is, when Bob and she weren't out dancing or at a party. Friends and family wondered about her dependency, though they had little idea she'd become a bona fide alcoholic.

Bob knew, of course, but kept it to himself, though he took it out on Catherine more and more over the years, especially after he'd been drinking on the weekends. During the early years when she'd over-imbibed, he hadn't minded and even found her funny because she became silly and girlishly awkward. At first, he'd enjoyed taking care of her — and even helping her to bed.

Now that Prohibition was over, they frequented actual bars. But increasingly, early in the day, Catherine would pour herself a drink (straight gin) and light a cigarette. At night, she'd pace the darkened rooms of their apartment, smoking, sipping, crying, and muttering about the unfairness of life. Naturally, this disturbed Bob's sleep. He'd call out to her to come back to bed and when she wouldn't, he'd try coaxing her. If she resisted, he'd drag her, or even shove her, back into the bedroom. If she was too drunk, Catherine would fall in a heap, sobbing on the floor. Almost always, she'd accuse him of not loving her. He'd try to rub her back and reassure her that he still did.

"Well, you sure got a helluva way to show it, fella!"

"I'm worried about you, Kate. When you drift off in your haze from the hooch, you're so far away."

"And being a brute with me is how to handle it?"

"I always ask you nicely to return to bed and then I have to insist. You don't give me much recourse."

"And when I resist, you use force. That sure doesn't add up to love in my book!"

"Look, Kiddo, I try. That's all I can do. Sorry if I get a little rough. You could've given me the boot by now."

"I'll show you, Bob Sage. Just you wait!"

'Showing him' sometimes meant taking a swing at Bob, but when she considered it rationally, the best way to get back at him was by using her brain, not brawn. He always seemed to appreciate it when Catherine used her smarts. Her mind still felt like a steel trap, but too often she became the one entrapped — ensnared by her thoughts. When she couldn't sleep, she'd think about how her career had stagnated. She missed going to law school and their early days together. She missed the bustling times of Sage & Sage. She wondered how life would be different if they had a child.

Bob was dealing with Catherine the best he could, or so he told himself. Anyone else would be at their wit's end. He knew he wasn't a prince: any other woman would've been frustrated by him, too. No one could fault Kate for not having tried harder at various times in their marriage. On the surface, it appeared like she'd given up, but she never did. She reminded him of the sort of boxer he'd always been and couldn't help but admire her for it.

They talked about changing the weekend pattern of going out to bars, but couldn't seem to break it. For the longest time, the physical abuse turned into a crazed passion afterward, but increasingly, their fights wound up in stiff hugs and empty apologies. He promised not to let his temper get the best of him and she promised not to drink so much. It was like the way her father treated her mother, though her mother goaded her father way more than she did Bob.

A couple more interviews came her way, but gone was Catherine's former enthusiasm and nervous anticipation beforehand. One was for a small downtown firm, and the other was for the firm where Bob now worked—Maile, Leach & Schrier. After brief interviews at both firms, she'd been told much the same: "Don't take this personally, but due to the tough economic times, we're not hiring women, no matter how well-qualified."

John Maile had been the more personable of the two men who interviewed her, no doubt because Bob worked for his firm, but also because he'd heard that Catherine "had one of the best legal minds in the city."

"For what it's worth, Mr. Maile," she'd responded.

"I'm sorry. You realize that you're married to an up-and-coming judge, right?"

Catherine did her best to smile and shook his hand. She bit her lip as she fought back the tears. As she was walking out of the office, another attorney, whistled and loudly said, "Where'd you get those great gams?"

She swiveled her head and grumbled, "Up yours, mister!"

. . .

Yet Catherine and Bob did their best to find enjoyment. On a late summer afternoon, they returned to Boblo Island and recollected their first trip there, now so many years ago. Life had seemed so innocent and madcap during the Roaring Twenties.

After the Columbia left shore, they roamed its interior. Catherine squealed with delight when she saw the large souvenir and snack stand. At least the hard times hadn't taken away all of life's frivolities. She eyed the fancy pencils, the wind-up mechanical mice, and postcards of the two steamboats and the island.

"Go ahead, Doll face, pick out whatever you'd like," Bob told her.

It made her feel like a girl again. Why not? Certainly, she deserved something for all the difficult times of late. It wasn't easy to decide.

Bob tapped his foot. A crowd of mostly children pushed their way to better view the little toys. Catherine furrowed her brows at one boy who almost knocked her over in his pursuit of a lollipop as large as a human face. Bob continued tapping his foot, but she couldn't hear it because of the growing crowd.

She finally found what she didn't even realize she'd been looking for: a rabbit foot keychain. She'd noticed them on their first trip to the island. While they were displayed in an array of artificially dyed colors, she settled on a white one that looked more natural. All of them promised to bring luck to their owner.

"Ironic isn't it? Poor rabbits run out of luck for us humans who believe in tricks of fate!" Catherine declared.

"Maybe rabbit feet simply don't make it into the pot of rabbit stew." Bob laughed and told her he thought a necklace would've made a better memento.

Captain Bob-lo stood near the snack bar. For once, he didn't have an audience. Bob convinced Catherine that this would be their only chance to talk to the locally famous captain. It bothered her that his popularity was mostly based on him being a dwarf.

The captain was friendly, at first. Then he stopped talking and gazed deeply into Bob's face and then Catherine's. The large, knowing, face on the little body grew exceedingly pale.

"Sorry, folks, I'm needed on the upper deck," Captain Bob-lo said curtly, bidding them both a good day — and good luck.

Had they imagined the look on the captain's face? Shivers went up and down Catherine's spine, though Bob dismissed the captain's changed mood, saying that he had no magical powers and was just another Irishman full of blarney.

They enjoyed the island, but discovered their stamina for amusement rides and dealing with crowds wasn't what it had once been. They danced in the large dance hall, but it seemed like all the songs the band played were sad ones. A cotton-candy and caramel apple concession stand now stood in place of the tree-lined enchanted bower where they'd first made love.

They never made it across the ocean on a larger ship that summer.

. . .

In early October, the two took a picnic lunch to Belle Isle. It was a golden fall day, and a warm breeze blew in off the river. They spotted a lake they hadn't known existed and Bob pointed out a small island. "How curious: an island on an island!" Catherine remarked. Before crossing a small wooden bridge over a tributary, they stopped at its center to gaze down at the water. At that moment, the breeze picked up and absconded with their hats: his — a black fedora and hers, a blue beret.

Both fedora and beret landed alongside each other in the water. They floated downstream; thankfully, the current was a lazy one. The two owners laughed and pointed at them.

"It's like our lives are going on without us, or the current of time is drifting us away. Doesn't it make you sad?" Catherine asked, holding back her long auburn curls that had been wildly dancing in the wind.

"At least they're side by side," Bob said, chuckling, as he rolled up his pant legs before wading into the water to retrieve the hats.

While their rescued hats were too drenched to be worn, their basket of bread, cheese, and wine at a picnic table was a sweet respite from an otherwise difficult day.

If only Catherine didn't always have that faraway look.

The following day, they joined Gene, Violet, and Bobby to see the Detroit Tigers play against the Chicago Cubs in the World Series. It was Bobby's first time attending a Tiger's game and Bob busied himself pointing out the players. He was surprised that Bobby knew the names of several of them.

Catherine chuckled at seeing the two brothers sitting side by side wearing baseball caps, nervously chewing their toothpicks. The Cubs had won the World Series against the Tigers back in '07 and '08. Did the Tigers now even stand a chance?

In the eleventh inning, the game was tied five to five. Few had ever seen such a nail-biting game. Tiger's player, Jo-Jo White made it to home plate and the Tigers won. The Detroit crowd went wild!

Everyone—except for Catherine—jumped for joy. She smiled, but had that same faraway look in her eyes, that later, Bob would think of as haunting.

. . .

Catherine slept for ten to twelve hours a night, often dreaming of fires. In some, Bob and she were suffocating. In others, she stood outside a house or building and watched it go up in flames. Frozen in place, she couldn't rescue the screaming victims stuck inside. She no longer mentioned her dreams to Bob. During her conscious life, she'd startle and feel her heart race whenever she'd hear a fire truck's siren.

Her dreams led her to research famous fires like the one in South Korea at the Jinhae Primary School which had killed 104 people in 1930, or the one in a wooden church in Romania that had killed 118...Then there was the one at the penitentiary in Columbus that had killed 322. The worst of them was the one in Japan in 1934—the Great Hakodate fire. Possibly more than 2,166 were burned to death. She tried to numb herself as she memorized the numbers, but couldn't help but visualize faces screaming in certain agony.

"Did you hear about the one in Japan, Bob?"

"You've mentioned it more than a few times. But yes, it was terrible."

CHAPTER FORTY-NINE

1937

"Excuse me, but vote for my boy, will you?" The question, almost as insistent as a command, came from the short, gray-haired lady. Her small blue eyes twinkled behind the round rims of her glasses. It was a question Nana repeated tirelessly. Daily, for weeks, she'd been campaigning for her son as she rode the Jefferson Avenue streetcar.

The leaflet she distributed read: *As he fought in the ring – he'll fight to do right! Vote for the Battling Barrister – Robert E. Sage for judge of the Common Pleas Court.* Next to the words was a photo of Bob in the boxing ring from a few years earlier. While his name wasn't known by all, most of the streetcar riders nodded in recognition and smiled at Nana, especially after seeing his picture.

"You're his mother?" they'd ask. She'd nod, dimpling with pride.

"Then you most certainly have my vote!"

Nana would often pat a prospective voter on the shoulder and thank them, before moving on to the next one. Sometimes she'd give a quick hug if the streetcar had come to a stop. She freely gave everyone her beaming smile.

Bob had five hard-working campaigners: his mother, wife, brother, sister-in-law, and nephew— though none more devoted to the cause than his mother. Although Catherine had been the first to encourage him to run for judge, she'd soon grown weary of knocking on doors and addressing postcards. She tried hard not to let it show.

Bob had developed an impressive new swagger, bravado like never before. Only Catherine knew the truth: it masked his fear of losing. She'd seen it before boxing matches with worthy opponents. None of the others running for the same seat had his name recognition, but it was pointless to remind Bob. Still, she'd repeat this, along with half a dozen other lines about what a great judge he'd soon become.

Despite having fallen a notch or two in Bob's eyes, he still respected his wife's opinion; her words mattered. He was truly thankful for all the family support and knew he could count on it. After a time, his phony campaign smile became real, as well as his confidence. Many city dwellers had known better times for the last couple years, so why not for Bob and his family? When he said his nightly prayers, he pleaded with God to shine a light on his dark path and show him the way to victory.

Bob didn't let on that his thoughts sometimes felt jumbled. He could get upset over the smallest things — or nothing at all. Maybe it was because of his frustration over not feeling clear-minded. Could it have been because he'd simply fallen on his head one too many times? He wasn't one for doctors unless he needed stitches, so he didn't dwell on the cause. Swimming seemed to help. It was undoubtedly for the best that his days in the ring were over.

Like others running for public office, Bob had a temporary pass to use the ritzy Detroit Athletic Club. During campaign season he swam there a few times a week. Going there made him feel classy, as it resembled Rome's, Palazzo Farnese. Not only did it have swimming pools but also gyms, bars, and restaurants.

He loved to mingle — now and then — with the hoity-toity. This he told no one.

One evening, taking a break from campaigning, Bob dove into the pool intending to swim his normal number of laps. Suddenly, he was sluggish. It took forever to finish a single lap. True, he'd had a few beers beforehand and little to eat that day. He stopped mid-crawl, gasping for breath right after a bolt of intense pain shot through his entire body. It was over before he knew it, but it was like the death-dog had gotten a good sniff of him. He couldn't stop shaking. Tomorrow, he'll make an appointment with his doctor. His mother had angina, so it could be he'd inherited a similar bad ticker.

Bob floated on his back to the poolside ladder. No way was he about to go down now because there were rounds to go in this life-match. He sure hoped so.

CHAPTER FIFTY

Wallace, Idaho

That fall, Bob and his nephew journeyed west by train on an unforgettable trip. He'd been promising Bobby for years and was feeling especially generous, having recently been elected as a judge for the Common Pleas Court. As he wouldn't be called the Honorable Robert Sage until the following year, it made perfect sense for him to make good on his promise. A fairly clean bill of health from his doctor helped restore his joie de vivre.

Bobby (soon to be known as Bob), would talk about the excursion for the rest of his life. He'd become the class clown in his freshman class at Mackenzie High School. Trip plans had fallen through the previous summer, so when Uncle Bob heard his namesake was flunking out of school—he had a talk with the boy's father. He reassured both parents that following the six-week adventure, Bobby would return home a changed young man. While Bob didn't have children of his own, he understood boys—especially of Bobby's age—ever since he'd begun coaching at the boxing gym.

"Don't show him too good a time or he'll want to drop out altogether," Violet told her brother-in-law.

"I've got a foolproof plan, so don't worry, Vi. Though he's a smart kid, I'll be subtle in my efforts. You've got my word."

Violet rolled her eyes, as she'd never quite trusted Bob, especially since hearing about his dalliance with Sophie. Still, she looked forward to having time alone with Gene.

Bobby had already confided in his uncle how he'd like to drop out of school. Maybe he could work at the boxing gym, and eventually become a boxer, too.

"Sure, kid, sure," was always his uncle's response. Bob didn't tell his nephew, but he had two strikes against him: childhood illnesses had robbed him of some of his physical stamina, plus he didn't have a suitable personality for a boxing career. It would be difficult to overcome those factors. True, Bobby had energy and spunk, but not in the right doses. Bobby was a sensitive boy and anyone at all perceptive could see right through his tough guy stance which he'd adopted from his uncle.

Bob claimed that he (himself) had been born with powerful fists. He'd constantly had to defend himself from his brothers. As he saw it, he had the necessary grit, unlike his nephew. Rather than tell him this directly, Bob would show the need for an education in this dog-eat-dog world. His parents readily agreed.

Six weeks wasn't much time to show the boy all the wonders of the West, but long enough to travel to the coast. They'd take a few side trips along the way: Chicago, San Francisco, and finally Idaho.

During their only night on the town in Chicago, Bob took Bobby by the club where Al Capone frequented. Bobby's jaw dropped in awe as his uncle regaled him with tales of the infamous gangster – even mentioning his encounters with Anna Sage. They took a quick walk through the shopping district, walked out on Navy Pier, and then a taxi took them to the famous Shedd Aquarium.

Next, still tired from the previous day, they boarded a westbound train heading through St. Paul, Minnesota. Bob would slam down one beer after another, smoke cigars, and converse with strangers in the club car. After only a few hours of sleep, he'd wake up with more energy than Bobby thought humanly possible. Although his uncle was coarse and gruff, everyone always seemed to like him. He sure had a magnetic personality. Before the trip, he had little idea of how fowl his uncle's language could be, though in the presence of women Bob was known to remark, "Excuse my French," after cursing. When Bob noticed his nephew had picked up a few of his expressions ("shit on a stick" and "sonofabitch!" —being his choice ones), he toned it down, as best he could, especially in the company of women.

One evening, his uncle got into a long conversation about the Hindenburg bursting into flames. The tragedy had happened the previous spring in New Jersey, and the nation was still talking about it. Bob's language was so colorful in describing the incident, that his nephew could not only picture the large floating sky-ship but how it must have appeared when engulfed by flames.

Bobby couldn't figure out his uncle's appeal to women, as the damage to his face from boxing injuries was extensive: his cartilage was nearly gone from his nose making it appear unnaturally flat; the skin beneath his eyes permanently scarred; and, only hats that were too large could hide his cauliflower ears. His face, too, had become heavy. Maybe women found the hoarseness of his voice appealing. Bobby had to admit that everyone found his uncle charming, and especially, the ladies. If only he could figure out how his uncle performed such magic.

Once they got to San Francisco, Bobby stared in amazement at the Golden Gate Bridge. It was the largest bridge in the entire world. They rode a ferry to the infamous Alcatraz Island. Bob told him it was a great place for a prison: if a prisoner escaped, there was little chance of them swimming to the mainland.

Bobby couldn't get over the glistening and wild waters of the bay.

"But what you want to bet, I could do it?" his uncle bragged, acting like he was truly going to attempt it, taking off his socks and shoes. "Meet me on the other side, okay, Bobby-me-boy?"

"You're not serious are you, Uncle Bob?"

"No, of course not," the joker finally confessed. "Just wanted to get your goat. Jiminy Cricket, kid, you're still pretty green, aren't you?"

This so upset the boy his nose bled. A soft-hearted guard handed him a handkerchief.

Bob told him how the infamous Al Capone was pacing in his cage there, no doubt planning his getaway. He was clearly impressed by this gangster. Such a fine line between men who upheld the law and those who broke it! In his gruff voice, his uncle added: "You know, Bobby, a good attorney has to think like a criminal."

Bobby realized he wanted to become an attorney like his uncle. Maybe one day, he, too, would run for elected office and become a judge. Before they got back to Detroit, Bobby would inform him of his decision.

They stayed a few nights at 'Sunset View' near Fisherman's Wharf. The run down hotel was the only one in the area. Bob would slip out, no doubt to a bar, leaving his nephew alone. The door would creak shut well past midnight. Bobby fought the urge to follow him. After sunrise, he woke with a start—not by his uncle, but the sea lions, crying on the rocks in the bay. It was the loneliest sound he'd ever heard.

After Bob finally returned, disheveled and cranky, he would collapse on the Murphy bed. Bobby got used to placing blankets over his unappreciative, yet unaware uncle. After minutes of listening to his uncle snoring louder than a sea lion, he'd make sure he had the room key, before wandering the wharf. Without being prompted by an adult, he'd wander into the local Catholic

Church and pray to Jesus, and all the saints, for their safety during the remainder of the journey.

Before heading back east, they stopped in Wallace, Idaho. His uncle hadn't visited in nine years but was excited to show his namesake the sights. Bobby knew his parents had met and married in Wallace, and that he'd been born there, though still a baby when they moved to Michigan. He was proud of himself for remembering his mother had been born in Missoula, Montana.

Bob pointed out a small house with a picket fence. It was where Gene and Violet first lived after getting married. Bobby claimed he recalled the picket fence, but his uncle didn't believe him.

"No, way, Bobby boy!"

"I swear up and down that I remember that fence."

"Aw, kid, don't pick up my bad habits." Bob's sarcasm was followed by a churlish grin.

They rented a car and drove to the nearby town of Burke, Bob and Gene's hometown. They'd lived there until Bob was fourteen and Gene, sixteen. Then the family moved to Michigan with only two of the original five boys.

Bob showed his nephew the silver, lead, and zinc mines and told him about the tough lives of the miners. Afterward, they drove to the closed-down mine where his twin, Raymond, had been killed from falling down a mine shaft. It was the same one in which Bobby's grandfather contracted miner's disease. Yes, Bob told him, his relatives had led even tougher lives than those who worked on the assembly line back in Michigan, though they didn't have it much easier.

"If you don't go to college, Bobby, you'll never see the sky." His uncle had said this before, but it had made little sense. Now it did. Yet as much as he loved his uncle — and was in awe of him — Bobby didn't want to follow in his exact footsteps;

otherwise, he, too, would wind up turning into a two-timing booze hound. No way would he let that happen.

One evening, over dinner in a *swanky* restaurant, Bob caught his nephew staring at a young, blond-haired waitress. In his gruff and gravelly voice, Bob asked if he was a virgin. Bobby's face reddened. He admitted he was, though he'd met a girl named Joyce, back at Mackenzie High. Someday, he told his uncle, "I'm going to marry her."

"Saving yourself for her, are you?" Bob asked, raising a brow.

"Not exactly."

"Well, all right, then. I was hoping you'd say that. There's a place I'd like to take you. Now's maybe the best time to see it."

His uncle hurriedly paid for the meal and Bobby caught him winking at the blonde on their way out. She reminded Bobby of Joyce, and while he didn't know Joyce well, he'd really missed her— especially since San Francisco. Not the best time to think about her, as he had to almost run to keep up with his uncle. He had no idea where they were going.

An older woman 'dolled-up' in lots of rouge, red cupid-bow lips, and wearing a fancy old-fashioned long dress—met the two Bobs at the door of a large Victorian house at the edge of town. A strong scent of perfume wafted out the door and tickled their noses. Bob and the woman embraced. At long last, he introduced Bobby to his "dear, old friend"—Isabelle Prevost. After rolling her eyes at Bob's words, she held Bobby to her bosom almost as long as she had his uncle. Bobby's cheeks burned.

Then Isabelle escorted them to an elaborately decorated sitting room with peacock feathers in Chinese vases and velvet-covered chairs and chaises. At the far end was a fireplace; two stone sphinxes guarded the hearth. Large tapestries of wilderness scenes hung on three of the four walls. On one wall there was the largest buffalo head Bobby had ever seen. It looked like the buffalo was watching him.

After growing tired of the animal's gaze, Bobby got a little bored. Would his uncle and that dame ever finish yapping? It was then he realized the where-and-why of their present circumstances.

"I've got someone for you to meet," Isabelle told Bobby. "She'll be with you soon."

His uncle had taken him to a brothel.

Before the boy could protest, his uncle announced he had an errand to run and would return shortly, adding that he hoped Bobby would relax a bit and have a fine time.

Bobby's throat suddenly felt parched. He thought of chasing after the older man, but Isabelle met him with a piece of chocolate cake and a glass of milk on a tray. Never one to resist cake, he sat back down. She smiled and mussed up his hair, only to disappear once more. Just as he finished wiping crumbs from his mouth, a blond-haired girl with ruby red lips sashayed into the room.

Why did she have to be so pretty? She had to be the most beautiful girl he'd seen since they'd left Detroit.

"You must be Bobby. I've heard so much about you. You're even more handsome in person than in the photos I've seen." The girl extended a cool hand with painted nails and led him up a flight of rickety stairs. She explained how Isabelle had shown her a picture Bob's uncle had sent little over a year ago. A couple was kissing passionately in the upstairs hallway. Bobby stared. He had a hard time walking and the girl about pushed him through an open doorway.

"My uncle will be back any minute. I really shouldn't," Bobby told the girl after she'd pushed him onto the bed and unbuttoned his shirt. Her perfume scent was even stronger and sweeter than that of the older woman. Bobby's throat felt like it was about to close up.

He burst out: "Hold on a second, I don't even know your name."

"Clara," she whispered, unzipping his fly. She licked his ear and then blew softly inside it. He'd never been so quickly aroused.

And then a cop burst into the room.

Bobby sat up with a start. What the hell?

"Don't you know, young man, this is a house of ill repute? You're under arrest!" The cop held a billy club.

Bobby's head whirled, and everything darkened. His life was ending before it had even begun. How could this be happening? He couldn't swallow or breathe.

The closet door opened and out popped his uncle like a jack-in-the-box.

Bobby sat on the bed, completely bewildered.

His uncle laughed — not in his usual soundless way — but emitting deep, loud guffaws like Bobby had never heard before. Then the cop and girl doubled over in hysterics.

•   •   •

"Let that teach you a lesson, Bobby me boy!" His uncle told him on the way out.

"What's that?" Bobby asked, now feeling livid with his uncle, but also embarrassed.

"Always zip up your trousers before leaving a room, son."

Bobby's hand felt his fly. Sure enough, he hadn't pulled it up. He wanted nothing more than to punch his uncle's lights out. Why had he even agreed to leave home with this scoundrel? Out in the dark fall night, Bobby took a swing but missed.

"Had to see what it would take to get your blood boiling. Turns out to be a hell of a lot more than it ever did me! Better than your average Irish Mick, you are Bobby."

Bob assumed a boxer's stance; his nephew did likewise.

"Go ahead, throw a punch!" the older man teased.

Instead, Bobby walked ahead of his uncle back to the hotel. He could still smell traces of Clara's perfume.

Later that night, settled in the bed of a more reputable establishment, Bobby realized he'd never been impressed by anyone more than he was with his uncle. He knew he'd never forget his afternoon at a bordello. Overall, he'd had a memorable time on the trip, but he was getting eager to return home. He'd missed Joyce, and also his several buddies. His uncle, always larger than life, had out-smarted him. Bobby had grown tired of tagging along after him. When he got home, he'd feel ready — more than ready — to buckle down with his schoolwork. Still, he would thank his uncle many times over for having taken him on this trip of a lifetime.

The aging boxer admitted that he'd had a good time, too, but tomorrow they'd have to begin their return journey. Their gals were waiting for them in Detroit. Not only did Bobby need to return to school, but Bob had to don his Santa Claus suit for Hudson's Department store, and then: the black robes of a judge.

CHAPTER FIFTY-ONE

Catherine sipped her coffee at Darla's Downtown Donuts while waiting for her two new friends to join her. Thinking about how Mary and Claire looked up to her, made her grin. How nice it was — for once — to be held in high regard! This hadn't happened often in her life, but when it did, it buoyed her spirits. In the past, she wouldn't have noticed or cared about how she'd been perceived by other women. Now, it mattered.

She met them a few weeks earlier at her new volunteer job at the League of Catholic Women's Home for Unwed Mothers. John had mentioned the job to her. He often recommended the place to young pregnant prostitutes, in hopes they wouldn't have back alley abortions.

The two other volunteers were around her age. Claire ran the small library in the live-in facility, and Mary helped young women manage their guilt about giving up their babies for adoption. Catherine's job was to provide legal advice, and also to gently coax those who reconsidered giving up their babies. "You'll have plenty of opportunities," she would tell girls in their teens, "to have and raise children when you're older."

The previous day, Rachel, an angry seventeen-year-old, had glared at Catherine. "How do you know what's best for you any of us? Do you even have children?" Catherine hadn't answered either question. She was so bothered by Rachel's questions that she tossed and turned for much of that night. Maybe Rachel was right. Who was she to give them advice? Well, she knew something of the law, and could imagine how hard it must be to raise children with little or no family support.

It had been almost a month since Bob had taken Bobby out West. According to the date circled on their calendar, they should be home in two days. The first week Bob had been gone hadn't been an easy one. The bed had seemed enormous. How important their dinnertime was: to tell him about how her day, and hear about his. It had been hard not having him around, even if his thoughts were elsewhere. It was damn lonely. Bob had every right to take a trip without her, and certainly a trip with their dear nephew. It was simply the idea that Bob had taken someone else, that made her feel rejected.

Then she received a postcard from him. It had been brief, of course; warm but gruff like him: "Missing you, Kiddo! Yours to the end...Love, Bob."

Catherine's initial loneliness came as a shock, but then her attitude improved. She went to bed ridiculously early to avoid drinking. Less alcohol had caused her to better manage her emotions and life. She volunteered twenty hours a week and discovered she still had time to visit friends and family.

The only problem – and perhaps a significant one – was that when she got together with others, they seemed far away. She was only feigning interest in them. Her dear sister, Molly, and little Rose - the name perfectly suited her little niece, as she looked much like a rosebud. Catherine would chalk up her disinterest due to envy. Strange, as she'd never envied Eileen for being a mother...She sure didn't envy the young unwed pregnant women. Their despair was palpable and jarred her numbed state of mind. She'd have to ask Claire and Mary if they felt the same. They'd been volunteering there for a few years. Maybe her heart would steel itself after she'd been there longer. She hoped so.

Catherine now waved at the two women standing in the doorway. She almost didn't recognize them with the brims of their dark hats almost covering their eyes. They joined her in the booth, both happy to be in from the chilly November wind.

"Hope you haven't been waiting long," said Mary, the prettier one. She rubbed her hands together and smiled at the waitress stopping by with piping hot coffee. Never one to indulge in idle chit-chat, Catherine told them about what Rachel had said. She wondered if they'd heard that sort of thing before.

"If she didn't curse you as a follow-up to what she said, then count yourself lucky," Claire told her.

"These girls lash out because they feel trapped—cornered by their unfortunate circumstances," added Mary, whose hands still looked raw from the bitter weather. Mary's bespectacled eyes were red-rimmed. Catherine guessed she had problems sleeping and, doubtless, read late into the night.

"I can only imagine they do. Guess I've got to work on hardening my heart. Just when I think I'm tougher than shoe leather, I find I'm not." Catherine sighed.

"Well, don't get too crusty. That's the problem with most who work there. The nuns can be the worst culprits because they can't relate," said Mary.

"Think it's too late for me to become a Sister?" Catherine asked, getting a laugh out of her two companions. Little did they know, but on some level she was serious.

CHAPTER FIFTY-TWO

On Thanksgiving, Catherine lay in the fetal position under several blankets. The bedroom smelled of stale smoke and bad breath. Her hair, dirty and snarled, looked like crows had been nesting in it. Little did Bob know, but she'd tried to get up—she truly had.

They were already an hour late for dinner at Nana's. Maybe he'd wait until tomorrow to mention the danger of smoking in bed.

Bob tried his best to rouse her for the last couple of hours, but had no luck. At first, he stood in the bedroom doorway, and whispered. Then, louder: "C'mon, Kate, rise and shine!" When those methods didn't work, he began thudding around the apartment, swearing loudly and opening the bedroom door, only to slam it shut.

His last attempt was the cold water trick.

Catherine sat bolt upright and snapped at him: "Bob Sage, go there by yourself, why don't you? Tell them I've got a massive headache, which I now most definitely do."

While he'd only sprinkled the water on her face, at least something finally worked. He wouldn't be surprised if she was having another nervous breakdown. Here we go again.

Gene, Violet, and Bobby would be at Nana's for dinner, too. Bob and Bobby, home for over two weeks, had separately planned to tell stories of the still-wild West. It had been a few years since his mother had made a holiday meal. Bob had been eagerly anticipating this one.

Maybe he should go without Catherine.

"Sorry, Kiddo, but you don't get off that easy! I'll wait. I'm going to sit here until you leave that bed."

Before doing so, Bob grabbed several of her garments that had piled up on the chair and threw them on the floor. Then he sat in the wingback chair glowering at her.

She growled and hid her face beneath the blanket.

Soon, he grew tired of waiting and stomped off, muttering obscenities. She meant to get up at that point, but she dozed off.

About an hour later, she got dressed, though he'd never seen her looking so life-weary and pale. He'd seen no one this pale except ghosts in the movies.

"You're going to slap some rouge onto those cheeks, right?" Bob didn't know why he bothered asking, as it was like talking to a sleepwalker.

He telephoned his mother to tell her they'd be late — he didn't know exactly when they'd get there, but it was okay for the family to have dinner without them. Nana's normally sweet little voice sounded terse: "No, son. Just get here when you can."

When Bob had first returned from the trip, Catherine had seemed fine — better than she had in some time. She told Bob all about her latest volunteer job with pregnant young women. It sounded like something she'd be good at doing. He told her maybe it could turn into a paid position. After telling her about the prank he'd played on Bobby at the brothel, she'd laughed and then scolded him appropriately.

She'd even admitted how much she'd missed him. He'd missed her, too, but after telling her so, he thought she'd looked at him dubiously. He wasn't sure how to convince her. On the second day after his return, she did something she hadn't done in a long time: she'd made him dinner — a meatloaf with baked potatoes. He'd complimented the perfectly made meal. She was truly a remarkable woman who continued to surprise him.

But then about a week ago, Catherine began hitting the sauce again and smoking her fool head off. She babbled on about how it wasn't fair that he was now a judge, while her legal career had fallen off the tracks. The train, she told him, had gone without her; it had left her sobbing on the platform. Bob tried to get her to realize that winning the election was his reward for a long and tough campaign, but she wouldn't. He felt sorry for her, he truly did, but had no use for her self-pity, of which she seemed in no short supply.

When Bob tried telling Catherine how she'd come a lot further than most women and was a victim of the times, it fell on deaf ears. Still, she agreed that counseling unwed mothers gave her a new sense of purpose. He remembered one of her pet phrases, something about how you're your own best friend and worst enemy.

What she didn't tell him was that once she got her drinking under control, she was considering adopting a baby. She didn't think it would take much to convince him to support the plan.

Then, on that Thanksgiving morning, Nana had heard the raven croak and the wren twitter. The shape of the clouds and her dreams had also confirmed her fears. Death was near. A little too near. She said nothing to her family. Maybe another sign would tell her whose, but she didn't want to know.

It was good she had dinner to prepare. She brought out her finest china and Irish linens. Cooking distracted her from dwelling on the messages she'd received.

Everyone at the table noticed how Catherine had been so much quieter than usual. Her hair didn't have its normal sheen and her dress was wrinkled. They were almost two hours late, so Nana didn't waste time before ringing the dinner bell.

"Ma, I'm sorry. You should've gone ahead without us," Bob said looking down at his hands folded for the dinner grace. But

Nana wouldn't have heard of it. She'd done her best to keep the turkey and side dishes warm, but most of the food wound up being overcooked and dry—especially the turkey. Thankfully, there'd been plenty of gravy.

Gene, as the eldest brother, began reciting the "Our Father..." and all chimed in at the end before digging into the platters and bowls of food.

Gene worried that their mother was feeling poorly. On the verge of passing out, Catherine hadn't noticed Nana's mood. Only Violet had been quietly delighted, as it gave her a chance to take over the table talk. Bobby was annoyed by his mother and worried about how tired his aunt seemed, as well as his silent Nana. He kept clearing his throat, a nervous habit he'd picked up from his mother. She was doing the same.

Nana looked around at her dear little family while Violet blathered. Her eyes rested on Catherine, who looked away and shivered. Did anyone else feel the chill? No one answered.

Bob told his wife on the car ride home she was an embarrassment. She hummed as she gazed out the window at the blurry world.

· · ·

That night, Nana knew the banshee would wail in her dreams, and again she'd be visited by the raven and the wren. She kept her bedside light on for the rest of the long night.

CHAPTER FIFTY-THREE

The following week, Bob tried to pique Catherine's interest in planning their trip overseas. It wouldn't take long before they'd have enough money saved up for the trip of a lifetime. If a European tour was both too costly and complex to arrange, they could travel to a tropical paradise. She nodded, smiled wanly, but preferred talking about how uncomfortably hot her skin felt at night—even though it was December.

Bob wanted to tell her it was because she spent most of her time in bed, but didn't bother.

"Why don't we have a lighter blanket? I can't just sleep with a sheet on me," Catherine complained. The look on her face told him she thought it was his fault. Wasn't it always? By morning blankets would be in a heap on the floor, and she'd be tangled in the top sheet.

It became too much for Bob to spend every evening with her. He began meeting up with friends at a bar, or staying after work to play cards with some of his co-workers. He always made it home before midnight. Catherine said she didn't mind. It was a relief not to argue so much. He knew she was drinking more again. Doubtless, she didn't have any interest in slowing down. And he'd be a fine one to lecture her when he enjoyed liquor almost as much as she did.

The previous year, he'd bought her a Victorian chaise. It was covered in plush burgundy velvet. Catherine called it her 'fainting couch,' and loved reading on it, while she smoked and drank. When her eyelids grew heavy, she'd set her book down and mull over memories and dreams. Having the plump Mr. Mercedes on her lap kept her from fidgeting and pacing. She was aware that her looks had faded, though sometimes she still felt attractive—especially if she wore her favorite blue silk kimono that Bob had given her. One evening when he was out, like usual, she roused herself from a stupor on the chaise and commended herself for taking a shower and fixing herself an egg for dinner.

Catherine was lower than a snail's belly, but she was certain it was a phase, a passing mood due to not working. It was only a matter of time before Bob met another woman.

The damn bottle needed to be emptied and thrown in the garbage.

Tomorrow will be the day. After doing so, she'd tell herself not to fret about Bob leaving her. She simply needed to refocus. Why not return to the home for unwed mothers? It had been difficult but rewarding work. It would be then that she'd broach adoption with Bob. In a few years, she'd be a practicing attorney again. She'd become a mother that a child could look up to. Hopefully, they'd adopt a girl whose life would turn out better than Catherine's. Yes, things were looking up again. She could feel her mood improving, her energy returning.

After washing up her plate, she played their Billie Holiday record on the Victrola, poured herself a nightcap, and lit a cigarette. It had been unseasonably warm outside, so she opened a few windows. An acrid odor wafted in off the river into the apartment, but she kept the windows partly open.

It had become her habit to listen to "Summertime" over and over. Such a soothing, though melancholy song…She recalled the best days with Bob – that summer after finishing law school; times on Belle Isle; their trips to Boblo Island (especially the first one); those picnics at lakes, and dancing beneath the stars. What a vibrant whirlwind of a romance! That magical night on Belle Isle when he'd first proposed…Then the successful days of Sage & Sage—all they'd done for the less fortunate. What a team they'd made—could still make—if only she wasn't so sad and sleepy.

She poured herself another drink and lit one cigarette off another. Where was Mr. Mercedes? Probably on the bed under a blanket—he seldom left her side these days. Hopefully, he hadn't jumped out one of the open windows. Shouldn't Bob be home by now? She couldn't blame him for not wanting to be around her. The stench from the river was too much, so she shut the windows. Her eyelids felt heavy, so she shut them.

Nana's face came into her mind, mouthing something. "Hush, Nana—let me sleep some. I'll get up soon."

Catherine drifted further and further out, then she smelled smoke. It wasn't coming from the river.

When she realized she was on fire, she got up and ran. It was the worst thing she could have done.

Bob would later say that her red hair turned white. Remarkably, her hair hadn't burned up, though her eyebrows had been completely erased.

He came home earlier than usual from a card game and found her lying on the floor. Thick smoke filled the apartment. Good thing the windows were shut—had they been open the entire apartment would have gone up in flames.

Catherine had been alive, but barely conscious, moaning and rolling on the floor. Rolling must have helped put out the flames. He didn't know what to do. Help would be there soon, he told her repeatedly.

Fingers shaking, he called for an ambulance. Thank God they had a telephone. Too bad she couldn't have placed the call before he got home.

Bob opened the windows wide. He could see that part of the carpet had burned.

After returning from the hospital, he found Mr. Mercedes crouching in their bedroom closet, seemingly unaffected by the smoke. "It's going to be okay, boy," he tried to reassure the cat.

But it wasn't. The third-degree burns had covered Catherine's entire body. A mummy stared up at Bob from the hospital bed. Her eyes and mouth were all that showed—eyes darting about, as if looking for a way out. Having little to do at her bedside besides talking, he mostly noticed her eyes. At first, the whites had turned red from the smoke. When they finally cleared up, her irises became more noticeable and were the deep gray of burned wood.

Morphine was administered. During her conscious moments, Catherine would mumble incoherently, and sometimes scream once the morphine wore off. No one but Bob could get her to calm down, especially when he sang her Irish lullabies. She responded best to a famous one:

Tura lura lural
Tura lura lie
Tura lura lural
Hush don't you cry
Tura lura lural
Tura lura lie
Tura lura lural
That's an Irish lullaby
Often in dreams I've wandered
Back to that cot again
And I feel her arms huggin' me
Just like when she held me then

Nurses and doctors admitted they'd never seen a patient so badly burned. Ever increasing doses of the drug were administered.

Bob, Nana, and Catherine's parents were her primary visitors. Others stopped by with flowers and cards, but found it too difficult to stay long because of her constant moaning or screaming. Bob visited every day and usually remained until visiting hours were over. Others guessed that she'd been drunk when she lit herself aflame, but Bob looked squarely into faces and said that "Catherine simply fell asleep with a lit cigarette. Let's leave it at that." No one dared to argue with him. It was his duty to stick by her – he would tell anyone who wondered how he had the stamina. She would have done no less for him.

Something told Catherine that it wasn't over. Sadly, there was no way she could convey it.

She hung on for two long weeks following the fire.

PART III
JUDGE SAGE

CHAPTER FIFTY-FOUR

1938

Bob had never known such difficult times, especially those first few months after his wife's death. He'd mourned for loved ones before, but never like this. It was like the bottom, top, and center had fallen out of his life. The punch that truly had him down for the count: had he been home that night, he wouldn't have lost her.

For the first time, he understood Catherine's desire to sleep around the clock. Mostly, he didn't dream, but one night he did. In it, he heard her voice, warning him about something, but he couldn't make out her words. That was the entire dream. Food tasted like cardboard, and the weight of daily living was so heavy he could barely breathe. If it weren't for having to feed Mr. Mercedes or his mother, he wouldn't have bothered getting out of bed. Would he ever not wake up blaming himself for Catherine's death? Never did they take that trip to Europe, buy a mansion, or a yacht. He doubted they'd have been any happier. Still, he'd made those promises…And yet they'd had some good times — even a few wonderful ones.

Old injuries caused him physical pain like never before. Once he'd enjoyed friends and meeting new people, but now he despised almost everyone, except his mother and brother — though even they could get on his nerves.

Bob had never been so angry.

Catherine's casket had been closed during the large funeral. Bob had carefully placed a single red tulip on its mahogany top. The chorus of weeping echoed around him; he buried his face in his hands and sobbed. Father Tim's voice quavered and a tear streamed down his pale face. When Bob could at last look around, he was taken aback. Every pew was full.

Bob sat in the front pew with the McIntoshes. Catherine's parents and their three children braced each other with their shoulders. Nieces and nephews were almost as somber as the adults, even the now four-year-old Rose. Stony faces winced as they crumbled. John, visibly shaken, had stepped up to help the others get through the ordeal. The other Sages sat in the pew directly behind them. Bobby looked uncomfortable in his only suit. He tugged at sleeves he'd long outgrown.

While Bobby had heard stories about the deaths of many relatives, he'd never lost one whom he'd known. He'd always been enamored by his aunt and knew he'd never forget her. Violet wailed louder than anyone. Not that her sorrow was any more intense than the others—it was simply in her nature to express sorrow or joy. Nana kept rubbing her arm and gently shushing her. Nana had always been one to buck up during difficult times.

Bob commended himself for doing somewhat better during the funeral home visitation, as greeting people gave him something to do. He felt like a party host. Part of him kept wondering what was keeping Catherine. Why had she left him there to do all the chit-chat? Still, she would've been pleased with the turnout. No one seemed to blame her for the downward turn her life had taken before the end. Loyalty of family and friends had been something to behold. But it wasn't up to them, or Bob, to forgive her transgressions—that was God's business, and everyone else better damn well stay out of it! She would've been especially proud to see Emily Schauber, Professor Higgins, Dean Hally there, as well as Aunt Vivian. He'd expected to see

Margaret and Joan, but also there were the two women from Catherine's last job at the home for unwed mothers, and countless others — many of whom Bob had never met.

It wasn't long before Bob moved back in with his mother after hearing that she'd been having an increasingly hard time getting around. Who couldn't admire the brave face she showed the world? All the more brave, as the fight had gone out of her. Unlike Catherine, she never complained. He marveled still over the great job she did making that last Thanksgiving dinner. Had Catherine's death further weakened her? The two women had been pretty close. His mother had always adored his ambitious, yet troubled wife — even though she'd always sided with him when Catherine and he had gone through rough times.

Caring for her during that first month after Catherine's death helped Bob get from one day to the next. Nana fell in love with Mr. Mercedes, who was less lonely than before. The orange cat purred so loud, Bob was embarrassed. Nana seemed a little better, though less spirited and slower. He sure wished he could have better cared for Catherine.

Then a much hoped for day arrived: he paid a visit to the Common Pleas Court and was given his black robe and a key to his chamber. Bob hadn't expected the chamber to be so grand. It contained a large mahogany desk, a built-in bookcase behind his desk (wide as the wall and tall as the ceiling), and also comfortable chairs for guests.

He sat in the swivel chair behind his desk and gazed out at the skyscrapers and the choppy Detroit River below. A freighter passed by, followed by a tug boat. Catherine would've so enjoyed the view! A wave of sadness knocked him to his knees; he struggled for breath. How could he possibly be worthy of a judgeship? Even though he felt far older, he was only thirty-eight. Most judges were older and doubtless, far wiser than he. Sure, he'd seen a lot in his day; in fact, he'd lived life pretty much to its fullest. He'd made the necessary connections in the world of both work and sports. And while he'd hung up his boxing gloves, the embers from those days still glowed. People he'd never met often greeted him by name when passing on the streets. He'd come to 'know' the law as well as other attorneys, though he knew he wasn't the smartest. He knew smart legal minds had to out-wit criminals. Mostly, he could do that, but not always — he'd never been as sharp as Catherine. Still, he was both fair-minded and passionate, so maybe he was up for the job. What he lacked in brain power, he'd make up for in grit, caring, and a sense of justice.

Once Bob became used to his role in the courtroom, he saved up money to buy a large city lot which he planned on turning into the Detroit Sports Park. There would be a memorial site in Catherine's honor, as she'd not only helped foster his dream but also with the fundraising. Since he presided over a courtroom, working there couldn't be a regular job. Still, he'd visit the park and make sure it lived up to its promise of hosting a variety of sports — from amateur boxing to baseball. Mostly, it would give area youths somewhere to go. Detroit desperately needed that. While he'd put away some money for the land purchase, he still needed to have fundraisers. He hoped to receive donations from judges, attorneys, and local businessmen. Could there be a worthier cause?

Bob knew two men from his early days in Corktown — the Nadell brothers. It was said they knew how to expedite loans. He'd need both loans, plus the cold cash from fundraisers, to see the project through to completion. Bob readily acknowledged that he had little financial acumen. Soon, he'd try to locate them.

He'd always gotten along with Catherine's parents; they'd always treated him nicely. One Sunday after mass, Bob visited them. While, at first, they seemed happy to see him, they soon became more cordial than friendly. It was a clear sign they no longer saw themselves as his in-laws. The couple sat next to each other on a sofa. They looked so much older. He probably did, too. While they didn't say as much, Bob got the feeling they blamed him for Catherine's death. They stared at him, as did their one-eyed cat. All three looked like they had it in for him.

An overcast sky darkened the room, but no one bothered turning on a light. He lacked the courage to do so. It was tough trying to hold his rough-skinned hands still in his lap.

Bob told them about how his mother was, and how he'd moved in with her. There was an awkward silence. They acted formal and impersonal, as if he was a mere acquaintance. He'd never felt more uncomfortable. After they'd barely reacted to a few of stories about colorful Detroit criminals, he stated what had been weighing heavily on his mind.

"You realize I did what I could to get Catherine off the bottle, right?"

"Sure you did," Bridget said flatly, with little conviction.

"Yes, I sure did!" Bob insisted. "And you remember how she was about smoking. No one could convince her to throw her cigarettes away."

The couple both nodded, but remained expressionless. All three sat in painful silence. The ticking of the mantel clock became increasingly louder.

"Glad to hear you're a judge now, Bob. Catherine would've been proud."

It was Bob's turn to nod. More silence.

"Well, guess I better get going. I've got cases to look over." It was clear they wouldn't invite him for supper. On one level he was relieved. His reason for seeing them beyond a social visit had been to let them know about the sports park, and how there'd be a memorial in their daughter's honor. He could tell them how a special part of it would be called The Catherine Sage Playground. Maybe add something about the fundraiser, but it wasn't the right time. They might want him to call it The Catherine McIntosh Sage Playground and he couldn't see doing that. Maybe he'd never see them again, as being there in Catherine's girlhood home was close to unbearable.

Bob wasted no time in saying his goodbyes. After returning to his room at his mother's flat, he punched a hole in the wall. God wasn't about to let him off the hook. No such place as Easy Street for Bob Sage.

When his mother asked him the following day about his visit with Catherine's parents, he couldn't recall much about it. Odd thing was that he'd had nothing to drink after seeing them.

"Must not have gone well, right me lad? Seeing as you came home and punched a hole in the wall."

"Yeah, I recall being upset, Ma, but not much about the day. I know I stopped by to see them, but I don't recall what was said. Sorry about the wall. I'll call somebody to come fix it."

"Glad you're on the go again, Bob, but don't over-do it."

"Now, Ma…"

"Since you're staying with your old mama, she's going to look out for you. You got that?"

Robert Sage, the manly man, and judge, nodded and bowed his head like a repentant child.

. . .

Bob's new life began to — if not cancel out his earlier one — at least make it seem remote, almost like someone else's. He recalled his late wife, but with each passing day, he couldn't see her quite as clearly. Her voice became muffled, too, except in dreams in which she often appeared like she had when they first dated. Catherine had certainly been his one true love. But in some of his nightmares, he'd take a swing at her, and then a jab. He couldn't stop until thick curls of flame burst from his boxing mitts. He'd wake up drowning in sweat, cursing himself.

One day Gene and his son visited Bob at court. Bob showed — young Robert — around both the courtroom and his chamber.

Afterward, he proudly introduced his nephew to a few attorneys and a couple of clerks. His well-mannered and nice-looking namesake was now almost through high school. Bob was pleased to learn how much he excelled in his classes and that he had a young sweetheart. Must have been the same one he'd mentioned on their trip west. Too bad she wasn't an Irish girl, but his nephew had proudly reported that "Joyce is half Swedish and smart as she is lovely." He hoped the country would stay out of the war overseas. Too many young lives needlessly lost, and how heartbreaking if something were to happen to young Bob.

"Where the hell were you last night?" Gene asked him when Bobby was out of earshot on a tour of nearby offices.

"What do you mean?"

"You were supposed to stop by for dinner. Vi—you know she never cooks—made you an entire fried chicken dinner."

Bob pled guilty after taking out his pocket appointment book. He'd written nothing down for yesterday. What had he done? He wasn't sure, but he'd probably gone to the gym.

"I sure am sorry, Gene. Guess I've got some memory issues. Must be the new job…"

"Or, you have a screw loose after being 'punch drunk' one too many times," Gene said in his usual even-toned voice.

"Dad, don't be so tough on him, he just forgets sometimes. It happens," said the younger Robert, looking embarrassed but amazed that his father would speak that way to his own brother. Strange for him to be embarrassed by his father—it was usually only his mother who caused him to cringe.

"Look, you two," Bob began in his gruff and gravelly voice, "Here are three tickets to the Friday fights. They're on me. Dinner, too. Please give my apologies to Violet."

CHAPTER FIFTY-FIVE

August, 1940

Almost three years had passed since Catherine's death. Some days it seemed like a decade, but on others, he half-expected her to walk into the room. This occurred to Bob as he sat in his chamber, his muscular arms crossed behind his head, as he waited for the two guys he knew from school — Herman and Jack Nadell. Tough kids who'd chased both Gene and him, back when they were new to the Corktown neighborhood. After standing up to the dreaded Nadell brothers, Bob and Gene never encountered much trouble. It was Herman who'd suggested Bob become a boxer since he got right back up after taking a pounding.

Bob ran into them once, years later, during Prohibition. They'd become rumrunners for a time and had purchased Canadian booze for a song and smuggled it across the border. While the brothers belonged to the Purple Gang, they turned out to be less violent than many other members. Of course, there'd been the time Jack sent Joel Sheen to collect money for booze he'd 'given' Bob for a family picnic. It soured Bob on having any further dealings with Jack or his brother.

Years later, Bob heard they'd become pretty good, if not decent, businessmen. They knew how to get deals on loans — how to connect with those who knew how to tie up loose ends in the banking world. Often less savory sorts, but oh well. Once a grifter, always a grifter. He should've known better.

When he met with the Nadell brothers the previous month, they convinced him they cared as much as he did about doing right by Detroit kids by building a sports park. Not only did they know how to cut red tape, they also promised to match Bob's amount. It seemed only right to make them business partners. Most of the $35,000 that Bob came up with was from his personal savings and also several fundraisers. At last, his goal would be realized! Already ticket booths had been made, and also a baseball diamond.

Then yesterday, Bob had gone to the bank with a question about the account. After checking, a banker told him the money was gone. All but one dollar remained. Was this their idea of a joke? But maybe his signature was also needed to close the account. What did he expect by dealing with former members of the Purple Gang? He had only himself to blame. Had Catherine been there, she would've slowed him down, but he'd grown impatient with the entire project. It shouldn't have taken so long.

Before leaving the bank, he punched his fist against the wall so hard his knuckles bled.

Bob had spent Friday night in his office, as he hadn't wanted to spill the beans to his mother; hadn't wanted her to see his rage and humiliation. After several shots of whiskey, he drank straight from the bottle as he'd walked around downtown in the moonlight. It was there he hatched a plan.

After getting little sleep, he called Jack Nadell. He played dumb and told Jack he got another nice check from the mayor's office and he needed the two brothers to endorse it before Bob could deposit it the following Monday. Jack didn't know that Bob had gone to the bank the previous day.

"Sure, no problem, Bob. How about we stop by around two? We'll stop by with our attorney Smiley. We're seeing him on another matter, but he can serve as a notary," Jack told him.

"They can do that at the bank, Jack, when I take the check."

"See you at 2:00, Bob," said Jack, skirting the issue.

As the scenario had played out in Bob's mind, he hadn't envisioned a third person there. He'd heard of the purported slimy Smiley but had never met him. It would've been better if he hadn't.

It was a long morning. He chewed on a toothpick, paced, and finally succumbed to a few swigs of whiskey from a bottle he kept in a desk drawer. He roamed the hallway to check if anyone else was working. There was a single guard in the lobby, and no one but Bob on the third floor.

At 1:45, again Bob paced in his chamber. Nothing worse than having been played a fool...It happened a lot when he'd been a young boy—those brothers of his, even his twin, had always played pranks on him, but he came back swinging; they toughened him up. Then, more than once, the Purple Gang had gotten his goat. Back in the early '20s, he'd been invited to parties, not by the Nadells, but by other gang members. Bob would arrive and no one would be there...All the mickey's that got slipped into his drinks over the years...Catherine with her two-timing ways—sneaking around behind his back, though that was different, and he supposed sometimes he'd deserved it. This was beyond anything that had happened before. It was way worse. Gene and their mother would tell him his anger was getting the best of him. They would advise him to take some time off and take a vacation.

Bob, fuming, paced some more.

At 2:00 he forced himself to sit in his desk chair. Toothpick perched precariously between his lips—a ladder from a window, an escape rope. What was it he wanted to escape from? For starters, the angry, gruff, and often drunken man he'd become. His voice box was as broken as his dreams.

He looked down at his soft, pale hands. He could still make a fist, but to what end?

At 2:05 they still hadn't arrived. Was he about to get stiffed again? He couldn't allow it— wouldn't allow it.

And then, there they were. All three men stood outside his open door, waiting to be invited into his chamber.

"Come in, by all means, gentlemen."

They shook hands, grinned, and unsuspectingly, sat across from Bob at his large desk. He smiled at them. They smiled back. At first, no one said anything, but then Bob's grin disappeared. They argued about what had happened to the funds.

As Bob was reaching inside his desk drawer, his last comment was: "Let this be the peacemaker." With that, he took out a small pistol from his desk drawer. Calmly, he shot one brother. After Bob fired the first shot, both the second brother and their attorney saw what was happening, but sat frozen from shock in their chairs. Bob reloaded and fired the second shot. Both were perfect shots right between the brother's eyes.

Then Bob fired a third shot at Smiley. Ned, clutching his stomach, escaped from the office without a moment to spare. No doubt he'd immediately phone the police. Bob could go after him and shoot him again, but he'd already killed the brothers. Catherine's brother, John, would show up and put the cuffs on him. No way would Bob allow that to happen.

He had to get out of town.

Bob ran down the three flights of stairs, then the few blocks to the river. He'd never run so fast without stopping. Gasping, he doubled over. People looked at him strangely.

The world whirled.

He stopped once he got to a walkway that ran next to the river. After catching his breath, he inched his way as close as possible to the water's edge. Then he took the pistol from his suit coat pocket. No difference between those who study the law and break the law. Not really. At least not for him.

His shaky hands threw his aim off. The bullet, like an opponent's punch, didn't bring Bob down for the count. He was strong and could still win the match; down, but not out. A searing pain—the bullet must have gone through his face. Not about to waste time to find out if he'd blown his cheek off his face, he dove deep into the cold water, only to resurface, gasping for breath. Why didn't his body sink to the river bottom?

Maybe God had other plans for him.

The current carried him downriver. He remembered how he once told Catherine about how much quicker the boat ride to Boblo was downstream, as opposed to the return trip.

He swam and swam and had no idea where he was. He knew to stay close to shore. What mattered now was to swim away from his crime—his life. Maybe he'd wind up on some tropical shore. There'd be mermaids and music and fruity drinks. Catherine's voice called to him: "See you soon in Paradise." It would be better than grand. She would be there. He knew it. So would Raymond, James, his father, grandparents, Kate's grandmother, and Uncle Gerry. They didn't have to know what he'd done. By the time he got there, Bob wouldn't recall either.

He had a dream many years ago when he had a fever. In it, he'd shot two guys and then himself. It had come true, after all. A self-fulfilling prophecy? Not that it mattered; nothing did, except getting to that awaiting island. He hadn't thought about that dream in quite some time.

The river carried Bob further downstream. There would be no return trip.

EPILOGUE

Two weeks later, on an August day, the missing body of Robert Sage, the 'Battling Barrister,' was discovered on the shores of Duck Island. The coroner determined he swam quite far before succumbing — fighter to the end. Joyce Lindall, the girlfriend of the younger Bob Sage, read the headlines 'Sage Kills Two, Then Self' and for a moment her heart skipped a beat, thinking it had been her fiancé.

Robert Edwardo Sage's funeral would be one of the largest Detroit had ever known.

Young Bob asked Nana if she had foreseen her son's tragic death. "No, I didn't have to because he saw it himself." Mary Ellen Sage (Nana) lived until 1943, three years after Bob's death. She would meet none of her three great-granddaughters. Had it not been for the tender ministrations of her remaining son, Gene, perhaps Nana couldn't have braved it alone for those three years following Bob's death. My father did his best to see more of her, but World War II landed him in the South Pacific. While Nana worried about him, as she did all the Sage men, she knew he'd make it home. Bob's wife, Joyce, took comfort in her words. To my knowledge, my mother never met Nana.

Curiously, I suffered from an appendicitis attack on a Halloween night in Detroit, though this is my only known connection to Harry Houdini.

Catherine passed away at age thirty-seven and Bob lived until he was forty. Their fighting and fiery spirits continue to live on in the Sage family to this day.

END NOTES

1. Page 28
Captain Bob-lo (Joe Short) was the beloved captain of the Boblo
boat for decades. I well recall him greeting passengers as they
boarded the boat when I was a girl in the 1960s.

2. Page 32
Lila Neuenfelt was also the first female appointed as a judge of
the Wayne County Circuit Court.
(michiganwomenshalloffame.org 2018-01-10)

3. Page 36
Billy Miske, Harry Greb, and Jack Dempsey were all actual
boxers.

4. Page 38
Billy Watson's a fictional character, but I used the last name of an
actual person, Bob Watson—a highly thought-of boxing referee
in Detroit for much of the last half of the Twentieth Century, and
a lifelong friend of my father's.

5. Page 73
Emily Schauber is based on the actual Emelia C. Schaub. Emelia
was the first female attorney to successfully defend a client in a
murder case and was Michigan's first elected female prosecutor
in Leelanau, Michigan. Catherine was probably acquainted with
Emelia, who graduated in 1924.

6. Page 112
Grace Murphy graduated from Detroit College of Law the same

year as Catherine, so I have little doubt that Catherine and she were acquainted. Grace G. Costavas Murphy was the first Black woman to practice law in Michigan. While Grace died in 1932, I do not know the precise cause of her death.

7. Page 136
I'm sure Bob had heard about Anna Sage (The Lady in Red) after the gangster, John Dillinger's arrest, but I have no evidence they'd ever met.

8. Page 148
My grandfather, Gene Sage, told me about his brother Bob's fever dream when I was in high school.

9. Page 151
My grandfather thought a great deal of Catherine, his sister-in-law. I've taken liberties with this scene. No doubt Bob wasn't always easy to live with. At this point and a few others, Catherine wonders if she married the wrong brother. Gene was a gentle soul and not at all a womanizer like his brother.

10. Page 158
Harry Greb was the world Middleweight champion boxer. Bob fought him the night before Catherine and he were married. I can only imagine how jittery Catherine must have felt getting married the day after a big fight which Bob lost!

11. Page 160
I could find nothing about where Bob and Catherine married, though their reception was held at the Belle Isle Yacht Club. They could have either gotten married in Most Holy Trinity church in Corktown or downtown at Old St. Mary's.

12. Page 160
My great uncle was friends with Judge Frank Murphy.

13. Page 162

Bob took the bar exam three times before passing it on his third try.

14. Page 164

While Catherine and Bob had a law practice together for a time, I don't know if it had a name, or how long they practiced together.

15. Page 188

I suffered an appendicitis attack one Halloween, as did Henry Houdini. I'm sure Nana was impressed by Houdini, though my story of him contacting her is fictitious.

16. Page 190

I don't know if Bob was acquainted with members of the Purple Gang. My father always acted like his uncle was secretive and knew more than admit about Detroit's crime family. It is sheer speculation on my part that he knew Abe Berntein, the gang's leader, or Joe Zerilli, a leading member.

17. Page 216

Bob used the word, palooka, in its now dated meaning: an inferior or average prizefighter.

18. Page 220

My father never let on if he knew details of Bob and Catherine's extra-marital affairs, though he mentioned that they'd both had them, placing most of the blame on Bob.

19. Page 225

Harry Henderson was an actual boxer.

20. Page 240

My father often spoke about how Bob sometimes lost his temper to the point of being abusive with Catherine. He didn't know — or didn't say — how often the abuse occurred. My hunch is they would argue after they'd been drinking, which — from stories told — worsened as time went on.

21. Page 305

My father and grandfather were partners the law firm of Maile, Leach & Schrier, though my grandfather wasn't a practicing attorney. I don't think my father received many cases from them. Bob might have been connected to this firm as well, but I was unable to find any documentation. Also, I don't know if Catherine was ever interviewed by any of the partners.

22. Page 319

My great uncle took my father to a brothel on their trip out West. I've heard the story countless times, as it was one of my father's favorite stories.

23. Page 346

The Nadell brothers were the surnames of the two men my great uncle shot and killed. I could not locate their first names. My father referred to the third man, their attorney, as Smiley, in his memoir.

ABOUT THE AUTHOR

Susan E. Sage is a fiction writer and poet. Born and raised in Detroit, she received an English degree from Wayne State University. An educator for twenty-three years, she wore many hats: an adult education teacher, educational coordinator, as well as an academic interventionist at both the elementary and secondary levels.

Susan has published two other novels: *Insominy* (2010) and *A Mentor and Her Muse* (2017). Her short fiction and poetry have appeared in many journals, including: Five on the Fifth, Arlington Literary Journal, Illuminations, Twisted Vines Literary Journal, The Birds We Piled Loosely, Referential Magazine, Storyacious, E.T.A. Literary Journal, Digital Papercut, and Black Denim Lit.

At present, she lives in Flushing, Michigan, with her husband and two cats.

NOTE FROM THE AUTHOR

Word-of-mouth is crucial for any author to succeed. If you enjoyed *Dancing in the Ring*, please leave a review online — anywhere you are able. Even if it's just a sentence or two. It would make all the difference and would be very much appreciated.

Thanks!
Susan E. Sage

We hope you enjoyed reading this title from:

BLACK ROSE
writing™

www.blackrosewriting.com

Subscribe to our mailing list – *The Rosevine* – and receive **FREE** books, daily deals, and stay current with news about upcoming releases and our hottest authors.
Scan the QR code below to sign up.

Already a subscriber? Please accept a sincere thank you for being a fan of Black Rose Writing authors.

View other Black Rose Writing titles at www.blackrosewriting.com/books and use promo code **PRINT** to receive a **20% discount** when purchasing.